THE WORLD'S CLASSICS

ALMAYER'S FOLLY

JOSEPH CONRAD was born Józef Teodor Konrad Korzeniowski in the Russian part of Poland in 1857. His parents were punished by the Russians for their Polish nationalist activities and both died while Conrad was still a child. In 1874 he left Poland for France and in 1878 began a career with the British merchant navy. He spent nearly twenty years as a sailor and did not begin writing novels until he was approaching forty. He became a British citizen in 1886 and settled permanently in England after his marriage to Jessie George in 1896.

Conrad is a writer of unique power and sophistication; works such as *Heart of Darkness*, *Lord Jim*, and *Nostromo* display technical complexities which have established him as one of the first English 'Modernists'. He is also noted for the unprecedented vividness with which he communicates a pessimist's view of man's personal and social destiny in such works as *The Secret Agent*, *Under Western Eyes*, and *Victory*. Despite the immediate critical recognition that they received in his life-time Conrad's major novels did not sell, and he lived in relative poverty until the commercial success of *Chance* (1913) secured for him a wider public and an assured income. In 1923 he visited America, with great acclaim, and he was offered a knighthood (which he declined) shortly before his death in 1924. He is now numbered among the greatest writers in English, both for the range and seriousness of his concerns and the revolutionary energy of his art. Many regard him as the most important single innovator of the twentieth century.

JACQUES BERTHOUD is Professor and Head of the Department of English and Related Literature at the University of York. His work on Conrad includes *Joseph Conrad, the Major Phase* (1978) and editions of *The Nigger of the 'Narcissus'* (1984) and *The Shadow Line* (1986).

ALMAYER'S FOLLY

JOSEPH CONRAD was born Józef Teodor Konrad Korzeniowski in the Russian part of Poland in 1857. His parents were punished by the Russians for their Polish nationalist activities and both died while Conrad was still a child. In 1874 he left Poland for France and in 1878 began a career with the British merchant navy. He spent nearly twenty years as a sailor and did not begin writing novels until he was approaching forty. He became a British citizen in 1886 and settled permanently in England after his marriage to Jessie George in 1896.

Conrad is a writer of unique power and sophistication: works such as *Heart of Darkness*, *Lord Jim*, and *Nostromo* display technical complexities which have established him as one of the first English 'Modernists'. He is also noted for the unprecedented vividness with which he communicates a pessimistic view of man's personal and social destiny in such works as *The Secret Agent*, *Under Western Eyes*, and *Victory*. Despite the immediate critical recognition that they received in his life-time Conrad's major novels did not sell, and he lived in near-poverty until the commercial success of *Chance* (1913) secured for him a wider public and an assured income. In 1923 he visited America, with great acclaim, and he was offered a knighthood (which he declined) shortly before his death in 1924. He is now numbered among the greatest writers in English, both for the range and seriousness of his concerns and the revolutionary energy of his art. Many regard him as the most important single innovator of the twentieth century.

JACQUES BERTHOUD is Professor and Head of the Department of English and Related Literature at the University of York. His work on Conrad includes *Joseph Conrad: the Major Phase* (1978) and editions of *The Nigger of the 'Narcissus'* (1984) and *The Shadow-Line* (1986).

THE WORLD'S CLASSICS

JOSEPH CONRAD

Almayer's Folly

A Story of an Eastern River

Edited with an Introduction by
JACQUES BERTHOUD

Oxford New York
OXFORD UNIVERSITY PRESS

Oxford University Press, Walton Street, Oxford OX2 6DP

Oxford New York
Athens Auckland Bangkok Bogota Bombay
Buenos Aires Calcutta Cape Town Dar es Salaam
Delhi Florence Hong Kong Istanbul Karachi
Kuala Lumpur Madras Madrid Melbourne
Mexico City Nairobi Paris Singapore
Taipei Tokyo Toronto

and associated companies in
Berlin Ibadan

Oxford is a trade mark of Oxford University Press

First published as a World's Classics paperback 1992

British Library Cataloguing in Publication Data
Data available

Library of Congress Cataloging in Publication Data
Conrad, Joseph, 1857-1924.
Almayer's folly : a story of an eastern river / Joseph Conrad : edited with an introduction by Jacques Berthoud.
p. cm.—(The World's classics)
Includes bibliographical references (p.).
I. Berthoud, Jacques A. II. Title. III. Series.
PR6005.04A8 1992 823'.912—dc20 91-39404

ISBN 0-19-281697-7

3 5 7 9 10 8 6 4 2

Printed in Great Britain by
BPC Paperbacks Ltd,
Aylesbury, Bucks

For my son Tristan

CONTENTS

ABBREVIATIONS

Texts of Almayer's Folly

MS	Autograph manuscript (Rosenbach Foundation Collection)
TS	Final typescript (Humanities Research Center)
U	First English Edition by T. Fisher Unwin (1895)
M	First American Edition by Macmillan New York (1895)
SU	First American Collected Edition by Doubleday Page, known as the 'Sun-Dial' (1920)
H	First English Collected Edition by William Heinemann (1921)

Bibliographical Studies

Higdon, *Typescript*	Floyd Eugene Eddleman and David Leon Higdon, 'The Typescript of Conrad's *Almayer's Folly*'
Higdon, *Proof*	Floyd Eugene Eddleman and David Leon Higdon, 'Proof Revisions in Conrad's *Almayer's Folly*'
Higdon, *First*	Floyd Eugene Eddleman, David Leon Higdon, and Robert W. Hobson, 'The First Editions of Joseph Conrad's *Almayer's Folly*'
Higdon, *Collected*	David Leon Higdon and Floyd Eugene Eddleman, 'Collected Edition Variants in Conrad's *Almayer's Folly*'

Other Works

Allen	Jerry Allen, *The Sea Years of Joseph Conrad* (London, 1967)
Furnivall	J. S. Furnivall, *Netherlands India: A Study of Plural Economy* (Cambridge, 1967)
Gordan	John Dozier Gordan, *Joseph Conrad: The Making of a Novelist* (New York, 1963)
Hall	G. D. E. Hall, *A History of South-East Asia* (London, 1964)
Handbook i, ii	Naval Intelligence Division, Geographical Handbook Series, *Netherlands East Indies*, 2 vols. (?London, 1944)

Koran	Arthur J. Arberry, *The Koran Interpreted* (Oxford, 1964)
Letters i, ii	Frederick R. Karl and Laurence Davies (eds.), *The Collected Letters of Joseph Conrad, 1861–1897*, 2 vols. (Cambridge, 1983, 1986)
Life and Letters i, ii	G. Jean-Aubry, *Joseph Conrad, Life and Letters*, 2 vols. (London, 1927)
Najder	Zdzisław Najder, *Joseph Conrad: A Chronicle* (Cambridge, 1983)
Sherry	Norman Sherry, *Conrad's Eastern World* (Cambridge, 1966)
Vlekke	Bernard H. M. Vlekke, *Nusantara: A History of Indonesia* (The Hague, 1959)
Winstedt	R. O. Winstedt, *An Unabridged Malay-English ... English-Malay Dictionary*, 2 vols. (Kuala Lumpur, 1963)

INTRODUCTION: CONRAD'S REALISM

I

Almayer's Folly is set in Eastern Borneo in the early 1880s. Conrad never says so in so many words, but he draws into his novel quite enough of the world outside it—what we call the 'real world' when we want to distinguish it from an 'imagined world'—to enable us to verify time and place. In fact, he is sufficiently committed to documentary exactness for us to identify the occasional mistake. For example, he provides his Borneo with the monsoon season that in truth prevails only in other parts of the Malay Archipelago. Had his visits to its eastern coast lasted longer, he would have discovered that its climate is equatorial, with daily rainfall and no seasonal variations. Moreover, he might well have corrected his error had he become aware of it, for, as the notes to this edition show, his attempt to integrate his fiction into the real world is astonishingly comprehensive, encompassing landscape, weather, plant and animal life, demography, material resources, commerce, politics, religion, architecture, dress, etc. Indeed, it is obvious that much of what he put into *Almayer's Folly* was derived either from observation and memory, or from conversation and reading.

Yet the novel remains an essentially fictional narrative for which, by definition, truth to fact should not be a decisive criterion of success. For example, although Conrad's attribution of monsoons to East Borneo is a factual error, the imminence of the seasonal rains plays an active part in the story in that it provides a deadline for Almayer's expedition up river to recover the mine that he believes will be his salvation. In other words, this error intensifies tension for reader and character alike, and creates the purely literary value of suspense. Or, more generally, after over forty years of patient effort, research has been able to uncover a number of real-life sources for the novel: for instance, a river known as the Berau, a settlement called Tanjong Redeb, the names of various persons who traded there at the time of Conrad's visits. Conrad's fictional Sambir, however, is not a depiction of the Tanjong Redeb he knew in October 1888, nor is his Kaspar Almayer a portrait of the Charles Olmeijer he met there. Any travellers having purchased *Almayer's Folly* as a guide would have been able to claim their money back, for it situates the settlement now on an island (p. 14), now on a promontory (p. 50); nor would Charles Olmeijer, a respectable father of eight children, have had much difficulty in suing the author for defamation of character. Yet no one would claim that such considerations have any bearing on the status of *Almayer's Folly* as one of the most remarkable first novels we possess.

Are we then to conclude that Conrad's documentary scruples contribute nothing to the success of his work? Three years after completing *Almayer's Folly* he produced an artistic credo which began by defining fiction as 'a single-minded attempt to render the highest kind of justice to the visible universe, by bringing to light the truth, manifest and one, underlying its every aspect'.[1] This statement is by no means pellucid, but it makes at least one thing clear: that Conrad regards truth to the way things are, not generally but perforce in a given place and time, as more than incidental to his purpose as a novelist. Yet how can this be, if even factual 'injustices' (in the sense that it is 'unjust' to Borneo to mistake its climate) are able to be turned to artistic advantage? It is scarcely surprising that contemporary critics have taken to deriding the claim to truthfulness made by all the nineteenth-century realists, from Balzac to Zola, and Scott to Gissing. Everyone now accepts that what defines realism, as opposed let us say to romance, is not fidelity to reality but fidelity to convention. In this view a genre is primarily determined by literary rules. For example, one such rule allows the use of documentation as a technique of plausibility. To quote a successful modern practitioner: '. . . place

[1] Preface to *The Nigger of the 'Narcissus'* (London, Dent Collected Edition, 1950), vii.

and names are genuine, but this is merely the novelist's cunning device to add authenticity to fictitious characters and events'.[2] In this formulation, 'truth' and 'fiction' become antagonistic categories, 'truth' turning into 'truth-effect', achievable by following the rules of the game of 'authenticity'.

This move solves many problems, but at the cost of silencing Conrad. Yet there are good reasons why his voice should not be muffled too quickly. First, as a man who started life as the son of a banned Polish patriot, who served early on six of the seven seas in two foreign merchant marines, and who rose to the rank of captain well before the idea of writing occurred to him, he brings to his first novel an unusual freight of extra-literary experience. Second, as his long-suppressed 'Author's Note' to *Almayer's Folly* reveals, he takes Borneo as seriously as he takes England, dissociating himself from 'that literature which preys on strange people and prowls in far-off countries' (p. lxi), on the grounds of its exploitative insensitivity—of the unreality of its exoticism and the reductiveness of its treatment of human beings. His Indonesia will not be like Rider Haggard's Africa—a place offering no resistance to the fantasies of ignorance and desire. As far as Conrad is concerned, therefore, any theory of fiction that prevents a novel from receiving its author's knowledge and experience of the world—what has become important to him on the basis of what he has seen for himself—requires further interrogation.

The young Almayer (a fictional character) works for a couple of years in Macassar (a real city). What is obvious about this statement is that there is nothing remarkable about it. Almayer in Macassar is no ghost in the machine, and his presence there causes neither him nor us the slightest ontological confusion. To extend the point: nothing about the novel Conrad was writing need have prevented him from making his Almayer meet and talk to the historical Dutch

[2] P. D. James, 'Author's Note' to *Devices and Desires* (London, Faber, 1989).

Resident of the district, had he found it necessary, nor would such an encounter have struck us as absurd. Yet more generally: historians confirm that in 1881 the Dutch war against the Sumatran Achinese suffered a reverse that spread unrest throughout the Archipelago, and especially in Bali. In the novel, it is this event that brings the Balinese prince, Dain Maroola (the most imaginary character in the book), to Sambir; but Dain's arrival precipitates the crisis of the plot and its characters. Thus the Achin wars cannot be dismissed as mere background required by the 'plausibility effect', for they are an integral part of the narrative. Dain goes to Sambir because historical Bali needs contraband gunpowder to resist the colonial government; but he also goes to Sambir because of what Conrad alone has put there: regular calls of a steamer from Singapore, the presence of a disaffected white man, the absence of a government Resident. This represents a complex interpenetration of fact and fiction, yet at no time do we even begin to feel that there is a muddling of the two. Indeed, a considerable editorial effort has been necessary to disentangle the strands.

What has to be deduced from our failure to perceive a clash of categories is that there is none. The language of fiction cannot be differentiated from the language of fact. We talk about a character, a place, an event in a novel in exactly the same way as we talk about them in daily life; although Kaspar Almayer and Charles Olmeijer are different persons, the first is as entitled to be called a man as the second; the sentence 'Indeed, he had a report to make', which Conrad applies to his Rajah's factotum, Babalatchi (p. 61), could with equal propriety have been used of Conrad himself, or indeed of me as I write this. Language itself does not recognize the frontier dividing an imagined world from the real world.

This means that we are not logically compelled to read the phrase 'realistic fiction' as a contradiction in terms. Narrative texts range from the historical to the escapist; the two categories that mark the outer limits of narrative may seem incompatible, but it does not follow that those occupying an intermediate position, such as the realistic text in its various forms, are disqualified from incorporating, not as an optional extra or a device of verisimilitude but as a paradigm and principle of structure, the contextualization of history. This does not imply that historical and realistic narratives obey the same criteria. Realistic fiction is not bound by the rules of evidence, nor does it demand documentary precision, though in practice it usually retains (as the whole of Conrad's *œuvre* does) close contact with its sources in life and books. But the freedom of the novelist is no sinecure. Every sentence Conrad has fabricated in *Almayer's Folly* is constrained by the threat of verbal cliché, the claims of narrative logic, and the pressure of everything he has learnt in the course of three decades of life as one of the more adventurous and receptive citizens of the late nineteenth century.

II

What kind of man was the 32-year-old Conrad when, in the Autumn of 1889, he sat down in Bessborough Gardens, Pimlico, to write the first words of the novel that he would take five years to complete? Primarily, one who had acquired a pervasive sense of the relativity of human affairs. The conviction that we as individuals are at the centre of our lives, and as human beings at the centre of creation, is sustainable only under specific conditions—in particular, those guaranteeing that change be too gradual to rupture the illusion of a steady-state existence, such as parental security, a constant environment, a permanent homeland. None of these conditions was available to Conrad. He was born at the end of 1857 in a country that had been deprived of political existence since its first partitioning in 1795 between Russia, Austria, and Germany. His father, one of the chief architects of the futile Polish insurrection of 1863, was arrested and exiled with his wife and son to Northern Russia in 1862. Conrad's mother died three years later; his father sank into a 'morbid consumption' that carried him off, now back in Cracow, in 1869. Five years later, in 1874, the 16-year-old

Conrad persuaded his guardian to let him go to sea. For four years thereafter he served on French merchant ships out of Marseilles. In April 1878, however, he reinvented his future by enlisting on a British steamer, thus inaugurating a career under the red ensign that was to last for about sixteen years.

What we take for granted we do not notice. An Englishman of the 1870s would have had no reason to question his assumption of individual and national self-sufficiency. At home in his environment, he would have simply failed to perceive, unless he was specially imaginative or unlucky, how far he owed his sense of identity to the conditions of his life, or his sense of reality—of the fitness of things—to his country's place in the world. Conrad, however, could take very little for granted. Taught by his early acquaintance with deprivation and insecurity how much he depended on what was external to the self, yet how little he could control it, he would quickly have acquired a strong sense of the relativity of identity. Similarly, as a Pole born into a nation erased from the map of Europe, starting life as an exile (in Russia), continuing it after an interval as an *émigré* (in France, then England), he would have gained an equally strong sense of the relativity of cultures. Thus, when he settled down to write his first novel, he would have been in no doubt that human beings are born in a condition of plurality.

But the characterization is not yet complete. By an extraordinary turn of the lottery of history, the man whose early life had prepared him for the knowledge that no one is an island was cast in a role that would allow him to make the most productive use of his education. For sixteen years he found himself on the front line of the most important development of the second half of the nineteenth century: the expansion of Europe into the furthest regions of the world. The atlas of his deep-sea voyages, always undertaken in the service of commercial interests, shows that he rounded Cape Horn once and the Cape of Good Hope thirteen times, that he got to know every ocean of the globe except the North Pacific, that he visited the Caribbean and the northern republics of Latin America, and, regularly, India, Malaysia, Indonesia, China, and Australia, and that he even penetrated into what were then thought of as the darkest places of the earth, the island of Borneo and the African Congo.

The remorseless encroachment which carried Conrad in its vanguard involved the subjection of distant peoples by invaders incapable of recognizing, let alone respecting, their victims' difference. However, as himself a victim of unseeing imperialism, he remained deeply sceptical of justifications invoking the spread of civilization; and despite the fact that his contact with foreign people was necessarily superficial, he never failed to acknowledge that their lives, even when he did not understand them, made at least as much sense to them as his own to himself. But he was also receptive to more indirect consequences. Its commercial success took Europe out of itself, exposing its culture to displacement and disorientation. Dutch, Belgian, or British colonial agents, whether they knew it or not, found themselves in places that undermined the assumptions on which their lives were based. Moreover, as European interests established themselves across the world, some Europeans paradoxically began to sense that their continent was only a part of the whole it sought to dominate. They began to collect information about primitive or alien societies, and established the foundation of what was to become anthropological science. But having done so they could scarcely fail to turn its relativizing gaze upon themselves.

This irresistible historical process, however, held one final irony in reserve, to which Conrad proved exceptionally receptive. The exploration of the earth (to use a Euro-centric phrase) radically altered Western man's perception of his place within nature. It is well known that Charles Darwin was active in that cxploration, mounting an expedition to the Galapagos Islands in 1831, where he found evidence of the instability of animal species. What is less familiar is that he had a rival. Nearly thirty years before Conrad went to Borneo, the fauna and flora of that island were investigated by the naturalist Alfred Wallace who, quite independently, came to conclusions anticipating Darwin's. Wallace's account of his eight-year travels in Indonesia was published in 1869 under the title *The Malay Archipelago*. This book became Conrad's favourite reading, and materially influenced his early fiction.[3] But by then the consequences of the new ideas were everywhere apparent. With the publication of *The Origin of Species* in 1859, the theory of evolution quickly became notorious, and provided a focus for anxieties that had been gathering for half a century. The doctrine of Nature as God's permanent creation was felt to be threatened by the hypothesis of evolutionary flux. Human beings who had long thought themselves privileged by the work of the seven days felt their traditional moorings beginning to give way; and as providence began to drain out of the cosmos, human consciousness was left exposed as an irrelevance on the face of life. By the time Conrad was writing *Almayer's Folly*, this malaise had achieved the status of a commonplace. In the year the novel was published, a future British prime minister informed the nation that it inhabited 'an irrational Universe which accidentally turns out a few reasoning animals in one corner of it'.[4] Nor, naturally, was this metaphysical dismay (when it was more than a mere fashion) confined to Victorian England. In his *Notes from Underground* of 1864, Dostoevsky stated: 'I am firmly persuaded that a great deal of consciousness, every sort of consciousness, in fact, is a disease';[5] and in 1883, Nietzsche's Zarathustra finally proclaimed the death of God. Whether prompted by the hypothesis of a mechanical or of a random world, the idea of the Absurd was now firmly implanted in

[3] Florence Clemens, 'Conrad's Favourite Bedside Book', *South Atlantic Quarterly*, 38 (1939), 301–15.

[4] Arthur Balfour, *Foundations of Belief* (London, Longmans & Co., 1895), 75.

[5] F. Dostoevsky, *Notes from Underground*, trans. Garnett (London, Heinemann, 1966 (1918)), 61.

European culture.[6] In 1889, in Bessborough Gardens, Conrad shared it.

III

Almayer's Folly owes its realism in large measure to the relativism I have attempted to evoke. Conrad conceives of the individual subject not as an autonomous unit but as belonging simultaneously to itself and to others, as at once the centre of its own perceptions and the product of group formations, whether social, sexual, racial, religious, or national. This means that no human life, however private, can be understood merely internally but has also to be construed in terms of its location in an external world, which extends from the self's most intimate familiarities to realities lying beyond its farthest horizons.

Consider the situation of the novel's protagonist, a second-generation Dutch colonial stranded in an obscure native settlement thirty miles up a virtually unknown equatorial river. He lives in commercial decay on its banks; behind him rises the house of his Arab rivals, who have ruined his prospects; across the river can be seen the campong of the Malay rajah who rules his backwater by courtesy of the Dutch; inland are found primitive Dyaks, or head-hunters, who regularly bring down their produce in canoes; in the settlement lives an unemployed Chinaman who in due course will addict him to opium; down-river works a Siamese slave-girl whose experience of loss will eventually intersect with his; his wife, of Sulu (Philippino) origin, has had an unsuccessful convent education; his daughter, of mixed blood, has received, with scarcely greater success, a Protestant upbringing. Conrad has placed his protagonist at a crossroads of cultures where the elements, old and new, that make up the life of the Archipelago converge and collide. If

[6] For a detailed documentation, see John A. Lester, *Journey Through Despair 1880–1914* (Princeton, NJ, Princeton University Press, 1968).

the primitive past comes downstream, the international future comes up-river. Decisions taken in London and Amsterdam affect every household in Sambir. Captain Ford's steamer, owned by a Singapore merchant, brings news and cargo; Dutch naval frigates assert the presence of foreign authority; and the brig of a Balinese prince (whose Brahminism adds yet another item to a religious list that includes totemism, two forms of Islam, and two forms of Christianity) appears, to disturb a desultory nationalism and to precipitate Almayer's final disintegration.

In this social density and variety, *Almayer's Folly* prefigures Conrad's masterpieces of the first decade of the twentieth century, especially *Nostromo* and *The Secret Agent*. But it does so in another, equally significant, way. By enmeshing the individual subject in a network of relationships and interests, Conrad does not, even in his first novel, reduce it to a mere 'effect of system', as structural or dialectical sociologists would say. Moreover, to recognize that the very content of a particular purpose may be constituted by social and historical determinants is not to remove that purpose from its emplacement in personal desire. For all his denial of the self's autonomy, Conrad continues to take its life seriously. This enables him to give his novel, whatever its incidental lapses, a new kind of realism, for he no longer conceives of history as an abstract force (evolutionary or revolutionary), but concretely, as the interaction of human beings bearing the stamp of determinate groups and classes.

This interaction is impelled by the principle that confers on individuals the right to the pursuit of happiness. Only, for Conrad, this right is an instinct. In a letter of 8 February 1899, he reacted to Cunninghame Graham's ideal of 'international fraternity' in the following way: 'C'est l'égoisme qui sauve tout—absolument tout—tout ce que nous abhorrons[,] tout ce que nous aimons. Et tout se tient.'[7] In this

[7] *Letters*, ii. 159. ('Egoism preserves everything—absolutely everything—everything we hate and everything we love. And everything holds together.')

view, the edifice of the human world is preserved ('qui sauve tout') by the interlocking ('tout se tient') of disparate interests. This declaration was made in the context of *Heart of Darkness*. Not surprisingly it caused something of a scandal among Conrad's earlier readers; but it represents a serious position, which had been fully worked out in fictional terms four years earlier.

By definition, self-generated purposes seek realization in the public domain, where they encounter other such purposes which deflect, alter, or defeat them. The execution of an intention, therefore, depends on the capacity to read the intentions of others; but even in the most favoured cases, complete success is impossible. For example, Dain Maroola, the most accomplished operator in the novel, knows he can safely throw himself on the mercy of Lakamba because he is able to detect that the rajah is too implicated in the gunpowder plot to risk betraying him to the Dutch (p. 81), and too covetous of Almayer's alleged treasure to have Almayer's confidant killed (p. 83). So Dain is able to secure his ultimate aim (elopement with Nina), but only at the cost of failing to discern the threat to her father. And indeed, after he has taken his leave, Lakamba decides to have Almayer poisoned to prevent him, were he to be arrested by the Dutch, from betraying his treasure in exchange for his liberty (pp. 87–8). In the event, it is only Mrs Almayer's own project in the masquerade of the drowned corpse—a scheme directed as much against her husband as in favour of her daughter—that, ironically, averts his fate.

Dain has often been regarded as a figure out of adventure romance. That he satisfies at least two criteria of such stories—a hair's breadth escape and the winning of the lady—is evident, but this should not tempt us into premature judgement. The defining condition of the genre is that the resistance offered to the hero by the fact of social plurality should in principle be unreal. In this respect, romance narrative is like the suspended scenarios of personal reverie: they too presuppose the world outside the self, but only as the support of solipsistic omnipotence. This amounts to saying that in romance the projects of others are not taken seriously: 'others' are never finally 'themselves'. *Almayer's Folly*, a deeply realistic text, works on different conditions. One could say that it has no protagonist, in the sense that all its characters, even the most insignificant, are presented as the protagonists of their own lives. Now, it is true that Dain, who as it were enters the novel from outside it, lacks social density. Thus Conrad can only bring him fully to life in the reactive present—for example, when, condemned helplessly to await Nina's arrival in Bulangi's clearing, he displays all the feverish restlessness of a man normally in command of events (pp. 165–70). However, the fact remains that once Dain has been inserted into the interactions of Sambir, he is obliged by his author to abide by their logic.

This is perhaps best shown in his relations with Almayer. His descent on Sambir is characteristically confident. Having rapidly assessed the situation, he fobs off the Dutch with his trader's disguise, pays off Lakamba with a handsome bribe, holds off the Arabs with empty courtesies, and appropriates Almayer's designs to serve his own. But no man is merely himself. Almayer's purposes may be pathetically transparent, but he is, as he must be, the target of other purposes, some too submerged to be manipulable. He has been mistakenly suspected by the Arabs, whose own earlier venture into gunpowder smuggling came to disaster, of having betrayed them to the Dutch. Accordingly they take the appropriate revenge (p. 123). By commandeering the apparently malleable Almayer, Dain loses in one stroke gunpowder, brig, and crew. Under the novel's egalitarian conditions of relativity, the strong Dain and the weak Almayer are one.

To be sure, Dain's failed political project is overtaken after his arrival in Sambir by a new and eventually successful one—his love for Nina, which brings to the surface unsuspected depths of feeling in him. But this does not contradict the egalitarian law, for it involves an increased dependence on Almayer. This is not because Nina is

Almayer's daughter, even less because once he has met her, his attention is diverted into a new direction, but because it is to Almayer, paradoxically, that he owes his escape into happiness. In this novel, even successful intentions are fulfilled, as it were, unintentionally, for they too remain entangled in the discrete, not to say antagonistic, motives of other people.

When Nina finally explains herself to her father, she tells him: 'No two human beings understand each other. They can understand but their own voices' (p. 179). This accurately reflects both her life with him, and the novel's conception of social relations. But she immediately goes on to contradict it. Describing her commitment to Dain, she says: 'In time . . . both our voices, that man's and mine, spoke together in a sweetness that was intelligible to our ears only' (p. 179). Does a reciprocal love, by whatever route it is achieved, constitute a counter-example? Conrad seems to concede that two distinct individuals can blend into a single subjectivity: if so, is this fatal to the principle of interlocking egoisms (which are solitudes) that 'saves everything'?

His treatment of the couple, however, manages to do justice to their love as (in Nina's words) the discovery of 'a land where no one could follow us' (p. 179) without sacrificing his premiss. First, the novel does not forget that these two-souls-which-are-one are socially constituted. Nina chooses Dain because he is a Malay; Dain chooses Nina because she is a European. For her, he represents the resolution of the paralysing divisions of her mixed racial and cultural inheritance: she opts for the Indonesian in her. For him, she represents the seduction of emancipated femininity, a quality to which everyone responds, from Babalatchi's 'She is a white woman and knows no shame' (p. 128) to Dain's transgressive rapture at her mouth-to-mouth kiss (p. 72). Hence his feeling, as she parts from her father, that 'No desire, no longing, no effort of will or length of life could destroy this vague feeling of their difference' (p. 187), has a prophetic resonance. Second, the novel suggests that their reciprocal intensity may be the expression of the elemental, if not the evolutionary, powers of nature.[8] Sexual arousal is consistently set in the luxuriant corruption of the virgin forest. Their first moment of ecstatic communion occurs under a shower of 'immense red blossoms' dropping from trees rooted in 'death and decay' (p. 71); the moment of carnal knowledge is concealed within the border of a jungle whose soaring trunks live the death of their 'entombed and rotting' predecessors (pp. 166–7), and which seem to know that 'human love' is 'human blindness' (p. 173). The familiar double (inner–outer) description thus begins to emerge; but it is only when their love is recognized as properly part of the realistic manœuvres of the narrative that its ambivalence is fully disclosed. To say that lovers hear a sweetness that is 'intelligible to their ears only' and enter a land where 'no one can follow them' is not only to describe their delight; it is also to represent love as an *égoisme-à-deux*, which, in its ruthless tenderness, destroys not one but two lives—Almayer's of course, but also, no less poignantly, Taminah's.

IV

To represent the interplay of discrepant purposes in a narrative action has two major consequences if the task is carried out consistently and in detail. On the one hand, it closes the gap, left open by illustrative or functionalist narratives, between form and content regarded as separate stages of composition, one preceding the other. On the other hand, it opens a gap, within the narrative, between intentions and actions kept closed by genres such as the romance,

[8] Two monographs have appeared on the subject of Conrad and Darwin or Darwinism: Allan Hunter, *Joseph Conrad and the Ethics of Darwinism* (London, Croom Helm, 1983), and Redmond O'Hanlon, *Joseph Conrad and Charles Darwin: the Influence of Scientific Thought on Conrad's Fiction* (Edinburgh, Salamander, 1984). Both envisage the relationship in terms of parallels and allegories that assume a connection between ideas and fiction quite different from the one recommended in this essay.

premised on the autonomous conception of the self. Together, these consequences produce a third: the possibility of a new level of engagement with extra-textual reality, or, as we prefer to say, history. We shall deal with each of these in turn.

It is well known that Conrad's fictions are marked by the exploitation of a variety of allegedly unrealistic narrative procedures, notably chronological fragmentation, the use of internal narrators, and a predilection for the *style indirecte libre*. It used to be thought that these narrative 'transgressions' were instrumental, in that they seemed to act as devices for the expression of unconventional ideas and conceptions already in the writer's possession. Today, the prevailing view seems to be that it is the narrative mode that determines thematic content. One of the reasons for this is the prestige accorded to 'narratology' (i.e. the theory, some say the grammar, of narrative as such) by what might be called 'Genette's Anatomy', which attempts to do for the novel what Gray's *Anatomy* did for the body.[9] Genette's remarkable treatise has greatly refined our perception of how particular narratives work; yet it remains in order to ask how far it is possible to theorize or anatomize narrative as such. To describe the musculature of one human body is *mutatis mutandis*, to include all bodies; but to specify the articulations of *Almayer's Folly* is plainly not to specify those of *Bleak House* or *Ulysses*. What characterizes a narrative is not that it is composed of narratological tropes (everything covered by Genette's paradigm 'tense/mood/voice'), but in what way these elements are used. It is not (to change the analogy) the notes themselves that produce the melody, but their arrangement. This may seem elementary, yet once the point is grasped, the received distinction between form and content as separable elements can no longer be held. A musician plays a sad tune expressively: if we respond, we may be tempted to regard the expressive sadness as the

[9] Gérard Genette, *Figures III* (Paris, Seuil, 1972) (trans. as *Narrative Discourse* (Oxford, Blackwell, 1980)).

content of the tune; but does it then make sense to ask him to give us the sadness without the tune?[10]

Following a narrative is not the same as anatomizing it, for a narrative is a performance in which the tropes are, as it were, made to speak. The episode of the disfigured corpse in Chapter Seven will serve as an illustration, for it puts to use several of the narrative devices, including discrepant perspectives, delayed decoding, flashbacks, and synchrony (simultaneity of scenes), at work in the novel. As we have seen, every motivated event in *Almayer's Folly* is always to some degree opaque to those outside it, for its roots spread far into the community. To be sure, the incident of the corpse involves deliberate deception, in that Dain's drowned boatman is made to pass for his master; nevertheless, the significance of the event remains the complex of motives leading to the deception, rather than the deception itself—a complex which remains as submerged as the true identity of the corpse. The body is discovered by one such spectator, the garrulous, superstitious, excitable and indolent villager, Mahmat Banjer, whose comic innocence measures the gap between appearance and reality. That discovery is framed by the perspective of another spectator, Almayer. Unlike Mahmat's, Almayer's point of view is familiar to us, as near in fictional time as the previous evening, when he experienced the relief and joy of Dain's return, as far, in narrative time, as the opening chapter, and its ensuing free-ranging retrospections, which have taught us not only what that return means to him, but also how remote he is from its true motive. Given his state of deluded security, therefore, it is appropriate that he should continue to inhabit it until the last possible moment: that he should be the last person in the settlement to wake up, that he should be bewildered by the silence and emptiness around him, that he should be puzzled by the sight of Babalatchi crossing the water decked out in the regalia of a minister of state charged with an important

[10] See L. Wittgenstein, *Lectures & Conversations on Aesthetics, Psychology and Religious Belief* (Oxford, Blackwell, 1966), 29.

duty (only the reader knows that this is an execution), and that he should be the last to see the corpse. But his role as a witness is quite unlike Mahmat Banjer's. It is not merely that what for the one is an opportunity for self-importance is for the other the destruction of his future. It is the difference in significance of the success of the deception in each case. Both are taken in by the lie the corpse is telling: Mahmat's deception represents the happy ignorance of unambitious ordinary life; Almayer's, however, is paradoxically a kind of insight, for if the discovery that Dain is dead abolishes his last hopes, the discovery that he is alive will reveal, even more disastrously, how irrelevant these hopes are to the man on whom they depend, and to the woman in whom they are invested.

Because the incident is presented to us through these two uninstructed perspectives, we find ourselves equally perspectivized. Two conclusions have been drawn from this fact. David Leon Higdon has argued that Conrad traps the reader into accepting that the dead man is Dain;[11] Ian Watt has gone further in claiming that Conrad's manipulation of us is an easy way of 'feeding our curiosity about the plot at the cost of starving our understanding of the protagonists':[12] all we want to know is what really happened—namely that during the night Mrs Almayer initiated the deception and, while Nina took Dain to the security of Bulangi's clearing, disfigured the face of the corpse beyond identification. However, if we take the trouble of following the narrative, we find that the postponement of the explanation is not primarily a device for creating tension, but a means of generating interpretative unease. The presentation of the episode involves more than delayed decoding (the retrospective reinterpretation of details that originally seemed innocuous: for example, we need to know what has really happened before we notice the slight automatism of Mrs

[11] David Leon Higdon, *Time and English Fiction* (London, Macmillan, 1977), 96.

[12] Ian Watt, *Conrad in the Nineteenth Century* (London, Chatto & Windus, 1980), 62.

Almayer's cries of grief (pp. 95, 96)). If we read with only moderate attentiveness, however, we must observe an unexplained alteration in Babalatchi between his instinctive attempt to hide the corpse's 'identity', when he first sees it, by putting his foot on the hand bearing Dain's ring (p. 97), and his contrivance, after the corpse has been brought to the house, to publicize this 'identity' by cueing Mahmat (p. 105). But much more disturbing of a naïve reading is our observation of Nina's behaviour. We know from the earlier chapters what Almayer does not: that Nina and Dain are passionately in love. We cannot therefore fail to see that her conduct is quite incompatible with a belief that her lover is dead. In fact, the only emotion she betrays is anxiety about her father's state of mind; otherwise, she remains quite unmoved by what should have been a calamity to her. We cannot yet account for her behaviour, but we are left in no doubt that there is something awry about the episode. We know that interpretation is required, yet we cannot produce it. In brief, Conrad has not so much deceived us as *relativized our understanding*.

The act of reading positions us in linear time, and so predisposes us in favour of consecutive action. No narrative, of course, is uniformly chronological, except perhaps for Genette's formulaic reduction, 'subject + predicate + complement' (as in the alleged 'He returned home' for the *Odyssey*). But an author who seeks to narrate the relativity of projects must, like those fresco painters who constructed three-dimensional space out of a two-dimensional surface, dislodge readers from linearity so as to evoke simultaneity. In order to keep the narrative counterpoint of his novel going, Conrad therefore breaks up chronology and allocates the pieces to the various participants, bringing out the synchrony in a number of ways. For instance, in the course of 'that long day of excitement' (p. 147) opened by the discovery of the corpse and closed by the couple's escape, the cannon shot proclaiming the arrival of the Dutch which startles Nina and Babalatchi at the end of the first episode (pp. 106–7) is the shot heard by Abdulla and Reshid in the next chapter as they interrogate Taminah (p. 111), and again, three chapters later, the shot that reaches Dain's ears as he waits in hiding downstream (p. 166). Or again, the various cross-purposes that have been building up throughout the narrative are made to converge and break on a single spot, Bulangi's clearing, which receives in accelerating sequence first Dain, then Nina, then Almayer and Ali, then Babalatchi and his war canoe, and finally Taminah and the Dutch long-boat.

But more is required of us than the perception of synchronic pattern, if the experience of simultaneity is to be fully respected. We cannot, as it were, remain on the hill watching the battle unfolding below; we must also descend into the plain and struggle with the combatants. But we cannot be in two places at once. Conrad is therefore compelled into what I have called 'relativized understanding', which keeps us in suspense between error and truth, between knowing more than a blinkered character yet less than an omniscient narrator. His handling of the corpse episode is doubtless his most obvious example of it; but he never entirely frees us from its effects. Even the disclosure of the body's identity retains some of its elements, for it is the characters themselves who mediate the disclosure. First, we see Reshid, the heir to the Arab business, receiving with great suspicion the news of Dain's death. He possesses privileged information that Dain has been blown up with his ship, so he does not know what to believe: 'He has been dead once before, and came to life to die again now' (p. 109). (Incidentally, this provides another instance of relativized understanding: we perceive the need for further explanation, and are made to wait until the Dutch officer puts pressure on Almayer by telling him that he has been betrayed by the Arabs.) Reshid therefore tries to get Taminah, who as Bulangi's cake-seller has access to the Dutch, to spy for him; but all he does is to secure the services of the one person, other than the plotters themselves, who knows that Dain is alive. We have entered the second stage of clarification, which again assumes subjective form, this time in a flash-back evoking the growth of

Taminah's mute adoration of Dain and the jealous anguish with which she sees him brought by Nina to her master's hideout (pp. 112–19). The final stage, in which the details of the plot are exposed, takes another interactive form—Babalatchi's report to Lakamba urging, in the light of the new development, an instant readjustment of their strategy for political survival (pp. 127–30). Thus, even the process of information has to go through the instabilities of partial perception and coincident events.

To attend to the process of narration as it unfolds in *Almayer's Folly* is to abolish the labour of having to reconcile form and content. Narrative form no longer presents itself as a vehicle for expressing pre-existing material, or as itself the determinant of what can be said. Instead, 'what Conrad is saying' becomes a *further description* of 'how he is saying it'; alternatively, his presentation becomes a further account of what he represents. No one questions that the same object can be viewed under different descriptions. Literary texts are no exception. We shall therefore conclude by examining the novel's 'realism' directly, on the understanding that the term is not used programmatically, but as a sign that, as we have argued, the frontier between fiction and history is not closed.

V

An account of the historical dimension of *Almayer's Folly* must begin by assuming that its text is more than a paragraph of a larger text called 'history'. The novel is not the product of the nineteenth century, but of the mind of a man of the nineteenth century. This does not imply that Conrad had a complete, or even a commanding, grasp of the context that formed him; but in so far as he is a writer of calibre, that context is inside him, so that he cannot be regarded as a mere ventriloquist's dummy. It follows that history belongs to his book, and not only to its determinants.

It has not been sufficiently noticed that Conrad's presentation of Almayer is to a high degree historically conditioned.

He belongs to a class of petty-bourgeois colonials who hold power over a native population for purely contingent reasons, and who therefore exhibit all the symptoms of unearned self-esteem. The son of a subordinate official in the Botanical Gardens of Batavia, and of the daughter of an Amsterdam cigar dealer who devotes the leisure of a colonial wife to bewailing the lost glories of her youth, he combines the mediocre complacency of the father with the fatuous discontent of the mother. Like the Batavia that has produced him, he belongs neither to Indonesia nor to the Netherlands. As a white man fated to exist among people he considers his inferiors he suffers an internal fracture. His self-image is fatally disaligned from his actual life, and his ambitions hopelessly outstrip his capacities.

The young Almayer, then, is a class victim who has been equipped for his future with nothing better than a predilection for the soft option and a commitment to the main chance. Accordingly, he falls under the spell of a very different, historically earlier, colonial type, the trader–adventurer Lingard who, in the irresponsibility of self-reliance, corrupts him further by bribing him to marry his half-savage ward, a pirate chief's daughter captured in the course of a bloody encounter. Almayer's greed having overcome his racist scruples, he weds the girl, settles in Sambir as Lingard's manager, and awaits his promised inheritance. But competitors arrive, and his benefactor, having turned gold prospector, goes bankrupt and disappears.

Almayer's legacy of self-alienation is now complete. He feels nothing but aversion for the foetid tropical outpost in which he is trapped, and distaste for the betel-chewing harridan that the woman he married has become; yet he is patronized by the whole settlement for his laziness and self-pity, and loathed by his wife for his sexual feebleness (she has never accepted the loss of the masterful Lingard, p. 22) and for his status as political oppressor. So while he indulges dreams of conspicuous consumption in Amsterdam, she pines for the lawless virility of her Sulu past. Their relationship recapitulates the political and psychological tensions of the Archipelago, less because it is a symbol than because it is a product of them.

Is Almayer, then, no more than a sample of a certain type of colonialism? Certainly, Conrad's diagnosis of his condition is nothing if not realistic. The very content of his inner life—his very conception of happiness—is a desolating repetition of the vulgar ideals of his class. Moreover, we are left in no doubt that his dream of success is unreal, and that the contradictions of his present existence would not disappear were he to return to Holland. However, we are left in even less doubt that he cannot be dismissed as a mere case. Like the other characters of the novel, he is completely embedded in the deeper realism of its interactive narrative, and hence possesses a point of view which is important to him. Whether or not he succeeds, he means to convert desire into action, and to reclaim at least a portion of the world outside himself in which to establish his self-image. Thus he invests his future in Lingard's mine and Nina's love. He possesses neither, of course: we never discover whether the mine is exploitable, or even whether it exists; we know that Nina is as much her mother's daughter as his (indeed, more so, after her experience of sexual and racial discrimination in Singapore). Moreover, the plot itself underlines this dispossession: the man who promises to bring the mine within his grasp is also the man who takes Nina beyond his reach. But the fact remains that his quest for happiness remains fully alive in him.

The significance of this can be brought out by comparing two scenes. From one point of view, as the novel's title indicates, the incongruity of his pretensions make him a figure of absurdity. When news reaches Sambir that the British Borneo Company has been floated, Almayer jumps to the conclusion that the period of Dutch hegemony is over, and he spends his last guilder building a new house for the use of prospective English officials; but British interests are confined to Sarawak, and most of Borneo remains under the authority of Holland. To confirm this, a naval frigate pays Sambir an official visit, and Almayer entertains the Dutch officers in his now useless house. In the course of the evening, he is unable to conceal his discomfiture, and he leaves a vivid impression of his 'wonderful simplicity' and 'foolish hopefulness'. As they return to their ships, the river, we are told, wakes up 'to the ringing laughter provoked by some reminiscences of Almayer's lamentable narrative'; and 'the half-finished house built for the reception of Englishmen received on that joyous night the name of "Almayer's Folly"' (pp. 35–7). This merriment, which expresses a nice blend of personal complacency and national self-satisfaction, defines Almayer as a joke for all the province.

Against this, we may set Almayer's reaction to Babalatchi's identification of the drowned body, which at last puts him into contact with the folly that has made his comic reputation:

> Almayer raised his hands to his head and let them fall listlessly by his side in the utter abandonment of despair. Babalatchi, looking at him curiously, was astonished to see him smile. A strange fancy had taken possession of Almayer's brain, distracted by this new misfortune. It seemed to him that for many years he had been falling into a deep precipice. Day after day, month after month, year after year, he had been falling, falling, falling; it was a smooth, round, black thing, and the black walls had been rushing upwards with wearisome rapidity. A great rush, the noise of which he fancied he could hear yet; and now, with an awful shock, he had reached the bottom, and behold! he was alive and whole, and Dain was dead with all his bones broken. It struck him as funny. A dead Malay; he had seen many dead Malays without any emotion; and now he felt inclined to weep, but it was over the fate of a white man he knew; a man that fell over a deep precipice and did not die. He seemed somehow to himself to be standing on one side, a little way off, looking at a certain Almayer who was in great trouble. Poor, poor fellow! Why doesn't he cut his throat? He wished to encourage him; he was very anxious to see him lying dead over that other corpse. (pp. 99–100)

The broken body at Almayer's feet shatters the dream inside him. The frail link connecting his project and its realization snaps, and the inner and outer halves of his existence fall apart. He is seen to smile. This response, whatever it may say about his state of mind, expresses the perception of an incongruity. It bears, however, no relation to the officers' laughter, for he has not suddenly acquired the capacity to see himself with their eyes. His sense of absurdity is quite different: he is overwhelmed by a feeling of vertigo, as if, having slowly ascended to a great height, he looks back to find nothing underneath him. Up to now, he has remained inside his life, which has consisted of a dream of rising fortunes. But now, his whole being goes into reverse.

The incongruity involved here is not that disclosed to detachment. Even if the moral shock were less violent, he would not see that it has been his ascent towards an imaginary future that has guaranteed his decline into degeneracy and failure. The incongruity consists in the fact that his inner self survives the discovery that it is meaningless.[13] He has been expelled so abruptly out of it that he now stands outside it, looking at it objectively as if it were not himself, wondering why it is not dead, like the body of Dain. The man who had promised to realize it has ceased to exist, so it should have ceased to exist too. But it won't die: it refuses to become the double of the dead Malay. But how could it? For Almayer's very sense of his own objectivity, his vision of himself lying in front of himself, is itself a subjective reaction. A man may come to feel that he has stepped out of his own life, but in fact he will not do so until he dies in earnest. The absurdity Almayer represents to others cannot be compared to the absurdity of simultaneously being and not being himself. Others laugh, secure in the solidarity of a good conscience; Almayer endures an impossible self-division. And if he does not observe himself as a comic spectacle, neither do we, for as we have learnt, Conrad's narrative has positioned us ambiguously, and so deprived us of the stance appropriate to mockery.

[13] For a most illuminating analysis of the concept, see Thomas Nagel, 'The Absurd', in *Mortal Questions* (Cambridge, Cambridge University Press, 1979), 11–23.

VI

One of the abiding problems facing readers trying to make sense of the novel has been how to reconcile Almayer's unredeemed moral seediness with his obvious authority as the subject of extreme experience. To see how radical the problem is, we need look no further than the novel's extraordinary climax. Almayer's inability to countenance his daughter's love for Dain shows that he cannot accept that she should have wishes independent of his own; but this takes a particularly unpleasant, if wholly characteristic, form: he cannot bear the disgrace of her commitment to a racial inferior. Yet this is the very reason why he rescues the lovers! It is because he cannot tolerate the shame of 'white men finding my daughter with this Malay' that he saves him from certain death and releases both into love and life (p. 184). How are we to understand a denouement at once so contemptible and so magnanimous?

The question may be approached by considering the fate of the slave-girl Taminah, which significantly parallels Almayer's. (Here too, the affinity is signalled by the plot, which brings them together in a scene where their shared predicament makes them incomprehensible to each other.) Her life is divided into two parts. Before she sees Dain she remains in what is presented as a state of nature, living 'like the tall palms . . . desiring the sunshine, fearing the storm, unconscious of either' (p. 112). Once awakened by her love for Dain and her jealousy of Nina, however, her world becomes incomprehensible to her: fixed in a desire impossible either to relinquish or to fulfil, she knows only 'the injustice of the suffering inflicted upon her without cause and without redress' (p. 119). Almayer's case is more complex, but it repeats the pattern. Until he sees the drowned body, he remains, despite his disappointments, defined by his hopes and fears. After he has seen it, however, he too is fixed in a condition he can neither eradicate nor accept. As we have seen, the sensation that his life means everything to him survives the discovery that its meaning is worthless. Unlike

Taminah, he does all he can to obliterate the inner perspective that creates his torment. With the loss of the mine, his unconscious energies become concentrated on Nina; but because she is really lost to him—because he can only consent to her release at the cost of his sense of self—he diverts all these energies into forgetting her. But to try to forget is to remember; and the more obsessive his attempt to cancel his past—incinerating her belongings with his house, addicting himself to the erasure of opium—the less is his success in exorcizing her image. Try what he can, he remains as helpless as Taminah. Indeed, his very decision to linger out his final days in the vacant architectural 'folly' he had erected on his dreams, serves only to confirm the impossibility of escaping those dreams.

But it is in the experience that distinguishes him that the explanation of why a moral failure should be respected is to be sought. The absurd is not a moral concept, and its discovery does not require self-knowledge. It should not be confused with the detection of a dubious motive or the recognition of past folly, for these actions presuppose a reordering of the self. The absurd is a disorder of identity, for which the only credential required is that one should have hopes, desires, purposes, and projects that one takes seriously. In short, it is enough to be Almayer.

The greatest defect in the reception of the novel has been a merely moralistic response to its protagonist. From this, even Conrad's more sympathetic critics, like Ian Watt, are not exempt. Watt professes himself 'disinclined to pay much heed to the particular case of Almayer', for he dies 'not in heroic exhaustion . . . but in petulant disappointment at the failure of the future to behave as he thinks it ought', and so, Watt concludes, becomes the object of his author's 'implacable disdain'.[14] But the disdain is Watt's, not Conrad's. In *A Personal Record*, published seventeen years after *Almayer's Folly*, Conrad recalls his meeting with the original Almayer, to whom he attributes not only his first novel but his career as

[14] Watt, op. cit., 66–7.

a writer. Such claims are interpretations, of course; but in this case they deserve to be attended to, for Conrad's later account reproduces the very ambiguities of tone and perspective that structured the novel, combining an affectionate, urbane amusement with—in an address to Almayer's shade whose habitation is the abode of the dead but also the pages of the book—respect for his 'very anguish of paternity' and his faith that 'nothing was quite worthy of you', adding: 'What made you so real to me was that you held this lofty theory with some force of conviction and with an admirable consistency.'[15] Fidelity to a lost cause is the Polish motto, as Conrad never tires of pointing out; it also constitutes, his critics notwithstanding, Almayer's capacity for suffering. Other characters too know suffering—Taminah as we have noted, Nina stagnating between her implacable parents, Mrs Almayer caught in the foreign oppression of her marriage, even Babalatchi mourning the tumult and freedom of his outlaw past. But Almayer alone is fated to endure the 'consistency' that cannot adapt itself to defeat.

Thwarted hopes are, as we know, an ineradicable part of a state of affairs that offers us life only in order to deprive us of it. In the way in which *Almayer's Folly* presents this it makes, as I have argued, an egalitarian gesture. Both Conrad's eloquent epigraph and his sardonic 'Author's Note' announce this gesture, the first in its implication that the loss of a promised land is an experience known to all, the second in its rejection of the view that the 'decivilized' inhabitants of far-off lands have nothing in common with the refined citizens of Europe. In Conrad's first novel, this common denominator, to which he gives the name of 'solidarity', is more precise than participation in a generalized human predicament. Almayer's sense of the absurd may be remote indeed from the philosophical afflictions of a Nietzsche or a Dostoevsky, but it retains the mark of a historical moment. For all his uneducated isolation he remains a product of the late nineteenth century. He is also the product of the mind of

[15] *A Personal Record* (Dent Collected Edition, 1946), 88.

a man who shared that century's anxieties in full measure—to the point of conceiving the creation as a 'knitting machine', and of denouncing reason itself as 'hateful' for its demonstration 'that we, living, are out of life—utterly out of it'.[16] But perhaps because he was also a novelist, that is, someone compelled to bring his understanding of the world he lived in to the test of narrative precision, he saw plainly that a dislocated life is not rendered more endurable because it is lived in Borneo rather than in Paris, or that exile is less exemplary in the intimacies of an obscure trading outpost than amid the imagined spaces of an indifferent cosmos.

[16] Respectively in letters to R. B. Cunninghame Graham 20 Dec. 1897 (*Letters*, i. 116), and 14 Jan. 1898 (*Letters*, ii. 116). According to Conrad's analogy, the functioning of the universe is self-generated, remorseless, indestructible, mindless, blind, and impervious to human desires and ideals.

NOTE ON THE TEXT

I

The composition of Conrad's first novel occupied the last years of his career in the merchant navy. Conrad encountered the man on whom he was to base his protagonist, one Charles William Olmeijer, in Berau, NE Borneo, when as first mate of the *Vidar* from 22 August 1887 to 2 January 1888, he traded out of Singapore in the Sea of Celebes. Next, from 19 January 1888 to 26 March 1889, he commanded the barque *Otago*, sailing from Bangkok to Sydney, from Sydney to Mauritius, and from Mauritius to the South Australian coast. Returning to England on 14 May 1889, he began to look for another command. In the period of waiting that followed, he found himself making a start on what was to become *Almayer's Folly*. He was 32 years of age.

The compositional history of *Almayer's Folly* has been blurred or confused by Conrad's careless or unreliable memory (the details given in *A Personal Record* are not always accurate), and by the credulity and idolization of his memorialists. The verifiable facts are as follows.

(*a*) 'Commenced in September 1889 in London' (memo to John Quinn, collector of Conrad's manuscripts, 15 March 1812 (Gordan, 177)); 'on an Autumn day' (*A Personal Record*, 73) in Bessborough Gardens, Pimlico, where he probably wrote the first three chapters (Najder, 117).

(*b*) March 1890, began 'Chapter Five' while visiting Tadeusz Bobrowski, his uncle, in the Polish Ukraine (the verso of page 1 of the MS of that chapter has the draft of a letter to G. Sobotkiewica, a distant relation, sent on about 17 March (Gordan, 178–9; *Letters*, i. 44–5)).

(*c*) December 1890, descending the Congo river, he had 'only seven chapters' with him (*A Personal Record*, 14); this however must have been six, in the light of the next entry.

(*d*) 21 May to 14 June 1891, while convalescing at Champel-les-Bains, near Geneva, he wrote part of Chapter Seven (on the verso of pp. 1 and 6 of the MS of that chapter is a draft computation of the cost of board at 'La Roseraie' (Gordan)).

(*e*) 4 August to 14 November 1891, while warehouse superintendent in Upper Thames Street, he worked on 'Chapter Nine' (in fact probably Chapter Eight since he could not have finished it in Champel, despite *A Personal Record*, 14) perhaps initially in 'sordid lodgings in Greenhythe' (Jessie Conrad, *Joseph Conrad as I Knew Him*, 1926, 101), and certainly after about 15 September at 17 Gillingham Street, SW, his London address for the next five years (Gordan, 179–80).

(*f*) 25 October 1892 to 30 January 1893, on his second voyage as first mate of the clipper *Torrens*, he showed the MS to a consumptive Cambridge student, one W. H. Jacques, who encouraged him to complete it (*A Personal Record*, 15–18, which specifies, 'it was in latitude 40 south, and nearly in the longitude of Greenwich', namely south of the Cape of Good Hope, and hence about 20 December).

(*g*) August 1893, on his second visit to Tadeusz Bobrowski, he nearly lost 'the MS, advanced now to the first words of the ninth chapter', in the Friedrichstrasse railway station, Berlin (*A Personal Record*, 19); he may have completed that chapter during his stay in the Ukraine (early August to about October 1893).

(*h*) 4 December 1893 to 10 January 1894, winterbound in Rouen as second officer of the steamer *Adowa*, he started on Chapter Ten (*A Personal Record*, 1–5); he resigned this post, in London, on 17 January 1894.

(*i*) March 1894, on a visit to Brussels, he left with Marguerite Poradowska a typescript of Chapters One to Ten (Gordan, 382–3).

(*j*) *c.*29 March 1894, probably in Gillingham Street, he was struggling with Chapter Eleven, the first page of which he sent to Mme Poradowska (*Letters*, i. 150–1).

(*k*) 16 April 1894, on a ten-day visit to Launcelot Sanderson at Elstree, Essex, he informed Mme Poradowska that he had completed Chapter Nine (*Letters*, i. 152).

(*l*) 24 April 1894, in Gillingham Street, he reported to Mme Poradowska that the novel had been completed at 3 a.m., promising to send her Chapters Eleven and Twelve when typed (*Letters*, i. 153).

(*m*) late April 1894, he told Mme Poradowska that he was rewriting Chapters One to Four (*Letters*, i. 154–5), sending her at the same time the typescript of Chapter Eleven (Gordan, 183); although on 2 May he promised to send her the typescript of Chapter Twelve (*Letters*, i. 155–6, 157–8) he never did so (*Letters*, i. 159).

(*n*) 17 May 1894, Conrad reported to Mme Poradowska that the (revised?) typescript was with the critic Edmund Gosse, editor of the 'International Library' for Heinemann (*Letters*, i. 157–8).

(*o*) 4 July 1894, Conrad sent the typescript, under the name of 'Kamudi' (approximate Malay for 'rudder') to T. Fisher Unwin for consideration for the Pseudonym Library (*Letters*, i. 160–1 to Poradowska; 172–3 to Fisher Unwin; and Ugo Mursia, 'The True "Discoverer" of Joseph Conrad's Literary Talent', *Conradiana*, 4: 2 (1972), 7). Conrad was 36.

The final TS was received by Wilfred Hugh Chesson on 5 July 1894, who passed it on to Unwin's other reader, Edward Garnett, with a strong recommendation. In a letter to the magazine *Today* of June 1919, which had attributed the 'discovery' of Conrad to Garnett, Chesson wrote: 'Perhaps I may add that the purely stylistic and academic merits of Mr Conrad's work were even in 1894 too obvious to make the "discovery" of him by a literary critic much more than an evidence of reasonable attention to his business.' Elsewhere, he wrote: 'I remember how the magical melancholy of that masterpiece submerged me . . .' (Ugo Mursia, 'True "Discoverer"', 6, 8). Edward Garnett was equally impressed; and Conrad, after having written at least once (8 September) to enquire about the fate of his MS, received notice on 4 October 1894 that it had been accepted, on the basis of an offer of £20 for the copyright (*Letters*, i. 176–8).

To ensure copyright in the USA, the Chase Act of 1891 required that the American version be set and printed in the United States. Macmillan (New York) was contracted for simultaneous publication, its reader, one 'MM' having been much more conventional and guarded than the Unwin readers. He reported: 'Mr Conrad knows how to write in English, and his work is true enough . . . in its scene and characters to the life; but it is a stagnant, half-savage, sordid life, which needs an artist instead of a photographer to make even picturesque. . . . Clever it is of a kind, certainly, but with a cheerless, unprofitable cleverness, from which I can conceive no pleasure to be got.' (David Leon Higdon, 'The Macmillan Reader's Report on Conrad's *Almayer's Folly*', *English Studies*, 59: 1–6 (1978), 518–20.) As Higdon notes, this may explain the much shorter American print run (see below § II).

Four days after receiving the news of the acceptance of his novel, Conrad asked Unwin for the typescript so that he could make 'a final revision' (*Letters*, i. 178). These last adjustments must have been made very quickly, for the typescript was required for preparation by the compositors. Conrad received the first 16 pages of the proofs, almost certainly after initial errors had been identified, on 24 December (*Letters*, i. 192), and he revised as well as corrected them. The proofs were sent to America for typesetting before these ultimate emendations had been made. In fact, Conrad did not see the Macmillan edition until November 1919 (Gordan, 116, 188).

II

The text of *Almayer's Folly* exists or existed in nine states.

(*a*) The autograph manuscript, corrected and revised, sold with the then unpublished preface of 1895, but minus the lost

Chapter Nine, to John Quinn in March 1912 (B. L. Reid, *The Man from New York* (1968), 124). These manuscripts are now in the Rosenbach Foundation Collection, Philadelphia.

(*b*) A presumed first typescript of at least the first four chapters, of which there remains no trace.

(*c*) The final typescript, with autograph corrections, and used as printer's copy (stint allocation markings are preserved), sold to John Quinn on 17 July 1913 (Reid, *Man from New York*, 169). It is now in the Humanities Research Center, University of Texas at Austin.

(*d*) The revised and corrected proofs for the Fisher Unwin (First English) edition, which Conrad received from 24 December 1894, but which are now lost.

(*e*) The first English Edition, by T. Fisher Unwin, published in London on 29 April 1895 (2000 copies), reprinted with corrections as the 'Colonial Edition', and reissued with equally minor further corrections as a third printing.

(*f*) The first American Edition, by Macmillan, published in New York on 3 May 1895 (650 copies), reprinted as a 'regular edition' of 1,530 copies in 1911–12.

(*g*) The first American Limited Collected Edition, by Doubleday Page, published in Garden City, NY, in 1920 (735 copies), as the 'Sun-Dial' Edition; with Author's Note of 1895.

(*h*) The first English Limited Collected Edition, by William Heinemann, published in London, in 1921 (780 copies); with Author's Note of 1895, expanded.

(*i*) The 'Concord' Edition, Doubleday Page, in 1923, correcting the 'Sun-Dial' text, partly by comparing it with the Heinemann text; with Author's Note of 1895.

(*j*) All subsequent Doubleday Collected 'Editions' (i.e. issues or impressions) derive from the 'Concord' text; these include the 'Complete' (1924), the 'Canterbury' (1924), the 'Kent' (1925), the 'Memorial' (1925), the 'Inclusive' (1925), the 'Special' (1928), and the 'Deep Sea' (1928).

(*k*) All British Collected 'Editions', after the Heinemann, derive from the 'Sun-Dial' plates; these include the 'Uniform' (1924, Dent, London), the 'Medallion' (1925, Gresham, London), the 'Grant' (1925, Grant, Edinburgh), and the 'Collected' (1946–54, Dent, London).

The extant versions have been analysed by professional bibliographers, as follows: (*a*) and (*c*) by John Dozier Gordan, *Joseph Conrad, the Making of a Novelist* (1940), 112–29; (*c*) by Floyd Eugene Eddleman and David Leon Higdon, 'The Typescript of Conrad's *Almayer's Folly*', *Texas Studies in Literature and Language*, 18: 1 (1976), 98–123; (*d*) through a collation of (*c*) with (*e*) and (*f*), by Floyd Eugene Eddleman and David Leon Higdon, 'Proof Revisions in Conrad's *Almayer's Folly*', *Papers of the Bibliographical Society of America*, 70 (1976), 407–16; (*e*) and (*f*) by Floyd Eugene Eddleman, David Leon Higdon, and Robert W. Hobson, 'The First Editions of Joseph Conrad's *Almayer's Folly*', *Proof 4* (1975), 83–109; (*g*), (*h*), and (*i*) by David Leon Higdon and Floyd Eugene Eddleman, 'Collected Edition Variants in Conrad's *Almayer's Folly*', *Conradiana*, 9:1 (1977), 77–103; and the 'Author's Note' in MS, TS, (*g*) and (*h*) by David Leon Higdon, 'The Text and Context of Conrad's First Critical Essay', *Polish Review*, 20: 2–3 (1975), 97–105. What follows is a summary of their principal findings, checked against an independent collation of (*e*), (*f*), (*g*), and (*h*).

Autograph Manuscript (a). Having compared the manuscript (MS), the final typescript (TS) and the Fisher Unwin edition (U), Gordan concluded that the differences between the MS and the TS pointed to the existence of a carefully corrected intermediate typescript—probably the one given to Mme Poradowska in March 1894. The TS reveals substantial subtractions from and additions to the MS: it alters in major ways the first five chapters of the MS, continuously modifies chapters 6, 7, and 8, and corrects most heavily chapters 10 and 11. These revisions generally serve to condense the material or to make it more vivid. For example: 'She stopped [listening intently MS] *straining her ears to catch the slightest sound*', or '. . . over the sunlit solitude [of that path generally usually so full of the awakening of daily life MS] of the settlement' (Gordan, 119). Elsewhere, they serve to rearrange a sentence: 'she slept well outside on the platform built over the river under the bright stars' (MS) becomes 'dreamlessly under the bright stars on the platform built outside the house and over the river' (Gordan, 122). The most significant alterations, which require the hypothesis of the lost typescript, show that Conrad's plot was not ready-made when he started the novel. The opening pages of the MS, for example, have no mention even by implication of Nina and Dain; and when they do appear, neither Almayer's love for Nina, nor Nina and Dain's passion for each other, is suggested. Almayer's desire to escape Sambir is unconnected with his daughter, and his relationship with Dain involves no collaborative scheme. His own plans concern the recovery of buried treasure, a commonplace of adventure stories: 'he was going to seek for the big diamond and the gold nuggets, the old seaman had buried' (Gordan, 128). As Conrad began to develop his fable, however, it started to assume a life of its own; the original demoralized trader in pursuit of a hidden hoard expanded into the complications and cross-purposes of a three-way relationship and the skill, organization, and effort required for the rediscovery and re-exploitation of an abandoned mine. Large-scale reworking of the opening of the old narrative was therefore required in order to bring it in line with the new.

Typescript (c). According to Eddleman and Higdon, the TS consists of 280 pages numbered consecutively, and contains revisions (in black ink, red ink, indelible pencil, and lead pencil) on every page and in virtually every sentence. Some revisions appear both in the Unwin (U) and the Macmillan (M) editions, but many, made late in the typesetting, were too late for the American (M) edition. What is clear is that M prints the TS readings only, U the proof revisions. The TS was used (by thirteen Unwin compositors) for the typesetting. The 440 changes in wording it contains (162 additions, 93 deletions, and 14 'oddities') attend to grammar and idiom, and to the focusing of detail and image. For example, Lakamba, who has decided that Almayer must be done away with, originally tells his factotum Babalatchi: 'Coffee is a good thing for that' (TS); Conrad replaces it with the much more sinister: 'He drinks much coffee' (p. 88). Or again, Almayer's original 'First one hope, then another, and this is my last. Gone!' (TS) becomes: '. . . this is my last. Nothing is left now.' (p. 144)—which intensifies the sense of emptiness and pathos. Or yet again, Babalatchi's 'There is a time for fighting and a time for peaceful lies' (TS) becomes 'A man knows when to fight and when to tell peaceful lies' (p. 155)—which is at once less sententious and more virile. Or finally, Babalatchi's 'Now I go' (TS) when his attempt to save Nina and Dain is defeated by what he regards as their hysterical emotionalism, is replaced by 'I shall not stay here any longer' (p. 183), which adds disgust to his anger (Higdon, *Typescript*, 99–100). Higdon's survey of the innumerable alterations with his own succinct and often just comments provide a course in the technique of the *mot juste*. The revisions, however, are almost entirely concerned with stylistic fine-tuning; they do not reshape the narrative except for some minor relocations, mostly to reinforce the Dutch setting: thus Almayer is married in Batavia, not Singapore (p. 23), the future Mrs Almayer goes to a convent in Samarang, not Singapore (p. 22), the scientist–adventurer returns to Batavia, not Singapore (p. 122). Even at this late stage, Conrad continued to extract his novel from his Singapore-centred experience and to embed it more deeply into the Dutch environment.

The Printer's Proofs (d). Eddleman and Higdon have also systematically analysed the Unwin proof revisions, as they are deducible from a collation of the TS with U and M. They identify 100 substantive alterations, 'most of them undoubtedly authorial in origin' (Higdon, *Proof*, 408). The TS, as we have seen, was used as the printer's copy, the proofs were sent to New York to set up M, and the *revised* proofs were used for U. Thus when both editions diverge from the TS, or M varies from U, proof revisions may be inferred. In the event, the editions share 24 common revisions; 73 are unique to U; 3 are 'oddities'. Conrad's responsibility for the English printed text can be established because (i) the common revisions, mostly grammatical and idiomatic, are so cautious that they point to an in-house proof reader, and (ii) more than half the revisions occur in the last three chapters, which Conrad had written in something of a rush and about which he had remained anxious. The single major editorial intervention (the recasting of a clumsy sentence) is discussed in the notes to p. 5. The 73 revisions exclusive to U and owed to Conrad, who was encouraged to the last to improve his text regardless of cost (*Letters*, i. 197, 198–9), continue the stylistic refinement undertaken in the revision of the TS. For example, 'You have trodden the poor fellows [sic]—whoever he is—hand . . .' (TS) reappears in U as 'Whoever he is, you have trodden the poor fellow's hand . . .' (p. 98). Elsewhere, inaccuracies are removed; for example, 'one barrel of the revolver went off' (TS) is corrected to 'one chamber . . .' (p. 176); or 'That was before a white Rajah ruled in Kuching' (TS) is politicized into '. . . an English Rajah . . .' (p. 206). The single significant *addition* to the TS is discussed in the note to p. 50.

The First Editions (e) and (f). The article by Eddleman, Higdon and Hobson comparing U and M necessarily covers the same material as the article on the proofs, finding 96 substantive variants (out of a total of 306) between the two texts (Higdon, *First*, 83), and confirming that the American edition is 'set from unrevised uncorrected advance sheets of the English edition' (Higdon, *First*, 84). Thus the American text preserves British spelling but overlays British punctuation with American house-styling. Unlike M, U proved slightly accident-prone, and the two subsequent English printings repaired the damage. The following details may be of interest: 'The "Colonial Edition" (the second (?) printing of the first English edition) supplies two letters and one comma omitted from the first printing. . . . The third (?)

printing retains those corrections and adds five of its own, supplying one missing period . . . and four missing commas . . .' (Higdon, *Proof*, 87). Most of the American variants were the result of what Higdon calls the 'Macmillan grammarian's rage for correctness' (Higdon, *First*, 98). The Unwin variants repeat the story already told: 'Conrad's revisions, astonishingly diverse and numerous, demonstrate his preoccupation with the problems of repetition and redundancy, idiomatic rephrasing . . . more precise images, and grammatical consistency' (Higdon, *First*, 89). Higdon's assertion, however, that U, representing a later stage than M, is the 'sophisticated product' of a writer now committed to his craft, is exaggerated, for the revisions of the U proofs simply carry on a process that began with Conrad's revisions of the MS and the TS.

The Collected Editions (g), (h), (i), (j), (k). Higdon and Eddleman's collation of the limited collected editions with the first editions produce clarifications as momentous as their earlier collation of the first editions with the typescript. The history of the collected editions, as they affect *Almayer's Folly*, can be briefly summarized.

In April 1913 Conrad was told that Doubleday of New York was interested in publishing a uniform set of his works (*Life and Letters*, ii. 145). In July 1914 Doubleday acquired the American rights and the unsold stock of *Almayer's Folly* from Macmillan, who in 19 years had sold only 1,794 copies of the novel (Higdon, *Collected*, 77–8). Conrad revised the novel in 1916 (the marked copy was sold at auction in 1924 and has disappeared).

Doubleday then reached an agreement with Heinemann of London for a simultaneous Limited Collected Edition based on Conrad's marked copy as printer's copy. By 4 December 1919, Doubleday had set the type, and by 2 February 1920 had sent the proofs to Conrad, who corrected them and returned them on 2 March (*Life and Letters*, ii. 221). *Almayer's Folly*, as part of Volume I of the 'Sun-Dial' Doubleday Collected Edition appeared later that year.

The Heinemann Collected Edition, published in 1921, was

set up in type from Conrad's marked copy, and punctuated far more prescriptively than the 'Sun-Dial'. It also incorporated a few substantive variants, almost certainly by Conrad, but often reverting to 'unidiomatic phrasing indefensible on either grammatical or rhetorical grounds' (Higdon, *Collected*, 79). After printing 780 copies, Heinemann distributed the type and his edition engendered no reprints.

In 1923 Doubleday decided to issue a new set to be called the 'Concord' edition. For the *Almayer's Folly* volume an attempt seems to have been made to reconcile the 'Sun-Dial' text with the Heinemann text. (Other collations confirm this conclusion; the *Nostromo* 'Concord', for example, exhibits 32 variants from the 'Sun-Dial', 27 of which agree with Heinemann (Higdon, *Collected*, 120, quoting Gordon Lindstrand, 'Joseph Conrad's *Nostromo*: The Transmission of the Text', unpublished dissertation, University of Illinois, 1967).)

The 'Sun-Dial' *Almayer's Folly* shows that one major and 34 minor deletions were made, 28 of which occur in the first four chapters (Higdon, *Collected*, 79–86). Most of the alterations are routine changes in verb form (including the 'lie'/'lay' distinction, which Conrad confused). The three variants contributed by H to the total of eight accepted by the Collected Editions are all dubious: 'volumes' for 'columns' (p. 119) is a misprint; 'impassive' for 'impassible' (p. 46) is a modernization; 'rushed out' for 'roused out' (p. 121) is a misreading. All the substantive variants between the 'Sun-Dial' and the Unwin texts are discussed in the notes to this edition.

The 'Author's Note'. On 4 January 1895, Conrad wrote to Edward Garnett: 'I shall send on the preface tomorrow (Sat:)' (*Letters*, i. 197). A few days later he wrote to W. H. Chesson: 'As to that preface (which I have shown you) I trust it may be dispensed with, but if it must appear you are quite right—"*aversion from*" not "aversion for" as I wrote—and stuck to like a lunatic. You will correct?' (*Letters*, i. 199). One can infer, then, that the note was written at the turn of the year, and that it was considered for inclusion by Unwin's readers. In the event, however, it did not appear, and it ultimately found its way into John Quinn's hands, along with the MS of the novel (in March 1912, not 1913, as Higdon says, Higdon, *Essay*, 98). On 10 April 1919, Conrad, who was preparing the 'Sun-Dial' Edition, wrote to Quinn to retrieve the Note for Doubleday. Quinn at once had two copies typed, introducing a number of alterations, which are discussed in the notes to this edition. Further variations were introduced by the 'Sun-Dial' printing. The Heinemann edition reflects the Quinn typescript more closely; it also introduces a concluding paragraph written by Conrad specifically for Heinemann, at some time before 3 September 1920 (*Life and Letters*, ii. 248).

The Present Edition. The series of which this edition is a part takes as its base text that of the Dent Collected Edition (*Almayer's Folly*, 1947). The Dent Collected reproduces the Doubleday 'Sun-Dial' text of 1920. Doubleday sold duplicate 'Sun-Dial' plates to J. M. Dent for his 1923 Uniform Edition (Higdon, *Collected*, 78)—an edition, incidentally, which Conrad disliked 'for typographical reasons' (*Life and Letters*, ii. 322). These 'Sun-Dial' plates were used again for the 1925 'Medallion' Edition, and all subsequent Dent editions (Higdon, *Collected*, 78). In particular, the Dent Collected Edition does not descend from the 1923 'Uniform' Edition, but derives 'directly from a new impression of Sun-Dial plates' (Roderick Davis, in a review article, *The Conradian*, 15: 1 (June 1990), 107).

Whatever merits the Dent Collected Edition may have as a textual basis for editions of other novels by Conrad, the history just outlined shows that it is less appropriate for *Almayer's Folly*. Although Conrad did revise the printer's copy and corrected the proofs of the 'Sun-Dial' edition, his alterations were incidental, sometimes unnecessary and even retrogressive; and his major interventions, in the form of deletions, impoverished the text. In no way can the Collected Edition be regarded, as Henry James's 'New York' Edition can be, as amounting to a new text. Indeed, none of Conrad's Collected Editions can furnish a base text. Conrad hardly amended the Heinemann edition (in fact, the evidence suggests that he did not read the proofs after Volume 1 (John H. Stape, 'The Textual History of *Notes on Life and Letters*: The Book Text', *Conradiana*, 19: 2 (1987), 121), while, as we have seen, the Doubleday 'Concord' is an *ad hoc* reconciliation of the 'Sun-Dial' and the Heinemann texts.

The textual history establishes that the only satisfactory base text for *Almayer's Folly* is provided by the Unwin (First English) Edition of 1895, with the very minor corrections made for its two subsequent printings. The Macmillan (First American) Edition is disqualified by its failure to incorporate Conrad's corrections and revisions of the proofs of the Unwin edition. However, I have made no attempt to make my text approximate the Unwin edition's; nor have I sought to incorporate readings from various sources in order to create a composite text. One cannot turn a collateral text into a primary text without producing unprincipled patchwork. Apart, then, from the correction of a few obvious misprints and errors (listed below), this edition faithfully reproduces the text of the 1947 Dent Collected Edition.

Instead, I have included in the notes virtually all the substantive variants exhibited by the Unwin edition, together with those few variants in the Heinemann edition where Conrad's hand might be discerned. Thus readers are given access to the Unwin readings. Any editor of *Almayer's Folly* must remain indebted to Higdon and his collaborators (why have they not produced an edition of their own?). Nevertheless I have recollated the text of the Dent Collected Edition with the Unwin and the Heinemann texts. With some exceptions, this exercise has confirmed the accuracy of Higdon's work. As one example of such exceptions, in the article 'Collected Edition Variants' I have found mistranscriptions on pp. 80 line 17, 84 line 6, 85 line 20, 87 line 39, 89 line 16, 89 line 19, 93 line 4 (the phrase is not 'identical'), 93 line 10, 98 line 22, 101 line 14. I have tried to be accurate, but no doubt my work is equally vulnerable. Unfortunately, I have not had access to the manuscript and the typescript.

I have corrected the following errors and inconsistencies:

vii.27 shadows *for* shadow (Quinn misread the MS)
viii.11 huts *for* tents (Quinn misread the MS)
14.11 after, *for* after
19.20 river bending . . . wind, the *for* river, bending . . . wind the
19.25 roar and *for* roar, and
23.2 Rajah-Laut *for* Rajah Laut (as at 7.10, 21.20)
24.30 combination *for* combination,
26.34 from *for* with (on grounds of usage, and to distinguish 'with greater dread')
27.22 Providence, *for* Providence
28.3 Rajah-Laut *for* Rajah Laut
36.15 salt-water *for* salt water (as at 36.31)
39.3 Rajah-Laut *for* Rajah Laut
44.19 and the *for* the (on grammatical grounds, following U)
46.10 cortège *for* cortege (following H and *OED*)
49.24 foresail. *for* foresail
52.6 scabbards *for* scabbards,
52.7 were *for* was (a plural subject of two distinct sounds)
54.28 cortège *for* cortege
56.3 know, Tuan *for* know Tuan
67.7 lay *for* laid
67.22 the so-called *for* the, so-called,
71.22 water, *for* water;
98.22 pig's *for* pigs (following H)
99.3 Almayer excitedly *for* Almayer, excitedly (to avoid ambiguity, following H)
99.16 taken *for* take
100.34 drank, his *for* drank his
104.26 lay *for* laid
110.7 jamb *for* lintel (see Explanatory Notes)
114.15 charmed, *for* charmed (following U)
115.18 lying *for* laying
121.29 officers' *for* officer's (two officers feature equally in the context)

126.8	coxwain *for* coxswain
141.29	Queer, this *for* Queer this (following U)
148.19	speak, her *for* speak her
149.25	deep *for* keep (U confirms the misprint)
155.15	carcass *for* carcase (as at 96.18)
156.29	had she *for* she had (on grammatical grounds, following M)
178.6	this, Dain *for* this Dain
180.33–5	along to sing—how did you say that?—the song of love to you! *for* along to sing; how did you say that? The song of live to you! (see 179.30)
181.25	alive, *for* alive (following U)
183.32	sadly, *for* sadly
185.6	land, white *for* land white
187.7	lay *for* laid
195.22	Above, the *for* Above the
197.26	roof stick *for* roof-stick (as at 16.7)
200.10	this done, *for* this done
200.16	rustling, sharp . . . snapping, *for* rustling sharp . . . snapping; (U confirms misprint)

SELECT BIBLIOGRAPHY

Primary Works

DENT'S collected edition (1946–55) contained almost all Conrad's works except for the dramatizations and some minor items. *Congo Diary and Other Uncollected Pieces*, edited by Zdisław Najder (1978) contains the Congo notebooks, the fragment called *The Sisters, The Nature of a Crime* written in collaboration with Ford Madox Hueffer (later Ford Madox Ford) and other writings. Cambridge University Press is currently publishing a critical edition of the canon, starting with *The Secret Agent* and *Almayer's Folly*.

Letters

The Collected Letters of Joseph Conrad, edited by Frederick R. Karl and Laurence Davies, began appearing in 1983. Other important editions are as follows: *Joseph Conrad: Life and Letters*, by G. Jean-Aubry (1927); *Letters from Joseph Conrad, 1895–1924*, ed. Edward Garnett (1928); *Letters of Joseph Conrad to Marguerite Poradowska*, ed. and trans. John A. Gee and Paul J. Sturm (1940); *Joseph Conrad: Letters to William Blackwood and David J. Meldrum*, ed. William Blackburn (1958); *Conrad's Polish Background: Letters to and from Polish Friends*, ed. Zdisław Najder (1964); *Joseph Conrad's Letters to Cunningham Graham* (1969), ed. C. T. Watts. There are further collections edited by Richard Curle (1928), G. Jean-Aubry (1929), Rene Rapin (1966) and Dale B. J. Randall (1968).

Memoirs, biographies, and biographical studies

The most important memoirs are those by Jessie Conrad (1926 and 1935), Richard Curle (1928), and Ford Madox Ford (1924), and there are further memoirs by Borys Conrad (1970) and John Conrad (1981). Owen Knowles's chronology (1989) and Martin Ray's collection of interviews and recollections (1990) are helpful reference works. Documents related to Conrad's Polish experience and relations are collected in Zdisław Najder (ed.), *Conrad under Familial Eyes* (1983).

The most reliable and scholarly biography is Zdisław Najder's *Joseph Conrad: A Chronicle* (1983). There are critical biographies by Jocelyn Baines (1960), Bernard Meyer (a 'psychoanalytic biography', 1967), Frederick Karl (1979), and Jeffrey Meyers (1991). The most recent critical biography is John Batchelor's *The Life of Joseph Conrad: A Critical Biography* (1994). There are further recommended biographies and biographical studies by J. D. Gordan, *Joseph Conrad: The Making of a Novelist* (1941), Norman Sherry, *Conrad's Eastern World* (1966) and *Conrad's Western World* (1971), Ian Watt, *Conrad in the Nineteenth Century* (1980), Roger Tennant (1981) and Cedric Watts (1989).

Critical studies

General studies to be recommended are Douglas Hewitt, *Joseph Conrad: A Reassessment* (1952), A. J. Guerard, *Conrad the Novelist* (1958), Jacques Berthoud, *Joseph Conrad: The Major Phase* (1978), Cedric Watts, *A Preface to Conrad* (1982) and Suresh Raval, *The Art of Failure: Conrad's Fiction* (1986). The following specialist studies can also be recommended: Eloise Knapp Hay, *The Political Novels of Joseph Conrad* (1963), Andrzej Busza, *Conrad's Polish Literary Background, Antemurale*, 10 (1966), J. Hillis Miller, 'Joseph Conrad' in his *Poets of Reality* (1966), Edward Said, *Joseph Conrad and the Fiction of Autobiography* (1966), Lawrence Graver, *Conrad's Short Fiction* (1969), Bruce Johnson, *Conrad's Models of Mind* (1971), David Thorburn, *Conrad's Romanticism* (1974), Allan Hunter, *Joseph Conrad and the Ethics of Darwinism* (1983), Redmond O'Hanlon, *Joseph Conrad and Charles Darwin* (1984), Jakob Lothe, *Conrad's Narrative Method* (1989), Jeremy Hawthorn, *Joseph Conrad: Narrative Technique and Ideological Commitment* (1990), Yves Hervouet, *The French Face of Joseph Conrad* (1990), Daphna Erdinast-Vulcan, *Joseph Conrad and the Modern Temper* (1991) and Robert Hampson, *Joseph Conrad: Betrayal and Identity* (1992).

The following collections of essays may be found helpful: R. W. Stallman (ed.), *The Art of Joseph Conrad*, (1960); Norman Sherry (ed.), *Conrad: The Critical Heritage* (1973); W. Zyla and W. M. Aycock (eds.), *Joseph Conrad: Theory and World Fiction* (1974); Norman Sherry (ed.), *Joseph Conrad: A Commemoration*, (1976); Ross C. Murfin (ed.), *Conrad Revisited: Essays for the Eighties* (1985); Mario Curreli (ed.), *The Ugo Mursia Memorial Lectures* (1988); Keith Carabine (ed.), *Joseph Conrad: Critical Assessments* (1992); and Gene M. Moore (ed.), *Conrad's Cities* (1992).

There are annotated bibliographies of Conrad by Bruce E. Teets, 1971 and 1990, and a selected annotated bibliography by Owen Knowles, 1992.

There are three scholarly journals devoted to Conrad studies: *Conradiana*, *The Conradian* and *L'Epoque Conradienne*.

On Almayer's Folly

From the above list the following are particularly recommended for *Almayer's Folly*: Norman Sherry (1966), Ian Watt (1980), Zdisław Najder (1983), Yves Hervouet (1990), and Robert Hampson (1992). See also Vernon Young, 'Lingard's Folly: The Lost Subject', *Kenyon Review* 15, 4 (1953; reprinted in Stallman, 1960); William W. E. Slights, 'Anagram, Myth, and Structure of *Almayer's Folly*', *Ariel* 11, 3 (1980); Marialuisa Bignami, 'Joseph Conrad, the Malay Archipelago, and the Decadent Hero,' *The Review of English Studies*, 37, 150 (May 1987); Heliena Krenn, *Conrad's Lingard Trilogy* (1990).

The Cambridge University Press edition of *Almayer's Folly*, eds. F. E. Eddleman and D. L. Higdon with an introduction by Ian Watt (1994), is strongly recommended.

A CHRONOLOGY OF JOSEPH CONRAD

1857 3 December: Born Józef Teodor Konrad Korzeniowski, of Polish parents in the Ukraine.

1861 His father, poet and translator Apollo Korzeniowski, arrested for patriotic conspiracy.

1862 Conrad's parents exiled to Vologda, Russia; their son accompanies them.

1865 Death of his mother.

1869 Death of Apollo Korzeniowski in Kraków; Conrad comes under the protection of his uncle, Tadeusz Bobrowski.

1874 Leaves Poland for Marseilles to become a trainee seaman with the French merchant navy.

1876 As a 'steward' on the *Sainte-Antoine*, becomes acquainted with Dominic Cervoni (who appears in *The Mirror of the Sea* and *The Arrow of Gold* and is the source for Nostromo, and Peyrol in *The Rover*).

1877 Possibly involved in smuggling arms to the 'Carlists' (Spanish royalists) from Marseilles.

1878 March: Shoots himself in the chest in Marseilles but is not seriously injured; as a direct result of this suicide attempt his uncle clears his debts. April: Joins his first British ship, the *Mavis*, and later in the same year joins *The Skimmer of the Sea*. Would have become liable for Russian military service if he had stayed with the French merchant navy.

1886 Becomes a British citizen and passes the examination for a Master's certificate.

1887 Is injured on the *Highland Forest* and hospitalized in Singapore.

1887–8 Gets to know the Malay archipelago as an officer of the *Vidar*.

1888 Master of the *Otago*, his only command.

1889 Resigns from the *Otago*, settles briefly in London and begins to write *Almayer's Folly*. Begins a lasting friendship with Marguerite Poradowska.

1890 Works in the Belgian Congo for the Société Anonyme pour le Commerce du Haut-Congo.

1891–3 His pleasantest experience at sea, as an officer of the

Torrens; meets John Galsworthy, who is among the passengers and becomes a loyal friend.

1893 Autumn: Meets Jessie George.

1894 February: Death of Tadeusz Bobrowski. October: *Almayer's Folly* accepted by Unwin. Meets Edward Garnett, Unwin's reader and an influential literary friend.

1895 *Almayer's Folly* published.

1896 *An Outcast of the Islands* published. Becomes acquainted with H. G. Wells. 24 March: marriage to Jessie George. Begins work on *The Rescue*.

1897 *The Nigger of the 'Narcissus'* published. Meets Henry James and R. B. Cunninghame Graham (to be a close friend and the source for Gould in *Nostromo*).

1898 *Tales of Unrest* ('Karain', 'The Idiots', 'An Outpost of Progress', 'The Return', 'The Lagoon') published. Enters into collaboration with Ford Madox Ford (then Hueffer). Takes over from Ford the lease of a Kentish farmhouse, 'The Pent'. Friendship with Stephen Crane. Borys Conrad born.

1898–9 'Heart of Darkness' serialized in *Blackwood's*.

1899 J. B. Pinker becomes Conrad's literary agent.

1899–1900 *Lord Jim* serialized in *Blackwood's*.

1900 Stephen Crane dies. *Lord Jim* published as a book.

1901 *The Inheritors* (collaboration with Ford) published.

1902 *Youth: and Two Other Stories* (*Youth*, 'Heart of Darkness', 'The End of the Tether') published.

1903 *Typhoon: And Other Stories* ('Typhoon', 'Amy Foster', 'Falk', 'Tomorrow') and *Romance* (collaboration with Ford) published.

1904 Jessie Conrad injures her knees and is partially disabled for life. *Nostromo* published.

1906 Meets Arthur Marwood, who becomes his closest friend. John Conrad born. *The Mirror of the Sea* published.

1907 The Conrads move to The Someries, Luton Hoo. *The Secret Agent* published.

1908 *A Set of Six* ('Gaspar Ruiz', 'The Informer', 'The Brute', 'An Anarchist', 'The Duel', 'Il Conde') published.

1909 Quarrels with Ford over his contributions to *The English*

Review. The Conrads move to a cottage at Aldington, near 'The Pent'.

1910 Completion of *Under Western Eyes* accompanied by a nervous breakdown; Conrad lies in bed holding 'converse with the characters' of the novel. On his recovery the Conrads move to Capel House, Orlestone.

1911 *Under Western Eyes* published.

1912 *A Personal Record* and *'Twixt Land and Sea* ('A Smile of Fortune', 'The Secret Sharer', 'Freya of the Seven Isles') published.

1913 *Chance* published.

1914 *Chance* has good sales, especially in America; the earlier work now finds a larger public. The Conrads visit Poland and are nearly trapped by the outbreak of war.

1915 *Within the Tides* ('The Planter of Malata', 'The Partner', 'The Inn of the Two Witches') and *Victory* published.

1917 *The Shadow-Line* published. Conrad begins to write Author's Notes for a collected edition of his works.

1919 *The Arrow of Gold* published. The Conrads move to Oswalds, Bishopsbourne, near Canterbury.

1920 *The Rescue* published, 24 years after it was begun.

1921 Visit to Corsica for research on *Suspense*. Conrad in poor health. *Notes on Life and Letters* published.

1923 Conrad visits America and is lionized. *The Rover* published.

1924 May: Declines the offer of a knighthood. 3 August: Dies of a heart attack at Oswalds.

1924 *The Nature of a Crime* (collaboration with Ford) published.

1925 *Tales of Hearsay* ('The Warrior's Soul', 'Prince Roman', 'The Tale', 'The Black Mate') and *Suspense* published.

1926 *Last Essays* published.

1928 *The Sisters* (fragment) published.

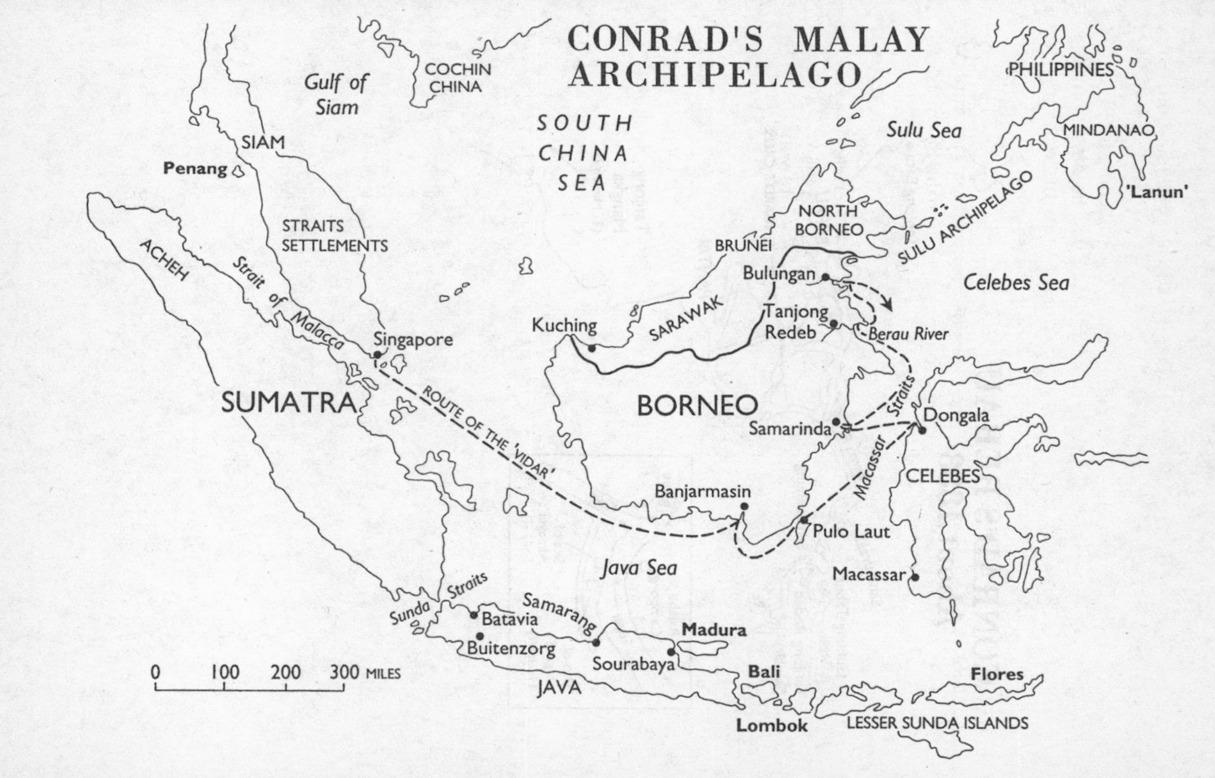
CONRAD'S MALAY ARCHIPELAGO
Gulf of Siam
COCHIN CHINA
SOUTH CHINA SEA
Sulu Sea
PHILIPPINES
MINDANAO
'Lanun'
SIAM
Penang
STRAITS SETTLEMENTS
ACHEH
Strait of Malacca
Singapore
SUMATRA
ROUTE OF THE 'VIDAR'
Kuching
SARAWAK
BRUNEI
NORTH BORNEO
SULU ARCHIPELAGO
Celebes Sea
Bulungan
Tanjong Redeb
Berau River
BORNEO
Samarinda
Dongala
Macassar Straits
CELEBES
Banjarmasin
Pulo Laut
Macassar
Java Sea
Sunda Straits
Batavia
Buitenzorg
Samarang
Sourabaya
Madura
JAVA
Bali
Lombok
Flores
LESSER SUNDA ISLANDS
0 100 200 300 MILES

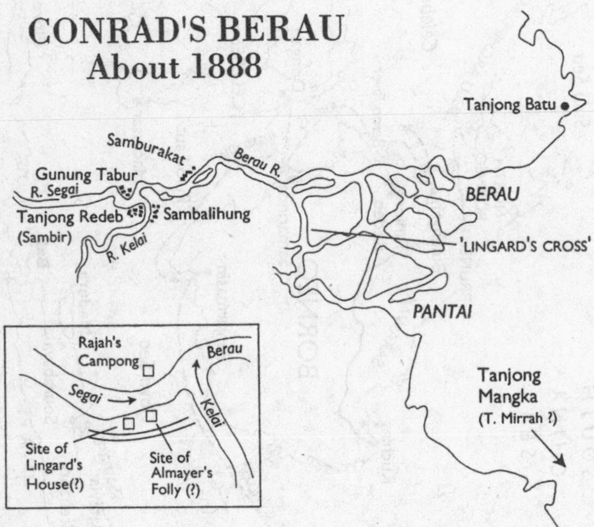
CONRAD'S BERAU
About 1888
Tanjong Batu
Samburakat
Berau R.
Gunung Tabur
R. Segai
Tanjong Redeb
(Sambir)
Sambalihung
R. Kelai
BERAU
'LINGARD'S CROSS'
PANTAI
Tanjong
Mangka
(T. Mirrah ?)
Rajah's
Campong
Berau
Segai
Kelai
Site of
Lingard's
House(?)
Site of
Almayer's
Folly (?)

AUTHOR'S NOTE

I AM informed that in criticizing that literature which preys on strange people and prowls in far-off countries, under the shade of palms, in the unsheltered glare of sunbeaten beaches, amongst honest cannibals and the more sophisticated pioneers of our glorious virtues, a lady*—distinguished in the world of letters—summed up her disapproval of* it by saying that the tales it produced were 'decivilized'.* And in that sentence not only the tales but, I apprehend, the strange people and the far-off countries also, are finally condemned in a verdict of contemptuous dislike.

A woman's judgment:* intuitive, clever, expressed with felicitous charm—infallible. A judgment that has nothing to do with justice. The critic and the judge seems* to think that in those distant lands all joy is a yell and a war dance, all pathos is a howl and a ghastly grin of filed teeth, and that the solution of all problems is found in the barrel of a revolver or on the point of an assegai. And yet it is not so. But the erring magistrate may plead in excuse the misleading nature of the evidence.

The picture of life, there as here, is drawn with the same elaboration of detail, coloured with the same tints. Only* in the cruel serenity of the sky, under the merciless brilliance of the sun, the dazzled eye misses the delicate detail, sees only the strong outlines, while the colours, in the steady light, seem crude and without shadows. Nevertheless it is the same picture.

And there is a bond between us and that humanity so far away. I am speaking here of men and women—not of the charming and graceful phantoms that move about in our mud and smoke and are softly luminous with the radiance of all our virtues; that are possessed of all refinements, of all sensibilities, of all wisdom—but, being only phantoms, possess no heart.

The sympathies of those are (probably) with the immortals: with the angels above or the devils below. I am content to sympathize with common mortals, no matter where they live; in houses or in huts, in the streets under a fog, or in the forests behind the dark line of dismal mangroves that fringe the vast solitude of the sea. For, their land—like ours—lies under the inscrutable eyes of the Most High. Their hearts—like ours—must endure the load of the gifts from Heaven: the curse of facts and the blessing of illusions, the bitterness of our wisdom and the deceptive consolation of our folly.*

J. C.

1895

Almayer's Folly

To the memory of T.B.*

Qui de nous n'a eu sa terre promise, son jour d'extase et sa fin en exil.

AMIEL*

ALMAYER'S FOLLY

CHAPTER ONE

"KASPAR! Makan!"*

The well-known shrill voice startled Almayer* from his dream of splendid future into the unpleasant realities of the present hour. An unpleasant voice too. He had heard it for many years, and with every year he liked it less. No matter; there would be an end to all this soon.

He shuffled uneasily, but took no further notice of the call. Leaning with both his elbows on the balustrade of the verandah, he went on looking fixedly at the great river that flowed—indifferent and hurried—before his eyes. He liked to look at it about the time of sunset; perhaps because at that time the sinking sun would spread a glowing gold tinge on the waters of the Pantai,* and Almayer's thoughts were often busy with gold;* gold he had failed to secure; gold the others had secured—dishonestly, of course—or gold he meant to secure yet, through his own honest exertions, for himself and Nina.* He absorbed himself in his dream of wealth and power away from this coast where he had dwelt for so many years, forgetting the bitterness of toil and strife in the vision of a great and splendid reward. They would live in Europe, he and his daughter. They would be rich and respected. Nobody would think of her mixed blood in the presence of her great beauty and of his immense wealth. Witnessing her triumphs he would grow young again, he would forget the twenty-five years of heart-breaking struggle on this coast where he felt like a prisoner. All this was nearly within his reach. Let only Dain* return! And return soon he must—in his own interest, for his own share. He was now more than a week late! Perhaps he would return to-night.

Such were Almayer's thoughts as, standing on the verandah of his new but already decaying house—* that last failure of his life—he looked on the broad river. There was no tinge of gold on it this evening, for it had been swollen by the rains, and rolled an angry and muddy flood under his inattentive eyes, carrying small drift-wood and big dead logs, and whole uprooted trees with branches and foliage, amongst which the water swirled and roared angrily.

One of those drifting trees grounded on the shelving shore, just by the house, and Almayer, neglecting his dream, watched it with languid interest. The tree swung slowly round, amid the hiss and foam of the water, and soon getting free of the obstruction began to move down stream again, rolling slowly over, raising upwards a long, denuded branch, like a hand lifted in mute appeal to heaven against the river's brutal and unnecessary violence. Almayer's interest in the fate of that tree increased rapidly. He leaned over to see if it would clear the low point below. It did; then he drew back, thinking that now its course was free down to the sea, and he envied the lot of that inanimate thing now growing small and indistinct in the deepening darkness. As he lost sight of it altogether he began to wonder how far out to sea it would drift. Would the current carry it north or south? South, probably, till it drifted in sight of Celebes, as far as Macassar,* perhaps!

Macassar! Almayer's quickened fancy distanced the

tree on its imaginary voyage, but his memory lagging behind some twenty years or more in point of time saw a young and slim Almayer, clad all in white and modest-looking, landing from the Dutch mail-boat on the dusty jetty of Macassar, coming to woo fortune in the godowns* of old Hudig.* It was an important epoch in his life, the beginning of a new existence for him. His father, a subordinate official employed in the Botanical Gardens of Buitenzorg,* was no doubt delighted to place his son in such a firm. The young man himself too was nothing loth to leave the poisonous shores of Java, and the meagre comforts of the parental bungalow, where the father grumbled all day at the stupidity of native gardeners, and the mother from the depths of her long easy-chair* bewailed the lost glories of Amsterdam, where she had been brought up, and of her position as the daughter of a cigar dealer there.*

Almayer had left his home with a light heart and a lighter pocket, speaking English well, and strong in arithmetic; ready to conquer the world, never doubting that he would.

After those twenty years, standing in the close and stifling heat of a Bornean evening, he recalled with pleasurable regret the image of Hudig's lofty and cool warehouses with their long and straight avenues of gin cases and bales of Manchester goods;* the big door swinging noiselessly; the dim light of the place, so delightful after the glare of the streets; the little railed-off spaces amongst piles of merchandise where the Chinese clerks, neat, cool, and sad-eyed, wrote rapidly and in silence amidst the din of the working gangs rolling casks or shifting cases to a muttered song, ending with a desperate yell. At the upper end, facing the great door, there was a larger space railed off, well lighted; there the noise was subdued by distance, and above it rose the soft and continuous clink of silver guilders which other discreet Chinamen were counting and piling up under the supervision of Mr. Vinck,* the cashier, the genius presiding in the place—the right hand of the Master.

In that clear space Almayer worked at his table not far from a little green painted door, by which always stood a Malay in a red sash and turban, and whose hand, holding a small string dangling from above, moved up and down with the regularity of a machine. The string worked a punkah* on the other side of the green door, where the so-called private office was, and where old Hudig—the Master—sat enthroned, holding noisy receptions. Sometimes the little door would fly open disclosing to the outer world, through the bluish haze of tobacco smoke, a long table loaded with bottles of various shapes and tall water pitchers, rattan* easy-chairs occupied by noisy men in sprawling attitudes, while the Master would put his head through and, holding by the handle, would grunt confidentially to Vinck; perhaps send an order thundering down the warehouse, or spy a hesitating stranger and greet him with a friendly roar, "Welgome, Gapitan! ver' you gome vrom? Bali, eh? Got bonies?* I vant bonies! Vant all you got; ha! ha! ha! Gome in!" Then the stranger was dragged in, in a tempest of yells, the door was shut, and the usual noises refilled the place; the song of the workmen, the rumble of barrels, the scratch of rapid pens; while above all rose the musical chink of broad silver pieces streaming ceaselessly through the yellow fingers of the attentive Chinamen.

At that time Macassar was teeming with life and commerce. It was the point in the islands where tended all those bold spirits who, fitting out schooners* on the Australian coast, invaded the Malay Archipelago in search of money and adventure. Bold, reckless, keen in business, not disinclined for a brush with the pirates that were to be found on many a coast as yet, making money fast, they used to have a general "rendezvous" in the bay for purposes of trade and dissipation. The Dutch merchants called those men English pedlars; some of them were undoubtedly gentlemen for whom that kind of life had a charm; most were seamen; the acknowledged king of them all was Tom Lingard,* he whom the Malays, honest or dishonest, quiet fishermen or desperate cut-throats, recognized as "the Rajah-Laut"*—the King of the Sea.

Almayer had heard of him before he had been three days in Macassar, had heard the stories of his smart business transactions, his loves, and also of his desperate fights with the Sulu pirates,* together with the romantic tale of some child—a girl—found in a piratical prau* by the victorious Lingard, when, after a long contest, he boarded the craft, driving the crew overboard. This girl, it was generally known, Lingard had adopted, was having her educated in some convent in Java, and spoke of her as "my daughter." He had sworn a mighty oath to marry her to a white man before he went home and to leave her all his money. "And Captain Lingard has lots of money," would say Mr. Vinck solemnly, with his head on one side, "lots of money; more than Hudig!" And after a pause—just to let his hearers recover from their astonishment at such an incredible assertion—he would add in an explanatory whisper, "You know, he has discovered a river."*

That was it! He had discovered a river! That was the fact placing old Lingard so much above the common crowd of sea-going adventurers who traded with Hudig in the daytime and drank champagne, gambled, sang noisy songs, and made love to half-caste girls under the broad verandah of the Sunda Hotel* at night. Into that river, whose entrances himself only knew, Lingard used to take his assorted cargo* of Manchester goods, brass gongs, rifles and gunpowder. His brig* *Flash*, which he commanded himself, would on those occasions disappear quietly during the night from the roadstead* while his companions were sleeping off the effects of the midnight carouse, Lingard seeing them drunk under the table before going on board, himself unaffected by any amount of liquor. Many tried to follow him and find that land of plenty for gutta-percha and rattans, pearl shells and birds' nests, wax and gum-dammar,* but the little *Flash* could outsail every craft in those seas. A few of them came to grief on hidden sandbanks and coral reefs,* losing their all and barely escaping with life from the cruel grip of this sunny and smiling sea; others got discouraged; and for many years the green and peaceful-looking islands guarding the entrances to the promised land kept their secret with all the merciless serenity of tropical nature. And so Lingard came and went on his secret or open expeditions, becoming a hero in Almayer's eyes by the boldness and enormous profits of his ventures, seeming to Almayer a very great man indeed as he saw him marching up the warehouse, grunting a "how are you?" to Vinck, or greeting Hudig, the Master, with a boisterous "Hallo, old pirate! Alive yet?" as a preliminary to transacting business behind the little green door. Often of an evening, in the silence of the then deserted warehouse, Almayer putting away his papers before driving home with Mr. Vinck, in whose household he lived, would pause listening to the noise of a hot discussion in the private office, would hear the deep and monotonous growl of the Master, and the roared-out interruptions of Lingard—two mastiffs fighting over a marrowy bone. But to Almayer's ears it sounded like a quarrel of Titans—a battle of the gods.

After a year or so Lingard, having been brought often in contact with Almayer in the course of business, took a sudden and, to the onlookers, a rather inexplicable fancy to the young man. He sang his praises, late at night, over a convivial glass to his cronies in the Sunda Hotel, and one fine morning electrified Vinck by declaring that he must have "that young fellow for a supercargo. Kind of captain's clerk. Do all my quill-driving for me." Hudig consented. Almayer, with youth's natural craving for change, was nothing loth, and packing his few belongings, started in the *Flash* on one of those long cruises when the old seaman was wont to visit almost every island in the archipelago. Months slipped by, and Lingard's friendship seemed to increase. Often pacing the deck with Almayer, when the faint night breeze, heavy with aromatic exhalations of the islands, shoved the brig gently along under the peaceful and sparkling sky, did the old seaman open his heart to his entranced listener. He spoke of his past life, of escaped dangers, of big profits in his trade, of new combinations that were in the future to bring profits bigger still. Often he had mentioned his daughter, the girl found in the pirate prau, speaking of her with a strange assumption of fatherly tenderness. "She must be a big girl now," he used to say. "It's nigh unto four years since I have seen her! Damme, Almayer, if I don't think we will run into Sourabaya* this trip." And after such a declaration he always dived into his cabin muttering to himself, "Something must be done—must be done." More than once he would astonish Almayer by walking up to him rapidly, clearing his throat with a powerful "Hem!" as if he intended* to say something, and then turning abruptly away to lean over the bulwarks in silence, and watch, motionless, for hours, the gleam and sparkle of the phosphorescent sea along the ship's side. It was the night before arriving in Sourabaya when one of those attempts at confidential communication succeeded. After clearing his throat he spoke. He spoke to some purpose. He wanted Almayer to marry his adopted daughter.* "And don't you kick because you're white!" he shouted, suddenly, not giving the surprised young man the time to say a word. "None of that with me! Nobody will see the colour of your wife's skin. The dollars are too thick for that, I tell you! And mind you, they will be thicker yet before I die. There will be millions, Kaspar! Millions I say! And all for her—and for you, if you do what you are told."

Startled by the unexpected proposal, Almayer hesitated, and remained silent for a minute. He was gifted with a strong and active imagination, and in that short space of time he saw, as in a flash of dazzling light, great piles of shining guilders, and realized all the possibilities of an opulent existence. The consideration, the indolent ease of life—for which he felt himself so well fitted—his ships, his warehouses, his merchandise (old Lingard would not live for ever), and, crowning all, in the far future gleamed like a fairy palace the big mansion in Amsterdam, that earthly paradise of his dreams, where made king amongst men by old Lingard's money, he would pass the evening of his days in inexpressible splendour. As to the other side of the picture—the companionship for life of a Malay girl, that legacy of a boatful of pirates—there was only within him a confused consciousness of shame that he a white man—— Still, a convent education of four years—and then she may mercifully die. He was always lucky, and money is powerful! Go through it. Why not? He had a vague idea of shutting her up somewhere, anywhere, out of his gorgeous future. Easy enough to dispose of a Malay woman, a slave, after all, to his Eastern mind, convent or no convent, ceremony or no ceremony.

He lifted his head and confronted the anxious yet irate seaman.

"I—of course—anything you wish, Captain Lingard."

"Call me father, my boy. She does," said the mollified old adventurer. "Damme, though, if I didn't think you were going to refuse. Mind you, Kaspar, I always get my way, so it would have been no use. But you are no fool."

He remembered well that time—the look, the accent, the words, the effect they produced on him, his very surroundings. He remembered the narrow slanting deck of the brig, the silent sleeping coast, the smooth black surface of the sea with a great bar of gold laid on it by the rising moon. He remembered it all, and he remembered his feelings of mad exultation at the thought of that fortune thrown into his hands. He was no fool then, and he was no fool now. Circumstances had been against him; the fortune was gone, but hope remained.

He shivered in the night air, and suddenly became aware of the intense darkness which, on the sun's departure, had closed in upon the river, blotting out the outlines of the opposite shore. Only the fire of dry branches lit outside the stockade of the Rajah's compound* called fitfully into view the ragged trunks of the surrounding trees, putting a stain of glowing red halfway across the river where the drifting logs were hurrying toward the sea through the impenetrable gloom. He had a hazy recollection of having been called some time during the evening by his wife. To his dinner probably. But a man busy contemplating the wreckage of his past in the dawn of new hopes cannot be hungry whenever his rice is ready. Time he went home, though; it was getting late.

He stepped cautiously on the loose planks towards the ladder. A lizard, disturbed by the noise, emitted a plaintive note and scurried through the long grass growing on the bank. Almayer descended the ladder carefully, now thoroughly recalled to the realities of life by the care necessary to prevent a fall on the uneven ground where the stones, decaying planks, and half-sawn beams were piled up in inextricable confusion. As he turned towards the house where he lived—"my old house" he called it—his ear detected the splash of paddles away in the darkness of the river. He stood still in the path, attentive and surprised at anybody being on the river at this late hour during such a heavy freshet.* Now he could hear the paddles distinctly, and even a rapidly exchanged word in low tones, the heavy breathing of men fighting with the current, and hugging the bank on which he stood. Quite close, too, but it was too dark to distinguish anything under the overhanging bushes.

"Arabs, no doubt," muttered Almayer to himself, peering into the solid blackness. "What are they up to now? Some of Abdulla's* business; curse him!"

The boat was very close now.

"Oh, ya! Man!"* hailed Almayer.

The sound of voices ceased, but the paddles worked as furiously as before. Then the bush in front of Almayer shook, and the sharp sound of the paddles falling into the canoe rang in the quiet night. They were holding on to the bush now; but Almayer could hardly make out an indistinct dark shape of a man's head and shoulders above the bank.

"You Abdulla?" said Almayer, doubtfully.

A grave voice answered—

"Tuan* Almayer is speaking to a friend. There is no Arab here."

Almayer's heart gave a great leap.

"Dain!" he exclaimed. "At last! at last! I have been waiting for you every day and every night. I had nearly given you up."

"Nothing could have stopped me from coming back here," said the other, almost violently. "Not even death," he whispered to himself.

"This is a friend's talk, and is very good," said Almayer, heartily. "Drop down* to the jetty and let your men cook their rice in my campong while we talk in the house."

There was no answer to that invitation.

"What is it?" asked Almayer, uneasily. "There is nothing wrong with the brig, I hope?"

"The brig is where no Orang Blanda* can lay his hands on her," said Dain, with a gloomy tone in his voice, which Almayer, in his elation, failed to notice.

"Right," he said. "But where are all your men? There are only two with you."

"Listen, Tuan Almayer," said Dain. "To-morrow's sun shall see me in your house, and then we will talk. Now I must go to the Rajah."

"To the Rajah! Why? What do you want with Lakamba?"*

"Tuan, to-morrow we talk like friends. I must see Lakamba to-night."

"Dain, you are not going to abandon me now, when all is ready?" asked Almayer, in a pleading voice.

"Have I not returned? But I must see Lakamba first for your good and mine."

The shadowy head disappeared abruptly. The bush, released from the grasp of the bowman,* sprung back with a swish, scattering a shower of muddy water over Almayer, as he bent forward, trying to see.

In a little while the canoe shot into the streak of light that streamed on the river from the big fire on the opposite shore, disclosing the outline of two men bending to their work, and a third figure in the stern flourishing the steering paddle, his head covered with an enormous round hat, like a fantastically exaggerated mushroom.

Almayer watched the canoe till it passed out of the line of light. Shortly after, the murmur of many voices reached him across the water. He could see the torches being snatched out of the burning pile, and rendering visible for a moment the gate in the stockade round which they crowded. Then they went in; the torches disappeared, and the scattered fire sent out only a dim and fitful glare.

Almayer stepped homewards with long strides and mind uneasy. Surely Dain was not thinking of playing him false. It was absurd. Dain and Lakamba were both too much interested in the success of his scheme. Trusting to Malays was poor work; but then even Malays have some sense and understand their own interest. All would be well—must be well. At this point in his meditation he found himself at the foot of the steps leading to the verandah of his home. From the low point of land where he stood he could see both branches of the river. The main stream of the Pantai was lost in complete darkness, for the fire at the Rajah's had gone out altogether; but up the Sambir* reach his eye could follow the long line of Malay houses crowding the bank, with here and there a dim light twinkling through bamboo walls, or a smoky torch burning on the platforms built out over the river.* Further away, where the island ended in a low cliff, rose a dark mass of buildings towering above the Malay structures. Founded solidly on a firm ground with plenty of space, starred by many lights burning strong and white, with a suggestion of paraffin and lamp-glasses, stood the house and the godowns of Abdulla bin Selim,* the great trader of Sambir. To Almayer the sight was very distasteful, and he shook his fist towards the buildings that in their evident prosperity looked to him cold and insolent, and contemptuous of his own fallen fortunes.

He mounted the steps of his house slowly.

In the middle of the verandah there was a round table. On it a paraffin lamp without a globe shed a hard glare on the three inner sides. The fourth side was open, and faced the river. Between the rough supports of the high-pitched roof hung torn rattan screens. There was no ceiling, and the harsh brilliance of the lamp was toned above into a soft half-light that lost itself in the obscurity amongst the rafters. The front wall was cut in two by the doorway of a central passage closed by a red curtain. The women's room opened into that passage, which led to the back courtyard and to the cooking shed. In one of the side walls there was a doorway. Half obliterated words—"Office: Lingard and Co."*—were still legible on the dusty door, which looked as if it had not been opened for a very long time. Close to the other side wall stood a bent-wood rocking chair, and by the table and about the verandah four wooden armchairs straggled forlornly, as if ashamed of their shabby surroundings. A heap of common mats lay in one corner, with an old hammock slung diagonally above. In the other corner, his head wrapped in a piece of red calico, huddled into a shapeless heap, slept a Malay, one of Almayer's domestic slaves—"my own people," he used to call them. A numerous and representative assembly of moths were holding high revels round the lamp to the spirited music of swarming mosquitoes. Under the palm-leaf thatch lizards raced on the beams calling softly. A monkey, chained to one of the verandah supports—retired for the night under the eaves—peered and grinned at Almayer, as it swung to one of the bamboo roof sticks and caused a shower of dust and bits of dried leaves to settle on the shabby table. The floor was uneven, with many withered plants and dried earth scattered about. A general air of squalid neglect pervaded the place.* The light breeze from the river swayed gently the tattered blinds, sending from the woods opposite a faint and sickly perfume as of decaying flowers.

Under Almayer's heavy tread the boards of the verandah creaked loudly. The sleeper in the corner moved uneasily, muttering indistinct words. There was a slight rustle behind the curtained doorway, and a soft voice asked in Malay, "Is it you, father?"

"Yes, Nina. I am hungry. Is everybody asleep in this house?"

Almayer spoke jovially and dropped with a contented sigh into the armchair nearest to the table. Nina Almayer came through the curtained doorway followed by an old Malay woman, who busied herself in setting upon the table a plateful of rice and fish, a jar of water and a bottle half full of genever.* After carefully placing before her master a cracked glass tumbler and a tin spoon she went away noiselessly. Nina stood by the table, one hand lightly resting on its edge, the other hanging listlessly by her side. Her face turned towards the outer darkness, through which her dreamy eyes seemed to see some entrancing picture, wore a look of impatient expectancy. She was tall for a half-caste, with the correct profile of the father, modified and strengthened by the squareness of the lower part of the face inherited from her maternal ancestors—the Sulu pirates. Her firm mouth, with the lips slightly parted and disclosing a gleam of white teeth, put a vague suggestion of ferocity into the impatient expression of her features. And yet her dark and perfect eyes had all the tender softness common to Malay women, but with a gleam of superior intelligence; they looked out gravely, wide open and steady, as if facing something invisible to all other eyes. She stood there all in white, straight, flexible, graceful, unconscious of herself, her low but broad forehead crowned with a shining mass of long black hair that fell in heavy tresses over her shoulders, and made her pale olive complexion look paler still by the contrast of its coal-black hue.

Almayer attacked his rice greedily, but after a few mouthfuls he paused, spoon in hand, and looked at his daughter curiously.

"Did you hear a boat pass about half an hour ago, Nina?" he asked.

The girl gave him a quick glance, and moving away from the light stood with her back to the table.

"I heard nothing," she said, slowly.

"There was a boat. At last! Dain himself; and he went on to Lakamba. I know it, for he told me so. I spoke to him, but he would not come here to-night. Promised to come to-morrow."

He swallowed another spoonful, then said—

"I am almost happy to-night, Nina. I can see the end of a long road, and it leads us away from this miserable swamp. We shall soon get away from here, I and you, my dear little girl, and then——"

He rose from the table and stood looking fixedly before him as if contemplating some enchanting vision.

"And then," he went on, "we shall be happy, you and I. Live rich and respected far from here, and forget this life, and all this struggle, and all this misery."

He approached his daughter and passed his hand caressingly over her hair.

"It is bad to have to trust a Malay," he said, "but I must own that this Dain is a perfect gentleman—a perfect gentleman," he repeated.

"Did you ask him to come here, father?" inquired Nina, not looking at him.

"Well, of course. We shall start on the day after to-morrow," said Almayer, joyously. "We must not lose any time. Are you glad, little girl?"

She was as tall as himself, but he liked to recall the time when she was little and they were all in all to each other.

"I am glad," she said, very low.

"Of course," said Almayer, vivaciously, "you cannot imagine what is before you. I myself have not been to Europe, but I have heard my mother talk so often that I seem to know all about it. We shall live a—a glorious life. You shall see."

Again he stood silent by his daughter's side looking at that enchanting vision. After a while he shook his fist towards the sleeping settlement.

"Ah! my friend Abdulla," he cried, "we shall see who will have the best of it after all these years!"

He looked up the river and remarked calmly:

"Another thunderstorm. Well! No thunder will keep me awake to-night, I know! Good-night, little girl," he whispered tenderly, kissing her cheek. "You do not seem to be very happy to-night, but to-morrow you will show a brighter face. Eh?"

Nina had listened to her father, unmoved, with her

half-closed eyes still gazing into the night now made more intense by a heavy thunder-cloud that had crept down from the hills blotting out the stars, merging sky, forest, and river into one mass of almost palpable blackness. The faint breeze had died out, but the distant rumble of thunder and pale flashes of lightning gave warning of the approaching storm. With a sigh the girl turned towards the table.

Almayer was in his hammock now, already half asleep.

"Take the lamp, Nina," he muttered, drowsily. "This place is full of mosquitoes. Go to sleep, daughter."

But Nina put the lamp out and turned back again towards the balustrade of the verandah. She stood with her arm round the wooden support looking eagerly towards the Pantai reach. And motionless there in the oppressive calm of the tropical night she could see at each flash of lightning the forest lining both banks up the river bending before the furious blast of wind, the upper reach of the river whipped into white foam, and the black clouds torn into fantastic shapes trailing low over the swaying trees. Round her all was as yet stillness and peace, but she could hear afar off the driving roar and hiss of heavy rain, the wash of the waves on the tormented river. It came nearer and nearer, with loud thunder-claps and long flashes of vivid lightning, followed by short periods of appalling blackness. When the storm reached the low point dividing the river, the whole house shook while the rain pattered loudly on the palm-leaf roof. The thunder spoke in one prolonged roll, and the incessant lightning disclosed a turmoil of leaping waters, driving logs, and the big trees bending before a brutal and merciless force.*

Undisturbed by the nightly event of the rainy monsoon,* the father slept quietly, oblivious alike of his hopes, his misfortunes, his friends, and his enemies; and the daughter stood motionless, at each flash of lightning eagerly scanning the broad river with a steady and anxious gaze.

CHAPTER TWO

When, in compliance with Lingard's abrupt demand, Almayer consented to wed the Malay girl, no one knew that on the day when the interesting young convert had lost all her natural relations and found a white father, she had been fighting desperately like the rest of them on board the prau, and was only prevented from leaping overboard, like the few other survivors, by a severe wound in the leg. There, on the fore-deck* of the prau, old Lingard found her under a heap of dead and dying pirates, and had her carried on the poop* of the *Flash* before the Malay craft was set on fire and sent adrift. She was conscious, and in the great peace and stillness of the tropical evening succeeding the turmoil of the battle, she watched all she held dear on earth after her own savage manner, drift away into the gloom in a great roar of flame and smoke. She lay there unheeding the careful hands attending to her wound, silent and absorbed in gazing at the funeral pile of those brave men she had so much admired and so well helped in their contest with the redoubtable "Rajah-Laut."

The light night breeze fanned the brig gently to the southwards, and the great blaze of light got smaller and smaller till it twinkled only on the horizon like a setting star. It set: the heavy canopy of smoke reflected the glare of hidden flames for a short time and then disappeared also.

She realized that with this vanishing gleam her old life departed too. Thenceforth there was slavery in the far countries, amongst strangers, in unknown and perhaps terrible surroundings.* There was in her the dread of the unknown; but otherwise she accepted her position calmly, after the manner of her people, and even considered it quite natural; for was she not a daughter of warriors, conquered in battle, and did she not belong rightfully to the victorious Rajah? Even the evident kindness of the terrible old man must spring, she thought, from admiration for his captive, and the flattered vanity eased for her the pangs of sorrow after such an awful calamity. Perhaps had she known of the high walls, the quiet gardens, and the silent nuns of the Samarang convent, where her destiny was leading her, she would have sought death in her dread and hate of such a restraint. But in imagination she pictured to herself the usual life of a Malay girl—the usual succession of heavy work and fierce love, of intrigues, gold ornaments, of domestic drudgery, and of that great but occult influence which is one of the few rights of half-savage womankind. But her destiny in the rough hands of the old sea-dog, acting under unreasoning impulses of the heart, took a strange and to her a terrible shape. She bore it all—the restraint and the teaching and the new faith—with calm submission, concealing her hate and contempt for all that new life. She learned the language very easily, yet understood but little of the new faith the good sisters taught her, assimilating quickly only the superstitious elements of the religion. She called Lingard father, gently and caressingly, at each of his short and noisy visits, under the clear impression that he was a great and dangerous power it was good to propitiate. Was he not now her master? And during those long four years she nourished a hope of finding favour in his eyes and ultimately becoming his wife, counsellor, and guide.

Those dreams of the future were dispelled by the Rajah-Laut's "fiat,"* which made Almayer's fortune, as that young man fondly hoped. And dressed in the hateful finery of Europe, the young convert* stood before the altar with an unknown and sulky-looking white man. For Almayer was uneasy, a little disgusted, and greatly inclined to run away. A judicious fear of the adopted father-in-law and a just regard for his own material welfare prevented him from making a scandal; yet, while swearing fidelity, he was concocting plans for getting rid of the pretty Malay girl in a more or less distant future. She, however, had retained enough of conventual teaching to understand well that according to white men's law* she was going to be Almayer's companion and not his slave, and promised to herself to act accordingly.

So when the *Flash* freighted with materials for building a new house left the harbour of Batavia,* taking away the young couple into the unknown Borneo, she did not carry on her deck so much love and happiness as old Lingard was wont to boast of before his casual friends in the verandahs of various hotels. The old seaman himself was perfectly happy. Now he had done his duty by the girl. "You know I made her an orphan," he often concluded solemnly, when talking about his own affairs to a scratch audience of shore loafers—as it was his habit to do. And the approbative shouts of his half-intoxicated auditors filled his simple soul with delight and pride. "I carry everything right through," was another of his sayings, and in pursuance of that principle he pushed the building of house and godowns on the Pantai River with feverish haste. The house for the young couple; the godowns for the big trade Almayer was going to develop while he (Lingard) would be able to give himself up to some mysterious work which was only spoken of in hints, but was understood to relate to gold and diamonds* in the interior of the island. Almayer was impatient too. Had he known what was before him he might not have been so eager and full of hope as he stood watching the last canoe of the Lingard expedition disappear in the bend up the river. When, turning round, he beheld the pretty little house, the godowns* built neatly by an army of Chinese carpenters,* the new jetty round which were clustered the trading canoes, he felt a sudden elation in the thought that the world was his.

But the world had to be conquered first, and its conquest was not so easy as he thought. He was very soon made to understand that he was not wanted in that corner of it where old Lingard and his own weak will placed him, in the midst of unscrupulous intrigues and of a fierce trade competition. The Arabs had found out the river,* had established a trading post in Sambir, and where they traded they would be masters and suffer no rival. Lingard returned unsuccessful from his first expedition, and departed again spending all the profits of the legitimate trade on his mysterious journeys. Almayer struggled with the difficulties of his position, friendless and unaided, save for the protection given to him for Lingard's sake by the old Rajah, the predecessor of Lakamba. Lakamba himself, then living as a private individual on a rice clearing, seven miles down the river, exercised all his influence towards the help of the white man's enemies, plotting against the old Rajah and Almayer with a certainty of combination pointing clearly to a profound knowledge of their most secret affairs. Outwardly friendly, his portly form was often to be seen on Almayer's verandah; his green turban* and gold-embroidered jacket shone in the front rank of the decorous throng of Malays coming to greet Lingard on his returns from the interior; his salaams were of the lowest, and his hand-shakings of the heartiest, when welcoming the old trader. But his small eyes took in the signs of the times, and he departed from those interviews with a satisfied and furtive smile to hold long consultations with his friend and ally, Syed* Abdulla, the chief of the Arab trading post, a man of great wealth and of great influence in the islands.

It was currently believed at that time in the settlement that Lakamba's visits to Almayer's house were not limited to those official interviews. Often on moonlight nights the belated fishermen* of Sambir saw a small canoe shooting out from the narrow creek at the back of the white man's house, and the solitary occupant paddle cautiously down the river in the deep shadows of the bank; and those events, duly reported, were discussed round the evening fires far into the night with the cynicism of expression common to Malays.* Almayer went on struggling desperately, but with a feebleness of purpose depriving him of all chance of success against men so unscrupulous and resolute as his rivals the Arabs. The trade fell away from the large godowns, and the godowns themselves rotted piecemeal. The old man's banker, Hudig of Macassar, failed,* and with this went the whole available capital. The profits of past years had been swallowed up in Lingard's exploring craze. Lingard was in the interior—perhaps dead—at all events giving no sign of life. Almayer stood alone in the midst of those adverse circumstances, deriving only a little comfort from the companionship of his little daughter, born two years after the marriage, and at the time some six years old. His wife had soon commenced to treat him with a savage contempt expressed by sulky silence, only occasionally varied by outbursts* of savage invective. He felt she hated him, and saw her jealous eyes watching himself and the child with almost an expression of hate. She was jealous of the little girl's evident preference for the father, and Almayer felt he was not safe with that woman in the house. While she was burning the furniture,* and tearing down the pretty curtains in her unreasoning hate of those signs of civilization, Almayer, cowed by these outbursts of savage nature, meditated in silence on the best way of getting rid of her. He thought of everything; even planned murder in an undecided and feeble sort of way, but dared do nothing—expecting every day the return of Lingard with news of some immense good fortune. Lingard returned indeed, but aged, ill, a ghost of his former self, with the fire of fever burning in his sunken eyes, almost the only survivor of the numerous expedition. But he was successful at last! Untold riches were in his grasp; he wanted more money—only a little more to realize a dream of fabulous fortune. And Hudig had failed! Almayer scraped all he could together, but the old man wanted more. If Almayer could not get it he would go to Singapore—to Europe even, but before all to Singapore; and he would take the little Nina with him. The child must be brought up decently. He had good friends in Singapore who would take care of her and have her taught properly. All would be well, and that girl, upon whom the old seaman seemed to have transferred all his former affection for the mother, would be the richest woman in the East—in the world even. So old Lingard shouted, pacing the verandah with his heavy quarter-deck* step, gesticulating with a smouldering cheroot; ragged, dishevelled, enthusiastic; and Almayer, sitting huddled up on a pile of mats, thought with dread of the separation from the only human being he loved—with greater dread still, perhaps, of the scene with his wife, the savage tigress deprived of her young. She will poison me, thought the poor wretch, well aware of that easy and final manner of solving the social, political, or family problems in Malay life.

To his great surprise she took the news very quietly, giving only him and Lingard a furtive glance, and saying not a word. This, however, did not prevent her the next day from jumping into the river and swimming after the boat in which Lingard was carrying away the nurse with the screaming child. Almayer had to give chase with his whale-boat* and drag her in by the hair in the midst of cries and curses enough to make heaven fall. Yet after two days spent in wailing, she returned to her former mode of life, chewing betel-nut,* and sitting all day amongst her women in stupefied idleness. She aged very rapidly after that, and only roused herself from her apathy to acknowledge by a scathing remark or an insulting exclamation the accidental presence of her husband. He had built for her a riverside hut in the compound* where she dwelt in perfect seclusion. Lakamba's visits had ceased when, by a convenient decree of Providence, the old ruler* of Sambir departed this life. Lakamba reigned in his stead now, having been well served* by his Arab friends with the Dutch authorities. Syed Abdulla was the great man and trader of the Pantai. Almayer lay ruined and helpless under the close-meshed net of their intrigues, owing his life only to his supposed knowledge of Lingard's valuable secret. Lingard had disappeared. He wrote once from Singapore saying the child was well, and under the care of a Mrs. Vinck,* and that he himself was going to Europe to raise money for the great enterprise. He was coming back soon. There would be no difficulties, he wrote. People would rush in with their money. Evidently they did not, for there was only one letter more from him saying he was ill, had found no relation living, but little else besides.* Then came a complete silence. Europe had swallowed up* the Rajah-Laut apparently, and Almayer looked vainly westward for a ray of light out of the gloom of his shattered hopes. Years passed, and the rare letters from Mrs. Vinck, later from the girl herself, were the only thing to be looked to to make life bearable amongst the triumphant savagery of the river. Almayer lived now alone, having even ceased to visit his debtors who would not pay, sure of Lakamba's protection. The faithful Sumatrese* Ali cooked his rice and made his coffee, for he dared not trust any one else, and least of all his wife. He killed time wandering sadly in the overgrown paths round the house, visiting the ruined godowns where a few brass guns covered with verdigris* and only a few broken cases of mouldering Manchester goods reminded him of the good early times when all this was full of life and merchandise, and he overlooked a busy scene on the river bank, his little daughter by his side. Now the up-country canoes glided past the little rotten wharf of Lingard and Co., to paddle up the Pantai branch, and cluster round the new jetty belonging to Abdulla. Not that they loved Abdulla, but they dared not trade with the man whose star had set. Had they done so they knew there was no mercy to be expected from Arab or Rajah; no rice to be got on credit in times of scarcity from either; and Almayer could not help them, having at times hardly enough for himself. Almayer, in his isolation and despair, often envied his near neighbour the Chinaman, Jim-Eng,* whom he could see stretched on a pile of cool mats, a wooden pillow under his head, an opium* pipe in his nerveless fingers. He did not seek, however, consolation in opium—perhaps it was too expensive—perhaps his white man's pride saved him from that degradation; but most likely it was the thought of his little daughter in the far-off Straits Settlements.* He heard from her oftener since Abdulla bought a steamer,* which ran now between Singapore and the Pantai settlement every three months or so. Almayer felt himself nearer his daughter. He longed to see her, and planned a voyage to Singapore, but put off his departure from year to year, always expecting some favourable turn of fortune. He did not want to meet her with empty hands and with no words of hope on his lips. He could not take her back into that savage life to which he was condemned himself. He was also a little afraid of her. What would she think of him? He reckoned the years. A grown woman. A civilized woman, young and hopeful; while he felt old and hopeless, and very much like those savages round him. He asked himself what was going to be her future. He could not answer that question yet, and he dared not face her. And yet he longed after her. He hesitated for years.

His hesitation was put an end to by Nina's unexpected appearance in Sambir. She arrived in the steamer under the captain's care. Almayer beheld her with surprise not unmixed with wonder. During those ten years the child had changed into a woman, black-haired, olive-skinned, tall, and beautiful, with great sad eyes, where the startled expression common to Malay womankind was modified by a thoughtful tinge inherited from her European ancestry. Almayer thought with dismay of the meeting of his wife and daughter, of what this grave girl in European clothes would think of her betel-nut chewing mother, squatting in a dark hut, disorderly, half naked, and sulky. He also feared an outbreak of temper on the part of that pest of a woman he had hitherto managed to keep tolerably quiet, thereby saving the remnants of his dilapidated furniture. And he stood there before the closed door of the hut in the blazing sunshine listening to the murmur of voices, wondering what went on inside, wherefrom all the servant-maids had been expelled at the beginning of the interview, and now stood clustered by the palings with half-covered faces in a chatter of curious speculation. He forgot himself there trying to catch a stray word through the bamboo walls, till the captain of the steamer (who had walked up with the girl) fearing a sunstroke, took him under the arm and led him into the shade of his own verandah where Nina's trunk stood already, having been landed by the steamer's men. As soon as Captain Ford*had his glass before him and his cheroot lighted, Almayer asked for the explanation of his daughter's unexpected arrival. Ford said little beyond generalizing in vague but violent terms upon the foolishness of women in general, and of Mrs. Vinck in particular.

"You know, Kaspar," said he, in conclusion, to the excited Almayer, "it is deucedly awkward to have a half-caste girl in the house. There's such a lot of fools about. There was that young fellow from the bank who used to ride to the Vinck bungalow early and late. That old woman thought it was for that Emma of hers. When she found out what he wanted exactly, there was a row, I can tell you. She would not have Nina—not an hour longer—in the house. Fact is, I heard of this affair and took the girl to my wife. My wife is a pretty good woman—as women go—and upon my word we would have kept the girl for you, only she would not stay. Now, then! Don't flare up, Kaspar. Sit still. What can you do? It is better so. Let her stay with you. She was never happy over there. Those two Vinck girls are no better than dressed-up monkeys.

They slighted her. You can't make her white. It's no use you swearing at me. You can't. She is a good girl for all that, but she would not tell my wife anything. If you want to know, ask her yourself; but if I was you I would leave her alone. You are welcome to her passage money, old fellow, if you are short now." And the skipper, throwing away his cigar, walked off to "wake them up on board," as he expressed it.

Almayer vainly expected to hear of the cause of his daughter's return from his daughter's lips. Not that day, not on any other day did she ever allude to her Singapore life. He did not care to ask, awed by the calm impassiveness of her face, by those solemn eyes looking past him on the great, still forests sleeping in majestic repose to the murmur of the broad river. He accepted the situation, happy in the gentle and protecting affection the girl showed him, fitfully enough, for she had (as he called it) her bad days when she used to visit her mother and remain long hours in the riverside hut, coming out as inscrutable as ever, but with a contemptuous look and a short word ready to answer any of his speeches. He got used even to that, and on those days kept quiet, although greatly alarmed by his wife's influence upon the girl. Otherwise Nina adapted herself wonderfully to the circumstances of a half-savage and miserable life. She accepted without question or apparent disgust the neglect, the decay, the poverty of the household, the absence of furniture, and the preponderance of rice diet on the family table. She lived with Almayer in the little house (now sadly decaying) built originally by Lingard for the young couple. The Malays discussed eagerly* her arrival. There were at the beginning crowded levées* of Malay women with their children, seeking eagerly after "Ubat"* for all the ills of the flesh from the young Mem Putih.* In the cool of the evening grave Arabs in long white shirts and yellow sleeveless jackets walked slowly on the dusty path by the riverside towards Almayer's gate, and made solemn calls upon that Unbeliever under shallow pretences of business, only to get a glimpse of the young girl in a highly decorous manner. Even Lakamba came out of his stockade in a great pomp of war canoes and red umbrellas, and landed on the rotten little jetty of Lingard and Co. He came, he said, to buy a couple of brass guns as a present to his friend the chief of Sambir Dyaks;* and while Almayer, suspicious but polite, busied himself in unearthing the old popguns in the godowns, the Rajah sat on an armchair in the verandah, surrounded by his respectful retinue waiting in vain for Nina's appearance. She was in one of her bad days, and remained in her mother's hut watching with her the ceremonious proceedings on the verandah. The Rajah departed, baffled but courteous, and soon Almayer began to reap the benefit of improved relations with the ruler in the shape of the recovery of some debts, paid to him with many apologies and many a low salaam by debtors till then considered hopelessly insolvent. Under these improving circumstances Almayer brightened up a little. All was not lost perhaps. Those Arabs and Malays saw at last that he was a man of some ability, he thought. And he began, after his manner, to plan great things, to dream of great fortunes for himself and Nina. Especially for Nina! Under these vivifying impulses he asked Captain Ford to write to his friends in England making inquiries after Lingard. Was he alive or dead? If dead, had he left any papers, documents; any indications or hints as to his great enterprise? Meantime he had found amongst the rubbish in one of the empty rooms a notebook belonging to the old adventurer. He studied the crabbed handwriting of its pages and often grew meditative over it. Other things also woke him up from his apathy. The stir made in the whole of the island by the establishment of the British Borneo Company* affected even the sluggish flow of the Pantai life. Great changes were expected; annexation was talked of; the Arabs grew civil. Almayer began building his new house for the use of the future engineers, agents, or settlers of the new Company. He spent every available guilder on it with a confiding* heart. One thing only disturbed his happiness; his wife came out of her seclusion, importing her green jacket, scant sarongs,* shrill voice, and witch-like appearance, into his quiet life in the small bungalow. And his daughter seemed to accept that savage intrusion into their daily existence with wonderful equanimity. He did not like it, but dared say nothing.

CHAPTER THREE

The deliberations conducted in London have a far-reaching importance, and so the decision issued from the fog-veiled offices of the Borneo Company darkened for Almayer the brilliant sunshine of the Tropics, and added another drop of bitterness to the cup of his disenchantments. The claim to that part of the East Coast was abandoned,* leaving the Pantai river under the nominal power of Holland. In Sambir there was joy and excitement. The slaves* were hurried out of sight into the forest and jungle, and the flags were run up to tall poles in the Rajah's compound in expectation of a visit from Dutch man-of-war boats.

The frigate* remained anchored outside the mouth of the river, and the boats came up in tow of the steam launch, threading their way cautiously amongst a crowd of canoes filled with gaily dressed Malays. The officer in command listened gravely to the loyal speeches of Lakamba, returned the salaams of Abdulla, and assured those gentlemen in choice Malay of the great Rajah's*—down in Batavia—friendship and good-will towards the ruler and inhabitants of this model state of Sambir.

Almayer from his verandah watched across the river the festive proceedings, heard the report of brass guns saluting the new flag presented to Lakamba, and the deep murmur of the crowd of spectators surging round the stockade. The smoke of the firing rose in white clouds on the green background of the forests, and he could not help comparing his own fleeting hopes to the rapidly disappearing vapour. He was by no means patriotically elated by the event, yet he had to force himself into a gracious behaviour when, the official reception being over, the naval officers of the Commission* crossed the river to pay a visit to the solitary white man of whom they had heard, no doubt wishing also to catch a glimpse of his daughter. In that they were disappointed, Nina refusing to show herself; but they seemed easily consoled by the gin and cheroots set before them by the hospitable Almayer; and sprawling comfortably on the lame armchairs* under the shade of the verandah, while the blazing sunshine outside seemed to set the great river simmering in the heat, they filled the little bungalow with the unusual sounds of European languages, with noise and laughter produced by naval witticisms at the expense of the fat Lakamba whom they had been complimenting so much that very morning. The younger men in an access of good fellowship made their host talk, and Almayer, excited by the sight of European faces, by the sound of European voices, opened his heart before the sympathizing strangers, unaware of the amusement the recital of his many misfortunes caused to those future admirals. They drank his health, wished him many big diamonds and a mountain of gold, expressed even an envy of the high destinies awaiting him yet. Encouraged by so much friendliness, the grey-headed and foolish dreamer invited his guests to visit his new house. They went there through the long grass in a straggling procession while their boats were got ready for the return down the river in the cool of the evening. And in the great empty rooms where the tepid wind entering through the sashless windows whirled gently the dried leaves and the dust of many days of neglect, Almayer in his white jacket and flowered sarong, surrounded by a circle of glittering uniforms, stamped his foot to show the solidity of the neatly-fitting floors and expatiated upon the beauties and convenience of the building. They listened and assented, amazed by the wonderful simplicity and the foolish hopefulness of the man, till Almayer, carried away by his excitement, disclosed his regret at the non-arrival of the English, "who knew how to develop a rich country," as he expressed it. There was a general laugh amongst the Dutch officers at that unsophisticated statement, and a move was made towards the boats; but when Almayer, stepping cautiously on the rotten boards of the Lingard jetty, tried to approach the chief of the Commission with some timid hints anent* the protection required by the Dutch subject against the wily Arabs, that salt-water diplomat told him significantly that the Arabs were better subjects than Hollanders who dealt illegally in gunpowder with the Malays. The innocent Almayer recognized there at once the oily tongue of Abdulla and the solemn persuasiveness of Lakamba, but ere he had time to frame an indignant protest the steam launch and the string of boats moved rapidly down the river leaving him on the jetty, standing open-mouthed in his surprise and anger. There are thirty miles of river from Sambir to the gem-like islands of the estuary where the frigate was awaiting the return of the boats. The moon rose long before the boats had traversed half that distance, and the black forest sleeping peacefully under her cold rays woke up that night to the ringing laughter in the small flotilla provoked by some reminiscence of Almayer's lamentable narrative. Salt-water jests at the poor man's expense were passed from boat to boat, the non-appearance of his daughter was commented upon with severe displeasure, and the half-finished house built for the reception of Englishmen received on that joyous night the name of "Almayer's Folly" by the unanimous vote of the lighthearted seamen.

For many weeks after this visit life in Sambir resumed its even and uneventful flow. Each day's sun shooting its morning rays above the tree-tops lit up the usual scene of daily activity. Nina walking on the path that formed the only street in the settlement saw the accustomed sight of men lolling on the shady side of the houses, on the high platforms; of women busily engaged in husking the daily rice; of naked brown children racing along the shady and narrow paths leading to the clearings. Jim-Eng, strolling before his house, greeted her with a friendly nod before climbing up indoors to seek his beloved opium pipe. The elder children clustered round her, daring from long acquaintance, pulling the skirts of her white robe with their dark fingers, and showing their brilliant teeth in expectation of a shower of glass beads. She greeted them with a quiet smile, but always had a few friendly words for a Siamese girl,* a slave owned by Bulangi,* whose numerous wives were said to be of a violent temper. Well-founded rumour said also that the domestic squabbles of that industrious cultivator ended generally in a combined assault of all his wives upon the Siamese slave. The girl herself never complained—perhaps from dictates of prudence, but more likely through the strange, resigned apathy of half-savage womankind. From early morning she was to be seen on the paths amongst the houses—by the riverside or on the jetties, the tray of pastry, it was her mission to sell, skilfully balanced on her head. During the great heat of the day she usually sought refuge in Almayer's campong, often finding shelter in a shady corner of the verandah, where she squatted with her tray before her, when invited by Nina. For "Mem Putih" she had always a smile, but the presence of

Mrs. Almayer, the very sound of her shrill voice, was the signal for a hurried departure.

To this girl Nina often spoke; the other inhabitants of Sambir seldom or never heard the sound of her voice. They got used to the silent figure moving in their midst calm and white-robed, a being from another world and incomprehensible to them. Yet Nina's life for all her outward composure, for all the seeming detachment from the things and people surrounding her, was far from quiet, in consequence of Mrs. Almayer being much too active for the happiness and even safety of the household. She had resumed some intercourse with Lakamba, not personally, it is true (for the dignity of that potentate kept him inside his stockade), but through the agency of that potentate's prime minister, harbour master, financial adviser, and general factotum. That gentleman*—of Sulu origin—was certainly endowed with statesmanlike qualities, although he was totally devoid of personal charms. In truth he was perfectly repulsive, possessing only one eye and a pock-marked face, with nose and lips horribly disfigured by the small-pox. This unengaging individual often strolled into Almayer's garden in unofficial costume, composed of a piece of pink calico round his waist. There at the back of the house, squatting on his heels on scattered embers, in close proximity to the great iron boiler, where the family daily rice was being cooked by the women under Mrs. Almayer's superintendence, did that astute negotiator carry on long conversations in Sulu language with Almayer's wife. What the subject of their discourses was might have been guessed from the subsequent domestic scenes by Almayer's hearthstone.

Of late Almayer had taken to excursions up the river. In a small canoe with two paddlers and the faithful Ali for a steersman he would disappear for a few days at a time. All his movements were no doubt closely watched by Lakamba and Abdulla, for the man once in the confidence of Rajah-Laut was supposed to be in possession of valuable secrets. The coast population of Borneo believes implicitly in diamonds of fabulous value, in gold mines of enormous richness in the interior. And all those imaginings are heightened by the difficulty of penetrating far inland, especially on the northeast coast, where the Malays and the river tribes of Dyaks or Head-hunters are eternally quarrelling.* It is true enough that some gold reaches the coast in the hands of those Dyaks when, during short periods of truce in the desultory warfare, they visit the coast settlements of Malays. And so the wildest exaggerations are built up and added to on the slight basis of that fact.

Almayer in his quality of *white man—as Lingard before him—had somewhat better relations with the up-river tribes.* Yet even his excursions were not without danger, and his returns were eagerly looked for by the impatient Lakamba. But every time the Rajah was disappointed. Vain were the conferences by the rice-pot of his factotum Babalatchi with the white man's wife. The white man himself was impenetrable—impenetrable to persuasion, coaxing, abuse; to soft words and shrill revilings; to desperate beseechings or murderous threats; for Mrs. Almayer, in her extreme desire to persuade her husband into an alliance with Lakamba, played upon the whole gamut of passion. With her soiled robe wound tightly under the armpits across her lean bosom, her scant greyish hair tumbled in disorder over her projecting cheek-bones, in suppliant attitude, she depicted with shrill volubility the advantages of close union with a man so good and so fair dealing.

"Why don't you go to the Rajah?" she screamed.

"Why do you go back to those Dyaks in the great forest? They should be killed. You cannot kill them, you cannot; but our Rajah's men are brave! You tell the Rajah where the old white man's treasure is. Our Rajah is good! He is our very grandfather.* He will kill those wretched Dyaks, and you shall have half the treasure. Oh, Kaspar, tell where the treasure is! Tell me! Tell me out of the old man's surat* where you read so often at night."

On those occasions Almayer sat with rounded shoulders bending to the blast of this domestic tempest, accentuating only each pause in the torrent of his wife's eloquence by an angry growl, "There is no treasure! Go away, woman!" Exasperated by the sight of his patiently bent back, she would at last walk round so as to face him across the table, and clasping her robe with one hand she stretched the other lean arm and claw-like hand to emphasize, in a passion of anger and contempt, the rapid rush of scathing remarks and bitter cursings heaped on the head of the man unworthy to associate with brave Malay chiefs. It ended generally by Almayer rising slowly, his long pipe in hand, his face set into a look of inward pain, and walking away in silence. He descended the steps and plunged into the long grass on his way to the solitude of his new house, dragging his feet in a state of physical collapse from disgust and fear before that fury. She followed to the head of the steps, and sent the shafts of indiscriminate abuse after the retreating form. And each of those scenes was concluded by a piercing shriek, reaching him far away. "You know, Kaspar, I am your wife! your own Christian wife after your own Blanda law!" For she knew that this was the bitterest thing of all; the greatest regret of that man's life.

All these scenes Nina witnessed unmoved. She

might have been deaf, dumb, without any feeling as far as any expression of opinion went. Yet oft when her father had sought the refuge of the great dusty rooms of "Almayer's Folly," and her mother, exhausted by rhetorical efforts, squatted wearily on her heels with her back against the leg of the table, Nina would approach her curiously, guarding her skirts from betel juice besprinkling the floor, and gaze down upon her as one might look into the quiescent crater of a volcano after a destructive eruption. Mrs. Almayer's thoughts after these scenes were usually turned into a channel of childhood reminiscences, and she gave them utterance in a kind of monotonous recitative—slightly disconnected, but generally describing the glories of the Sultan of Sulu, his great splendour, his power, his great prowess, the fear which benumbed the hearts of white men at the sight of his swift piratical praus. And these muttered statements of her grandfather's might were mixed up with bits of later recollections, where the great fight with the "White Devil's" brig and the convent life in Samarang occupied the principal place. At that point she usually dropped the thread of her narrative, and pulling out the little brass cross, always suspended round her neck, she contemplated it with superstitious awe. That superstitious feeling connected with some vague talismanic properties of the little bit of metal and the still more hazy but terrible notion of some bad Djinns* and horrible torments invented, as she thought, for her especial punishment by the good Mother Superior in case of the loss of the above charm, were Mrs. Almayer's only theological outfit* for the stormy road of life. Mrs. Almayer had at least something tangible to cling to, but Nina, brought up under the Protestant* wing of the proper Mrs. Vinck, had not even a little piece of brass to remind her of past teaching.

And listening to the recital of those savage glories, those barbarous fights and savage feasting, to the story of deeds valorous, albeit somewhat bloodthirsty, where men of her mother's race shone far above the Orang Blanda, she felt herself irresistibly fascinated, and saw with vague surprise the narrow mantle of civilized morality, in which good-meaning people had wrapped her young soul, fall away and leave her shivering and helpless as if on the edge of some deep and unknown abyss. Strangest of all, this abyss did not frighten her when she was under the influence of the witch-like being she called her mother. She seemed to have forgotten in civilized surroundings her life before the time when Lingard had, so to speak, kidnapped her from Brow.* Since then she had had Christian teaching, social education, and a good glimpse of civilized life. Unfortunately her teachers did not understand her nature, and the education ended in a scene of humiliation, in an outburst of contempt from white people for her mixed blood.* And now she had lived on the river for three years with a savage mother and a father walking about amongst pitfalls, with his head in the clouds, weak, irresolute, and unhappy. She had lived a life devoid of all the decencies of civilization, in miserable domestic conditions; she had breathed* the atmosphere of sordid plottings for gain, of the no less disgusting intrigues and crimes for lust or money; and those things, together with the domestic quarrels, were the only events of her three years' existence. She did not die from despair and disgust the first month, as she expected and almost hoped for. On the contrary, at the end of half a year it had seemed to her that she had known no other life. Her young mind having been unskilfully permitted to glance at better things, and then thrown back again into the hopeless quagmire of barbarism, full of strong and uncontrolled passions, had lost the power to discriminate. It seemed to Nina that there was no change and no difference Whether they traded in brick godowns or on the muddy river bank; whether they reached after much or little; whether they made love under the shadows of the great trees or in the shadow of the cathedral* on the Singapore promenade; whether they plotted for their own ends under the protection of laws and according to the rules of Christian conduct, or whether they sought the gratification of their desires with the savage cunning and the unrestrained fierceness of natures as innocent of culture as their own immense and gloomy forests, Nina saw only the same manifestations of love and hate and of sordid greed chasing the uncertain dollar* in all its multifarious and vanishing shapes. To her resolute nature, however, after all these years, the savage and uncompromising sincerity of purpose shown by her Malay kinsmen seemed at last preferable to the sleek hypocrisy, to the polite disguises, to the virtuous pretences of such white people as she had had the misfortune to come in contact with. After all it was her life; it was going to be her life, and so thinking she fell more and more under the influence of her mother. Seeking, in her ignorance, a better side to that life, she listened with avidity to the old woman's tales of the departed glories of the Rajahs, from whose race she had sprung, and she became gradually more indifferent, more contemptuous of the white side of her descent represented by a feeble and traditionless father.

Almayer's difficulties were by no means diminished by the girl's presence in Sambir. The stir caused by her arrival had died out, it is true, and Lakamba had not renewed his visits; but about a year after the departure of the man-of-war boats the nephew of Abdulla, Syed

Reshid,* returned from his pilgrimage to Mecca, rejoicing in a green jacket* and the proud title of Hadji.* There was a great letting off of rockets on board the steamer which brought him in, and a great beating of drums all night in Abdulla's compound, while the feast of welcome was prolonged far into the small hours of the morning. Reshid was the favourite nephew and heir of Abdulla, and that loving uncle, meeting Almayer one day by the riverside, stopped politely to exchange civilities and to ask solemnly for an interview. Almayer suspected some attempt at a swindle, or at any rate something unpleasant, but of course consented with a great show of rejoicing. Accordingly the next evening, after sunset, Abdulla came, accompanied by several other grey-beards and by his nephew. That young man—of a very rakish and dissipated appearance—affected the greatest indifference as to the whole of the proceedings. When the torch-bearers had grouped themselves below the steps, and the visitors had seated themselves on various lame chairs,* Reshid stood apart in the shadow, examining his aristocratically small hands with great attention. Almayer, surprised by the great solemnity of his visitors, perched himself on the corner of the table with a characteristic want of dignity quickly noted by the Arabs with grave disapproval. But Abdulla spoke now, looking straight past Almayer at the red curtain hanging in the doorway, where a slight tremor disclosed the presence of women on the other side. He began by neatly complimenting Almayer upon the long years they had dwelt together in cordial neighbourhood, and called upon Allah to give him many more years to gladden the eyes of his friends by his welcome presence. He made a polite allusion to the great consideration shown him (Almayer) by the Dutch "Commissie,"* and drew thence the flattering inference of Almayer's great importance amongst his own people. He—Abdulla—was also important amongst all the Arabs, and his nephew Reshid would be heir of that social position and of great riches. Now Reshid was a Hadji. He was possessor of several Malay women, went on Abdulla, but it was time he had a favourite wife, the first of the four allowed by the Prophet. And, speaking with well-bred politeness, he explained further to the dumbfounded Almayer that, if he would consent to the alliance of his offspring with that true believer and virtuous man Reshid, she would be mistress of all the splendours of Reshid's house, the first wife of the first Arab in the Islands, when he—Abdulla—had been called to the joys of Paradise by Allah the All-merciful. "You know, Tuan," he said, in conclusion, "the other women would be her slaves, and Reshid's house is great. From Bombay he has brought great divans, and costly carpets, and European furniture. There is also a great looking-glass in a frame shining like gold. What could a girl want more?" And while Almayer looked upon him in silent dismay Abdulla spoke in a more confidential tone, waving his attendants away, and finished his speech by pointing out the material advantages of such an alliance, and offering to settle upon Almayer three thousand dollars as a sign of his sincere friendship and the price of the girl.

Poor Almayer was nearly having a fit. Burning with the desire of taking Abdulla by the throat, he had but to think of his helpless position in the midst of lawless men to comprehend the necessity of diplomatic conciliation. He mastered his impulses, and spoke politely and coldly, saying the girl was young and was the apple of his eye. Tuan Reshid, a Faithful and a Hadji, would not want an infidel woman in his harem;

and, seeing Abdulla smile sceptically at that last objection, he remained silent, not trusting himself to speak more, not daring to refuse point-blank, nor yet to say anything compromising. Abdulla understood the meaning of that silence, and rose to take leave with a grave salaam.* He wished his friend Almayer "a thousand years," and moved down the steps, helped dutifully by Reshid. The torch-bearers shook their torches, scattering a shower of sparks into the river, and the cortège moved off, leaving Almayer agitated but greatly relieved by their departure. He dropped into a chair and watched the glimmer of the lights amongst the tree trunks till they disappeared and complete silence succeeded the tramp of feet and the murmur of voices. He did not move till the curtain rustled and Nina came out on the verandah and sat in the rocking-chair, where she used to spend many hours every day. She gave a slight rocking motion to her seat, leaning back with half-closed eyes, her long hair shading her face from the smoky light of the lamp on the table. Almayer looked at her furtively, but the face was as impassible as ever. She turned her head slightly towards her father, and, speaking, to his great surprise, in English, asked—

"Was that Abdulla here?"

"Yes," said Almayer—"just gone."

"And what did he want, father?"

"He wanted to buy you for Reshid," answered Almayer, brutally, his anger getting the better of him, and looking at the girl as if in expectation of some outbreak of feeling. But Nina remained apparently unmoved, gazing dreamily into the black night outside.

"Be careful, Nina," said Almayer, after a short silence and rising from his chair, "when you go paddling alone into the creeks in your canoe. That Reshid is a violent scoundrel, and there is no saying what he may do. Do you hear me?"

She was standing now, ready to go in, one hand grasping the curtain in the doorway. She turned round, throwing her heavy tresses back by a sudden gesture.

"Do you think he would dare?" she asked, quickly, and then turned again to go in, adding in a lower tone, "He would not dare. Arabs are all cowards."

Almayer looked after her, astonished. He did not seek the repose of his hammock. He walked the floor absently, sometimes stopping by the balustrade to think. The lamp went out. The first streak of dawn broke over the forest; Almayer shivered in the damp air. "I give it up," he muttered to himself, lying down wearily. "Damn those women! Well! If the girl did not look as if she wanted to be kidnapped!"

And he felt a nameless fear creep into his heart, making him shiver again.

CHAPTER FOUR

THAT year, towards the breaking up of the southwest monsoon,* disquieting rumours reached Sambir. Captain Ford, coming up to Almayer's house for an evening's chat, brought late numbers of the *Straits Times** giving the news of Acheen war* and of the unsuccessful Dutch expedition. The Nakhodas* of the rare trading praus ascending the river paid visits to Lakamba, discussing with that potentate the unsettled state of affairs, and wagged their heads gravely over the recital of Orang Blanda exaction, severity, and general tyranny, as exemplified in the total stoppage of gunpowder* trade and the rigorous visiting of all suspicious craft trading in the straits of Macassar. Even the loyal soul of Lakamba was stirred into a state of inward discontent by the withdrawal of his license for powder and by the abrupt confiscation of one hundred and fifty barrels of that commodity by the gunboat *Princess Amelia*,* when, after a hazardous voyage, it had almost reached the mouth of the river. The unpleasant news was given him by Reshid, who, after the unsuccessful issue of his matrimonial projects, had made a long voyage amongst the islands for trading purposes; had bought the powder for his friend, and was overhauled and deprived of it on his return when actually congratulating himself on his acuteness in avoiding detection. Reshid's wrath was principally directed against Almayer,* whom he suspected of having notified the Dutch authorities of the desultory warfare carried on by the Arabs and the Rajah with the up-river Dyak tribes.

To Reshid's great surprise the Rajah received his complaints very coldly, and showed no signs of vengeful disposition towards the white man. In truth, Lakamba knew very well that Almayer was perfectly innocent of any meddling in state affairs; and besides, his attitude towards that much persecuted individual was wholly changed in consequence of a reconciliation effected between him and his old enemy by Almayer's newly-found friend, Dain Maroola.

Almayer had now a friend. Shortly after Reshid's departure on his commercial journey, Nina, drifting slowly with the tide in the canoe on her return home after one of her solitary excursions, heard in one of the small creeks a splashing of* heavy ropes dropping in the water and the prolonged song of Malay seamen when some heavy pulling is to be done. Through the thick fringe of bushes hiding the mouth of the creek she saw the tall spars of some European-rigged sailing vessel overtopping the summits of the Nipa palms.* A brig was being hauled out of the small creek into the main stream. The sun had set, and during the short moments of twilight Nina saw the brig, aided by the evening breeze and the flowing tide, head towards Sambir under her set foresail. The girl turned her canoe out of the main river into one of the many narrow channels amongst the wooded islets, and paddled vigorously over the black and sleepy backwaters towards Sambir. Her canoe brushed the water-palms, skirted the short spaces of muddy bank where sedate alligators* looked at her with lazy unconcern, and, just as darkness was setting in, shot out into the broad junction of the two main branches of the river, where the brig was already at anchor with sails furled, yards squared,* and decks seemingly untenanted by any human being. Nina had to cross the river and pass pretty close to the brig in order to reach home on the low promontory between the two branches of the Pantai. Up both branches, in the houses built on the banks and over the water, the lights twinkled already, reflected in the still waters below. The hum of voices, the occasional cry of a child, the rapid and abruptly interrupted roll of a wooden drum, together with some distant hailing in the darkness by the returning fishermen, reached her over the broad expanse of the river. She hesitated a little before crossing, the sight of such an unusual object as an European-rigged vessel causing her some uneasiness, but the river in its wide expansion was dark enough to render a small canoe invisible. She urged her small craft with swift strokes of her paddle, kneeling in the bottom and bending forward to catch any suspicious sound while she steered towards the little jetty of Lingard and Co., to which the strong light of the paraffin lamp shining on the whitewashed verandah of Almayer's bungalow served as a convenient guide. The jetty itself, under the shadow of the bank overgrown by drooping bushes, was hidden in darkness. Before even she could see it she heard the hollow bumping of a large boat against its rotten posts, and heard also the murmur of whispered conversation in that boat whose white paint and great dimensions, faintly visible on nearer approach, made her rightly guess that it belonged to the brig just anchored. Stopping her course by a rapid motion of her paddle, with another swift stroke she sent it whirling away from the wharf and steered for a little rivulet which gave access to the back courtyard of the house.* She landed at the muddy head of the creek and made her way towards the house over the trodden grass of the courtyard. To the left, from the cooking shed, shone a red glare through the banana plantation she skirted, and the noise of feminine laughter reached her from there in the silent evening. She rightly judged her mother was not near, laughter and Mrs. Almayer not being close neighbours. She must be in the house, thought Nina, as she ran lightly up the inclined plane of shaky planks leading to the back door of the narrow passage dividing the house in two. Outside the doorway, in the black shadow, stood the faithful Ali.

"Who is there?" asked Nina.

"A great Malay man has come," answered Ali, in a tone of suppressed excitement. "He is a rich man. There are six men with lances. Real Soldat,* you understand. And his dress is very brave. I have seen his dress. It shines! What jewels! Don't go there, Mem Nina. Tuan said not; but the old Mem is gone. Tuan will be angry. Merciful Allah! what jewels that man has got!"

Nina slipped past the outstretched hand of the slave into the dark passage where, in the crimson glow of the hanging curtain, close by its other end, she could see a small dark form crouching near the wall. Her mother was feasting her eyes and ears with what was taking place on the front verandah, and Nina approached to take her share in the rare pleasure of some novelty. She was met by her mother's extended arm and by a low murmured warning not to make a noise.

"Have you seen them, mother?" asked Nina, in a breathless whisper.

Mrs. Almayer turned her face towards the girl, and her sunken eyes shone strangely in the red half-light of the passage.

"I saw him," she said, in an almost inaudible tone, pressing her daughter's hand with her bony fingers. "A great Rajah has come to Sambir—a Son of Heaven,"* muttered the old woman to herself. "Go away, girl!"

The two women stood close to the curtain, Nina wishing to approach the rent in the stuff, and her mother defending the position with angry obstinacy. On the other side there was a lull in the conversation, but the occasional* light tinkling of some ornaments, the clink of metal scabbards or of brass siri-vessels* passed from hand to hand, was audible during the short pause. The women struggled silently, when there was a shuffling noise and the shadow of Almayer's burly form fell on the curtain.

The women ceased struggling and remained motionless. Almayer had stood up to answer his guest, turning his back to the doorway, unaware of what was going on on the other side. He spoke in a tone of regretful irritation.

"You have come to the wrong house, Tuan Maroola, if you want to trade as you say. I was a trader once, not now, whatever you may have heard about me in Macassar. And if you want anything, you will not find it here; I have nothing to give, and want nothing myself. You should go to the Rajah here; you can see in the daytime his houses across the river, there, where those fires are burning on the shore. He will help you and trade with you. Or, better still, go to the Arabs over there," he went on bitterly, pointing with his hand towards the houses of Sambir. "Abdulla is the man you want. There is nothing he would not buy, and there is nothing he would not sell; believe me, I know him well."

He waited for an answer a short time, then added—

"All that I have said is true, and there is nothing more."

Nina, held back by her mother, heard a soft voice reply with a calm evenness of intonation peculiar to the better class Malays—

"Who would doubt a white Tuan's words? A man seeks his friends where his heart tells him. Is this not true also? I have come, although so late, for I have something to say which you may be glad to hear. To-morrow I shall go to the Sultan; a trader wants the friendship of great men. Then I shall return here to speak serious words, if Tuan permits. I shall not go to the Arabs; their lies are very great! What are they? Chelakka!"*

Almayer's voice sounded a little more pleasantly in reply.

"Well, as you like. I can hear you to-morrow at any time if you have anything to say. Bah! After you have seen the Sultan Lakamba you will not want to return here, Inchi* Dain. You will see. Only mind, I will have nothing to do with Lakamba. You may tell him so. What is your business with me, after all?"

"To-morrow we talk, Tuan, now I know you," answered the Malay. "I speak English a little, so we can talk and nobody will understand, and then——"

He interrupted himself suddenly, asking surprised, "What's that noise, Tuan?"

Almayer had also heard the increasing noise of the scuffle recommenced on the women's side of the curtain. Evidently Nina's strong curiosity was on the point of overcoming Mrs. Almayer's exalted sense of social proprieties. Hard breathing was distinctly audible, and the curtain shook during the contest, which was mainly physical, although Mrs. Almayer's voice was heard in angry remonstrance with its usual want of strictly logical reasoning, but with the well-known richness of invective.

"You shameless woman! Are you a slave?" shouted shrilly the irate matron. "Veil your face,* abandoned wretch! You white snake, I will not let you!"

Almayer's face expressed annoyance and also doubt as to the advisability of interfering between mother and daughter. He glanced at his Malay visitor, who was waiting silently for the end of the uproar in an attitude of amused expectation, and waving his hand contemptuously he murmured—

"It is nothing. Some women."

The Malay nodded his head gravely, and his face assumed an expression of serene indifference, as etiquette demanded after such an explanation. The contest was ended behind the curtain, and evidently the younger will had its way, for the rapid shuffle and click of Mrs. Almayer's high-heeled sandals died away in the distance. The tranquillized master of the house was going to resume the conversation when, struck by an unexpected change in the expression of his guest's countenance, he turned his head and saw Nina standing in the doorway.

After Mrs. Almayer's retreat from the field of battle, Nina, with a contemptuous exclamation, "It's only a trader," had lifted the conquered curtain and now stood in full light, framed in the dark background of the passage, her lips slightly parted, her hair in disorder* after the exertion, the angry gleam not yet faded out of her glorious and sparkling eyes. She took in at a glance the group of white-clad lancemen standing motionless in the shadow of the far-off end of the verandah, and her gaze rested curiously on the chief of that imposing cortège. He stood, almost facing her, a little on one side, and struck by the beauty of the unexpected apparition had bent low, elevating his joint hands above his head in a sign of respect accorded by Malays only to the great of this earth. The crude light of the lamp shone on the gold embroidery of his black silk jacket, broke in a thousand sparkling rays on the jewelled hilt of his kriss* protruding from under the many folds of the red sarong gathered into a sash round his waist, and played on the precious stones of the many rings on his dark fingers. He straightened himself up quickly after the low bow, putting his hand with a graceful ease on the hilt of his heavy short sword ornamented with brilliantly dyed fringes of horsehair.* Nina, hesitating on the threshold, saw an erect lithe figure of medium height with a breadth of shoulder suggesting great power. Under the folds of a blue turban, whose fringed ends hung gracefully over the left shoulder, was a face full of determination and expressing a reckless good-humour, not devoid, however, of some dignity. The squareness of lower jaw, the full red lips, the mobile nostrils, and the proud carriage of the head gave the impression of a being half-savage, untamed, perhaps cruel, and corrected the liquid softness of the almost feminine eye, that general characteristic of the race. Now, the first surprise over, Nina saw those eyes fixed upon her with such an uncontrolled expression of admiration and desire that she felt a hitherto unknown feeling of shyness, mixed with alarm and some delight, enter and penetrate her whole being. Confused by those unusual sensations she stopped in the doorway and instinctively drew the lower part of the curtain across her face, leaving only half a rounded cheek, a stray tress, and one eye exposed, wherewith to contemplate the gorgeous and bold being so unlike in appearance to the rare specimens of traders she had seen before on that same verandah.

Dain Maroola, dazzled by the unexpected vision, forgot the confused Almayer, forgot his brig, his escort staring in open-mouthed admiration, the object of his visit and all things else, in his overpowering desire to prolong the contemplation of so much loveliness met so suddenly in such an unlikely place—as he thought.*

"It is my daughter," said Almayer, in an embarrassed manner. "It is of no consequence. White women have their customs, as you know, Tuan, having travelled much, as you say. However, it is late; we will finish our talk to-morrow."

Dain bent low trying to convey in a last glance towards the girl the bold expression of his overwhelming admiration. The next minute he was shaking Almayer's hand with grave courtesy, his face wearing a look of stolid unconcern as to any feminine presence. His men filed off, and he followed them quickly, closely attended by a thick-set, savage-looking Sumatrese* he had introduced before as the commander of his brig. Nina walked to the balustrade of the verandah and saw the sheen of moonlight on the steel spear-heads and heard the rhythmic jingle of brass anklets as the men moved in single file towards the jetty. The boat shoved off after a little while, looming large in the full light of the moon, a black shapeless mass in the slight haze hanging over the water. Nina fancied she could distinguish the graceful figure of the trader standing erect in the stern sheets,* but in a little while all the outlines got blurred, confused, and soon disappeared in the folds of white vapour shrouding the middle of the river.

Almayer had approached his daughter, and leaning with both arms over the rail, was looking moodily down on the heap of rubbish* at the foot of the verandah.

"What was all that noise just now?" he growled peevishly, without looking up. "Confound you and your mother! What did she want? What did you come out for?"

"She did not want to let me come out," said Nina. "She is angry. She says the man just gone is some Rajah. I think she is right now."

"I believe all you women are crazy," snarled Almayer. "What's that to you, to her, to anybody? The man wants to collect trepang* and birds' nests on the islands. He told me so, that Rajah of yours. He will come to-morrow. I want you both to keep away from the house, and let me attend to my business in peace."

Dain Maroola came the next day and had a long conversation with Almayer. This was the beginning of a close and friendly intercourse which, at first, was much remarked in Sambir, till the population got used to the frequent sight of many fires burning in Almayer's campong, where Maroola's men were warming themselves during the cold nights of the northeast monsoon, while their master had long conferences with the Tuan Putih—as they styled Almayer amongst themselves. Great was the curiosity in Sambir on the subject of the new trader. Had he seen the Sultan? What did the Sultan say? Had he given any presents? What would he sell? What would he buy? Those were the questions broached eagerly by the inhabitants of bamboo houses built over the river. Even in more substantial buildings, in Abdulla's house, in the residences of principal traders, Arab, Chinese, and Bugis,* the excitement ran high, and lasted many days. With inborn suspicion they would not believe the simple account of himself the young trader was always ready to give. Yet it had all the appearance of truth. He said he was a trader, and sold rice. He did not want to buy gutta-percha or beeswax, because he intended to employ his numerous crew in collecting trepang on the coral reefs outside the river, and also in seeking for birds' nests on the mainland.* Those two articles he professed himself ready to buy if there were any to be obtained in that way. He said he was from Bali, and a Brahmin,* which last statement he made good by refusing all food* during his often repeated visits to Lakamba's and Almayer's houses. To Lakamba he went generally at night and had long audiences. Babalatchi, who was always a third party at those meetings of potentate and trader, knew how to resist all attempts on the part of the curious to ascertain the subject of so many long talks. When questioned with languid courtesy by the grave Abdulla he sought refuge in a vacant stare of his one eye, and in the affectation of extreme simplicity.

"I am only my master's slave," murmured Babalatchi, in a hesitating manner. Then as if making up his mind suddenly for a reckless confidence he would inform Abdulla of some transaction in rice, repeating the words, "A hundred big bags the Sultan bought; a hundred, Tuan!" in a tone of mysterious solemnity. Abdulla, firmly persuaded of the existence of some more important dealings, received, however, the information with all the signs of respectful astonishment. And the two would separate, the Arab cursing inwardly the wily dog, while Babalatchi went on his way walking on the dusty path, his body swaying, his chin with its few grey hairs pushed forward, resembling an inquisitive goat bent on some unlawful expedition. Attentive eyes watched his movements. Jim-Eng, descrying Babalatchi far away, would shake off the stupor of an habitual opium smoker and, tottering on to the middle of the road, would await the approach of that important person, ready with hospitable invitation. But Babalatchi's discretion was proof even against the combined assaults of good fellowship and of strong gin generously administered by the openhearted Chinaman. Jim-Eng, owning himself beaten, was left uninformed with the empty bottle, and gazed sadly after the departing form of the statesman of

Sambir pursuing his devious and unsteady way, which, as usual, led him to Almayer's compound. Ever since a reconciliation had been effected by Dain Maroola between his white friend and the Rajah, the one-eyed diplomatist had again become a frequent guest in the Dutchman's house. To Almayer's great disgust he was to be seen there at all times, strolling about in an abstracted kind of way on the verandah, skulking in the passages, or else popping round unexpected corners, always willing to engage Mrs. Almayer in confidential conversation. He was very shy of the master himself, as if suspicious that the pent-up feelings of the white man towards his person might find vent in a sudden kick. But the cooking shed was his favourite place, and he became an habitual guest there, squatting for hours amongst the busy women, with his chin resting on his knees, his lean arms clasped round his legs, and his one eye roving uneasily—the very picture of watchful ugliness. Almayer wanted more than once to complain to Lakamba of his Prime Minister's intrusion, but Dain dissuaded him. "We cannot say a word here that he does not hear," growled Almayer.

"Then come and talk on board the brig," retorted Dain, with a quiet smile. "It is good to let the man come here. Lakamba thinks he knows much. Perhaps the Sultan thinks I want to run away. Better let the one-eyed crocodile sun himself in your campong, Tuan."

And Almayer assented unwillingly muttering vague threats of personal violence, while he eyed malevolently the aged statesman sitting with quiet obstinacy by his domestic rice-pot.

CHAPTER FIVE

At last the excitement had died out in Sambir. The inhabitants got used to the sight of comings and goings between Almayer's house and the vessel, now moored to the opposite bank, and speculation as to the feverish activity displayed by Almayer's boatmen in repairing old canoes ceased to interfere with the due discharge of domestic duties by the women of the Settlement. Even the baffled Jim-Eng left off troubling his muddled brain with secrets of trade, and relapsed by the aid of his opium pipe into a state of stupefied bliss, letting Babalatchi pursue his way past his house uninvited and seemingly unnoticed.

So on that warm afternoon, when the deserted river sparkled under the vertical sun,* the statesman of Sambir could, without any hindrance from friendly inquirers, shove off his little canoe from under the bushes, where it was usually hidden during his visits to Almayer's compound. Slowly and languidly Babalatchi paddled, crouching low in the boat, making himself small under his enormous sun hat to escape the scorching heat reflected from the water. He was not in a hurry; his master, Lakamba, was surely reposing at this time of the day. He would have ample time to cross over and greet him on his waking with important news. Will he be displeased? Will he strike his ebony wood staff angrily on the floor, frightening him by the incoherent violence of his exclamations; or will he squat down with a good-humoured smile, and, rubbing his hands gently over his stomach with a familiar gesture, expectorate copiously into the brass síri-vessel, giving vent to a low, approbative murmur? Such were Babalatchi's thoughts as he skilfully handled his paddle, crossing the river on his way to the Rajah's campong, whose stockades showed from behind the dense foliage of the bank just opposite to Almayer's bungalow.

Indeed, he had a report to make. Something certain at last to confirm the daily tale of suspicions, the daily hints of familiarity, of stolen glances he had seen, of short and burning words he had overheard exchanged between Dain Maroola and Almayer's daughter. Lakamba had, till then, listened to it all, calmly and with evident distrust; now he was going to be convinced, for Babalatchi had the proof; had it this very morning, when fishing at break of day in the creek over which stood Bulangi's house. There from his skiff he saw Nina's long canoe drift past, the girl sitting in the stern bending over Dain, who was stretched in the bottom with his head resting on the girl's knees. He saw it. He followed them, but in a short time they took to the paddles and got away from under his observant eye. A few minutes afterwards he saw Bulangi's slave-girl paddling in a small dug-out to the town with her cakes for sale. She also had seen them in the grey dawn. And Babalatchi grinned confidentially to himself at the recollection of the slave-girl's discomposed face, of the hard look in her eyes, of the tremble in her voice, when answering his questions. That little Taminah evidently admired Dain Maroola. That was good! And Babalatchi laughed aloud at the notion; then becoming suddenly serious, he began by some strange association of ideas to speculate upon the price for which Bulangi would, possibly, sell the girl. He shook his head sadly at the thought that Bulangi was a hard man, and had refused one hundred dollars for that same Taminah only a few weeks ago; then he became suddenly aware that the canoe had drifted too far down during his meditation. He shook off the despondency caused by the certitude of Bulangi's mercenary disposition, and, taking up his paddle, in a few strokes sheered alongside the water-gate of the Rajah's house.

That afternoon Almayer, as was his wont lately, moved about on the water-side, overlooking the repairs to his boats. He had decided at last. Guided by the scraps of information contained in old Lingard's pocket-book, he was going to seek for the rich gold-mine, for that place where he had only to stoop to gather up an immense fortune and realize the dream of his young days. To obtain the necessary help he had shared his knowledge with Dain Maroola, he had consented to be reconciled with Lakamba, who gave his support to the enterprise on condition of sharing the profits; he had sacrificed his pride, his honour, and his loyalty* in the face of the enormous risk of his undertaking, dazzled by the greatness of the results to be achieved by this alliance so distasteful yet so necessary. The dangers were great, but Maroola was brave; his men seemed as reckless as their chief, and with Lakamba's aid success seemed assured.

For the last fortnight Almayer was absorbed in the preparations, walking amongst his workmen and slaves in a kind of waking trance, where practical details as to the fitting out of the boats were mixed up with vivid dreams of untold wealth, where the present misery of burning sun, of the muddy and malodorous river bank disappeared in a gorgeous vision of a splendid future existence for himself and Nina. He hardly saw Nina during these last days, although the beloved daughter was ever present in his thoughts. He hardly took notice of Dain, whose constant presence in his house had become a matter of course to him now they were connected by a community of interests. When meeting the young chief he gave him an absent greeting and passed on, seemingly wishing to avoid him, bent upon forgetting the hated reality of the present by absorbing himself in his work, or else by letting his imagination soar far above the tree-tops into the great white clouds away to the westward, where the paradise of Europe was awaiting the future Eastern millionaire. And Maroola, now the bargain was struck and there was no more business to be talked over, evidently did not care for the white man's company. Yet Dain was always about the house, but he seldom stayed long by the riverside. On his daily visits to the white man the Malay chief preferred to make his way quietly through the central passage of the house, and would come out into the garden at the back, where the fire was burning in the cooking shed, with the rice kettle swinging over it, under the watchful supervision of Mrs. Almayer. Avoiding that shed, with its black smoke and the warbling of soft, feminine voices, Dain would turn to the left. There, on the edge of a banana plantation, a clump of palms and mango trees* formed a shady spot, a few scattered bushes giving it a certain seclusion into which only the serving women's chatter or an occasional burst of laughter could penetrate. Once in, he was invisible; and hidden there, leaning against the smooth trunk of a tall palm, he waited with gleaming eyes and an assured smile to hear the faint rustle of dried grass under the light footsteps of Nina.

From the very first moment when his eyes beheld this—to him—perfection of loveliness he felt in his inmost heart the conviction that she would be his; he felt the subtle breath of mutual understanding passing between their two savage natures, and he did not want

Mrs. Almayer's encouraging smiles to take every opportunity of approaching the girl; and every time he spoke to her, every time he looked into her eyes, Nina, although averting her face, felt as if this bold-looking being who spoke burning words into her willing ear was the embodiment of her fate, the creature of her dreams—reckless, ferocious, ready with flashing kriss for his enemies, and with passionate embrace for his beloved—the ideal Malay chief of her mother's tradition.

She recognized with a thrill of delicious fear the mysterious consciousness of her identity with that being. Listening to his words, it seemed to her she was born only then to a knowledge of a new existence, that her life was complete only when near him, and she abandoned herself to a feeling of dreamy happiness, while with half-veiled face and in silence—as became a Malay girl—she listened to Dain's words giving up to her the whole treasure of love and passion his nature was capable of with all the unrestrained enthusiasm of a man totally untrammelled by any influence of civilized self-discipline.

And they used to pass many a delicious and fast fleeting hour under the mango trees behind the friendly curtain of bushes till Mrs. Almayer's shrill voice gave the signal of unwilling separation. Mrs. Almayer had undertaken the easy task of watching her husband lest he should interrupt the smooth course of her daughter's love affair, in which she took a great and benignant interest. She was happy and proud to see Dain's infatuation, believing him to be a great and powerful chief, and she found also a gratification of her mercenary instincts in Dain's open-handed generosity.

On the eve of the day when Babalatchi's suspicions were confirmed by ocular demonstration, Dain and Nina had remained longer than usual in their shady retreat. Only Almayer's heavy step on the verandah and his querulous clamour for food decided Mrs. Almayer to lift a warning cry. Maroola leaped lightly over the low bamboo fence, and made his way* through the banana plantation down to the muddy shore of the back creek, while Nina walked slowly towards the house to minister to her father's wants, as was her wont every evening. Almayer felt happy enough that evening; the preparations were nearly completed; to-morrow he would launch his boats. In his mind's eye he saw the rich prize in his grasp; and, with tin spoon in his hand, he was forgetting the plateful of rice before him in the fanciful arrangement of some splendid banquet to take place on his arrival in Amsterdam. Nina, reclining in the long chair,* listened absently to the few disconnected words escaping from her father's lips. Expedition! Gold! What did she care for all that? But at the name of Maroola mentioned by her father she was all attention. Dain was going down the river with his brig to-morrow to remain away for a few days, said Almayer. It was very annoying, this delay. As soon as Dain returned they would have to start without loss of time, for the river was rising. He would not be surprised if a great flood was coming. And he pushed away his plate with an impatient gesture on rising from the table. But now Nina heard him not. Dain going away! That's why he had ordered her, with that quiet masterfulness it was her delight to obey, to meet him at break of day in Bulangi's creek. Was there a paddle in her canoe? she thought. Was it ready? She would have to start early—at four in the morning, in a very few hours.

She rose from her chair, thinking she would require rest before the long pull in the early morning. The lamp was burning dimly, and her father, tired with the day's labour, was already in his hammock. Nina put the lamp out and passed into a large room she shared with her mother on the left of the central passage. Entering, she saw that Mrs. Almayer had deserted the pile of mats serving her as bed in one corner of the room, and was now bending over the opened lid of her large wooden chest. Half a shell of cocoanut filled with oil, where a cotton rag floated for a wick, stood on the floor, surrounding her with a ruddy halo of light shining through the black and odorous smoke. Mrs. Almayer's back was bent, and her head and shoulders hidden in the deep box. Her hands rummaged in the interior, where a soft clink as of silver money could be heard. She did not notice at first her daughter's approach, and Nina, standing silently by her, looked down on many little canvas bags ranged in the bottom of the chest, wherefrom her mother extracted handfuls of shining guilders* and Mexican dollars,* letting them stream slowly back again through her claw-like fingers. The music of tinkling silver seemed to delight her, and her eyes sparkled with the reflected gleam of freshly-minted coins. She was muttering to herself: "And this, and this, and yet this! Soon he will give more*—as much more as I ask. He is a great Rajah—a Son of Heaven! And she will be a Ranee—* he gave all this for her! Who ever gave anything for me? I am a slave! Am I? I am the mother of a great Ranee!" She became aware suddenly of her daughter's presence, and ceased her droning, shutting the lid down violently; then, without rising from her crouching position, she looked up at the girl standing by with a vague smile on her dreamy face.

"You have seen. Have you?" she shouted, shrilly. "That is all mine, and for you. It is not enough! He will have to give more before he takes you away to the southern island where his father is king. You hear me? You are worth more, granddaughter of Rajahs! More! More!"

The sleepy voice of Almayer was heard on the verandah recommending silence. Mrs. Almayer extinguished the light and crept into her corner of the room. Nina lay down on her back on a pile of soft mats, her hands entwined under her head, gazing through the shutterless hole, serving as a window at the stars twinkling on the black sky; she was awaiting the time of start* for her appointed meeting-place. With quiet happiness she thought of that meeting in the great forest, far from all human eyes and sounds. Her soul, lapsing again into the savage mood, which the genius of civilization working by the hand of Mrs. Vinck could never destroy, experienced a feeling of pride and of some slight trouble at the high value her worldly-wise mother had put upon her person; but she remembered the expressive glances and words of Dain, and, tranquillized, she closed her eyes in a shiver of pleasant anticipation.

There are some situations where the barbarian and the so-called civilized man meet upon the same ground. It may be supposed that Dain Maroola was not exceptionally delighted with his prospective mother-in-law, nor that he actually approved of that worthy woman's appetite for shining dollars. Yet on that foggy morning when Babalatchi, laying aside the cares of state, went to visit his fish-baskets in the Bulangi creek, Maroola had no misgivings, experienced no feelings but those of impatience and longing, when paddling to the east side of the island forming the backwater in question. He hid his canoe in the bushes and strode rapidly across the islet, pushing with impatience through the twigs of heavy undergrowth intercrossed over his path. From motives of prudence he would not take his canoe to the meeting-place, as Nina had done. He had left it in the main stream till his return from the other side of the island. The heavy warm fog was closing rapidly round him, but he managed to catch a fleeting glimpse of a light away to the left, proceeding from Bulangi's house. Then he could see nothing in the thickening vapour, and kept to the path only by a sort of instinct, which also led him to the very point on the opposite shore he wished to reach. A great log had stranded there, at right angles to the bank, forming a kind of jetty against which the swiftly flowing stream broke with a loud ripple. He stepped on it with a quick but steady motion, and in two strides found himself at the outer end, with the rush and swirl of the foaming water at his feet.

Standing there alone, as if separated from the world; the heavens, earth; the very water roaring under him swallowed up in the thick veil of the morning fog, he breathed out the name of Nina before him into the apparently limitless space, sure of being heard, instinctively sure of the nearness of the delightful creature; certain of her being aware of his near presence as he was aware of hers.

The bow of Nina's canoe loomed up close to the log, canted high out of the water by the weight of the sitter in the stern. Maroola laid his hand on the stem and leaped lightly in, giving it a vigorous shove off. The light craft, obeying the new impulse, cleared the log by a hair's breadth, and the river, with obedient complicity, swung it broadside to the current, and bore it off silently and rapidly between the invisible banks. And once more Dain, at the feet of Nina, forgot the world, felt himself carried away helpless by a great wave of supreme emotion, by a rush of joy, pride, and desire; understood once more with overpowering certitude that there was no life possible without that being he held clasped in his arms with passionate strength in a prolonged embrace.

Nina disengaged herself gently with a low laugh.

"You will overturn the boat, Dain," she whispered.

He looked into her eyes eagerly for a minute and let her go with a sigh, then lying down in the canoe he put his head on her knees, gazing upwards and stretching his arms backwards till his hands met round the girl's waist. She bent over him, and, shaking her head, framed both their faces in the falling locks of her long black hair.

And so they drifted on, he speaking with all the rude eloquence of a savage nature giving itself up without restraint to an overmastering passion, she bending low to catch the murmur of words sweeter to her than life itself. To those two nothing existed then outside the gunwales* of the narrow and fragile craft. It was their world, filled with their intense and all-absorbing love. They took no heed of thickening mist, or of the breeze dying away before sunrise; they forgot the existence of the great forests surrounding them, of all the tropical nature awaiting the advent of the sun in a solemn and impressive silence.

Over the low river-mist hiding the boat with its freight of young passionate life and all-forgetful happiness, the stars paled, and a silvery-grey tint crept over the sky from the eastward. There was not a breath of wind, not a rustle of stirring leaf, not a splash of leaping fish to disturb the serene repose of all living things on the banks of the great river. Earth, river, and sky were wrapped up in a deep sleep from which it seemed there would be no waking. All the seething life and movement of tropical nature seemed concentrated in the ardent eyes, in the tumultuously beating hearts of the two beings drifting in the canoe, under the white canopy of mist, over the smooth surface of the river.

Suddenly a great sheaf of yellow rays shot upwards from behind the black curtain of trees lining the banks of the Pantai. The stars went out; the little black clouds at the zenith glowed for a moment with crimson tints, and the thick mist, stirred by the gentle breeze, the sigh of waking nature, whirled round and broke into fantastically torn pieces, disclosing the wrinkled surface of the river sparkling in the broad light of day. Great flocks of white birds* wheeled screaming above the swaying tree-tops. The sun had risen on the east coast.

Dain was the first to return to the cares of everyday life. He rose and glanced rapidly up and down the river. His eye detected Babalatchi's boat astern, and another small black speck on the glittering water, which was Taminah's canoe. He moved cautiously forward, and, kneeling, took up a paddle; Nina at the stern took hers. They bent their bodies to the work, throwing up the water at every stroke, and the small craft went swiftly ahead, leaving a narrow wake fringed with a lacelike border of white and gleaming foam. Without turning his head, Dain spoke.

"Somebody behind us, Nina. We must not let him gain. I think he is too far to recognize us."

"Somebody before us also," panted out Nina, without ceasing to paddle.

"I think I know," rejoined Dain. "The sun shines over there, but I fancy it is the girl Taminah. She comes down every morning to my brig to sell cakes—stays often all day. It does not matter; steer more into the bank; we must get under the bushes. My canoe is hidden not far from here."

As he spoke his eyes watched the broad-leaved nipas

which they were brushing in their swift and silent course.

"Look out, Nina," he said at last; "there, where the water palms end and the twigs hang down under the leaning tree. Steer for the big green branch."

He stood up attentive, and the boat drifted slowly in shore, Nina guiding it by a gentle and skilful movement of her paddle. When near enough Dain laid hold of the big branch, and leaning back shot the canoe under a low green archway of thickly matted creepers giving access to a miniature bay formed by the caving in of the bank during the last great flood. His own boat was there anchored by a stone, and he stepped into it, keeping his hand on the gunwale of Nina's canoe. In a moment the two little nutshells with their occupants floated quietly side by side, reflected by the black water in the dim light struggling through a high canopy of dense foliage;* while above, away up in the broad day, flamed immense red blossoms* sending down on their heads a shower of great dew-sparkling petals that descended rotating slowly in a continuous and perfumed stream; and over them, under them, in the sleeping water,* all around them in a ring of luxuriant vegetation bathed in the warm air charged with strong and harsh perfumes, the intense work of tropical nature went on: plants shooting upward, entwined, interlaced in inextricable confusion, climbing madly and brutally over each other in the terrible silence of a desperate struggle towards the life-giving sunshine above—as if struck with sudden horror at the seething mass of corruption below, at the death and decay from which they sprang.

"We must part now," said Dain, after a long silence. "You must return at once, Nina. I will wait till the brig drifts down here, and shall get on board then."

"And will you be long away, Dain?" asked Nina, in a low voice.

"Long!" exclaimed Dain. "Would a man willingly remain long in a dark place? When I am not near you, Nina, I am like a man that is blind. What is life to me without light?"

Nina leaned over, and with a proud and happy smile took Dain's face between her hands, looking into his eyes with a fond yet questioning gaze. Apparently she found there the confirmation of the words just said, for a feeling of grateful security lightened for her the weight of sorrow at the hour of parting. She believed that he, the descendant of many great Rajahs, the son of a great chief, the master of life and death, knew the sunshine of life only in her presence. An immense wave of gratitude and love welled forth out of her heart towards him. How could she make an outward and visible sign of all she felt for the man who had filled her heart with so much joy and so much pride? And in the great tumult of passion, like a flash of lightning came to her the reminiscence of that despised and almost forgotten civilization she had only glanced at in her days of restraint, of sorrow, and of anger. In the cold ashes of that hateful and miserable past she would find the sign of love, the fitting expression of the boundless felicity of the present, the pledge of a bright and splendid future. She threw her arms around Dain's neck and pressed her lips to his in a long and burning kiss.* He closed his eyes, surprised and frightened at the storm raised in his breast by the strange and to him hitherto unknown contact, and long after Nina had pushed her canoe into the river he remained motionless, without daring to open his eyes, afraid to lose the sensation of intoxicating delight he had tasted for the first time.

Now he wanted but immortality, he thought, to be the

equal of gods, and the creature that could open so the gates of paradise must be his—soon would be his for ever!

He opened his eyes in time to see through the archway of creepers the bows of his brig come slowly into view, as the vessel drifted past on its way down the river. He must go on board now, he thought; yet he was loth to leave the place where he had learned to know what happiness meant. "Time yet. Let them go," he muttered to himself; and he closed his eyes again under the red shower of scented petals, trying to recall the scene with all its delight and all its fear.

He must have been able to join his brig in time, after all, and found much occupation outside, for it was in vain that Almayer looked for his friend's speedy return. The lower reach of the river where he so often and so impatiently directed his eyes remained deserted, save for the rapid flitting of some fishing canoe; but down the upper reaches came black clouds and heavy showers heralding the final setting in of the rainy season with its thunderstorms and great floods making the river almost impossible of ascent for native canoes.

Almayer, strolling along the muddy beach between his houses, watched uneasily the river rising inch by inch, creeping slowly nearer to the boats, now ready and hauled up in a row under the cover of dripping Kajang-mats.* Fortune seemed to elude his grasp, and in his weary tramp backwards and forwards under the steady rain falling from the lowering sky, a sort of despairing indifference took possession of him. What did it matter? It was just his luck! Those two infernal savages, Lakamba and Dain, induced him, with their promises of help, to spend his last dollar in the fitting out of boats, and now one of them was gone somewhere, and the other shut up in his stockade would give no sign of life. No, not even the scoundrelly

Babalatchi, thought Almayer, would show his face near him, now they had sold him all the rice, brass gongs, and cloth necessary for his expedition. They had his very last coin, and did not care whether he went or stayed. And with a gesture of abandoned* discouragement Almayer would climb up slowly to the verandah of his new house to get out of the rain, and leaning on the front rail with his head sunk between his shoulders he would abandon himself to the current of bitter thoughts, oblivious of the flight of time and the pangs of hunger, deaf to the shrill cries of his wife calling him to the evening meal. When, roused from his sad meditations by the first roll of the evening thunderstorm, he stumbled slowly towards the glimmering light of his old house, his half-dead hope made his ears preternaturally acute to any sound on the river. Several nights in succession he had heard the splash of paddles and had seen the indistinct form of a boat, but when hailing the shadowy apparition, his heart bounding with sudden hope of hearing Dain's voice, he was disappointed each time by the sulky answer conveying to him the intelligence that the Arabs were on the river, bound on a visit to the home-staying Lakamba. This caused him many sleepless nights, spent in speculating upon the kind of villainy those estimable personages were hatching now. At last, when all hope seemed dead, he was overjoyed on hearing Dain's voice; but Dain also appeared very anxious to see Lakamba, and Almayer felt uneasy owing to a deep and ineradicable distrust as to that ruler's disposition towards himself. Still, Dain had returned at last. Evidently he meant to keep to his bargain. Hope revived, and that night Almayer slept soundly, while Nina watched the angry river under the lash of the thunderstorm sweeping onward towards the sea.

CHAPTER SIX

DAIN was not long in crossing the river after leaving Almayer. He landed at the water-gate of the stockade enclosing the group of houses which composed the residence of the Rajah of Sambir. Evidently somebody was expected there, for the gate was open, and men with torches were ready to precede the visitor up the inclined plane of planks leading to the largest house where Lakamba actually resided, and where all the business of state was invariably transacted. The other buildings within the enclosure served only to accommodate the numerous household and the wives of the ruler.

Lakamba's own house was a strong structure of solid planks, raised on high piles, with a verandah of split bamboos surrounding it on all sides; the whole was covered in by an immensely high-pitched roof of palm-leaves, resting on beams blackened by the smoke of many torches.

The building stood parallel to the river, one of its long sides facing the water-gate of the stockade. There was a door in the short side looking up the river, and the inclined plank-way led straight from the gate to that door. By the uncertain light of smoky torches, Dain noticed the vague outlines of a group of armed men in the dark shadows to his right. From that group Babalatchi stepped forward to open the door, and Dain entered the audience chamber of the Rajah's residence. About one-third of the house was curtained off, by heavy stuff of European manufacture, for that purpose; close to the curtain there was a big arm-chair of some black wood, much carved, and before it a rough deal table. Otherwise the room was only furnished with mats in great profusion. To the left of the entrance stood a rude arm-rack, with three rifles with fixed bayonets in it. By the wall, in the shadow, the body-guard of Lakamba—all friends or relations—slept in a confused heap of brown arms, legs, and multi-coloured garments, from whence issued an occasional snore or a subdued groan of some uneasy sleeper. An European lamp with a green shade standing on the table made all this indistinctly visible to Dain.

"You are welcome to your rest here," said Babalatchi, looking at Dain interrogatively.

"I must speak to the Rajah at once," answered Dain.

Babalatchi made a gesture of assent, and, turning to the brass gong suspended under the arm-rack, struck two sharp blows.

The ear-splitting din woke up the guard. The snores ceased; outstretched legs were drawn in; the whole heap moved, and slowly resolved itself into individual forms with much yawning and rubbing of sleepy eyes; behind the curtains there was a burst of feminine chatter; then the bass voice of Lakamba was heard.

"Is that the Arab trader?"

"No, Tuan," answered Babalatchi; "Dain has returned at last. He is here for an important talk, bitcharra*—if you mercifully consent."

Evidently Lakamba's mercy went so far—for in a short while he came out from behind the curtain—but it did not go to the length of inducing him to make an extensive toilet. A short red sarong tightened hastily round his hips was his only garment. The merciful ruler of Sambir looked sleepy and rather sulky. He sat in the arm-chair, his knees well apart, his elbows on the arm-rests, his chin on his breast, breathing heavily and waiting malevolently for Dain to open the important talk.

But Dain did not seem anxious to begin. He directed his gaze towards Babalatchi, squatting comfortably at the feet of his master, and remained silent with a slightly bent head as if in attentive expectation of coming words of wisdom.

Babalatchi coughed discreetly, and, leaning forward, pushed over a few mats for Dain to sit upon, then lifting up his squeaky voice he assured him with eager volubility of everybody's delight at this long-looked-for return. His heart had hungered for the sight of Dain's face, and his ears were withering for the want of the refreshing sound of his voice. Everybody's hearts and ears were in the same sad predicament, according to Babalatchi, as he indicated with a sweeping gesture the other bank of the river where the settlement slumbered peacefully, unconscious of the great joy awaiting it on the morrow when Dain's presence amongst them would be disclosed. "For"—went on Babalatchi—"what is the joy of a poor man if not the open hand of a generous trader or of a great——"

Here he checked himself abruptly with a calculated embarrassment of manner, and his roving eye sought the floor, while an apologetic smile dwelt for a moment on his misshapen lips. Once or twice during this opening speech an amused expression flitted across Dain's face, soon to give way, however, to an appearance of grave concern. On Lakamba's brow a heavy frown had settled, and his lips moved angrily as he listened to his Prime Minister's oratory. In the silence that fell upon the room when Babalatchi ceased speaking arose a chorus of varied snores from the corner where the body-guard had resumed their interrupted slumbers, but the distant rumble of thunder filling then Nina's heart with apprehension for the safety of her lover passed unheeded by those three men intent each on their own purposes,* for life or death.

After a short silence, Babalatchi, discarding now the flowers of polite eloquence, spoke again, but in short and hurried sentences and in a low voice. They had been very uneasy. Why did Dain remain so long absent? The men dwelling on the lower reaches of the river heard the reports of big guns and saw a fire-ship* of the Dutch amongst the islands of the estuary. So they were anxious. Rumours of a disaster had reached Abdulla a few days ago, and since then they had been waiting for Dain's return under the apprehension of some misfortune. For days they had closed their eyes in fear, and woke up alarmed, and walked abroad trembling, like men before an enemy. And all on account of Dain. Would he not allay their fears for his safety, not for themselves? They were quiet and faithful, and devoted to the great Rajah in Batavia—may his fate lead him ever to victory for the joy and profit of his servants! "And here," went on Babalatchi, "Lakamba my master was getting thin in his anxiety for the trader he had taken under his protection; and so was Abdulla, for what would wicked men not say if perchance——"

"Be silent, fool!" growled Lakamba, angrily.

Babalatchi subsided into silence with a satisfied smile, while Dain, who had been watching him as if fascinated, turned with a sigh of relief towards the ruler of Sambir. Lakamba did not move, and, without raising his head, looked at Dain from under his eyebrows, breathing audibly, with pouted lips, in an air of general discontent.

"Speak! O Dain!" he said at last. "We have heard many rumours. Many nights in succession has my friend Reshid come here with bad tidings. News travels fast along the coast. But they may be untrue; there are more lies in men's mouths in these days than when I was young, but I am not easier to deceive now."

"All my words are true," said Dain, carelessly. "If you want to know what befell my brig, then learn that it is in the hands of the Dutch. Believe me, Rajah," he went on, with sudden energy, "the Orang Blanda have good friends in Sambir, or else how did they know I was coming thence?"

Lakamba gave Dain a short and hostile glance. Babalatchi rose quietly, and, going to the arm-rack, struck the gong violently.

Outside the door there was a shuffle of bare feet; inside, the guard woke up and sat staring in sleepy surprise.

"Yes, you faithful friend of the white Rajah," went on Dain, scornfully, turning to Babalatchi, who had returned to his place, "I have escaped, and I am here to gladden your heart. When I saw the Dutch ship I ran the brig inside the reefs and put her ashore. They did not dare to follow with the ship, so they sent the boats. We took to ours and tried to get away, but the ship dropped fireballs* at us, and killed many of my men. But I am left, O Babalatchi! The Dutch are coming here. They are seeking for me. They're coming to ask their faithful friend Lakamba and his slave Babalatchi. Rejoice!"

But neither of his hearers appeared to be in a joyful mood. Lakamba had put one leg over his knee. and went on gently scratching it with a meditative air, while Babalatchi, sitting cross-legged, seemed suddenly to become smaller and very limp, staring straight before him vacantly. The guard evinced some interest in the proceedings, stretching themselves full length on the mats to be nearer the speaker. One of them got up and now stood leaning against the arm-rack, playing absently with the fringes of his sword-hilt.

Dain waited till the crash of thunder had died away in distant mutterings before he spoke again.

"Are you dumb, O ruler of Sambir, or is the son of a great Rajah unworthy of your notice? I am come here to seek refuge and to warn you, and want to know what you intend doing."

"You came here because of the white man's daughter," retorted Lakamba, quickly. "Your refuge was with your father, the Rajah of Bali, the Son of Heaven, the 'Anak Agong'* himself. What am I to protect great princes? Only yesterday I planted rice in a burnt clearing; to-day you say I hold your life in my hand."

Babalatchi glanced at his master. "No man can escape his fate," he murmured piously. "When love enters a man's heart he is like a child—without any understanding. Be merciful, Lakamba," he added, twitching the corner of the Rajah's sarong warningly.

Lakamba snatched away the skirt of the sarong angrily. Under the dawning comprehension of intolerable embarrassments caused by Dain's return to Sambir he began to lose such composure as he had been, till then, able to maintain; and now he raised his voice loudly above the whistling of the wind and the patter of rain on the roof in the hard squall passing over the house.

"You came here first as a trader with sweet words and great promises, asking me to look the other way while you worked your will on the white man there. And I did. What do you want now? When I was young I fought. Now I am old, and want peace. It is easier for me to have you killed than to fight the Dutch. It is better for me."

The squall had now passed, and, in the short stillness of the lull in the storm, Lakamba repeated softly, as if to himself, "Much easier. Much better."

Dain did not seem greatly discomposed by the Rajah's threatening words. While Lakamba was speaking he had glanced once rapidly over his shoulder, just to make sure that there was nobody behind him, and, tranquillized in that respect, he had extracted a siri-box* out of the folds of his waist-cloth, and was wrapping carefully the little bit of betel-nut and a small pinch of lime in the green leaf tendered him politely by the watchful Babalatchi. He accepted this as a peace-offering from the silent statesman—a kind of mute protest against his master's undiplomatic violence, and as an omen of a possible understanding to be arrived at yet. Otherwise Dain was not uneasy. Although recognizing the justice of Lakamba's surmise that he had come back to Sambir only for the sake of the white man's daughter, yet he was not conscious of any childish lack of understanding, as suggested by Babalatchi. In fact, Dain knew very well that Lakamba was too deeply implicated in the gunpowder smuggling to care for an investigation by the Dutch authorities into that matter. When sent off by his father, the independent Rajah of Bali,* at the time when the hostilities between Dutch and Malays threatened to spread from Sumatra over the whole archipelago, Dain had found all the big traders deaf to his guarded proposals, and above the temptation of the great prices he was ready to give for gunpowder. He went to Sambir as a last and almost hopeless resort, having heard in Macassar of the white man there, and of the regular steamer trading from Singapore—allured also by the fact that there was no Dutch resident* on the river, which would make things easier, no doubt. His hopes got nearly wrecked against the stubborn loyalty of Lakamba arising from well-understood self-interest; but at last the young man's generosity, his persuasive enthusiasm, the prestige of his father's great name, overpowered the prudent hesitation of the ruler of Sambir. Lakamba would have nothing to do himself with any illegal traffic. He also objected to the Arabs being made use of in that matter; but he suggested Almayer, saying that he was a weak man easily persuaded, and that his friend, the English captain of the steamer, could be made very useful—very likely even would join in the business, smuggling the powder in the steamer without Abdulla's knowledge. There again Dain met in Almayer an unexpected resistance; Lakamba had to send Babalatchi over with the solemn promise that his eyes would be shut in friendship for the white man, Dain paying for the promise and the friendship in good silver guilders of the hated Orang Blanda. Almayer, at last consenting, said the powder would be obtained, but Dain must trust him with dollars to send to Singapore in payment for it. He would induce Ford to buy and smuggle it in the steamer on board the brig. He did not want any money for himself out of the transaction, but Dain must help him in his great enterprise after sending off the brig. Almayer had explained to Dain that he could not trust Lakamba alone in that matter; he would be afraid of losing his treasure and his life through the cupidity of the Rajah; yet the Rajah had to be told, and insisted on taking a share in that operation, or else his eyes would remain shut no longer. To this Almayer had to submit. Had Dain not seen Nina he would have probably refused to engage himself and his men in the projected expedition to Gunong Mas*—the mountain of gold. As it was he intended to return with half of his men as soon as the brig was clear of the reefs, but the persistent chase given him by the Dutch frigate had forced him to run south and ultimately to wreck and destroy his vessel in order to preserve his liberty or perhaps even his life. Yes, he had come back to Sambir for Nina, although aware that the Dutch would look for him there, but he had also calculated his chances of safety in Lakamba's hands. For all his ferocious talk, the merciful ruler would not kill him, for he had long ago been impressed with the notion that Dain possessed the secret of the white man's treasure; neither would he give him up to the Dutch, for fear of some fatal disclosure of complicity in the treasonable trade. So Dain felt tolerably secure as he sat meditating quietly his answer to the Rajah's bloodthirsty speech. Yes, he would point out to him the aspect of his position should he—Dain—fall into the hands of the Dutch and should he speak the truth. He would have nothing more to lose then, and he would speak the truth. And if he did return to Sambir, disturbing thereby Lakamba's peace of mind, what then? He came to look after his property. Did he not pour a stream of silver into Mrs. Almayer's greedy lap? He had paid, for the girl, a price worthy of a great prince, although unworthy of that delightfully maddening creature for whom his untamed soul longed in an intensity of desire far more tormenting than the sharpest pain. He wanted his happiness. He had the right to be in Sambir.

He rose, and, approaching the table, leaned both his elbows on it; Lakamba responsively edged his seat a little closer, while Babalatchi scrambled to his feet and thrust his inquisitive head between his master's and Dain's. They interchanged their ideas rapidly, speaking in whispers into each other's faces, very close now, Dain suggesting, Lakamba contradicting, Babalatchi conciliating and anxious in his vivid apprehension of coming difficulties. He spoke most, whispering earnestly, turning his head slowly from side to side so as to bring his solitary eye to bear upon each of his interlocutors in turn. Why should there be strife? said he. Let Tuan Dain, whom he loved only less than his master, go trustfully into hiding. There were many places for that. Bulangi's house away in the clearing was best. Bulangi was a safe man. In the network of crooked channels no white man could find his way. White men were strong, but very foolish. It was undesirable to fight them, but deception was easy. They were like silly women—they did not know the use of reason, and he was a match for any of them—went on Babalatchi, with all the confidence of deficient experience. Probably the Dutch would seek Almayer. Maybe they would take away their countryman if they were suspicious of him. That would be good. After the Dutch went away Lakamba and Dain would get the treasure without any trouble, and there would be one person less to share it. Did he not speak wisdom? Will Tuan Dain go to Bulangi's house till the danger is over, go at once?

Dain accepted this suggestion of going into hiding with a certain sense of conferring a favour upon Lakamba and the anxious statesman, but he met the proposal of going at once with a decided no, looking Babalatchi meaningly in the eye. The statesman sighed as a man accepting the inevitable would do, and pointed silently towards the other bank of the river. Dain bent his head slowly.

"Yes, I am going there," he said.

"Before the day comes?" asked Babalatchi.

"I am going there now," answered Dain, decisively. "The Orang Blanda will not be here before to-morrow night, perhaps, and I must tell Almayer of our arrangements."

"No, Tuan. No; say nothing," protested Babalatchi. "I will go over myself at sunrise and let him know."

"I will see," said Dain, preparing to go.

The thunderstorm was recommencing outside, the heavy clouds hanging low overhead now. There was a constant rumble of distant thunder punctuated by the nearer sharp crashes, and in the continuous play of blue lightning the woods and the river showed fitfully, with all the elusive distinctness of detail characteristic of such a scene. Outside the door of the Rajah's house Dain and Babalatchi stood on the shaking verandah as if dazed and stunned by the violence of the storm. They stood there amongst the cowering forms of the Rajah's slaves and retainers seeking shelter from the rain, and Dain called aloud to his boatmen, who responded with an unanimous "Ada!* Tuan!" while they looked uneasily at the river.

"This is a great flood!" shouted Babalatchi into Dain's ear. "The river is very angry. Look! Look at the drifting logs! Can you go?"

Dain glanced doubtfully on the livid expanse of seething water bounded far away on the other side by the narrow black line of the forests. Suddenly, in a vivid white flash, the low point of land with the bending trees on it and Almayer's house, leaped into view, flickered and disappeared. Dain pushed Babalatchi aside and ran down to the water-gate followed by his shivering boatmen.

Babalatchi backed slowly in and closed the door, then turned round and looked silently upon Lakamba. The Rajah sat still, glaring stonily upon the table, and Babalatchi gazed curiously at the perplexed mood of the man he had served so many years through good and evil fortune. No doubt the one-eyed statesman felt within his savage and much sophisticated breast the unwonted feelings of sympathy with, and perhaps even pity for, the man he called his master. From the safe position of a confidential adviser, he could, in the dim vista of past years, see himself—a casual cut-throat—finding shelter under that man's roof in the modest rice-clearing of early beginnings. Then came a long period of unbroken success, of wise counsels, and deep plottings resolutely carried out by the fearless Lakamba, till the whole east coast from Poulo Laut to Tanjong Batu* listened to Babalatchi's wisdom speaking through the mouth of the ruler of Sambir. In those long years how many dangers escaped, how many enemies bravely faced, how many white men successfully circumvented! And now he looked upon the result of so many years of patient toil: the fearless Lakamba cowed by the shadow of an impending trouble. The ruler was growing old, and Babalatchi, aware of an uneasy feeling at the pit* of his stomach, put both his hands there with a suddenly vivid and sad perception of the fact that he himself was growing old too; that the time of reckless daring was past for both of them, and that they had to seek refuge in prudent cunning. They wanted peace; they were disposed to reform; they were ready even to retrench so as to have the wherewithal to bribe the evil days away, if bribed away they could be. Babalatchi sighed for the second time that night as he squatted again at his master's feet and tendered him his betel-nut box in mute sympathy. And they sat there in close yet silent communion of betel-nut chewers, moving their jaws slowly, expectorating decorously into the wide-mouthed brass vessel they passed to one another, and listening to the awful din of the battling elements outside.

"There is a very great flood," remarked Babalatchi, sadly.

"Yes," said Lakamba. "Did Dain go?"

"He went, Tuan. He ran down to the river like a man possessed of the Sheitan* himself."

There was another long pause.

"He may get drowned," suggested Lakamba at last, with some show of interest.

"The floating logs are many," answered Babalatchi, "but he is a good swimmer," he added languidly.

"He ought to live," said Lakamba; "he knows where the treasure is."

Babalatchi assented with an ill-humoured grunt. His want of success in penetrating the white man's secret as to the locality where the gold was to be found was a sore point with the statesman of Sambir, as the only conspicuous failure in an otherwise brilliant career.

A great peace had now succeeded the turmoil of the storm. Only the little belated clouds, which hurried past overhead to catch up the main body flashing silently in the distance, sent down short showers that pattered softly with a soothing hiss over the palm-leaf roof.

Lakamba roused himself from his apathy with an appearance of having grasped the situation at last.

"Babalatchi," he called briskly, giving him a slight kick.

"Ada Tuan! I am listening."

"If the Orang Blanda come here, Babalatchi, and take Almayer to Batavia to punish him for smuggling gunpowder, what will he do, you think?"

"I do not know, Tuan."

"You are a fool," commented Lakamba, exultingly. "He will tell them where the treasure is, so as to find mercy. He will."

Babalatchi looked up at his master and nodded his head with by no means a joyful surprise. He had not thought of this; there was a new complication.

"Almayer must die," said Lakamba, decisively, "to make our secret safe. He must die quietly, Babalatchi. You must do it."

Babalatchi assented, and rose wearily to his feet. "To-morrow?" he asked.

"Yes; before the Dutch come. He drinks much coffee," answered Lakamba, with seeming irrelevancy.

Babalatchi stretched himself yawning, but Lakamba, in the flattering consciousness of a knotty problem solved by his own unaided intellectual efforts, grew suddenly very wakeful.

"Babalatchi," he said to the exhausted statesman, "fetch the box of music the white captain gave me. I cannot sleep."

At this order a deep shade of melancholy settled upon Babalatchi's features. He went reluctantly behind the curtain and soon reappeared carrying in his arms a small hand-organ, which he put down on the table with an air of deep dejection. Lakamba settled himself comfortably in his arm-chair.

"Turn, Babalatchi, turn," he murmured, with closed eyes.

Babalatchi's hand grasped the handle with the energy of despair, and as he turned, the deep gloom on his countenance changed into an expression of hopeless resignation. Through the open shutter the notes of Verdi's music floated out on the great silence over the river and forest. Lakamba listened with closed eyes and a delighted smile; Babalatchi turned, at times dozing off and swaying over, then catching himself up in a great fright with a few quick turns of the handle. Nature slept in an exhausted repose after the fierce turmoil, while under the unsteady hand of the statesman of Sambir the Trovatore fitfully wept, wailed, and bade good-bye to his Leonore* again and again in a mournful round of tearful and endless iteration.

CHAPTER SEVEN

THE bright sunshine of the clear mistless morning, after the stormy night, flooded the main path of the settlement leading from the low shore of the Pantai branch of the river to the gate of Abdulla's compound. The path was deserted this morning; it stretched its dark yellow surface, hard beaten by the tramp of many bare feet, between the clusters of palm trees, whose tall trunks barred it with strong black lines at irregular intervals, while the newly risen sun threw the shadows of their leafy heads far away over the roofs of the buildings lining the river, even over the river itself as it flowed swiftly and silently past the deserted houses. For the houses were deserted too. On the narrow strip of trodden grass intervening between their open doors and the road, the morning fires smouldered untended, sending thin fluted columns of smoke into the cool air, and spreading the thinnest veil of mysterious blue haze over the sunlit solitude of the settlement. Almayer, just out of his hammock, gazed sleepily at the unwonted appearance of Sambir, wondering vaguely at the absence of life. His own house was very quiet; he could not hear his wife's voice, nor the sound of Nina's footsteps in the big room, opening on the verandah, which he called his sitting-room, whenever, in the company of white men, he wished to assert his claims to the commonplace decencies of civilization. Nobody ever sat there; there was nothing there to sit upon, for Mrs. Almayer in her savage moods, when excited by the reminiscences of the piratical period of her life, had torn off the curtains to make sarongs for the slave-girls, and had burnt the showy furniture piecemeal to cook the family rice. But Almayer was not thinking of his furniture now. He was thinking of Dain's return, of Dain's nocturnal interview with Lakamba, of its possible influence on his long-matured plans, now nearing the period of their execution. He was also uneasy at the non-appearance of Dain who had promised him an early visit. "The fellow had plenty of time to cross the river," he mused, "and there was so much to be done to-day. The settling of details for the early start on the morrow; the launching of the boats; the thousand and one finishing touches. For the expedition must start complete, nothing should be forgotten, nothing should——"

The sense of the unwonted solitude grew upon him suddenly, and in the unusual silence he caught himself longing even for the usually unwelcome sound of his wife's voice to break the oppressive stillness which seemed, to his frightened fancy, to portend the advent of some new misfortune. "What has happened?" he muttered half aloud, as he shuffled in his imperfectly adjusted slippers towards the balustrade of the verandah. "Is everybody asleep or dead?"

The settlement was alive and very much awake. It was awake ever since the early break of day, when Mahmat Banjer, in a fit of unheard-of energy, arose and, taking up his hatchet, stepped over the sleeping forms of his two wives and walked shivering to the water's edge to make sure that the new house he was building had not floated away during the night.

The house was being built by the enterprising Mahmat on a large raft,* and he had securely moored it just inside the muddy point of land at the junction of the two branches of the Pantai so as to be out of the way of drifting logs that would no doubt strand on the point during the freshet. Mahmat walked through the wet grass saying bourrouh,* and cursing softly to himself the hard necessities of active life that drove him from his warm couch into the cold of the morning. A glance showed him that his house was still there, and he congratulated himself on his foresight in hauling it out of harm's way, for the increasing light showed him a confused wrack of drift-logs, half-stranded on the muddy flat, interlocked into a shapeless raft by their branches, tossing to and fro and grinding together in the eddy caused by the meeting currents of the two branches of the river. Mahmat walked down to the water's edge to examine the rattan moorings of his house just as the sun cleared the trees of the forest on the opposite shore. As he bent over the fastenings he glanced again carelessly at the unquiet jumble of logs and saw there something that caused him to drop his hatchet and stand up, shading his eyes with his hand from the rays of the rising sun. It was something red, and the logs rolled over it, at times closing round it, sometimes hiding it. It looked to him at first like a strip of red cloth. The next moment Mahmat had made it out and raised a great shout.

"Ah ya! There!" yelled Mahmat. "There's a man amongst the logs." He put the palms of his hand to his lips and shouted, enunciating distinctly, his face turned towards the settlement: "There's a body of a man in the river! Come and see! A dead—stranger!"

The women of the nearest house were already outside kindling the fires and husking the morning rice. They took up the cry shrilly, and it travelled so from house to house, dying away in the distance. The men rushed out excited but silent, and ran towards the muddy point where the unconscious logs tossed and ground and bumped and rolled over the dead stranger with the stupid persistency of inanimate things. The women followed, neglecting their domestic duties and disregarding the possibilities of domestic discontent, while groups of children brought up the rear, warbling joyously, in the delight of unexpected excitement.

Almayer called aloud for his wife and daughter, but receiving no response, stood listening intently. The murmur of the crowd reached him faintly, bringing with it the assurance of some unusual event. He glanced at the river just as he was going to leave the verandah and checked himself at the sight of a small canoe crossing over from the Rajah's landing-place. The solitary occupant (in whom Almayer soon recognized Babalatchi) effected the crossing a little below the house and paddled up to the Lingard jetty in the dead water under the bank. Babalatchi clambered out slowly and went on fastening his canoe with fastidious care, as if not in a hurry to meet Almayer, whom he saw looking at him from the verandah. This delay gave Almayer time to notice and greatly wonder at Babalatchi's official get-up.* The statesman of Sambir was clad in a costume befitting his high rank. A loudly checkered sarong encircled his waist and from its many folds peeped out the silver hilt of the kriss that saw the light only on great festivals or during official receptions. Over the left shoulder and across the otherwise unclad breast of the aged diplomatist glistened a patent leather belt bearing a brass plate with the arms of Netherlands under the inscription, "Sultan of Sambir." Babalatchi's head was covered by a red turban, whose fringed ends falling over the left cheek and shoulder gave to his aged face a ludicrous expression of joyous recklessness. When the canoe was at last fastened to his satisfaction he straightened himself up, shaking down the folds of his sarong, and moved with long strides towards Almayer's house, swinging regularly his long ebony staff, whose gold head ornamented with precious stones flashed in the morning sun. Almayer waved his hand to the right towards the point of land, to him invisible, but in full view from the jetty.

"Oh, Babalatchi! oh!" he called out; "what is the matter there? can you see?"

Babalatchi stopped and gazed intently at the crowd on the river bank, and after a little while the astonished Almayer saw him leave the path, gather up his sarong in one hand, and break into a trot through the grass towards the muddy point. Almayer, now greatly interested, ran down the steps of the verandah. The murmur of men's voices and the shrill cries of women reached him quite distinctly now, and as soon as he turned the corner of his house he could see the crowd on the low promontory swaying and pushing round some object of interest. He could indistinctly hear Babalatchi's voice, then the crowd opened before the aged statesman and closed after him with an excited hum, ending in a loud shout.

As Almayer approached the throng a man ran out and rushed past him towards the settlement, unheeding his call to stop and explain the cause of this excitement. On the very outskirts of the crowd Almayer found himself arrested by an unyielding mass of humanity, regardless of his entreaties for a passage, insensible to his gentle pushes as he tried to work his way through it towards the riverside.

In the midst of his gentle and slow progress he fancied suddenly he had heard his wife's voice in the thickest of the throng. He could not mistake very well Mrs. Almayer's high-pitched tones, yet the words were too indistinct for him to understand their purport. He paused in his endeavours to make a passage for himself, intending to get some intelligence from those around him, when a long and piercing shriek rent the air, silencing the murmurs of the crowd and the voices of his informants. For a moment Almayer remained as if turned into stone with astonishment and horror, for he was certain now that he had heard his wife wailing for the dead. He remembered Nina's unusual absence, and maddened by his apprehensions as to her safety, he pushed blindly and violently forward, the crowd falling back with cries of surprise and pain before his frantic advance.

On the point of land in a little clear space lay the body of the stranger just hauled out from amongst the logs. On one side stood Babalatchi, his chin resting on the head of his staff and his one eye gazing steadily at the shapeless mass of broken limbs, torn flesh, and bloodstained rags. As Almayer burst through the ring of horrified spectators, Mrs. Almayer threw her own head-veil over the upturned face of the drowned man, and, squatting by it, with another mournful howl, sent a shiver through the now silent crowd. Mahmat, dripping wet, turned to Almayer, eager to tell his tale.

In the first moment of reaction from the anguish of his fear the sunshine seemed to waver before Almayer's eyes, and he listened to words spoken around him without comprehending their meaning. When, by a strong effort of will, he regained the possession of his senses, Mahmat was saying—

"That is the way, Tuan. His sarong was caught in the broken branch, and he hung with his head under water. When I saw what it was I did not want it here. I wanted it to get clear and drift away. Why should we bury a stranger in the midst of our houses for his ghost to frighten our women and children? Have we not enough ghosts about this place?"

A murmur of approval interrupted him here. Mahmat looked reproachfully at Babalatchi.

"But the Tuan Babalatchi ordered me to drag the body ashore"—he went on looking round at his audience, but addressing himself only to Almayer—"and I dragged him by the feet; in through the mud I have dragged him, although my heart longed to see him float down the river to strand perchance on Bulangi's clearing—may his father's grave be defiled!"

There was subdued laughter at this, for the enmity of Mahmat and Bulangi was a matter of common notoriety and of undying interest to the inhabitants of Sambir. In the midst of that mirth Mrs. Almayer wailed suddenly again.

"Allah! What ails the woman!" exclaimed Mahmat, angrily. "Here, I have touched this carcass which came from nobody knows where, and have most likely defiled myself before eating rice. By orders of Tuan Babalatchi I did this thing to please the white man. Are you pleased, O Tuan Almayer? And what will be my recompense? Tuan Babalatchi said a recompense there will be, and from you. Now consider. I have been defiled and if not defiled I may be under the spell. Look at his anklets! Who ever heard of a corpse appearing during the night amongst the logs with gold anklets on its legs? There is witchcraft there. However," added Mahmat, after a reflective pause, "I will have the anklet if there is permission, for I have a charm against the ghosts and am not afraid. God is great!"

A fresh outburst of noisy grief from Mrs. Almayer checked the flow of Mahmat's eloquence. Almayer, bewildered, looked in turn at his wife, at Mahmat, at

Babalatchi, and at last arrested his fascinated gaze on the body lying on the mud with covered face in a grotesquely unnatural contortion of mangled and broken limbs, one twisted and lacerated arm, with white bones protruding in many places through the torn flesh, stretched out; the hand with outspread fingers nearly touching his foot.[*]

"Do you know who this is?" he asked of Babalatchi, in a low voice.

Babalatchi, staring straight before him, hardly moved his lips, while Mrs. Almayer's persistent lamentations drowned the whisper of his murmured reply intended only for Almayer's ear.

"It was fate. Look at your feet, white man. I can see a ring on those torn fingers which I know well."

Saying this, Babalatchi stepped carelessly forward, putting his foot as if accidentally on the hand of the corpse and pressing it into the soft mud. He swung his staff menacingly towards the crowd, which fell back a little.

"Go away," he said sternly, "and send your women to their cooking fires, which they ought not to have left to run after a dead stranger. This is men's work here. I take him now in the name of the Rajah. Let no man remain here but Tuan Almayer's slaves. Now go!"

The crowd reluctantly began to disperse. The women went first, dragging away the children that hung back with all their weight on the maternal hand. The men strolled slowly after them in ever forming and changing groups that gradually dissolved as they neared the settlement and every man regained his own house with steps quickened by the hungry anticipation of the morning rice. Only on the slight elevation where the land sloped down towards the muddy point a few men, either friends or enemies of Mahmat, remained gazing curiously for some time longer at the small group standing around the body on the river bank.

"I do not understand what you mean, Babalatchi," said Almayer. "What is the ring you are talking about? Whoever he is, you have trodden the poor fellow's hand right into the mud. Uncover his face," he went on, addressing Mrs. Almayer, who, squatting by the head of the corpse, rocked herself to and fro, shaking from time to time her dishevelled grey locks, and muttering mournfully.

"Hai!"* exclaimed Mahmat, who had lingered close by. "Look, Tuan; the logs came together so," and here he pressed the palms of his hands together, "and his head must have been between them, and now there is no face for you to look at. There are his flesh and his bones, the nose, and the lips, and maybe his eyes, but nobody could tell the one from the other. It was written the day he was born that no man could look at him in death and be able to say, 'This is my friend's face.'"

"Silence, Mahmat; enough!" said Babalatchi, "and take thy eyes off his anklet, thou eater of pig's flesh.* Tuan Almayer," he went on, lowering his voice, "have you seen Dain this morning?"

Almayer opened his eyes wide and looked alarmed. "No," he said quickly; "haven't you seen him? Is he not with the Rajah? I am waiting; why does he not come?"

Babalatchi nodded his head sadly.

"He is come, Tuan. He left last night when the storm was great and the river spoke angrily. The night was very black, but he had within him a light that showed the way to your house as smooth as a narrow backwater, and the many logs no bigger than wisps of dried grass. Therefore he went; and now he lies here." And Babalatchi nodded his head towards the body.

"How can you tell?" said Almayer excitedly, pushing his wife aside. He snatched the cover off and looked at the formless* mass of flesh, hair, and drying mud, where the face of the drowned man should have been. "Nobody can tell," he added, turning away with a shudder.

Babalatchi was on his knees wiping the mud from the stiffened fingers of the outstretched hand. He rose to his feet and flashed before Almayer's eyes a gold ring set with a large green stone.

"You know this well," he said. "This never left Dain's hand. I had to tear the flesh now to get it off. Do you believe now?"

Almayer raised his hands to his head and let them fall listlessly by his side in the utter abandonment of despair. Babalatchi, looking at him curiously, was astonished to see him smile. A strange fancy had taken possession of Almayer's brain, distracted by this new misfortune. It seemed to him that for many years he had been falling into a deep precipice. Day after day, month after month, year after year, he had been falling, falling, falling; it was a smooth, round, black thing, and the black walls had been rushing upwards with wearisome rapidity. A great rush, the noise of which he fancied he could hear yet; and now, with an awful shock, he had reached the bottom, and behold! he was alive and whole, and Dain was dead with all his bones broken. It struck him as funny. A dead Malay; he had seen many dead Malays without any emotion; and now he felt inclined to weep, but it was over the fate of a white man he knew; a man that fell over a deep precipice and did not die. He seemed somehow to himself to be standing on one side, a little way off, looking at a certain Almayer who was in great trouble. Poor, poor fellow! Why doesn't he cut his throat? He wished to encourage him; he was very anxious to see him lying dead over that other corpse. Why does he not die and end this suffering? He groaned aloud unconsciously and started with affright at the sound of his own voice. Was he going mad? Terrified by the thought he turned away and ran towards his house repeating to himself, "I am not going mad; of course not, no, no, no!" He tried to keep a firm hold of the idea. Not mad, not mad. He stumbled as he ran blindly up the steps repeating fast and ever faster those words wherein seemed to lie his salvation. He saw Nina standing there, and wished to say something to her, but could not remember what, in his extreme anxiety not to forget that he was not going mad, which he still kept repeating mentally as he ran round the table, till he stumbled against one of the arm-chairs and dropped into it exhausted. He sat staring wildly at Nina, still assuring himself mentally of his own sanity and wondering why the girl shrank from him in open-eyed alarm. What was the matter with her? This was foolish. He struck the table violently with his clenched fist and shouted hoarsely, "Give me some gin! Run!" Then, while Nina ran off, he remained in the chair, very still and quiet, astonished at the noise he had made.

Nina returned with a tumbler half filled with gin, and found her father staring absently before him. Almayer felt very tired now, as if he had come from a long journey. He felt as if he had walked miles and miles that morning and now wanted to rest very much. He took the tumbler with a shaking hand, and as he drank, his teeth chattered against the glass which he drained and set down heavily on the table. He turned his eyes slowly towards Nina standing beside him, and said steadily—

"Now all is over, Nina. He is dead, and I may as well burn all my boats."

He felt very proud of being able to speak so calmly. Decidedly he was not going mad. This certitude was very comforting, and he went on talking about the finding of the body, listening to his own voice complacently. Nina stood quietly, her hand resting lightly on her father's shoulder, her face unmoved, but every line of her features, the attitude of her whole body expressing the most keen and anxious attention.

"And so Dain is dead," she said coldly, when her father ceased speaking.

Almayer's elaborately calm demeanour gave way in a moment to an outburst of violent indignation.

"You stand there as if you were only half alive, and talk to me," he exclaimed angrily, "as if it was a matter of no importance. Yes, he is dead! Do you understand? Dead! What do you care? You never cared; you saw me struggle, and work, and strive, unmoved; and my suffering you could never see. No, never. You have no heart, and you have no mind, or you would have understood that it was for you, for your happiness I was working. I wanted to be rich; I wanted to get away from here. I wanted to see white men bowing low before the power of your beauty and your wealth. Old as I am I wished to seek a strange land, a civilization to which I am a stranger, so as to find a new life in the contemplation of your high fortunes, of your triumphs, of your happiness. For that I bore patiently the burden of work, of disappointment, of humiliation amongst these savages here, and I had it all nearly in my grasp."

He looked at his daughter's attentive face and jumped to his feet upsetting the chair.

"Do you hear? I had it all there; so; within reach of my hand."

He paused, trying to keep down his rising anger, and failed.

"Have you no feeling?" he went on. "Have you lived without hope?" Nina's silence exasperated him; his voice rose, although he tried to master his feelings.

"Are you content to live in this misery and die in this wretched hole? Say something, Nina; have you no sympathy? Have you no word of comfort for me? I that loved you so."

He waited for a while for an answer, and receiving none shook his fist in his daughter's face.

"I believe you are an idiot!" he yelled.

He looked round for the chair, picked it up and sat down stiffly. His anger was dead within him, and he felt ashamed of his outburst, yet relieved to think that now he had laid clear before his daughter the inner meaning of his life. He thought so in perfect good faith, deceived by the emotional estimate of his motives, unable to see the crookedness of his ways, the unreality of his aims, the futility of his regrets. And now his heart was filled only with a great tenderness and love for his daughter. He wanted to see her miserable, and to share with her his despair; but he wanted it only as all weak natures long for a companionship in misfortune with beings innocent of its cause. If she suffered herself she would understand and pity him; but now she would not, or could not, find one word of comfort or love for him in his dire extremity. The sense of his absolute loneliness came home to his heart with a force that made him shudder. He swayed and fell forward with his face on the table, his arms stretched straight out, extended and rigid. Nina made a quick movement towards her father and stood looking at the grey head, on the broad shoulders shaken convulsively by the violence of feelings that found relief at last in sobs and tears.

Nina sighed deeply and moved away from the table. Her features lost the appearance of stony indifference that had exasperated her father into his outburst of anger and sorrow. The expression of her face, now unseen by her father, underwent a rapid change. She had listened to Almayer's appeal for sympathy, for one word of comfort, apparently indifferent, yet with her breast torn by conflicting impulses raised unexpectedly by events she had not foreseen, or at least did not expect to happen so soon. With her heart deeply moved by the sight of Almayer's misery, knowing it in her power to end it with a word, longing to bring peace to that troubled heart, she heard with terror the voice of her overpowering love commanding her to be silent. And she submitted after a short and fierce struggle of her old self against the new principle of her life. She wrapped herself up in absolute silence, the only safeguard against some fatal admission. She could not trust herself to make a sign, to murmur a word for fear of saying too much; and the very violence of the feelings that stirred the innermost recesses of her soul seemed to turn her person into a stone. The dilated nostrils and the flashing eyes were the only signs of the storm raging within, and those signs of his daughter's emotion Almayer did not see, for his sight was dimmed by self-pity, by anger, and by despair.

Had Almayer looked at his daughter as she leant over the front rail of the verandah he could have seen the expression of indifference give way to a look of pain and that again pass away, leaving the glorious beauty of her face marred by deep-drawn lines of watchful anxiety. The long grass in the neglected courtyard stood very straight before her eyes in the noonday heat. From the river-bank there were voices and a shuffle of bare feet approaching the house; Babalatchi could be heard giving directions to Almayer's men, and Mrs. Almayer's subdued wailing became audible as the small procession bearing the body of the drowned man and headed by that sorrowful matron turned the corner of the house. Babalatchi had taken the broken anklet off the man's leg, and now held it in his hand as he moved by the side of the bearers, while Mahmat lingered behind timidly, in the hopes of the promised reward.

"Lay him there," said Babalatchi to Almayer's men, pointing to a pile of drying planks in front of the verandah. "Lay him there. He was a Kaffir* and the son of a dog, and he was the white man's friend. He drank the white man's strong water,"* he added, with affected horror. "That I have seen myself."

The men stretched out the broken limbs on two planks they had laid level, while Mrs. Almayer covered the body with a piece of white cotton cloth, and after whispering for some time with Babalatchi departed to her domestic duties. Almayer's men, after laying down their burden, dispersed themselves in quest of shady spots wherein to idle the day away. Babalatchi was left alone by the corpse that lay rigid under the white cloth in the bright sunshine.

Nina came down the steps and joined Babalatchi, who put his hand to his forehead, and squatted down with great deference.

"You have a bangle there," said Nina, looking down on Babalatchi's upturned face and into his solitary eye.

"I have, Mem Putih," returned the polite statesman. Then turning towards Mahmat he beckoned him closer, calling out, "Come here!"

Mahmat approached with some hesitation. He avoided looking at Nina, but fixed his eyes on Babalatchi.

"Now, listen," said Babalatchi, sharply. "The ring and the anklet you have seen, and you know they belonged to Dain the trader, and to no other. Dain returned last night in a canoe. He spoke with the Rajah, and in the middle of the night left to cross over to the white man's house. There was a great flood, and this morning you found him in the river."

"By his feet I dragged him out," muttered Mahmat under his breath. "Tuan Babalatchi, there will be a recompense!" he exclaimed aloud.

Babalatchi held up the gold bangle before Mahmat's eyes. "What I have told you, Mahmat, is for all ears. What I give you now is for your eyes only. Take."

Mahmat took the bangle eagerly and hid it in the folds of his waist-cloth. "Am I a fool to show this thing in a house with three women in it?" he growled. "But I shall tell them about Dain the trader, and there will be talk enough."

He turned and went away, increasing his pace as soon as he was outside Almayer's compound.

Babalatchi looked after him till he disappeared behind the bushes. "Have I done well, Mem Putih?" he asked, humbly addressing Nina.

"You have," answered Nina. "The ring you may keep yourself."

Babalatchi touched his lips and forehead,* and scrambled to his feet. He looked at Nina, as if expecting her to say something more, but Nina turned towards the house and went up the steps, motioning him away with her hand.

Babalatchi picked up his staff and prepared to go. It was very warm, and he did not care for the long pull to the Rajah's house. Yet he must go and tell the Rajah—tell of the event; of the change in his plans; of all his suspicions. He walked to the jetty and began casting off the rattan painter* of his canoe.

The broad expanse of the lower reach, with its shimmering surface dotted by the black specks of the fishing canoes, lay before his eyes. The fishermen seemed to be racing. Babalatchi paused in his work, and looked on with sudden interest. The man in the foremost canoe, now within hail of the first houses of Sambir, laid in his paddle and stood up shouting—

"The boats! the boats! The man-of-war's boats are coming! They are here!"

In a moment the settlement was again alive with people rushing to the riverside. The men began to unfasten their boats, the women stood in groups looking towards the bend down the river. Above the trees lining the reach a slight puff of smoke appeared like a black stain on the brilliant blue of the cloudless sky.

Babalatchi stood perplexed, the painter in his hand. He looked down the reach, then up towards Almayer's house, and back again at the river as if undecided what to do. At last he made the canoe fast again hastily, and ran towards the house and up the steps of the verandah.

"Tuan! Tuan!" he called, eagerly. "The boats are coming. The man-of-war's boats. You had better get ready. The officers will come here, I know."

Almayer lifted his head slowly from the table, and looked at him stupidly.

"Mem Putih!" exclaimed Babalatchi to Nina, "look at him. He does not hear. You must take care," he added meaningly.

Nina nodded to him with an uncertain smile, and was going to speak, when a sharp report from the gun mounted in the bow of the steam launch that was just then coming into view arrested the words on her parted lips. The smile died out, and was replaced by the old look of anxious attention. From the hills far away the echo came back like a long-drawn and mournful sigh, as if the land had sent it in answer to the voice of its masters.

CHAPTER EIGHT

THE news as to the identity of the body lying now in Almayer's compound spread rapidly over the settlement. During the forenoon most of the inhabitants remained in the long street discussing the mysterious return and the unexpected death of the man who had become known to them as the trader. His arrival during the northeast monsoon, his long sojourn in their midst, his sudden departure with his brig, and, above all, the mysterious appearance of the body, said to be his, amongst the logs, were subjects to wonder at and to talk over and over again with undiminished interest. Mahmat moved from house to house and from group to group, always ready to repeat his tale: how he saw the body caught by the sarong in a forked log; how Mrs. Almayer coming, one of the first, at his cries, recognized it, even before he had it hauled on shore; how Babalatchi ordered him to bring it out of the water. "By the feet I dragged him in, and there was no head," exclaimed Mahmat, "and how could the white man's wife know who it was? She was a witch, it was well known. And did you see how the white man himself ran away at the sight of the body? Like a deer he ran!" And here Mahmat imitated Almayer's long strides, to the great joy of the beholders. And for all his trouble he had nothing. The ring with the green stone Tuan Babalatchi kept. "Nothing! Nothing!" He spat down at his feet in sign of disgust, and left that group to seek further on a fresh audience.

The news spreading to the furthermost parts of the

settlement found out Abdulla in the cool recess of his godown, where he sat overlooking his Arab clerks and the men loading and unloading the up-country canoes. Reshid, who was busy on the jetty, was summoned into his uncle's presence and found him, as usual, very calm and even cheerful, but very much surprised. The rumour of the capture or destruction of Dain's brig had reached the Arab's ears three days before from the sea-fishermen and through the dwellers on the lower reaches of the river. It had been passed upstream from neighbour to neighbour till Bulangi, whose clearing was nearest to the settlement, had brought that news himself to Abdulla whose favour he courted. But rumour also spoke of a fight and of Dain's death on board his own vessel. And now all the settlement talked of Dain's visit to the Rajah and of his death when crossing the river in the dark to see Almayer. They could not understand this. Reshid thought that it was very strange. He felt uneasy and doubtful. But Abdulla, after the first shock of surprise, with the old age's dislike for solving riddles, showed a becoming resignation. He remarked that the man was dead now at all events, and consequently no more dangerous. Where was the use to wonder at the decrees of Fate, especially if they were propitious to the True Believers? And with a pious ejaculation to Allah the Merciful, the Compassionate,* Abdulla seemed to regard the incident as closed for the present.

Not so Reshid. He lingered by his uncle, pulling thoughtfully his neatly trimmed beard.

"There are many lies," he murmured. "He has been dead once before, and came to life to die again now. The Dutch will be here before many days and clamour for the man. Shall I not believe my eyes sooner than the tongues of women and idle men?"

"They say that the body is being taken to Almayer's compound," said Abdulla. "If you want to go there you must go before the Dutch arrive here. Go late. It should not be said that we have been seen inside that man's enclosure lately."

Reshid assented to the truth of this last remark and left his uncle's side. He leaned against the jamb of the big doorway and looked idly across the courtyard through the open gate on to the main road of the settlement. It lay empty, straight, and yellow under the flood of light. In the hot noontide the smooth trunks of palm trees, the outlines of the houses, and away there at the other end of the road the roof of Almayer's house visible over the bushes on the dark background of forest, seemed to quiver in the heat radiating from the steaming earth. Swarms of yellow butterflies rose, and settled to rise again in short flights before Reshid's half-closed eyes. From under his feet arose the dull hum of insects in the long grass of the courtyard. He looked on sleepily.

From one of the side paths amongst the houses a woman stepped out on the road, a slight girlish figure walking under the shade of a large tray balanced on its head. The consciousness of something moving stirred Reshid's half-sleeping senses into a comparative wakefulness. He recognized Taminah, Bulangi's slave-girl, with her tray of cakes for sale—an apparition of daily recurrence and of no importance whatever. She was going towards Almayer's house. She could be made useful. He roused himself up and ran towards the gate calling out, "Taminah O!" The girl stopped, hesitated, and came back slowly. Reshid waited, signing to her impatiently to come nearer.

When near Reshid Taminah stood with downcast eyes. Reshid looked at her a while before he asked—

"Are you going to Almayer's house? They say in the settlement that Dain the trader, he that was found drowned this morning, is lying in the white man's campong."

"I have heard this talk," whispered Taminah; "and this morning by the riverside I saw the body. Where it is now I do not know."

"So you have seen it?" asked Reshid, eagerly. "Is it Dain? You have seen him many times. You would know him."

The girl's lips quivered and she remained silent for a while breathing quickly.

"I have seen him, not a long time ago," she said at last. "The talk is true; he is dead. What do you want from me, Tuan? I must go."

Just then the report of the gun fired on board the steam launch was heard, interrupting Reshid's reply. Leaving the girl he ran to the house, and met in the courtyard Abdulla coming towards the gate.

"The Orang Blanda are come," said Reshid, "and now we shall have our reward."

Abdulla shook his head doubtfully. "The white men's rewards are long in coming," he said. "White men are quick in anger and slow in gratitude. We shall see."

He stood at the gate stroking his grey beard and listening to the distant cries of greeting at the other end of the settlement. As Taminah was turning to go he called her back.

"Listen, girl," he said: "there will be many white men in Almayer's house. You shall be there selling your cakes to the men of the sea. What you see and what you hear you may tell me. Come here before the sun sets and I will give you a blue handkerchief with red spots. Now go, and forget not to return."

He gave her a push with the end of his long staff as she was going away and made her stumble.

"This slave is very slow," he remarked to his nephew, looking after the girl with great disfavour.

Taminah walked on, her tray on the head, her eyes fixed on the ground. From the open doors of the houses were heard, as she passed, friendly calls inviting her within for business purposes, but she never heeded them, neglecting her sales in the preoccupation of intense thinking. Since the very early morning she had heard much, she had also seen much that filled her heart with a joy mingled with great suffering and fear. Before the dawn, before she left Bulangi's house to paddle up to Sambir she had heard voices outside the house when all in it, but herself were asleep. And now, with her knowledge of the words spoken in the darkness, she held in her hand a life and carried in her breast a great sorrow. Yet from her springy step, erect figure, and face veiled over by the every-day look of apathetic indifference, nobody could have guessed of the double load she carried under the visible burden of the tray piled up high with cakes manufactured by the thrifty hands of Bulangi's wives. In that supple figure straight as an arrow, so graceful and free in its walk, behind those soft eyes that spoke of nothing but of unconscious resignation, there slept all feelings and all passions, all hopes and all fears, the curse of life and the consolation of death. And she knew nothing of it all. She lived like the tall palms amongst whom* she was passing now, seeking the light, desiring the sunshine, fearing the storm, unconscious of either. The slave had no hope, and knew of no change. She knew of no other sky, no other water, no other forest, no other world, no other life. She had no wish, no hope, no love, no fear except of a blow, and no vivid feeling but that of occasional hunger, which was seldom, for Bulangi was rich and rice was plentiful in the solitary house in his clearing. The absence of pain and hunger was her happiness, and when she felt unhappy she was simply tired, more than usual, after the day's labour. Then in the hot nights of the southwest monsoon she slept dreamlessly under the bright stars on the platform built outside the house and over the river. Inside they slept too: Bulangi by the door; his wives further in; the children with their mothers. She could hear their breathing; Bulangi's sleepy voice; the sharp cry of a child soon hushed with tender words. And she closed her eyes to the murmur of the water below her, to the whisper of the warm wind above, ignorant of the never-ceasing life of that tropical nature that spoke to her in vain with the thousand faint voices of the near forest, with the breath of tepid wind; in the heavy scents that lingered around her head; in the white wraiths of morning mist that hung over her in the solemn hush of all creation before the dawn.

Such had been her existence before the coming of the brig with the strangers. She remembered well that time; the uproar in the settlement, the never-ending wonder, the days and nights of talk and excitement. She remembered her own timidity with the strange men, till the brig moored to the bank became in a manner part of the settlement, and the fear wore off in the familiarity of constant intercourse. The call on board then became part of her daily round. She walked hesitatingly up the slanting planks of the gangway amidst the encouraging shouts and more or less decent jokes of the men idling over the bulwarks. There she sold her wares to those men that spoke so loud and carried themselves so free. There was a throng, a constant coming and going; calls interchanged, orders given and executed with shouts; the rattle of blocks,* the flinging about of coils of rope. She sat out of the way under the shade of the awning, with her tray before her, the veil drawn well over her face, feeling shy amongst so many men. She smiled at all buyers, but spoke to none, letting their jests pass with stolid unconcern. She heard many tales told around her of far-off countries, of strange customs, of events stranger still. Those men were brave; but the most fearless of them spoke of their chief with fear. Often the man they called their master passed before her, walking erect and indifferent, in the pride of youth, in the flash of rich dress, with a tinkle of gold ornaments, while everybody stood aside watching anxiously for a movement of his lips, ready to do his bidding. Then all her life seemed to rush into her eyes, and from under her veil she gazed at him, charmed, yet fearful to attract attention. One day he noticed her and asked, "Who is that girl?" "A slave, Tuan! A girl that sells cakes," a dozen voices replied together. She rose in terror to run on shore, when he called her back; and as she stood trembling with head hung down before him, he spoke kind words, lifting her chin with his hand and looking into her eyes with a smile. "Do not be afraid," he said. He never spoke to her any more. Somebody called out from the river-bank; he turned away and forgot her existence. Taminah saw Almayer standing on the shore with Nina on his arm. She heard Nina's voice calling out gaily, and saw Dain's face brighten with joy as he leaped on shore. She hated the sound of that voice ever since.

After that day she left off visiting Almayer's compound, and passed the noon hours under the shade of the brig awning. She watched for his coming with heart beating quicker and quicker, as he approached, into a wild tumult of newly-aroused feelings of joy and hope and fear that died away with Dain's retreating figure, leaving her tired out, as if after a struggle, sitting still for a long time in dreamy languor. Then she paddled home slowly in the afternoon, often letting her canoe float with the lazy stream in the quiet backwater of the river. The paddle hung idle in the water as she sat in the stern, one hand supporting her chin, her eyes wide open, listening intently to the whispering of her heart that seemed to swell at last into a song of extreme sweetness. Listening to that song she husked the rice at home; it dulled her ears to the shrill bickerings of Bulangi's wives, to the sound of angry reproaches addressed to herself. And when the sun was near its setting she walked to the bathing-place and heard it as she stood on the tender grass of the low bank, her robe at her feet, and looked at the reflection of her figure on the glass-like surface of the creek. Listening to it she walked slowly back, her wet hair hanging over her shoulders; lying down to rest under the bright stars, she closed her eyes to the murmur of the water below, of the warm wind above; to the voice of nature speaking through the faint noises of the great forest, and to the song of her own heart.

She heard, but did not understand, and drank in the dreamy joy of her new existence without troubling about its meaning or its end, till the full consciousness of life came to her through pain and anger. And she suffered horribly the first time she saw Nina's long canoe drift silently past the sleeping house of Bulangi, bearing the two lovers into the white mist of the great river. Her jealousy and rage culminated into a paroxysm of physical pain that left her lying panting on the river-bank, in the dumb agony of a wounded animal. But she went on moving patiently in the enchanted circle of slavery, going through her task day after day with all the pathos of the grief she could not express, even to herself, locked within her breast. She shrank from Nina as she would have shrunk from the sharp blade of a knife cutting into her flesh, but she kept on visiting the brig to feed her dumb, ignorant soul on her own despair. She saw Dain many times. He never spoke, he never looked. Could his eyes see only one woman's image? Could his ears hear only one woman's voice? He never noticed her; not once.

And then he went away. She saw him and Nina for the last time on that morning when Babalatchi, while visiting his fish baskets, had his suspicions of the white man's daughter's love affair with Dain confirmed beyond the shadow of doubt. Dain disappeared, and Taminah's heart, where lay useless and barren the seeds of all love and of all hate, the possibilities of all passions and of all sacrifices, forgot its joys and its sufferings when deprived of the help of the senses. Her half-formed, savage mind, the slave of her body—as her body was the slave of another's will—forgot the faint and vague image of the ideal that had found its beginning in the physical promptings of her savage nature. She dropped back into the torpor of her former life and found consolation—even a certain kind of happiness—in the thought that now Nina and Dain were separated, probably for ever. He would forget. This thought soothed the last pangs of dying jealousy that had nothing now to feed upon, and Taminah found peace. It was like the dreary tranquillity of a desert, where there is peace only because there is no life.

And now he had returned. She had recognized his voice calling aloud in the night for Bulangi. She had crept out after her master to listen closer to the intoxicating sound. Dain was there, in a boat, talking to Bulangi. Taminah, listening with arrested breath, heard another voice. The maddening joy, that only a second before she thought herself incapable of containing within her fast-beating heart, died out, and left her shivering in the old anguish of physical pain that she had suffered once before at the sight of Dain and Nina. Nina spoke now, ordering and entreating in turns, and Bulangi was refusing, expostulating, at last consenting. He went in to take a paddle from the heap lying behind the door. Outside the murmur of two voices went on, and she caught a word here and there. She understood that he was fleeing from white men, that he was seeking a hiding-place, that he was in some danger. But she heard also words which woke the rage of jealousy that had been asleep for so many days in her bosom. Crouching low on the mud in the black darkness amongst the piles, she heard the whisper in the boat that made light of toil, of privation, of danger, of life itself, if in exchange there could be but a short moment of close embrace, a look from the eyes, the feel of light breath, the touch of soft lips. So spoke Dain as he sat in the canoe holding Nina's hands while waiting for Bulangi's return; and Taminah, supporting herself by the slimy pile, felt as if a heavy weight was crushing her down, down into the black oily water at her feet. She wanted to cry out; to rush at them and tear their vague shadows apart; to throw Nina into the smooth water, cling to her close, hold her to the bottom where that man could not find her. She could not cry, she could not move. Then footsteps were heard on the bamboo platform above her head; she saw Bulangi get into his smallest canoe and take the lead, the other boat following, paddled by Dain and Nina. With a slight splash of the paddles dipped stealthily into the water, their indistinct forms passed before her aching eyes and vanished in the darkness of the creek.

She remained there in the cold and wet, powerless to

move, breathing painfully under the crushing weight that the mysterious hand of Fate had laid so suddenly upon her slender shoulders, and shivering, she felt within a burning fire, that seemed to feed upon her very life. When the breaking day had spread a pale golden ribbon over the black outline of the forests, she took up her tray and departed towards the settlement, going about her task purely from the force of habit. As she approached Sambir she could see the excitement and she heard with momentary surprise of the finding of Dain's body. It was not true, of course. She knew it well. She regretted that he was not dead. She should have liked Dain to be dead, so as to be parted from that woman—from all women. She felt a strong desire to see Nina, but without any clear object. She hated her, and feared her, and she felt an irresistible impulse pushing her towards Almayer's house to see the white woman's face, to look close at those eyes, to hear again that voice, for the sound of which Dain was ready to risk his liberty, his life even. She had seen her many times; she had heard her voice daily for many months past. What was there in her? What was there in that being to make a man speak as Dain had spoken, to make him blind to all other faces, deaf to all other voices?

She left the crowd by the riverside, and wandered aimlessly among the empty houses, resisting the impulse that pushed her towards Almayer's campong to seek there in Nina's eyes the secret of her own misery. The sun mounting higher, shortened the shadows and poured down upon her a flood of light and of stifling heat as she passed on from shadow to light, from light to shadow amongst the houses, the bushes, the tall trees, in her unconscious flight from the pain in her own heart. In the extremity of her distress she could find no words to pray for relief, she knew of no heaven to send her prayer to, and she wandered on with tired feet in the dumb surprise and terror at the injustice of the suffering inflicted upon her without cause and without redress.

The short talk with Reshid, the proposal of Abdulla steadied her a little and turned her thoughts into another channel. Dain was in some danger. He was hiding from white men. So much she had overheard last night. They all thought him dead. She knew he was alive, and she knew of his hiding-place. What did the Arabs want to know about the white men? The white men want with Dain? Did they wish to kill him? She could tell them all—no, she would say nothing, and in the night she would go to him and sell him his life for a word, for a smile, for a gesture even, and be his slave in far-off countries, away from Nina. But there were dangers. The one-eyed Babalatchi who knew everything; the white man's wife!—she was a witch. Perhaps they would tell. And then there was Nina. She must hurry on and see.

In her impatience she left the path and ran towards Almayer's dwelling through the undergrowth between the palm trees. She came out at the back of the house, where a narrow ditch, full of stagnant water that overflowed from the river, separated Almayer's campong from the rest of the settlement. The thick bushes growing on the bank were hiding from her sight the large courtyard with its cooking shed. Above them rose several thin columns of smoke, and from behind the sound of strange voices informed Taminah that the Men of the Sea belonging to the warship had already landed and were camped between the ditch and the house. To the left one of Almayer's slave-girls came down to the ditch and bent over the shiny water, washing a kettle. To the right the tops of the banana plantation, visible above the bushes, swayed and shook under the touch of invisible hands gathering the fruit. On the calm water several canoes moored to a heavy stake were crowded together, nearly bridging the ditch just at the place where Taminah stood. The voices in the courtyard rose at times into an outburst of calls, replies, and laughter, and then died away into a silence that soon was broken again by a fresh clamour. Now and again the thin blue smoke rushed out thicker and blacker, and drove in odorous masses over the creek, wrapping her for a moment in a suffocating veil; then, as the fresh wood caught well alight, the smoke vanished in the bright sunlight, and only the scent of aromatic wood drifted afar, to leeward* of the crackling fires.

Taminah rested her tray on a stump of a tree, and remained standing with her eyes turned towards Almayer's house, whose roof and part of a whitewashed wall were visible over the bushes. The slave-girl finished her work, and after looking for a while curiously at Taminah, pushed her way through the dense thicket back to the courtyard. Round Taminah there was now a complete solitude. She threw herself down on the ground, and hid her face in her hands. Now when so close she had no courage to see Nina. At every burst of louder voices from the courtyard she shivered in the fear of hearing Nina's voice. She came to the resolution of waiting where she was till dark, and then going straight to Dain's hiding-place. From where she was she could watch the movements of white men, of Nina, of all Dain's friends, and of all his enemies. Both were hateful alike to her, for both would take him away beyond her reach. She hid herself in the long grass to wait anxiously for the sunset that seemed so slow to come.

On the other side of the ditch, behind the bush, by

the clear fires, the seamen of the frigate had encamped on the hospitable invitation of Almayer. Almayer, roused out of his apathy by the prayers and importunity of Nina, had managed to get down in time to the jetty so as to receive the officers at their landing. The lieutenant in command accepted his invitation to his house with the remark that in any case their business was with Almayer—and perhaps not very pleasant, he added. Almayer hardly heard him. He shook hands with them absently and led the way towards the house. He was scarcely conscious of the polite words of welcome he greeted the strangers with, and afterwards repeated several times over again in his efforts to appear at ease. The agitation of their host did not escape the officer's eyes, and the chief confided to his subordinate, in a low voice, his doubts as to Almayer's sobriety. The young sub-lieutenant laughed and expressed in a whisper the hope that the white man was not intoxicated enough to neglect the offer of some refreshments. "He does not seem very dangerous," he added, as they followed Almayer up the steps of the verandah.

"No, he seems more of a fool than a knave; I have heard of him," returned the senior.

They sat around the table. Almayer with shaking hands made gin cocktails, offered them all round, and drank himself, with every gulp feeling stronger, steadier, and better able to face all the difficulties of his position. Ignorant of the fate of the brig he did not suspect the real object of the officers' visit. He had a general notion that something must have leaked out about the gunpowder trade, but apprehended nothing beyond some temporary inconvenience. After emptying his glass he began to chat easily, lying back in his chair with one of his legs thrown negligently over the arm. The lieutenant astride on his chair, a glowing cheroot in the corner of his mouth, listened with a sly smile from behind the thick volumes of smoke that escaped from his compressed lips. The young sub-lieutenant, leaning with both elbows on the table, his head between his hands, looked on sleepily in the torpor induced by fatigue and the gin. Almayer talked on—

"It is a great pleasure to see white faces here. I have lived here many years in great solitude. The Malays, you understand, are not company for a white man; moreover they are not friendly; they do not understand our ways. Great rascals they are. I believe I am the only white man on the east coast that is a settled resident. We get visitors from Macassar or Singapore sometimes—traders, agents, or explorers, but they are rare. There was a scientific explorer* here a year or more ago. He lived in my house: drank from morning to night. He lived joyously for a few months, and when the liquor he brought with him was gone he returned to Batavia with a report on the mineral wealth of the interior. Ha, ha, ha! Good, is it not?"

He ceased abruptly and looked at his guests with a meaningless stare. While they laughed he was reciting to himself the old story: "Dain dead, all my plans destroyed. This is the end of all hope and of all things." His heart sank within him. He felt a kind of deadly sickness.

"Very good. Capital!" exclaimed both officers.

Almayer came out of his despondency with another burst of talk.

"Eh! what about the dinner? You have got a cook with you. That's all right. There is a cooking shed in the other courtyard. I can give you a goose. Look at my geese*—the only geese on the east coast—perhaps on the whole island. Is that your cook? Very good. Here, Ali, show this Chinaman the cooking place and tell Mem Almayer to let him have room there. My wife, gentlemen, does not come out; my daughter may. Meantime have some more drink. It is a hot day."

The lieutenant took the cigar out of his mouth, looked at the ash critically, shook it off and turned towards Almayer.

"We have a rather unpleasant business with you," he said.

"I am sorry," returned Almayer. "It can be nothing very serious, surely."

"If you think an attempt to blow up forty men at least, not a serious matter you will not find many people of your opinion," retorted the officer sharply.

"Blow up! What? I know nothing about it," exclaimed Almayer. "Who did that, or tried to do it?"

"A man with whom you had some dealings," answered the lieutenant. "He passed here under the name of Dain Maroola. You sold him the gunpowder he had in that brig we captured."

"How did you hear about the brig?" asked Almayer. "I know nothing about the powder he may have had."

"An Arab trader of this place has sent the information about your goings on here to Batavia, a couple of months ago," said the officer. "We were waiting for the brig outside, but he slipped past us at the mouth of the river, and we had to chase the fellow to the southward. When he sighted us he ran inside the reefs and put the brig ashore. The crew escaped in boats before we could take possession. As our boats neared the craft it blew up with a tremendous explosion; one of the boats being too near got swamped. Two men drowned—that is the result of your speculation, Mr. Almayer. Now we want this Dain. We have good grounds to suppose he is hiding in Sambir. Do you know where he is? You had better put yourself right with the authorities as much as possible by being perfectly frank with me. Where is this Dain?"

Almayer got up and walked towards the balustrade of the verandah. He seemed not to be thinking of the officer's question. He looked at the body laying straight and rigid under its white cover on which the sun, declining amongst the clouds to the westward, threw a pale tinge of red. The lieutenant waited for the answer, taking quick pulls at his half-extinguished cigar. Behind them Ali moved noiselessly laying the table, ranging solemnly the ill-assorted and shabby crockery, the tin spoons, the forks with broken prongs, and the knives with saw-like blades and loose handles. He had almost forgotten how to prepare the table for white men. He felt aggrieved; Mem Nina would not help him. He stepped back to look at his work admiringly, feeling very proud. This must be right; and if the master afterwards is angry and swears, then so much the worse for Mem Nina. Why did she not help? He left the verandah to fetch the dinner.

"Well, Mr. Almayer, will you answer my question as frankly as it is put to you?" asked the lieutenant, after a long silence.

Almayer turned round and looked at his interlocutor steadily. "If you catch this Dain what will you do with him?" he asked.

The officer's face flushed. "This is not an answer," he said, annoyed.

"And what will you do with me?" went on Almayer, not heeding the interruption.

"Are you inclined to bargain?" growled the other. "It would be bad policy, I assure you. At present I have no orders about your person, but we expected your assistance in catching this Malay."

"Ah!" interrupted Almayer, "just so: you can do

nothing without me, and I, knowing the man well, am to help you in finding him."

"This is exactly what we expect," assented the officer. "You have broken the law, Mr. Almayer, and you ought to make amends."

"And save myself?"

"Well, in a sense yes. Your head is not in any danger," said the lieutenant, with a short laugh.

"Very well," said Almayer, with decision, "I shall deliver the man up to you."

Both officers rose to their feet quickly, and looked for their side-arms which they had unbuckled. Almayer laughed harshly.

"Steady, gentlemen!" he exclaimed. "In my own time and in my own way. After dinner, gentlemen, you shall have him."

"This is preposterous," urged the lieutenant. "Mr. Almayer, this is no joking matter. The man is a criminal. He deserves to hang. While we dine he may escape; the rumour of our arrival——"

Almayer walked towards the table. "I give you my word of honour, gentlemen, that he shall not escape; I have him safe enough."

"The arrest should be effected before dark," remarked the young sub.

"I shall hold you responsible for any failure. We are ready, but can do nothing just now without you," added the senior, with evident annoyance.

Almayer made a gesture of assent. "On my word of honour," he repeated vaguely. "And now let us dine," he added briskly.

Nina came through the doorway and stood for a moment holding the curtain aside for Ali and the old Malay woman bearing the dishes; then she moved towards the three men by the table.

"Allow me," said Almayer, pompously. "This is my daughter. Nina, these gentlemen, officers of the frigate outside, have done me the honour to accept my hospitality."

Nina answered the low bows of the two officers by a slow inclination of the head and took her place at the table opposite her father. All sat down. The coxwain* of the steam launch came up carrying some bottles of wine.

"You will allow me to have this put upon the table?" said the lieutenant to Almayer.

"What! Wine! You are very kind. Certainly. I have none myself. Times are very hard."

The last words of his reply were spoken by Almayer in a faltering voice. The thought that Dain was dead recurred to him vividly again, and he felt as if an invisible hand was gripping his throat. He reached for the gin bottle while they were uncorking the wine and swallowed a big gulp. The lieutenant, who was speaking to Nina, gave him a quick glance. The young sub began to recover from the astonishment and confusion caused by Nina's unexpected appearance and great beauty. "She was very beautiful and imposing," he reflected, "but after all a half-caste girl." This thought caused him to pluck up heart and look at Nina sideways. Nina, with composed face, was answering in a low, even voice the elder officer's polite questions as to the country and her mode of life. Almayer pushed his plate away and drank his guest's wine in gloomy silence.

CHAPTER NINE

"CAN I believe what you tell me? It is like a tale for men that listen only half awake by the camp fire, and it seems to have run off a woman's tongue."

"Who is there here for me to deceive, O Rajah?" answered Babalatchi. "Without you I am nothing. All I have told you I believe to be true. I have been safe for many years in the hollow of your hand. This is no time to harbour suspicions. The danger is very great. We should advise and act at once, before the sun sets."

"Right. Right," muttered Lakamba, pensively.

They had been sitting for the last hour together in the audience chamber of the Rajah's house, for Babalatchi, as soon as he had witnessed the landing of the Dutch officers, had crossed the river to report to his master the events of the morning, and to confer with him upon the line of conduct to pursue in the face of altered circumstances. They were both puzzled and frightened by the unexpected turn the events had taken. The Rajah, sitting crosslegged on his chair, looked fixedly at the floor; Babalatchi was squatting close by in an attitude of deep dejection.

"And where did you say he is hiding now?" asked Lakamba, breaking at last the silence full of gloomy forebodings in which they both had been lost for a long while.

"In Bulangi's clearing—the furthest one, away from the house. They went there that very night. The white man's daughter took him there. She told me so herself, speaking to me openly, for she is half white and has no decency. She said she was waiting for him while he was here; then, after a long time, he came out of the darkness and fell at her feet exhausted. He lay like one dead, but she brought him back to life in her arms, and made him breathe again with her own breath. That is what she said, speaking to my face, as I am speaking now to you, Rajah. She is like a white woman and knows no shame."

He paused, deeply shocked. Lakamba nodded his head. "Well, and then?" he asked.

"They called the old woman," went on Babalatchi, "and he told them all—about the brig, and how he tried to kill many men. He knew the Orang Blanda were very near, although he had said nothing to us about that; he knew his great danger. He thought he had killed many, but there were only two dead, as I have heard from the men of the sea that came in the warship's boats."

"And the other man, he that was found in the river?" interrupted Lakamba.

"That was one of his boatmen. When his canoe was overturned by the logs those two swam together, but the other man must have been hurt. Dain swam, holding him up. He left him in the bushes when he went up to the house. When they all came down his heart had ceased to beat; then the old woman spoke; Dain thought it was good. He took off his anklet and broke it, twisting it round the man's foot. His ring he put on that slave's hand. He took off his sarong and clothed that thing that wanted no clothes, the two women holding it up meanwhile, their intent being to deceive all eyes and to mislead the minds in the settlement, so that they could swear to the thing that was not, and that there could be no treachery when the white men came. Then Dain and the white woman departed to call up Bulangi and find a hiding-place. The old woman remained by the body."

"Hai!" exclaimed Lakamba. "She has wisdom."

"Yes, she has a Devil of her own to whisper counsel in her ear," assented Babalatchi. "She dragged the body with great toil to the point where many logs were stranded. All these things were done in the darkness after the storm had passed away. Then she waited. At the first sign of daylight she battered the face of the dead with a heavy stone, and she pushed him amongst the logs. She remained near, watching. At sunrise Mahmat Banjer came and found him. They all believed; I myself was deceived, but not for long. The white man believed, and, grieving, fled to his house. When we were alone, I, having doubts, spoke to the woman, and she, fearing my anger and your might, told me all, asking for help in saving Dain."

"He must not fall into the hands of the Orang Blanda," said Lakamba; "but let him die, if the thing can be done quietly."

"It cannot, Tuan! Remember there is that woman who, being half white, is ungovernable, and would raise a great outcry. Also the officers are here. They are angry enough already. Dain must escape; he must go. We must help him now for our own safety."

"Are the officers very angry?" inquired Lakamba, with interest.

"They are. The principal chief used strong words when speaking to me—to me when I salaamed in your name. I do not think," added Babalatchi, after a short pause and looking very worried—"I do not think I saw a white chief so angry before. He said we were careless or even worse. He told me he would speak to the Rajah, and that I was of no account."

"Speak to the Rajah!" repeated Lakamba, thoughtfully. "Listen, Babalatchi: I am sick, and shall withdraw; you cross over and tell the white men."

"Yes," said Babalatchi, "I am going over at once; and as to Dain?"

"You get him away as you can best. This is a great trouble in my heart," sighed Lakamba.

Babalatchi got up, and, going close to his master, spoke earnestly.

"There is one of our praus at the southern mouth of the river. The Dutch warship is to the northward watching the main entrance.* I shall send Dain off to-night in a canoe, by the hidden channels, on board the prau. His father is a great prince, and shall hear of our generosity. Let the prau take him to Ampanam.* Your glory shall be great, and your reward in powerful friendship. Almayer will no doubt deliver the dead body as Dain's to the officers, and the foolish white men shall say, 'This is very good; let there be peace.' And the trouble shall be removed from your heart, Rajah."

"True! true!" said Lakamba.

"And, this being accomplished by me who am your slave, you shall reward with a generous hand. That I know! The white man is grieving for the lost treasure, in the manner of white men who thirst after dollars. Now, when all other things are in order, we shall perhaps obtain the treasure from the white man. Dain must escape, and Almayer must live."

"Now go, Babalatchi, go!" said Lakamba, getting off his chair. "I am very sick, and want medicine. Tell the white chief so."

But Babalatchi was not to be got rid of in this summary manner. He knew that his master, after the manner of the great, liked to shift the burden of toil and danger on to his servants' shoulders, but in the difficult straits in which they were now the Rajah must play his part. He may be very sick for the white men, for all the world if he liked, as long as he would take upon himself the execution of part at least of Babalatchi's carefully thought-of plan. Babalatchi wanted a big canoe manned by twelve men to be sent out after dark towards Bulangi's clearing. Dain may have to be overpowered. A man in love cannot be expected to see clearly the path of safety if it leads him away from the object of his affections, argued Babalatchi, and in that case they would have to use force in order to make him go. Would the Rajah see that trusty men manned the canoe? The thing must be done secretly. Perhaps the Rajah would come himself, so as to bring all the weight of his authority to bear upon Dain if he should prove obstinate and refuse to leave his hiding-place. The Rajah would not commit himself to a definite promise, and anxiously pressed Babalatchi to go, being afraid of the white men paying him an unexpected visit. The aged statesman reluctantly took his leave and went into the courtyard.

Before going down to his boat Babalatchi stopped for a while in the big open space where the thick-leaved trees put black patches of shadow which seemed to float on a flood of smooth, intense light that rolled up to the houses and down to the stockade and over the river, where it broke and sparkled in thousands of glittering wavelets, like a band woven of azure and gold edged with the brilliant green of the forests guarding both banks of the Pantai. In the perfect calm before the coming of the afternoon breeze the irregularly jagged line of tree-tops stood unchanging, as if traced by an unsteady hand on the clear blue of the hot sky. In the space sheltered by the high palisades there lingered the smell of decaying blossoms from the surrounding forest, a taint of drying fish; with now and then a whiff of acrid smoke from the cooking fires when it eddied down from under the leafy boughs and clung lazily about the burnt-up grass.

As Babalatchi looked up at the flagstaff overtopping a group of low trees in the middle of the courtyard the tricolour flag of the Netherlands stirred slightly for the first time since it had been hoisted that morning on the arrival of the man-of-war boats. With a faint rustle of trees the breeze came down in light puffs, playing capriciously for a time with this emblem of Lakamba's power, that was also the mark of his servitude; then the breeze freshened in a sharp gust of wind, and the flag flew out straight and steady above the trees. A dark shadow ran along the river, rolling over and covering up the sparkle of declining sunlight. A big white cloud sailed slowly across the darkening sky, and hung to the westward as if waiting for the sun to join it there. Men and things shook off the torpor of the hot afternoon and stirred into life under the first breath of the sea breeze.

Babalatchi hurried down to the water-gate; yet before he passed through it he paused to look round the courtyard, with its light and shade, with its cheery fires, with the groups of Lakamba's soldiers and retainers scattered about. His own house stood amongst the other buildings in that enclosure, and the statesman of Sambir asked himself with a sinking heart when and how would it be given him to return to that house. He had to deal with a man more dangerous than any wild beast of his experience: a proud man, a man wilful after the manner of princes, a man in love. And he was going forth to speak to that man words of cold and worldly wisdom. Could anything be more appalling? What if that man should take umbrage at some fancied slight to his honour or disregard of his affections and suddenly "amok"? The wise adviser would be the first victim, no doubt, and death would be his reward. And underlying the horror of this situation there was the danger of those meddlesome fools, the white men. A vision of comfortless exile in far-off Madura* rose up before Babalatchi. Wouldn't that be worse than death itself? And there was that half-white woman with threatening eyes. How could he tell what an incomprehensible creature of that sort would or would not do? She knew so much that she made the killing of Dain an impossibility. That much was certain. And yet the sharp, rough-edged kriss is a good and discreet friend, thought Babalatchi, as he examined his own lovingly, and put it back in the sheath, with a sigh of regret, before unfastening his canoe. As he cast off the painter, pushed out into the stream, and took up his paddle, he realized vividly how unsatisfactory it was to have women mixed up in state affairs. Young women, of course. For Mrs. Almayer's mature wisdom, and for the easy aptitude in intrigue that comes with years to the feminine mind, he felt the most sincere respect.

He paddled leisurely, letting the canoe drift down as he crossed towards the point. The sun was high yet, and nothing pressed.* His work would commence only with the coming of darkness. Avoiding the Lingard jetty, he rounded the point, and paddled up the creek at the back of Almayer's house. There were many canoes lying there, their noses all drawn together, fastened all to the same stake. Babalatchi pushed his little craft in amongst them and stepped on shore. On the other side of the ditch something moved in the grass.

"Who's that hiding?" hailed Babalatchi. "Come out and speak to me."

Nobody answered. Babalatchi crossed over, passing from boat to boat, and poked his staff viciously in the suspicious place. Taminah jumped up with a cry.

"What are you doing here?" he asked, surprised. "I have nearly stepped on your tray. Am I a Dyak that you should hide at my sight?"

"I was weary, and—I slept," whispered Taminah, confusedly.

"You slept! You have not sold anything to-day, and you will be beaten when you return home," said Babalatchi.

Taminah stood before him abashed and silent. Babalatchi looked her over carefully with great satisfaction. Decidedly he would offer fifty dollars more to that thief Bulangi. The girl pleased him.

"Now you go home. It is late," he said sharply. "Tell Bulangi that I shall be near his house before the night is half over, and that I want him to make all things ready for a long journey. You understand? A long journey to the southward. Tell him that before sunset, and do not forget my words."

Taminah made a gesture of assent, and watched Babalatchi recross the ditch and disappear through the bushes bordering Almayer's compound. She moved a little further off the creek and sank in the grass again, lying down on her face, shivering in dry-eyed misery.

Babalatchi walked straight towards the cooking-shed looking for Mrs. Almayer. The courtyard was in a great uproar. A strange Chinaman had possession of the kitchen fire and was noisily demanding another saucepan. He hurled objurgations, in the Canton* dialect and bad Malay, against the group of slave-girls standing a little way off, half frightened, half amused, at his violence. From the camping fires round which the seamen of the frigate were sitting came words of encouragement, mingled with laughter and jeering. In the midst of this noise and confusion Babalatchi met Ali, an empty dish in his hand.

"Where are the white men?" asked Babalatchi.

"They are eating in the front verandah," answered Ali. "Do not stop me, Tuan. I am giving the white men their food and am busy."

"Where's Mem Almayer?"

"Inside the passage.* She is listening to the talk."

Ali grinned and passed on; Babalatchi ascended the plankway to the rear verandah, and beckoning out Mrs. Almayer, engaged her in earnest conversation. Through the long passage,* closed at the further end by the red curtain, they could hear from time to time Almayer's voice mingling in conversation with an abrupt loudness that made Mrs. Almayer look significantly at Babalatchi.

"Listen," she said. "He has drunk much."

"He has," whispered Babalatchi. "He will sleep heavily to-night."

Mrs. Almayer looked doubtful.

"Sometimes the devil of strong gin makes him keep awake, and he walks up and down the verandah all night, cursing; then we stand afar off," explained Mrs. Almayer, with the fuller knowledge born of twenty odd years of married life.

"But then he does not hear, nor understand, and his hand, of course, has no strength. We do not want him to hear to-night."

"No," assented Mrs. Almayer, energetically, but in a cautiously subdued voice. "If he hears he will kill."

Babalatchi looked incredulous.

"Hai Tuan, you may believe me. Have I not lived many years with that man? Have I not seen death in that man's eyes more than once when I was younger and he guessed at many things.* Had he been a man of my own people I would not have seen such a look twice; but he——"

With a contemptuous gesture she seemed to fling unutterable scorn on Almayer's weak-minded aversion to sudden bloodshed.

"If he has the wish but not the strength, then what do we fear?" asked Babalatchi, after a short silence during which they both listened to Almayer's loud talk till it subsided into the murmur of general conversation. "What do we fear?" repeated Babalatchi again.

"To keep the daughter whom he loves he would strike into your heart and mine without hesitation," said Mrs. Almayer. "When the girl is gone he will be like the devil unchained. Then you and I had better beware."

"I am an old man and fear not death," answered Babalatchi, with a mendacious assumption of indifference. "But what will you do?"

"I am an old woman, and wish to live," retorted Mrs. Almayer. "She is my daughter also. I shall seek safety at the feet of our Rajah, speaking in the name of the past when we both were young, and he——"

Babalatchi raised his hand.

"Enough. You shall be protected," he said soothingly.

Again the sound of Almayer's voice was heard, and again interrupting their talk, they listened to the confused but loud utterance coming in bursts of unequal strength, with unexpected pauses and noisy repetitions that made some words and sentences fall clear and distinct on their ears out of the meaningless jumble of excited shoutings emphasized by the thumping of Almayer's fist upon the table. On the short intervals of silence, the high complaining note of tumblers, standing close together and vibrating to the shock, lingered, growing fainter, till it leapt up again into tumultuous ringing, when a new idea started a new rush of words and brought down the heavy hand again. At last the quarrelsome shouting ceased, and the thin plaint of disturbed glass died away into reluctant quietude.

Babalatchi and Mrs. Almayer had listened curiously, their bodies bent and their ears turned towards the passage. At every louder shout they nodded at each other with a ridiculous affectation of scandalized propriety, and they remained in the same attitude for some time after the noise had ceased.

"This is the devil of gin," whispered Mrs. Almayer. "Yes; he talks like that sometimes when there is nobody to hear him."

"What does he say?" inquired Babalatchi, eagerly. "You ought to understand."

"I have forgotten their talk. A little I understood. He spoke without any respect of the white ruler in Batavia, and of protection, and said he had been wronged; he said that several times. More I did not understand. Listen! Again he speaks!"

"Tse! tse! tse!" clicked Babalatchi, trying to appear shocked, but with a joyous twinkle of his solitary eye. "There will be great trouble between those white men. I will go round now and see. You tell your daughter that there is a sudden and a long journey before her, with much glory and splendour at the end. And tell her that Dain must go, or he must die, and that he will not go alone."

"No, he will not go alone," slowly repeated Mrs. Almayer, with a thoughtful air, as she crept into the passage after seeing Babalatchi disappear round the corner of the house.

The statesman of Sambir, under the impulse of vivid curiosity, made his way quickly to the front of the house, but once there he moved slowly and cautiously as he crept step by step up the stairs of the verandah. On the highest step he sat down quietly, his feet on the steps below, ready for flight should his presence prove unwelcome. He felt pretty safe so. The table stood nearly endways to him, and he saw Almayer's back; at Nina he looked full face, and had a side view of both officers; but of the four persons sitting at the table only Nina and the younger officer noticed his noiseless arrival. The momentary dropping of Nina's eyelids acknowledged Babalatchi's presence; she then spoke at once to the young sub, who turned towards her with attentive alacrity, but her gaze was fastened steadily on her father's face while Almayer was speaking uproariously.

". . . disloyalty and unscrupulousness! What have you ever done to make me loyal? You have no grip on this country. I had to take care of myself, and when I asked for protection I was met with threats and contempt, and had Arab slander* thrown in my face. I! a white man!"

"Don't be violent, Almayer," remonstrated the lieutenant; "I have heard all this already."

"Then why do you talk to me about scruples? I wanted money, and I gave powder in exchange. How could I know that some of your wretched men were going to be blown up? Scruples! Pah!"

He groped unsteadily amongst the bottles, trying one after another, grumbling to himself the while. "No more wine," he muttered discontentedly.

"You have had enough, Almayer," said the lieutenant, as he lighted a cigar. "Is it not time to deliver to us your prisoner? I take it you have that Dain Maroola stowed away safely somewhere. Still we had better get that business over, and then we shall have more drink. Come! don't look at me like this."

Almayer was staring with stony eyes, his trembling fingers fumbling about his throat.

"Gold," he said with difficulty. "Hem! A hand on the windpipe, you know. Sure you will excuse. I wanted to say—a little gold for a little powder. What's that?"

"I know, I know," said the lieutenant soothingly.

"No! You don't know. Not one of you knows!" shouted Almayer. "The government is a fool, I tell you. Heaps of gold. I am the man that knows; I and another one. But he won't speak. He is——"

He checked himself with a feeble smile, and, making an unsuccessful attempt to pat the officer on the shoulder, knocked over a couple of empty bottles.

"Personally you are a fine fellow," he said very distinctly, in a patronizing manner. His head nodded drowsily as he sat muttering to himself.

The two officers looked at each other helplessly.

"This won't do," said the lieutenant, addressing his junior. "Have the men mustered in the compound here. I must get some sense out of him. Hi! Almayer! Wake up, man. Redeem your word. You gave your word. You gave your word of honour, you know."

Almayer shook off the officer's hand with impatience, but his ill-humour vanished at once, and he looked up, putting his forefinger to the side of his nose.

"You are very young; there is time for all things," he said, with an air of great sagacity.

The lieutenant turned towards Nina, who, leaning back in her chair, watched her father steadily.

"Really I am very much distressed by all this for your sake," he exclaimed. "I do not know," he went on, speaking with some embarrassment, "whether I have any right to ask you anything, unless, perhaps, to withdraw from this painful scene, but I feel that I must—for your father's good—suggest that you should —I mean if you have any influence over him you ought to exert it now to make him keep the promise he gave me before he—before he got into this state."

He observed with discouragement that she seemed not to take any notice of what he said, sitting still with half-closed eyes.

"I trust——" he began again.

"What is the promise you speak of?" abruptly asked Nina, leaving her seat and moving towards her father.

"Nothing that is not just and proper. He promised to deliver to us a man who in time of profound peace took the lives of innocent men to escape the punishment he deserved for breaking the law. He planned his mischief on a large scale. It is not his fault if it failed, partially. Of course you have heard of Dain Maroola. Your father secured him, I understand. We know he escaped up this river. Perhaps you——"

"And he killed white men!" interrupted Nina.

"I regret to say they were white. Yes, two white men lost their lives through that scoundrel's freak."*

"Two only!" exclaimed Nina.

The officer looked at her in amazement.

"Why! why! You——" he stammered, confused.

"There might have been more," interrupted Nina. "And when you get this—this scoundrel, will you go?"

The lieutenant, still speechless, bowed his assent.

"Then I would get him for you if I had to seek him in a burning fire," she burst out with intense energy. "I hate the sight of your white faces. I hate the sound of your gentle voices. That is the way you speak to women, dropping sweet words before any pretty face.

I have heard your voices before. I hoped to live here without seeing any other white face but this," she added in a gentler tone, touching lightly her father's cheek.

Almayer ceased his mumbling and opened his eyes. He caught hold of his daughter's hand and pressed it to his face, while Nina with the other hand smoothed his rumpled grey hair looking defiantly over her father's head at the officer, who had now regained his composure and returned her look with a cool, steady stare. Below, in front of the verandah, they could hear the tramp of seamen mustering there according to orders. The sub-lieutenant came up the steps, while Babalatchi stood up uneasily and, with finger on lip, tried to catch Nina's eye.

"You are a good girl," whispered Almayer, absently, dropping his daughter's hand.

"Father! father!" she cried, bending over him with passionate entreaty. "See those two men looking at us. Send them away. I cannot bear it any more. Send them away. Do what they want and let them go."

She caught sight of Babalatchi and ceased speaking suddenly, but her foot tapped the floor with rapid beats in a paroxysm of nervous restlessness. The two officers stood close together looking on curiously.

"What has happened? What is the matter?" whispered the younger man.

"Don't know," answered the other, under his breath. "One is furious, and the other is drunk. Not so drunk, either. Queer, this. Look!"

Almayer had risen, holding on to his daughter's arm. He hesitated a moment, then he let go his hold and lurched half-way across the verandah. There he pulled himself together, and stood very straight, breathing hard and glaring round angrily.

"Are the men ready?" asked the lieutenant.

"All ready, sir."

"Now, Mr. Almayer, lead the way," said the lieutenant.

Almayer rested his eyes on him as if he saw him for the first time.

"Two men," he said thickly. The effort of speaking seemed to interfere with his equilibrium. He took a quick step to save himself from a fall, and remained swaying backwards and forwards. "Two men," he began again, speaking with difficulty. "Two white men—men in uniform—honourable men. I want to say—men of honour. Are you?"

"Come! None of that," said the officer impatiently. "Let us have that friend of yours."

"What do you think I am?" asked Almayer, fiercely.

"You are drunk, but not so drunk as not to know what you are doing. Enough of this tomfoolery," said the officer sternly, "or I will have you put under arrest in your own house."

"Arrest!" laughed Almayer, discordantly. "Ha! ha! ha! Arrest! Why, I have been trying to get out of this infernal place for twenty years, and I can't. You hear, man! I can't, and never shall! Never!"

He ended his words with a sob, and walked unsteadily down the stairs. When in the courtyard the lieutenant approached him, and took him by the arm. The sub-lieutenant and Babalatchi followed close.

"That's better, Almayer," said the officer encouragingly. "Where are you going to? There are only planks there. Here," he went on, shaking him slightly, "do we want the boats?"

"No," answered Almayer, viciously. "You want a grave."

"What? Wild again! Try to talk sense."

"Grave!" roared Almayer, struggling to get himself

free. "A hole in the ground. Don't you understand? You must be drunk. Let me go! Let go, I tell you!"

He tore away from the officer's grasp, and reeled towards the planks where the body lay under its white cover; then he turned round quickly, and faced the semicircle of interested faces. The sun was sinking rapidly, throwing long shadows of house and trees over the courtyard, but the light lingered yet on the river, where the logs went drifting past in midstream, looking very distinct and black in the pale red glow. The trunks of the trees in the forest on the east bank were lost in gloom while their highest branches swayed gently in the departing sunlight. The air felt heavy and cold in the breeze, expiring in slight puffs that came over the water.

Almayer shivered as he made an effort to speak, and again with an uncertain gesture he seemed to free his throat from the grip of an invisible hand. His bloodshot eyes wandered aimlessly from face to face.

"There!" he said at last. "Are you all there? He is a dangerous man."

He dragged at the cover with hasty violence, and the body rolled stiffly off the planks and fell at his feet in rigid helplessness.

"Cold, perfectly cold," said Almayer, looking round with a mirthless smile. "Sorry can do no better. And you can't hang him, either. As you observe, gentlemen," he added gravely, "there is no head, and hardly any neck."

The last ray of light was snatched away from the tree-tops, the river grew suddenly dark, and in the great stillness the murmur of the flowing water seemed to fill the vast expanse of grey shadow that descended upon the land.

"This is Dain," went on Almayer to the silent group

that surrounded him. "And I have kept my word. First one hope, then another, and this is my last. Nothing is left now. You think there is one dead man here? Mistake, I 'sure you. I am much more dead. Why don't you hang me?" he suggested suddenly, in a friendly tone, addressing the lieutenant. "I assure, assure you it would be a mat—matter of form altog—altogether."

These last words he muttered to himself, and walked zigzagging towards his house. "Get out!" he thundered at Ali, who was approaching timidly with offers of assistance. From afar, scared groups of men and women watched his devious progress. He dragged himself up the stairs by the banister, and managed to reach a chair into which he fell heavily. He sat for awhile panting with exertion and anger, and looking round vaguely for Nina; then making a threatening gesture towards the compound, where he had heard Babalatchi's voice, he overturned the table with his foot in a great crash of smashed crockery. He muttered yet menacingly to himself, then his head fell on his breast, his eyes closed, and with a deep sigh he fell asleep.

That night—for the first time in its history—the peaceful and flourishing settlement of Sambir saw the lights shining about "Almayer's Folly." These were the lanterns of the boats hung up by the seamen under the verandah where the two officers were holding a court of inquiry into the truth of the story related to them by Babalatchi. Babalatchi had regained all his importance. He was eloquent and persuasive, calling Heaven and Earth to witness the truth of his statements. There were also other witnesses. Mahmat Banjer and a good many others underwent a close examination that dragged its weary length far into the evening. A messenger was sent for Abdulla, who excused himself from coming on the score of his venerable age, but sent Reshid. Mahmat had to produce the bangle, and saw with rage and mortification the lieutenant put it in his pocket as one of the proofs of Dain's death, to be sent in with the official report of the mission. Babalatchi's ring was also impounded for the same purpose, but the experienced statesman was resigned to that loss from the very beginning. He did not mind as long as he was sure that the white men believed. He put that question to himself earnestly as he left, one of the last, when the proceedings came to a close. He was not certain. Still, if they believed only for a night, he would put Dain beyond their reach and feel safe himself. He walked away fast, looking from time to time over his shoulder in the fear of being followed, but he saw and heard nothing.

"Ten o'clock," said the lieutenant, looking at his watch and yawning. "I shall hear some of the captain's complimentary remarks when we get back. Miserable business, this."

"Do you think all this is true?" asked the younger man.

"True! It is just possible. But if it isn't true what can we do? If we had a dozen boats we could patrol the creeks; and that wouldn't be much good. That drunken madman was right; we haven't enough hold on this coast. They do what they like. Are our hammocks slung?"

"Yes, I told the coxswain. Strange couple over there," said the sub, with a wave of his hand towards Almayer's house.

"Hem! Queer, certainly. What have you been telling her? I was attending to the father most of the time."

"I assure you I have been perfectly civil," protested the other warmly.

"All right. Don't get excited. She objects to civility, then, from what I understand. I thought you might have been tender. You know we are on service."

"Well, of course. Never forget that. Coldly civil. That's all."

They both laughed a little, and not feeling sleepy began to pace the verandah side by side. The moon rose stealthily above the trees, and suddenly changed the river into a stream of scintillating silver. The forest came out of the black void and stood sombre and pensive over the sparkling water. The breeze died away into a breathless calm.

Seamanlike, the two officers tramped measuredly up and down without exchanging a word. The loose planks rattled rhythmically under their steps with obtrusive dry sound in the perfect silence of the night. As they were wheeling round again the younger man stood attentive.

"Did you hear that?" he asked.

"No!" said the other. "Hear what?"

"I thought I heard a cry. Ever so faint. Seemed a woman's voice. In that other house. Ah! Again! Hear it?"

"No," said the lieutenant, after listening awhile. "You young fellows always hear women's voices. If you are going to dream you had better get into your hammock. Good-night."

The moon mounted higher, and the warm shadows grew smaller and crept away as if hiding before the cold and cruel light.

CHAPTER TEN

"It has set at last," said Nina to her mother pointing towards the hills behind which the sun had sunk. "Listen, mother, I am going now to Bulangi's creek, and if I should never return——"

She interrupted herself, and something like doubt dimmed for a moment the fire of suppressed exaltation that had glowed in her eyes and had illuminated the serene impassiveness of her features with a ray of eager life during all that long day of excitement—the day of joy and anxiety, of hope and terror, of vague grief and indistinct delight. While the sun shone with that dazzling light in which her love was born and grew till it possessed her whole being, she was kept firm in her unwavering resolve by the mysterious whisperings of desire which filled her heart with impatient longing for the darkness that would mean the end of danger and strife, the beginning of happiness, the fulfilling of love, the completeness of life. It had set at last! The short tropical twilight went out before she could draw the long breath of relief; and now the sudden darkness seemed to be full of menacing voices calling upon her to rush headlong into the unknown; to be true to her own impulses to give herself up to the passion she had evoked and shared. He was waiting! In the solitude of the secluded clearing, in the vast silence* of the forest he was waiting alone, a fugitive in fear of his life. Indifferent to his danger he was waiting for her. It was for her only that he had come; and now as the time approached when he should have his reward, she asked herself with dismay what meant that chilling doubt of her own will and of her own desire? With an effort she shook off the fear of the passing weakness. He should have his reward. Her woman's love and her woman's honour overcame the faltering distrust of that unknown future waiting for her in the darkness of the river.

"No, you will not return," muttered Mrs. Almayer, prophetically. "Without you he will not go, and if he remains here——" She waved her hand towards the lights of "Almayer's Folly," and the unfinished sentence died out in a threatening murmur.

The two women had met behind the house, and now were walking slowly together towards the creek where all the canoes were moored. Arrived at the fringe of bushes they stopped by a common impulse, and Mrs. Almayer, laying her hand on her daughter's arm, tried in vain to look close into the girl's averted face. When she attempted to speak, her first words were lost in a stifled sob that sounded strangely coming from that woman who, of all human passions, seemed to know only those of anger and hate.

"You are going away to be a great Ranee," she said at last, in a voice that was steady enough now, "and if you be wise you shall have much power that will endure many days, and even last into your old age. What have I been? A slave all my life, and I have cooked rice for a man who had no courage and no wisdom. Hai! I! even I, was given in gift by a chief and a warrior to a man that was neither. Hai! Hai!"

She wailed to herself softly, lamenting the lost possibilities of murder and mischief that could have fallen to her lot had she been mated with a congenial spirit. Nina bent down over Mrs. Almayer's slight form and scanned attentively, under the stars that had rushed out on the black sky and now hung breathless over that strange parting, her mother's shrivelled features, and looked close into the sunken eyes that could see into her own dark future by the light of a long and a painful experience. Again she felt herself fascinated, as of old, by her mother's exalted mood and by the oracular certainty of expression which, together with her fits of violence, had contributed not a little to the reputation for witchcraft she enjoyed in the settlement.

"I was a slave, and you shall be a queen," went on Mrs. Almayer, looking straight before her; "but remember men's strength and their weakness. Tremble before his anger, so that he may see your fear in the light of day; but in your heart you may laugh, for after sunset he is your slave."

"A slave! He! The master of life! You do not know him, mother."

Mrs. Almayer condescended to laugh contemptuously.

"You speak like a fool of a white woman," she exclaimed. "What do you know of men's anger and of men's love? Have you watched the sleep of men weary of dealing death? Have you felt about you the strong arm that could drive a kriss deep into a beating heart? Yah! you are a white woman, and ought to pray to a woman god!"*

"Why do you say this? I have listened to your words so long that I have forgotten my old life. If I was white would I stand here, ready to go? Mother, I shall return to the house and look once more at my father's face."

"No!" said Mrs. Almayer, violently. "No, he sleeps now the sleep of gin; and if you went back he might awake and see you. No, he shall never see you.

When the terrible old man took you away from me when you were little, you remember——"

"It was such a long time ago," murmured Nina.

"I remember," went on Mrs. Almayer, fiercely. "I wanted to look at your face again. He said no! I heard you cry and jumped into the river. You were his daughter then; you are my daughter now. Never shall you go back to that house; you shall never cross this courtyard again. No! no!"

Her voice rose almost to a shout. On the other side of the creek there was a rustle in the long grass. The two women heard it, and listened for a while in startled silence.

"I shall go," said Nina, in a cautious but intense whisper. "What is your hate or your revenge to me?"

She moved towards the house, Mrs. Almayer clinging to her and trying to pull her back.

"Stop, you shall not go!" she gasped.

Nina pushed away her mother impatiently and gathered up her skirts for a quick run, but Mrs. Almayer ran forward and turned round, facing her daughter with outstretched arms.

"If you move another step," she exclaimed, breathing quickly, "I shall cry out. Do you see those lights in the big house? There sit two white men, angry because they cannot have the blood of the man you love. And in those dark houses," she continued, more calmly as she pointed towards the settlement, "my voice could wake up men that would lead the Orang Blanda soldiers to him who is waiting—for you."

She could not see her daughter's face, but the white figure before her stood silent and irresolute in the darkness. Mrs. Almayer pursued her advantage.

"Give up your old life! Forget!" she said in entreating tones. "Forget that you ever looked at a white face; forget their words; forget their thoughts. They speak lies. And they think lies because they despise us that are better than they are, but not so strong. Forget their friendship and their contempt; forget their many gods. Girl, why do you want to remember the past when there is a warrior and a chief ready to give many lives—his own life—for one of your smiles?"

While she spoke she pushed gently her daughter towards the canoes, hiding her own fear, anxiety, and doubt under the flood of passionate words that left Nina no time to think and no opportunity to protest, even if she had wished it. But she did not wish it now. At the bottom of that passing desire to look again at her father's face there was no strong affection. She felt no scruples and no remorse at leaving suddenly that man whose sentiment towards herself she could not understand, she could not even see. There was only an instinctive clinging to old life, to old habits, to old faces; that fear of finality which lurks in every human breast and prevents so many heroisms and so many crimes. For years she had stood between her mother and her father, the one so strong in her weakness, the other so weak where he could have been strong. Between those two beings so dissimilar, so antagonistic, she stood with mute heart wondering and angry at the fact of her own existence. It seemed so unreasonable, so humiliating to be flung there in that settlement and to see the days rush by into the past, without a hope, a desire, or an aim that would justify the life she had to endure in ever-growing weariness. She had little belief and no sympathy for her father's dreams; but the savage ravings of her mother chanced to strike a responsive chord, deep down somewhere in her despairing heart; and she dreamed dreams of her own with the persistent absorption of a captive thinking of liberty within the walls of his prison cell. With the coming of Dain she found the road to freedom by obeying the voice of the new-born impulses, and with surprised joy she thought she could read in his eyes the answer to all the questionings of her heart. She understood now the reason and the aim of life; and in the triumphant unveiling of that mystery she threw away disdainfully her past with its sad thoughts, its bitter feelings and its faint affections, now withered and dead in contact with her fierce passion.

Mrs. Almayer unmoored Nina's own canoe and, straightening herself painfully, stood, painter in hand, looking at her daughter.

"Quick," she said; "get away before the moon rises, while the river is dark. I am afraid of Abdulla's slaves. The wretches prowl in the night often, and might see and follow you. There are two paddles in the canoe."

Nina approached her mother and touched lightly with her lips the wrinkled forehead. Mrs. Almayer snorted contemptuously in protest against that tenderness which she, nevertheless, feared could be contagious.

"Shall I ever see you again, mother?" murmured Nina.

"No," said Mrs. Almayer, after a short silence. "Why should you return here where it is my fate to die? You will live far away in splendour and might. When I hear of white men driven from the islands, then I shall know that you are alive, and that you remember my words."

"I shall always remember," returned Nina, earnestly; "but where is my power, and what can I do?"

"Do not let him look too long in your eyes, nor lay his head on your knees without reminding him that men should fight before they rest. And if he lingers, give him his kriss yourself and bid him go, as the wife of a mighty prince should do when the enemies are near. Let him slay the white men that come to us to trade, with prayers on their lips and loaded guns in their hands. Ah"—she ended with a sigh—"they are on every sea, and on every shore; and they are very many!"

She swung the bow of the canoe towards the river, but did not let go the gunwale, keeping her hand on it in irresolute thoughtfulness. Nina put the point of the paddle against the bank, ready to shove off into the stream.

"What is it, mother?" she asked, in a low voice. "Do you hear anything?"

"No," said Mrs. Almayer, absently. "Listen, Nina," she continued, abruptly, after a slight pause, "in after years there will be other women——"

A stifled cry in the boat interrupted her, and the paddle rattled in the canoe as it slipped from Nina's hands, which she put out in a protesting gesture. Mrs. Almayer fell on her knees on the bank and leaned over the gunwale so as to bring her own face close to her daughter's.

"There will be other women," she repeated firmly; "I tell you that, because you are half white, and may forget that he is a great chief, and that such things must be. Hide your anger, and do not let him see on your face the pain that will eat your heart. Meet him with joy in your eyes and wisdom on your lips, for to you he will turn in sadness or in doubt. As long as he looks upon many women your power will last, but should there be one, one only with whom he seems to forget you, then——"

"I could not live," exclaimed Nina, covering her face with both her hands. "Do not speak so, mother; it could not be."

"Then," went on Mrs. Almayer, steadily, "to that woman, Nina, show no mercy."

She moved the canoe down towards the stream by the gunwale, and gripped it with both her hands, the bow pointing into the river.

"Are you crying?" she asked sternly of her daughter, who sat still with covered face. "Arise, and take your paddle, for he has waited long enough. And remember, Nina, no mercy; and if you must strike, strike with a steady hand."

She put out all her strength, and swinging her body over the water, shot the light craft far into the stream. When she recovered herself from the effort she tried vainly to catch a glimpse of the canoe that seemed to have dissolved suddenly into the white mist trailing over the heated waters of the Pantai. After listening for a while intently on her knees, Mrs. Almayer rose with a deep sigh, while two tears wandered slowly down her withered cheeks. She wiped them off quickly with a wisp of her grey hair as if ashamed of herself, but could not stifle another loud sigh, for her heart was heavy and she suffered much, being unused to tender emotions. This time she fancied she had heard a faint noise, like the echo of her own sigh, and she stopped, straining her ears to catch the slightest sound, and peering apprehensively towards the bushes near her.

"Who is there?" she asked, in an unsteady voice, while her imagination peopled the solitude of the riverside with ghost-like forms. "Who is there?" she repeated faintly.

There was no answer: only the voice of the river murmuring in sad monotone behind the white veil seemed to swell louder for a moment, to die away again in a soft whisper of eddies washing against the bank.

Mrs. Almayer shook her head as if in answer to her

own thoughts, and walked quickly away from the bushes, looking to the right and left watchfully. She went straight towards the cooking-shed, observing that the embers of the fire there glowed more brightly than usual, as if somebody had been adding fresh fuel to the fires during the evening. As she approached, Babalatchi, who had been squatting in the warm glow, rose and met her in the shadow outside.

"Is she gone?" asked the anxious statesman, hastily.

"Yes," answered Mrs. Almayer. "What are the white men doing? When did you leave them?"

"They are sleeping now, I think. May they never wake!" exclaimed Babalatchi, fervently. "Oh! but they are devils, and made much talk and trouble over that carcass. The chief threatened me twice with his hand, and said he would have me tied up to a tree. Tie me up to a tree! Me!" he repeated, striking his breast violently.

Mrs. Almayer laughed tauntingly.

"And you salaamed and asked for mercy. Men with arms by their side acted otherwise when I was young."

"And where are they, the men of your youth? You mad woman!" retorted Babalatchi, angrily. "Killed by the Dutch. Aha! But I shall live to deceive them. A man knows when to fight and when to tell peaceful lies. You would know that if you were not a woman."

But Mrs. Almayer did not seem to hear him. With bent body and outstretched arm she appeared to be listening to some noise behind the shed.

"There are strange sounds," she whispered, with evident alarm. "I have heard in the air the sounds of grief, as of a sigh and weeping. That was by the riverside. And now again I heard——"

"Where?" asked Babalatchi, in an altered voice. "What did you hear?"

"Close here. It was like a breath long drawn. I wish I had burnt the paper* over the body before it was buried."

"Yes," assented Babalatchi. "But the white men had him thrown into a hole at once. You know he found his death on the river," he added cheerfully, "and his ghost may hail the canoes, but would leave the land alone."

Mrs. Almayer, who had been craning her neck to look round the corner of the shed, drew back her head.

"There is nobody there," she said, reassured. "Is it not time for the Rajah war-canoe to go to the clearing?"

"I have been waiting for it here, for I myself must go," explained Babalatchi. "I think I will go over and see what makes them late. When will you come? The Rajah gives you refuge."

"I shall paddle over before the break of day. I cannot leave my dollars behind," muttered Mrs. Almayer.

They separated. Babalatchi crossed the courtyard towards the creek to get his canoe, and Mrs. Almayer walked slowly to the house, ascended the plankway, and passing through the back verandah entered the passage leading to the front of the house; but before going in she turned in the doorway and looked back at the empty and silent courtyard, now lit up by the rays of the rising moon. No sooner had she disappeared, however, than a vague shape flitted out from amongst the stalks of the banana plantation, darted over the moonlit space, and fell in the darkness at the foot of the verandah. It might have been the shadow of a driving cloud, so noiseless and rapid was its passage, but for the trail of disturbed grass, whose feathery heads trembled and swayed for a long time in the moonlight before they rested motionless and gleaming, like a design of silver sprays embroidered on a sombre background.

Mrs. Almayer lighted the cocoanut lamp, and lifting cautiously the red curtain, gazed upon her husband, shading the light with her hand. Almayer, huddled up in the chair, one of his arms hanging down, the other thrown across the lower part of his face as if to ward off an invisible enemy, his legs stretched straight out, slept heavily, unconscious of the unfriendly eyes that looked upon him in disparaging criticism. At his feet lay the overturned table, amongst a wreck of crockery and broken bottles. The appearance as of traces left by a desperate struggle was accentuated by the chairs, which seemed to have been scattered violently all over the place, and now lay about the verandah with a lamentable aspect of inebriety in their helpless attitudes. Only Nina's big rocking-chair, standing black and motionless on its high runners, towered above the chaos of demoralized furniture, unflinchingly dignified and patient, waiting for its burden.

With a last scornful look towards the sleeper, Mrs. Almayer passed behind the curtain into her own room. A couple of bats, encouraged by the darkness and the peaceful state of affairs, resumed their silent and oblique gambols above Almayer's head, and for a long time the profound quiet of the house was unbroken, save for the deep breathing of the sleeping man and the faint tinkle of silver in the hands of the woman preparing for flight. In the increasing light of the moon that had risen now above the night mist, the objects on the verandah came out strongly outlined in black splashes of shadow with all the uncompromising ugliness of their disorder, and a caricature of the sleeping Almayer appeared on the dirty whitewash of the wall behind him in a grotesquely exaggerated detail of attitude and feature enlarged to a heroic size. The discontented bats departed in quest of darker places, and a lizard came out in short, nervous rushes, and, pleased with the white table-cloth, stopped on it in breathless immobility that would have suggested sudden death had it not been for the melodious call he exchanged with a less adventurous friend hiding amongst the lumber in the courtyard. Then the boards in the passage creaked, the lizard vanished, and Almayer stirred uneasily with a sigh: slowly, out of the senseless annihilation of drunken sleep, he was returning, through the land of dreams, to waking consciousness. Almayer's head rolled from shoulder to shoulder in the oppression of his dream; the heavens had descended upon him like a heavy mantle, and trailed in starred folds far under him. Stars above, stars all round him; and from the stars under his feet rose a whisper full of entreaties and tears, and sorrowful faces flitted amongst the clusters of light filling the infinite space below. How escape from the importunity of lamentable cries and from the look of staring, sad eyes in the faces which pressed round him till he gasped for breath under the crushing weight of worlds that hung over his aching shoulders? Get away! But how? If he attempted to move he would step off into nothing, and perish in the crashing fall of that universe of which he was the only support. And what were the voices saying? Urging him to move! Why? Move to destruction! Not likely! The absurdity of the thing filled him with indignation. He got a firmer foothold and stiffened his muscles in heroic resolve to carry his burden to all eternity. And ages passed in the superhuman labour, amidst the rush of circling worlds; in the plaintive murmur of sorrowful voices urging him to desist before it was too late—till the mysterious power that had laid upon him the giant task seemed at last to seek his destruction. With terror he felt an irresistible hand shaking him by the shoulder, while the chorus of voices swelled louder into an agonized prayer to go, go before it is too late. He felt himself slipping, losing his balance, as something dragged at his legs, and he fell. With a faint cry he glided out of the anguish of perishing creation into an imperfect waking that seemed to be still under the spell of his dream.

"What? What?" he murmured sleepily, without moving or opening his eyes. His head still felt heavy, and he had not the courage to raise his eyelids. In his ears there still lingered the sound of entreating whisper. —"Am I awake?—Why do I hear the voices?" he argued to himself, hazily.—"I cannot get rid of the horrible nightmare yet.—I have been very drunk.—What is that shaking me? I am dreaming yet.—I must open my eyes and be done with it. I am only half awake, it is evident."

He made an effort to shake off his stupor and saw a face close to his, glaring at him with staring eyeballs. He closed his eyes again in amazed horror and sat up straight in the chair, trembling in every limb. What was this apparition?—His own fancy, no doubt.—His nerves had been much tried the day before—and then the drink! He would not see it again if he had the courage to look.—He would look directly.—Get a little steadier first.—So.—Now.

He looked. The figure of a woman standing in the steely light, her hands stretched forth in a suppliant gesture, confronted him from the far-off end of the verandah; and in the space between him and the obstinate phantom floated the murmur of words that fell on his ears in a jumble of torturing sentences, the meaning of which escaped the utmost efforts of his brain. Who spoke the Malay words? Who ran away? Why too late—and too late for what? What meant those words of hate and love mixed so strangely together, the ever-recurring names falling on his ears again and again—Nina, Dain; Dain, Nina? Dain was dead, and Nina was sleeping, unaware of the terrible experience through which he was now passing. Was he going to be tormented for ever, sleeping or waking, and have no peace either night or day? What was the meaning of this?

He shouted the last words aloud. The shadowy woman seemed to shrink and recede a little from him towards the doorway, and there was a shriek. Exasperated by the incomprehensible nature of his torment, Almayer made a rush upon the apparition, which eluded his grasp, and he brought up heavily against the wall. Quick as lightning he turned round and pursued fiercely the mysterious figure fleeing from him with piercing shrieks that were like fuel to the flames of his anger. Over the furniture, round the overturned table, and now he had it cornered behind Nina's chair. To the left, to the right they dodged, the chair rocking madly between them, she sending out shriek after shriek at every feint, and he growling meaningless curses through his hard set teeth. "Oh! the fiendish noise that split his head and seemed to choke his breath.—It would kill him.—It must be stopped!" An insane desire to crush that yelling thing induced him to cast himself recklessly over the chair with a desperate grab, and they came down together in a cloud of dust amongst the splintered wood. The last shriek died out under him in a faint gurgle, and he had secured the relief of absolute silence.

He looked at the woman's face under him. A real woman. He knew her. By all that is wonderful! Taminah! He jumped up ashamed of his fury and stood perplexed, wiping his forehead. The girl struggled to a kneeling posture and embraced his legs in a frenzied prayer for mercy.

"Don't be afraid," he said, raising her. "I shall not hurt you. Why do you come to my house in the night? And if you had to come, why not go behind the curtain where the women sleep?"

"The place behind the curtain is empty," gasped Taminah, catching her breath between the words. "There are no women in your house any more, Tuan. I saw the old Mem go away before I tried to wake you. I did not want your women, I wanted you."

"Old Mem!" repeated Almayer. "Do you mean my wife?"

She nodded her head.

"But of my daughter you are not afraid?" said Almayer.

"Have you not heard me?" she exclaimed. "Have I not spoken for a long time when you lay there with eyes half open? She is gone too."

"I was asleep. Can you not tell when a man is sleeping and when awake?"

"Sometimes," answered Taminah in a low voice; "sometimes the spirit lingers close to a sleeping body and may hear. I spoke a long time before I touched you, and I spoke softly for fear it would depart at a sudden noise and leave you sleeping for ever. I took you by the shoulder only when you began to mutter words I could not understand. Have you not heard, then, and do you know nothing?"

"Nothing of what you said. What is it? Tell again if you want me to know."

He took her by the shoulder and led her unresisting to the front of the verandah into a stronger light. She wrung her hands with such an appearance of grief that he began to be alarmed.

"Speak," he said. "You made noise enough to wake even dead men. And yet nobody living came," he added to himself in an uneasy whisper. "Are you mute? Speak!" he repeated.

In a rush of words which broke out after a short struggle from her trembling lips she told him the tale of Nina's love and her own jealousy. Several times he looked angrily into her face and told her to be silent; but he could not stop the sounds that seemed to him to run out in a hot stream, swirl about his feet, and rise in scalding waves about him, higher, higher, drowning his heart, touching his lips with a feel of molten lead, blotting out his sight in scorching vapour, closing over his head, merciless and deadly. When she spoke of the deception as to Dain's death of which he had been the victim only that day, he glanced again at her with terrible eyes, and made her falter for a second, but he turned away directly, and his face suddenly lost all expression in a stony stare far away over the river. Ah! the river! His old friend and his old enemy, speaking always with the same voice as he runs from year to year bringing fortune or disappointment, happiness or pain, upon the same varying but unchanged surface of glancing currents and swirling eddies. For many years he had listened to the passionless and soothing murmur that sometimes was the song of hope, at times the song of triumph, of encouragement; more often the whisper of consolation that spoke of better days to come. For so many years! So many years! And now to the accompaniment of that murmur he listened to the slow and painful beating of his heart. He listened attentively, wondering at the regularity of its beats. He began to count mechanically. One, two. Why count? At the next beat it must stop. No heart could suffer so and beat so steadily for long. Those regular strokes as of a muffled hammer that rang in his ears must stop soon. Still beating unceasing and cruel. No man can bear this: and is this the last, or will the next one be the last?—How much longer? O God! how much longer? His hand weighed heavier unconsciously on the girl's shoulder, and she spoke the last words of her story crouching at his feet with tears of pain and shame and anger. Was her revenge to fail her? This white man was like a senseless stone. Too late! Too late!

"And you saw her go?" Almayer's voice sounded harshly above her head.

"Did I not tell you?" she sobbed, trying to wriggle gently out from under his grip. "Did I not tell you that I saw the witchwoman push the canoe? I lay hidden in the grass and heard all the words. She that we used to call the white Mem wanted to return to look at your face, but the witchwoman forbade her, and——"

She sank lower yet on her elbow, turning half round under the downward push of the heavy hand, her face lifted up to him with spiteful eyes.

"And she obeyed," she shouted out in a half-laugh, half-cry of pain. "Let me go, Tuan. Why are you angry with me? Hasten, or you will be too late to show your anger to the deceitful woman."

Almayer dragged her up to her feet and looked close into her face while she struggled, turning her head away from his wild stare.

"Who sent you here to torment me?" he asked, violently. "I do not believe you. You lie."

He straightened his arm suddenly and flung her across the verandah towards the doorway, where she lay immobile and silent, as if she had left her life in his grasp, a dark heap, without a sound or a stir.

"Oh! Nina!" whispered Almayer, in a voice in which reproach and love spoke together in pained tenderness. "Oh! Nina! I do not believe."

A light draught from the river ran over the courtyard in a wave of bowing grass and, entering the verandah, touched Almayer's forehead with its cool breath, in a caress of infinite pity. The curtain in the women's doorway blew out and instantly collapsed with startling helplessness. He stared at the fluttering stuff.

"Nina!" cried Almayer. "Where are you, Nina?"

The wind passed out of the empty house in a tremulous sigh, and all was still.

Almayer hid his face in his hands as if to shut out a loathsome sight. When, hearing a slight rustle, he uncovered his eyes, the dark heap by the door was gone.

CHAPTER ELEVEN

In the middle of a shadowless square of moonlight, shining on a smooth and level expanse of young rice-shoots,* a little shelter-hut perched on high posts, the pile of brushwood near by and the glowing embers of a fire with a man stretched before it, seemed very small and as if lost in the pale green iridescence reflected from the ground. On three sides of the clearing, appearing very far away in the deceptive light, the big trees of the forest, lashed together with manifold bonds by a mass of tangled creepers, looked down at the growing young life at their feet with the sombre resignation of giants that had lost faith in their strength. And in the midst of them the merciless creepers clung to the big trunks in cable-like coils, leaped from tree to tree, hung in thorny festoons from the lower boughs, and, sending slender tendrils on high to seek out the smallest branches, carried death to their victims in an exulting riot of silent destruction.

On the fourth side, following the curve of the bank of that branch of the Pantai that formed the only access to the clearing, ran a black line of young trees, bushes, and thick second growth, unbroken save for a small gap chopped out in one place. At that gap began the narrow footpath leading from the water's edge to the grass-built shelter used by the night watchers when the ripening crop had to be protected from the wild pigs.* The pathway ended at the foot of the piles on which the hut was built, in a circular space covered with ashes and bits of burnt wood. In the middle of that space, by the dim fire, lay Dain.

He turned over on his side with an impatient sigh, and, pillowing his head on his bent arm, lay quietly with his face to the dying fire. The glowing embers shone redly in a small circle, throwing a gleam into his wide-open eyes.* His body was weary with the exertion of the past few days, his mind more weary still with the strain of solitary waiting for his fate. Never before had he felt so helpless. He had heard the report of the gun fired on board the launch, and he knew that his life was in untrustworthy hands, and that his enemies were very near.

During the slow hours of the afternoon he had roamed about on the edge of the forest, or, hiding in the bushes, watched the creek with unquiet eyes for some sign of danger. He feared not death, yet he desired ardently to live, for life to him was Nina. She had promised to come, to follow him, to share his danger and his splendour. But with her by his side he cared not for danger, and without her there could be no splendour and no joy in existence. Crouching in his shady hiding-place, he closed his eyes, trying to evoke the gracious and charming image of the white figure that for him was the beginning and the end of life. With eyes shut tight, his teeth hard set, he tried in a great effort of passionate will to keep his hold on that vision of supreme delight. In vain! His heart grew heavy as the figure of Nina faded away to be replaced by another vision this time—a vision of armed men, of angry faces, of glittering arms—and he seemed to hear the hum of excited and triumphant voices as they discovered him in his hiding-place. Startled by the vividness of his fancy, he would open his eyes, and, leaping out into the sunlight, resume his aimless wanderings around the clearing. As he skirted in his weary march the edge of the forest he glanced now and then into its dark shade, so enticing in its deceptive appearance of coolness, so repellent with its unrelieved gloom, where lay, entombed and rotting, countless generations of trees, and where their successors stood as if mourning, in dark green foliage, immense and helpless, awaiting their turn. Only the parasites seemed to live there in a sinuous rush upwards into the air and sunshine, feeding on the dead and the dying alike, and crowning their victims with pink and blue flowers* that gleamed amongst the boughs, incongruous and cruel, like a strident and mocking note in the solemn harmony of the doomed trees.

A man could hide there, thought Dain, as he approached a place where the creepers had been torn and hacked into an archway that might have been the beginning of a path. As he bent down to look through he heard angry grunting, and a sounder* of wild pig crashed away in the undergrowth. An acrid smell of damp earth and of decaying leaves took him by the throat, and he drew back with a scared face, as if he had been touched by the breath of Death itself. The very air seemed dead in there—heavy and stagnating, poisoned with the corruption of countless ages. He went on, staggering on his way, urged by the nervous restlessness that made him feel tired yet caused him to loathe the very idea of immobility and repose. Was he a wild man to hide in the woods and perhaps be killed there—in the darkness—where there was no room to breathe? He would wait for his enemies in the sunlight, where he could see the sky and feel the breeze. He knew how a Malay chief should die. The sombre and desperate fury,* that peculiar inheritance of his race, took possession of him, and he glared savagely across the clearing towards the gap in the bushes by the riverside. They would come from there.

In imagination he saw them now. He saw the bearded faces and the white jackets of the officers, the light on the levelled barrels of the rifles. What is the bravery of the greatest warrior before the firearms in the hand of a slave? He would walk towards them with a smiling face, with his hands held out in a sign of submission till he was very near them. He would speak friendly words—come nearer yet—yet nearer—so near that they could touch him with their hands and stretch them out to make him a captive. That would be the time; with a shout and a leap he would be in the midst of them, kriss in hand, killing, killing, killing, and would die with the shouts of his enemies in his ears, their warm blood spurting before his eyes.

Carried away by his excitement, he snatched the kriss hidden in his sarong, and, drawing a long breath, rushed forward, struck at the empty air, and fell on his face. He lay as if stunned in the sudden reaction from his exaltation, thinking that, even if he died thus gloriously, it would have to be before he saw Nina. Better so. If he saw her again he felt that death would be too terrible. With horror he, the descendant of Rajahs and of conquerors, had to face the doubt of his own bravery. His desire of life tormented him in a paroxysm of agonizing remorse. He had not the courage to stir a limb. He had lost faith in himself, and there was nothing else in him of what makes a man. The suffering remained, for it is ordered that it should abide in the human body even to the last breath, and fear remained. Dimly he could look into the depths of his passionate love, see its strength and its weakness, and felt afraid.

The sun went down slowly. The shadow of the western forest marched over the clearing, covered the man's scorched shoulders with its cool mantle, and went on hurriedly to mingle with the shadows of other forests on the eastern side. The sun lingered for a while amongst the light tracery of the higher branches, as if in friendly reluctance to abandon the body stretched in the green paddy-field. Then Dain, revived by the cool of the evening breeze, sat up and stared round him. As he did so the sun dipped sharply, as if ashamed of being detected in a sympathizing attitude, and the clearing, which during the day was all light, became suddenly all darkness, where the fire gleamed like an eye. Dain walked slowly towards the creek, and, divesting himself of his torn sarong, his only garment, entered the water cautiously. He had had nothing to eat that day, and had not dared show himself in daylight by the water-side to drink. Now, as he swam silently, he swallowed a few mouthfuls of water that lapped about his lips. This did him good, and he walked with greater confidence in himself and others as he returned towards the fire. Had he been betrayed by Lakamba all would have been over by this. He made up a big blaze, and while it lasted dried himself, and then lay down by the embers. He could not sleep, but he felt a great numbness in all his limbs. His restlessness was gone, and he was content to lie still, measuring the time by watching the stars that rose in endless succession above the forests, while the slight puffs of wind under the cloudless sky seemed to fan their twinkle into a greater brightness. Dreamily he assured himself over and over again that she would come, till the certitude crept into his heart and filled him with a great peace. Yes, when the next day broke, they would be together on the great blue sea that was like life—away from the forests that were like death. He murmured the name of Nina into the silent space with a tender smile: this seemed to break the spell of stillness, and far away by the creek a frog croaked loudly as if in answer. A chorus of loud roars and plaintive calls rose from the mud along the line of bushes. He laughed heartily; doubtless it was their love-song. He felt affectionate towards the frogs and listened, pleased with the noisy life near him.

When the moon peeped above the trees he felt the old impatience and the old restlessness steal over him. Why was she so late? True, it was a long way to come with a single paddle. With what skill and what endurance could those small hands manage a heavy paddle! It was very wonderful—such small hands, such soft little palms that knew how to touch his cheek with a feel lighter than the fanning of a butterfly's wing. Wonderful! He lost himself lovingly in the contemplation of this tremendous mystery, and when he looked at the moon again it had risen a hand's breadth above the trees. Would she come? He forced himself to lie still, overcoming the impulse to rise and rush round the clearing again. He turned this way and that; at last, quivering with the effort, he lay on his back, and saw her face among the stars looking down on him.

The croaking of frogs suddenly ceased. With the watchfulness of a hunted man Dain sat up, listening anxiously, and heard several splashes in the water as the frogs took rapid headers into the creek. He knew that they had been alarmed by something, and stood up suspicious and attentive. A slight grating noise, then the dry sound as of two pieces of wood struck against each other. Somebody was about to land! He took up an armful of brushwood, and, without taking his eyes from the path, held it over the embers of his fire. He waited, undecided, and saw something gleam amongst the bushes; then a white figure came out of the shadows and seemed to float towards him in the pale light. His heart gave a great leap and stood still, then went on shaking his frame in furious beats. He dropped the brushwood upon the glowing coals, and had an impression of shouting her name—of rushing to meet her; yet he emitted no sound, he stirred not an inch, but he stood silent and motionless like chiselled bronze under the moonlight that streamed over his naked shoulders. As he stood still, fighting with his breath, as if bereft of his senses by the intensity of his delight, she walked up to him with quick, resolute steps, and, with the appearance of one about to leap from a dangerous height, threw both her arms round his neck with a sudden gesture. A small blue gleam crept amongst the dry branches, and the crackling of reviving fire was the only sound as they faced each other in the speechless emotion of that meeting; then the dry fuel caught at once, and a bright hot flame shot upwards in a blaze as high as their heads, and in its light they saw each other's eyes.

Neither of them spoke. He was regaining his senses in a slight tremor that ran upwards along his rigid body and hung about his trembling lips. She drew back her head and fastened her eyes on his in one of those long looks that are a woman's most terrible weapon; a look that is more stirring than the closest touch, and more dangerous than the thrust of a dagger, because it also whips the soul out of the body, but leaves the body alive and helpless, to be swayed here and there by the capricious tempests of passion and desire; a look that enwraps the whole body, and that penetrates into the innermost recesses of the being, bringing terrible defeat in the delirious uplifting of accomplished conquest. It has the same meaning for the man of the forests and the sea as for the man threading the paths of the more dangerous wilderness of houses and streets.

Men that had felt in their breasts the awful exultation such a look awakens become mere things of to-day—which is paradise; forget yesterday—which was suffering; care not for to-morrow—which may be perdition. They wish to live under that look for ever. It is the look of woman's surrender.

He understood, and, as if suddenly released from his invisible bonds, fell at her feet with a shout of joy, and, embracing her knees, hid his head in the folds of her dress, murmuring disjointed words of gratitude and love. Never before had he felt so proud as now, when at the feet of that woman that half belonged to his enemies. Her fingers played with his hair in an absent-minded caress as she stood absorbed in thought. The thing was done. Her mother was right. The man was her slave. As she glanced down at his kneeling form she felt a great pitying tenderness for that man she was used to call—even in her thoughts—the master of life. She lifted her eyes and looked sadly at the southern heavens under which lay the path of their lives—her own, and that man's at her feet. Did he not say himself that she was the light of his life? She would be his light and his wisdom; she would be his greatness and his strength; yet hidden from the eyes of all men she would be, above all, his only and lasting weakness. A very woman! In the sublime vanity of her kind she was thinking already of moulding a god from the clay at her feet. A god for others to worship. She was content to see him as he was now, and to feel him quiver at the slightest touch of her light fingers. And while her eyes looked sadly at the southern stars a faint smile seemed to be playing about her firm lips. Who can tell in the fitful light of a camp fire? It might have been a smile of triumph, or of conscious power, or of tender pity, or, perhaps, of love.

She spoke softly to him, and he rose to his feet, putting his arm round her in quiet consciousness of his ownership; she laid her head on his shoulder with a sense of defiance to all the world in the encircling protection of that arm. He was hers with all his qualities and his faults.* His strength and his courage, his recklessness and his daring, his simple wisdom and his savage cunning—all were hers. As they passed together out of the red light of the fire into the silver shower of rays that fell upon the clearing he bent his head over her face, and she saw in his eyes the dreamy intoxication of boundless felicity from the close touch of her slight figure clasped to his side. With a rhythmical swing of their bodies they walked through the light towards the outlying shadows of the forests that seemed to guard their happiness in solemn immobility. Their forms melted in the play of light and shadow at the foot of the big trees, but the murmur of tender words lingered over the empty clearing, grew faint, and died out. A sigh as of immense sorrow passed over the land in the last effort of the dying breeze, and in the deep silence which succeeded, the earth and the heavens were suddenly hushed up in the mournful contemplation of human love and human blindness.

They walked slowly back to the fire. He made for her a seat out of the dry branches, and, throwing himself down at her feet, lay his head in her lap and gave himself up to the dreamy delight of the passing hour. Their voices rose and fell, tender or animated as they spoke of their love and of their future. She, with a few skilful words spoken from time to time, guided his thoughts, and he let his happiness flow in a stream of talk passionate and tender, grave or menacing, according to the mood which she evoked. He spoke to her of his own island,* where the gloomy forests and the muddy rivers were unknown. He spoke of its terraced fields, of the murmuring clear rills of sparkling water that flowed down the sides of great mountains, bringing life to the land and joy to its tillers. And he spoke also of the mountain peak that rising lonely above the belt of trees knew the secrets of the passing clouds, and was the dwelling-place of the mysterious spirit of his race, of the guardian genius of his house. He spoke of vast horizons swept by fierce winds that whistled high above the summits of burning mountains. He spoke of his forefathers that conquered ages ago the island of which he was to be the future ruler. And then as, in her interest, she brought her face nearer to his, he, touching lightly the thick tresses of her long hair, felt a sudden impulse to speak to her of the sea he loved so well; and he told her of its never-ceasing voice, to which he had listened as a child, wondering at its hidden meaning that no living man has penetrated yet; of its enchanting glitter; of its senseless and capricious fury; how its surface was for ever changing, and yet always enticing, while its depths were for ever the same, cold and cruel, and full of the wisdom of destroyed life. He told her how it held men slaves of its charm for a lifetime, and then, regardless of their devotion, swallowed them up, angry at their fear of its mystery, which it would never disclose, not even to those that loved it most. While he talked, Nina's head had been gradually sinking lower, and her face almost touched his now. Her hair was over his eyes, her breath was on his forehead, her arms were about his body. No two beings could be closer to each other, yet she guessed rather than understood the meaning of his last words that came out after a slight hesitation in a faint murmur, dying out imperceptibly into a profound and significant silence: "The sea, O Nina, is like a woman's heart."

She closed his lips with a sudden kiss, and answered in a steady voice—

"But to the men that have no fear, O master of my life, the sea is ever true."

Over their heads a film of dark, thread-like clouds, looking like immense cobwebs drifting under the stars, darkened the sky with the presage of the coming thunderstorm. From the invisible hills the first distant rumble of thunder came in a prolonged roll which, after tossing about from hill to hill, lost itself in the forests of the Pantai. Dain and Nina stood up, and the former looked at the sky uneasily.

"It is time for Babalatchi to be here," he said. "The night is more than half gone. Our road is long, and a bullet travels quicker than the best canoe."

"He will be here before the moon is hidden behind the clouds," said Nina. "I heard a splash in the water," she added. "Did you hear it too?"

"Alligator," answered Dain shortly, with a careless glance towards the creek. "The darker the night," he continued, "the shorter will be our road, for then we could keep in the current of the main stream, but if it is light—even no more than now—we must follow the small channels of sleeping water, with nothing to help our paddles."

"Dain," interposed Nina, earnestly, "it was no alligator. I heard the bushes rustling near the landing-place."

"Yes," said Dain, after listening awhile. "It cannot be Babalatchi, who would come in a big war canoe, and openly. Those that are coming, whoever they are, do not wish to make much noise. But you have heard, and now I can see," he went on quickly. "It is but one man. Stand behind me, Nina. If he is a friend he is welcome; if he is an enemy you shall see him die."

He laid his hand on his kriss, and waited the approach of his unexpected visitor. The fire was burning very low, and small clouds—precursors of the storm—crossed the face of the moon in rapid succession, and their flying shadows darkened the clearing. He could not make out who the man might be, but he felt uneasy at the steady advance of the tall figure walking on the path with a heavy tread, and hailed it with a command to stop. The man stopped at some little distance, and Dain expected him to speak, but all he could hear was his deep breathing. Through a break in the flying clouds a sudden and fleeting brightness descended upon the clearing. Before the darkness closed in again Dain saw a hand holding some glittering object extended towards him, heard Nina's cry of "Father!" and in an instant the girl was between him and Almayer's revolver. Nina's loud cry woke up the echoes of the sleeping woods, and the three stood still as if waiting for the return of silence before they would give expression to their various feelings. At the appearance of Nina, Almayer's arm fell by his side, and he made a step forward. Dain pushed the girl gently aside.

"Am I a wild beast that you should try to kill me suddenly and in the dark, Tuan Almayer?" said Dain, breaking the strained silence. "Throw some brushwood on the fire," he went on, speaking to Nina, "while I watch my white friend, lest harm should come to you or to me, O delight of my heart!"

Almayer ground his teeth and raised his arm again. With a quick bound Dain was at his side: there was a short scuffle, during which one chamber of the revolver went off harmlessly, then the weapon, wrenched out of Almayer's hand, whirled through the air and fell in the bushes. The two men stood close together, breathing hard. The replenished fire threw out an unsteady circle of light and shone on the terrified face of Nina, who looked at them with outstretched hands.

"Dain!" she cried out warningly, "Dain!"

He waved his hand towards her in a reassuring gesture, and, turning to Almayer, said with great courtesy—

"Now we may talk, Tuan. It is easy to send out death, but can your wisdom recall the life? She might have been harmed," he continued, indicating Nina. "Your hand shook much; for myself I was not afraid."*

"Nina!" exclaimed Almayer, "come to me at once. What is this sudden madness? What bewitched you? Come to your father, and together we shall try to forget this horrible nightmare!"

He opened his arms with the certitude of clasping her to his breast in another second. She did not move. As it dawned upon him that she did not mean to obey he felt a deadly cold creep into his heart, and pressing the palms of his hands to his temples, he looked down on the ground in mute despair. Dain took Nina by the arm and led her towards her father.

"Speak to him in the language of his people," he said. "He is grieving—as who would not grieve at losing thee, my pearl! Speak to him the last words he shall hear spoken by that voice, which must be very sweet to him, but is all my life to me."

He released her, and, stepping back a few paces out of the circle of light, stood in the darkness looking at them with calm interest. The reflection of a distant flash of lightning lit up the clouds over their heads, and was followed after a short interval by the faint rumble of thunder, which mingled with Almayer's voice as he began to speak.

"Do you know what you are doing? Do you know what is waiting for you if you follow that man? Have you no pity for yourself? Do you know that you shall be at first his plaything and then a scorned slave, a drudge, and a servant of some new fancy of that man?"

She raised her hand to stop him, and turning her head slightly, asked—

"You hear this, Dain! Is it true?"

"By all the gods!" came the impassioned answer from the darkness—"by heaven and earth, by my head and thine I swear: this is a white man's lie. I have delivered my soul into your hands for ever; I breathe with your breath, I see with your eyes, I think with your mind, and I take you into my heart for ever."

"You thief!" shouted the exasperated Almayer.

A deep silence succeeded this outburst, then the voice of Dain was heard again.

"Nay, Tuan," he said in a gentle tone, "that is not true also. The girl came of her own will. I have done no more but to show her my love like a man; she heard the cry of my heart, and she came, and the dowry* I have given to the woman you call your wife."

Almayer groaned in his extremity of rage and shame. Nina laid her hand lightly on his shoulder, and the contact, light as the touch of a falling leaf, seemed to calm him. He spoke quickly, and in English this time.

"Tell me," he said—"tell me, what have they done to you, your mother and that man? What made you give yourself up to that savage? For he is a savage. Between him and you there is a barrier that nothing can remove. I can see in your eyes the look of those who commit suicide when they are mad. You are mad. Don't smile. It breaks my heart. If I were to see you drowning before my eyes, and I without the power to help you, I could not suffer a greater torment. Have you forgotten the teaching of so many years?"

"No," she interrupted, "I remember it well. I remember how it ended also. Scorn for scorn, contempt for contempt, hate for hate. I am not of your race. Between your people and me there is also a barrier that nothing can remove. You ask why I want to go, and I ask you why I should stay."

He staggered as if struck in the face, but with a quick, unhesitating grasp she caught him by the arm and steadied him.

"Why you should stay!" he repeated slowly, in a dazed manner, and stopped short, astounded at the completeness of his misfortune.

"You told me yesterday," she went on again, "that I could not understand or see your love for me: it is so. How can I? No two human beings understand each other. They can understand but their own voices. You wanted me to dream your dreams, to see your own visions—the visions of life amongst the white faces of those who cast me out from their midst in angry contempt. But while you spoke I listened to the voice of my own self; then this man came, and all was still; there was only the murmur of his love. You call him a savage! What do you call my mother, your wife?"

"Nina!" cried Almayer, "take your eyes off my face."

She looked down directly, but continued speaking only a little above a whisper.

"In time," she went on, "both our voices, that man's and mine, spoke together in a sweetness that was intelligible to our ears only. You were speaking of gold then, but our ears were filled with the song of our love, and we did not hear you. Then I found that we could see through each other's eyes: that he saw things that nobody but myself and he could see. We entered a land where no one could follow us, and least of all you. Then I began to live."

She paused. Almayer sighed deeply. With her eyes still fixed on the ground she began speaking again. "And I mean to live. I mean to follow him. I have been rejected with scorn by the white people, and now I am a Malay! He took me in his arms, he laid his life at my feet. He is brave; he will be powerful, and I hold his bravery and his strength in my hand, and I shall make him great. His name shall be remembered long after both our bodies are laid in the dust. I love you no less than I did before, but I shall never leave him, for without him I cannot live."

"If he understood what you have said," answered Almayer, scornfully, "he must be highly flattered. You want him as a tool for some incomprehensible ambition of yours. Enough, Nina. If you do not go down at once to the creek, where Ali is waiting with my canoe, I shall tell him to return to the settlement and bring the Dutch officers here. You cannot escape from this clearing, for I have cast adrift your canoe. If the Dutch catch this hero of yours they will hang him as sure as I stand here. Now go."

He made a step* towards his daughter and laid hold of her by the shoulder, his other hand pointing down the path to the landing-place.

"Beware!" exclaimed Dain; "this woman belongs to me!"

Nina wrenched herself free and looked straight at Almayer's angry face.

"No, I will not go," she said with desperate energy. "If he dies I shall die too!"

"You die?" said Almayer, contemptuously. "Oh, no! You shall live a life of lies and deception till some other vagabond comes along to sing—how did you say that?—the song of love to you! Make up your mind quickly."

He waited for a while, and then added meaningly—"Shall I call out to Ali?"

"Call out," she answered in Malay, "you that cannot be true to your own countrymen. Only a few days ago you were selling the powder of their destruction;* now you want to give up to them the man that yesterday you called your friend. Oh, Dain," she said, turning towards the motionless but attentive figure in the darkness, "instead of bringing you life I bring you death, for he will betray* unless I leave you for ever!"

Dain came into the circle of light, and, throwing his arm around Nina's neck, whispered in her ear—

"I can kill him where he stands, before a sound can pass his lips. For you it is to say yes or no. Babalatchi cannot be far now."

He straightened himself up, taking his arm off her shoulder, and confronted Almayer, who looked at them both with an expression of concentrated fury.

"No!" she cried, clinging to Dain in wild alarm. "No! Kill me! Then perhaps he will let you go. You do not know the mind of a white man. He would rather see me dead than standing where I am. Forgive me, your slave, but you must not." She fell at his feet sobbing violently and repeating, "Kill me! Kill me!"

"I want you, alive" said Almayer, speaking also in Malay, with sombre calmness. "You go, or he hangs. Will you obey?"

Dain shook Nina off, and, making a sudden lunge, struck Almayer full in the chest with the handle of his kriss, keeping the point towards himself.

"Hai, look! It was easy for me to turn the point the other way," he said in his even voice. "Go, Tuan Putih," he added with dignity. "I give you your life, my life, and her life. I am the slave of this woman's desire, and she wills it so."

There was not a glimmer of light in the sky now, and the tops of the trees were as invisible as their trunks, being lost in the mass of clouds that hung low over the woods, the clearing, and the river. Every outline had disappeared in the intense blackness that seemed to have destroyed everything but space. Only the fire glimmered like a star forgotten in this annihilation of all visible things, and nothing was heard after Dain ceased speaking but the sobs of Nina, whom he held in his arms, kneeling beside the fire. Almayer stood looking down at them in gloomy thoughtfulness. As he was opening his lips to speak they were startled by a cry of warning by the riverside, followed by the splash of many paddles and the sound of voices.

"Babalatchi!" shouted Dain, lifting up Nina as he got upon his feet quickly.

"Ada!* Ada!" came the answer from the panting statesman who ran up the path and stood amongst them. "Run to my canoe," he said to Dain excitedly, without taking any notice of Almayer. "Run! we must go. That woman has told them all!"

"What woman?" asked Dain, looking at Nina. Just then there was only one woman in the whole world for him.

"The she-dog with white teeth; the seven times accursed slave of Bulangi. She yelled at Abdulla's gate till she woke up all Sambir. Now the white officers are coming guided by her and Reshid. If you want to live, do not look at me, but go!"

"How do you know this?" asked Almayer.

"Oh, Tuan! what matters how I know! I have only one eye, but I saw lights in Abdulla's house and in his campong as we were paddling past. I have ears, and while we lay under the bank I have heard the messengers sent out to the white men's house."

"Will you depart without that woman who is my daughter?" said Almayer, addressing Dain, while Babalatchi stamped with impatience, muttering, "Run! Run at once!"

"No," answered Dain, steadily, "I will not go; to no man will I abandon this woman."

"Then kill me and escape yourself," sobbed out Nina.

He clasped her close, looking at her tenderly, and whispered, "We will never part, O Nina!"

"I shall not stay here any longer," broke in Babalatchi, angrily. "This is great foolishness. No woman is worth a man's life. I am an old man, and I know."

He picked up his staff, and, turning to go, looked at Dain as if offering him his last chance of escape. But Dain's face was hidden amongst Nina's black tresses, and he did not see this last appealing glance.

Babalatchi vanished in the darkness. Shortly after his disappearance they heard the war canoe leave the landing-place in the swish of the numerous paddles dipped in the water together. Almost at the same time Ali came up from the riverside, two paddles on his shoulder.

"Our canoe is hidden up the creek, Tuan Almayer," he said, "in the dense bush where the forest comes down to the water. I took it there because I heard from Babalatchi's paddlers that the white men are coming here."

"Wait for me there," said Almayer, "but keep the canoe hidden."

He remained silent, listening to Ali's footsteps, then turned to Nina.

"Nina," he said sadly, "will you have no pity for me?"

There was no answer. She did not even turn her head, which was pressed close to Dain's breast.

He made a movement as if to leave them and stopped. By the dim glow of the burning-out fire he saw their two motionless figures. The woman's back turned to him with the long black hair streaming down over the white dress, and Dain's calm face looking at him above her head.

"I cannot," he muttered to himself. After a long pause he spoke again a little lower, but in an unsteady voice, "It would be too great a disgrace. I am a white man." He broke down completely there, and went on tearfully, "I am a white man, and of good family. Very good family," he repeated, weeping bitterly. "It would be a disgrace . . . all over the island,* . . . the only white man on the east coast. No, it cannot be . . . white men finding my daughter with this Malay. My daughter!" he cried aloud, with a ring of despair in his voice.

He recovered his composure after a while and said distinctly—

"I will never forgive you, Nina—never! If you were to come back to me now, the memory of this night would poison all my life. I shall try to forget. I have no daughter. There used to be a half-caste woman in my house, but she is going even now. You, Dain, or whatever your name may be,* I shall take you and that woman to the island at the mouth of the river myself. Come with me."

He led the way, following the bank as far as the forest. Ali answered to his call, and, pushing their way through the dense bush, they stepped into the canoe hidden under the overhanging branches. Dain laid Nina in the bottom, and sat holding her head on his knees. Almayer and Ali each took up a paddle. As they were going to push out Ali hissed warningly. All listened.

In the great stillness before the bursting out of the

thunderstorm they could hear the sound of oars working regularly in their row-locks.* The sound approached steadily, and Dain, looking through the branches, could see the faint shape of a big white boat. A woman's voice said in a cautious tone—

"There is the place where you may land, white men; a little higher—there!"

The boat was passing them so close in the narrow creek that the blades of the long oars nearly touched the canoe.

"Way enough!* Stand by to jump on shore! He is alone and unarmed," was the quiet order in a man's voice, and in Dutch.

Somebody else whispered: "I think I can see a glimmer of a fire through the bush." And then the boat floated past them, disappearing instantly in the darkness.

"Now," whispered Ali, eagerly, "let us push out and paddle away."

The little canoe swung into the stream, and as it sprung forward in response to the vigorous dig of the paddles they could hear an angry shout.

"He is not by the fire. Spread out, men, and search for him!"

Blue lights blazed out in different parts of the clearing, and the shrill voice of a woman cried in accents of rage and pain—

"Too late! O senseless white men! He has escaped!"

CHAPTER TWELVE

"THAT is the place," said Dain, indicating with the blade of his paddle a small islet about a mile ahead of the canoe—"that is the place where Babalatchi promised that a boat from the prau would come for me when the sun is overhead. We will wait for that boat there."

Almayer, who was steering, nodded without speaking, and by a slight sweep of his paddle laid the head of the canoe in the required direction.

They were just leaving the southern outlet of the Pantai, which lay behind them in a straight and long vista of water shining between two walls of thick verdure that ran downwards and towards each other, till at last they joined and sank together in the far-away distance. The sun, rising above the calm waters of the Straits,* marked its own path by a streak of light that glided upon the sea and darted up the wide reach of the river, a hurried messenger of light and life to the gloomy forests of the coast; and in this radiance of the sun's pathway floated the black canoe heading for the islet which lay bathed in sunshine, the yellow sands of its encircling beach shining like an inlaid golden disc on the polished steel of the unwrinkled sea. To the north and south of it rose other islets, joyous in their brilliant colouring of green and yellow, and on the main coast the sombre line of mangrove bushes ended to the southward in the reddish cliffs of Tanjong Mirrah,* advancing into the sea, steep and shadowless under the clear light of the early morning.

The bottom of the canoe grated upon the sand as the little craft ran upon the beach. Ali leaped on shore and held on while Dain stepped out carrying Nina in his arms, exhausted by the events and the long travelling during the night. Almayer was the last to leave the boat, and together with Ali ran it higher up on the beach. Then Ali, tired out by the long paddling, lay down in the shade of the canoe, and incontinently fell asleep. Almayer sat sideways on the gunwale, and with his arms crossed on his breast, looked to the southward upon the sea.

After carefully laying Nina down in the shade of the bushes growing in the middle of the islet, Dain threw himself beside her and watched in silent concern the tears that ran down from under her closed eyelids, and lost themselves in that fine sand upon which they both were lying face to face. These tears and this sorrow were for him a profound and disquieting mystery. Now, when the danger was past, why should she grieve? He doubted her love no more than he would have doubted the fact of his own existence, but as he lay looking ardently in her face, watching her tears, her parted lips, her very breath, he was uneasily conscious of something in her he could not understand. Doubtless she had the wisdom of perfect beings. He sighed. He felt something invisible that stood between them, something that would let him approach her so far, but no farther. No desire, no longing, no effort of will or length of life could destroy this vague feeling of their difference. With awe but also with great pride he concluded that it was her own incomparable perfection. She was his, and yet she was like a woman from another world. His! His! He exulted in the glorious thought; nevertheless her tears pained him.

With a wisp of her own hair which he took in his hand

with timid reverence he tried in an access* of clumsy tenderness to dry the tears that trembled on her eyelashes. He had his reward in a fleeting smile that brightened her face for the short fraction of a second, but soon the tears fell faster than ever, and he could bear it no more. He rose and walked towards Almayer, who still sat absorbed in his contemplation of the sea. It was a very, very long time since he had seen the sea—that sea that leads everywhere, brings everything, and takes away so much. He had almost forgotten why he was there, and dreamily he could see all his past life on the smooth and boundless surface that glittered before his eyes.

Dain's hand laid on Almayer's shoulder recalled him with a start from some country very far away indeed. He turned round, but his eyes seemed to look rather at the place where Dain stood than at the man himself. Dain felt uneasy under the unconscious gaze.

"What do you want?" asked Almayer.*

"She is crying," murmured Dain, softly.

"She is crying! Why?" asked Almayer, indifferently.

"I came to ask you. My Ranee smiles when looking at the man she loves. It is the white woman that is crying now. You would know."

Almayer shrugged his shoulders and turned away again towards the sea.

"Go, Tuan Putih," urged Dain. "Go to her; her tears are more terrible to me than the anger of gods."

"Are they? You will see them more than once. She told me she could not live without you," answered Almayer, speaking without the faintest spark of expression in his face, "so it behoves you to go to her quick, for fear you may find her dead."

He burst into a loud and unpleasant laugh which

made Dain stare at him with some apprehension, but got off the gunwale of the boat and moved slowly towards Nina, glancing up at the sun as he walked.

"And you go when the sun is overhead?" he said.

"Yes, Tuan. Then we go," answered Dain.

"I have not long to wait," muttered Almayer. "It is most important for me to see you go. Both of you. Most important," he repeated, stopping short and looking at Dain fixedly.

He went on again towards Nina, and Dain remained behind. Almayer approached his daughter and stood for a time looking down on her. She did not open her eyes, but hearing footsteps near her, murmured in a low sob, "Dain."

Almayer hesitated for a minute and then sank on the sand by her side. She, not hearing a responsive word, not feeling a touch, opened her eyes—saw her father, and sat up suddenly with a movement of terror.

"Oh, father!" she murmured faintly, and in that word there was expressed regret and fear and dawning hope.

"I shall never forgive you, Nina," said Almayer, in a dispassionate voice. "You have torn my heart from me while I dreamt of your happiness. You have deceived me. Your eyes that for me were like truth itself lied to me in every glance—for how long? You know that best. When you were caressing my cheek you were counting the minutes to the sunset that was the signal for your meeting with that man—there!"

He ceased, and they both sat silent side by side, not looking at each other, but gazing at the vast expanse of the sea. Almayer's words had dried Nina's tears, and her look grew hard as she stared before her into the limitless sheet of blue that shone limpid, unwaving, and steady like heaven itself. He looked at it also, but his features had lost all expression, and life in his eyes seemed to have gone out. The face was a blank, without a sign of emotion, feeling, reason, or even knowledge of itself. All passion, regret, grief, hope, or anger—all were gone, erased by the hand of fate, as if after this last stroke everything was over and there was no need for any record. Those few who saw Almayer during the short period of his remaining days were always impressed by the sight of that face that seemed to know nothing of what went on within: like the blank wall of a prison enclosing sin, regrets, and pain, and wasted life, in the cold indifference of mortar and stones.

"What is there to forgive?" asked Nina, not addressing Almayer directly, but more as if arguing with herself. "Can I not live my own life as you have lived yours? The path you would have wished me to follow has been closed to me by no fault of mine."

"You never told me," muttered Almayer.

"You never asked me," she answered, "and I thought you were like the others and did not care. I bore the memory of my humiliation alone, and why should I tell you that it came to me because I am your daughter? I knew you could not avenge me."

"And yet I was thinking of that only," interrupted Almayer, "and I wanted to give you years of happiness for the short day of your suffering. I only knew of one way."

"Ah! but it was not my way!" she replied. "Could you give me happiness without life? Life!" she repeated with sudden energy that sent the word ringing over the sea. "Life that means power and love," she added in a low voice.

"That!" said Almayer, pointing his finger at Dain standing close by and looking at them in curious wonder.

"Yes, that!" she replied, looking her father full in the face and noticing for the first time with a slight gasp of fear the unnatural rigidity of his features.

"I would have rather strangled you with my own hands," said Almayer, in an expressionless voice which was such a contrast to the desperate bitterness of his feelings that it surprised even himself. He asked himself who spoke, and, after looking slowly round as if expecting to see somebody, turned again his eyes towards the sea.

"You say that because you do not understand the meaning of my words," she said sadly. "Between you and my mother there never was any love. When I returned to Sambir I found the place which I thought would be a peaceful refuge for my heart, filled with weariness and hatred—and mutual contempt. I have listened to your voice and to her voice. Then I saw that you could not understand me; for was I not part of that woman? Of her who was the regret and shame of your life? I had to choose—I hesitated. Why were you so blind? Did you not see me struggling before your eyes? But, when he came, all doubt disappeared, and I saw only the light of the blue and cloudless heaven——"

"I will tell you the rest," interrupted Almayer: "when that man came I also saw the blue and the sunshine of the sky. A thunderbolt has fallen from that sky, and suddenly all is still and dark around me for ever. I will never forgive you, Nina; and to-morrow I shall forget you! I shall never forgive you," he repeated with mechanical obstinacy while she sat, her head bowed down as if afraid to look at her father.

To him it seemed of the utmost importance that he should assure her of his intention of never forgiving. He was convinced that his faith in her had been the foundation of his hopes, the motive of his courage, of his determination to live and struggle, and to be victorious for her sake. And now his faith was gone, destroyed by her own hands; destroyed cruelly, treacherously, in the dark; in the very moment of success. In the utter wreck of his affections and of all his feelings, in the chaotic disorder of his thoughts, above the confused sensation of physical pain that wrapped him up in a sting as of a whiplash curling round him from his shoulders down to his feet, only one idea remained clear and definite—not to forgive her; only one vivid desire—to forget her. And this must be made clear to her—and to himself—by frequent repetition. That was his idea of his duty to himself—to his race—to his respectable connections; to the whole universe unsettled and shaken by this frightful catastrophe of his life. He saw it clearly and believed he was a strong man. He had always prided himself upon his unflinching firmness. And yet he was afraid. She had been all in all to him. What if he should let the memory of his love for her weaken the sense of his dignity? She was a remarkable woman; he could see that; all the latent greatness of his nature—in which he honestly believed—had been transfused into that slight, girlish figure. Great things could be done! What if he should suddenly take her to his heart, forget his shame, and pain, and anger, and—follow her! What if he changed his heart if not his skin and made her life easier between the two loves that would guard her from any mischance! His heart yearned for her. What if he should say that his love for her was greater than . . .

"I will never forgive you, Nina!" he shouted, leaping up madly in the sudden fear of his dream.

This was the last time in his life that he was heard to raise his voice. Henceforth he spoke always in a monotonous whisper like an instrument of which all the strings but one are broken in a last ringing clamour under a heavy blow.

She rose to her feet and looked at him. The very violence of his cry soothed her in an intuitive conviction of his love, and she hugged to her breast the lamentable remnants of that affection with the unscrupulous greediness of women who cling desperately to the very scraps and rags of love, any kind of love, as a thing that of right belongs to them and is the very breath of their life. She put both her hands on Almayer's shoulders, and looking at him half tenderly, half playfully, she said—

"You speak so because you love me."

Almayer shook his head.

"Yes, you do," she insisted softly; then after a short pause she added, "and you will never forget me."

Almayer shivered slightly. She could not have said a more cruel thing.

"Here is the boat coming now," said Dain, his arm outstretched towards a black speck on the water between the coast and the islet.

They all looked at it and remained standing in silence till the little canoe came gently on the beach and a man landed and walked towards them. He stopped some distance off and hesitated.

"What news?" asked Dain.

"We have had orders secretly and in the night to take off from this islet a man and a woman. I see the woman. Which of you is the man?"

"Come, delight of my eyes," said Dain to Nina. "Now we go, and your voice shall be for my ears only. You have spoken your last words to the Tuan Putih, your father. Come."

She hesitated for a while, looking at Almayer, who

kept his eyes steadily on the sea, then she touched his forehead in a lingering kiss, and a tear—one of her tears—fell on his cheek and ran down his immovable face.

"Good-bye," she whispered, and remained irresolute till he pushed her suddenly into Dain's arms.

"If you have any pity for me," murmured Almayer, as if repeating some sentence learned by heart, "take that woman away."

He stood very straight, his shoulders thrown back, his head held high, and looked at them as they went down the beach to the canoe, walking enlaced in each other's arms. He looked at the line of their footsteps marked in the sand. He followed their figures moving in the crude blaze of the vertical sun, in that light violent and vibrating, like a triumphal flourish of brazen trumpets. He looked at the man's brown shoulders, at the red sarong round his waist; at the tall, slender, dazzling white figure he supported. He looked at the white dress, at the falling masses of the long black hair. He looked at them embarking, and at the canoe growing smaller in the distance, with rage, despair, and regret in his heart, and on his face a peace as that of a carved image of oblivion. Inwardly he felt himself torn to pieces, but Ali who—now aroused—stood close to his master, saw on his features the blank expression of those who live in that hopeless calm which sightless eyes only can give.

The canoe disappeared, and Almayer stood motionless with his eyes fixed on its wake. Ali from under the shade of his hand examined the coast curiously. As the sun declined, the sea-breeze sprang up from the northward and shivered with its breath the glassy surface of the water.

"Dapat!"* exclaimed Ali, joyously. "Got him,

master! Got prau! Not there! Look more Tanah Mirrah* side. Aha! That way! Master, see? Now plain. See?"

Almayer followed Ali's forefinger with his eyes for a long time in vain. At last he sighted a triangular patch of yellow light on the red background of the cliffs of Tanjong Mirrah. It was the sail of the prau that had caught the sunlight and stood out, distinct with its gay tint, on the dark red of the cape. The yellow triangle crept slowly from cliff to cliff, till it cleared the last point of land and shone brilliantly for a fleeting minute on the blue of the open sea. Then the prau bore up to the southward: the light went out of the sail, and all at once the vessel itself disappeared, vanishing in the shadow of the steep headland that looked on, patient and lonely, watching over the empty sea.

Almayer never moved. Round the little islet the air was full of the talk of the rippling water. The crested wavelets ran up the beach audaciously, joyously, with the lightness of young life, and died quickly, unresistingly, and graciously, in the wide curves of transparent foam on the yellow sand. Above, the white clouds sailed rapidly southwards as if intent upon overtaking something. Ali seemed anxious.

"Master," he said timidly, "time to get house now. Long way off to pull. All ready, sir."

"Wait," whispered Almayer.

Now she was gone his business was to forget, and he had a strange notion that it should be done systematically and in order. To Ali's great dismay he fell on his hands and knees, and, creeping along the sand, erased carefully with his hand all traces of Nina's footsteps. He piled up small heaps of sand, leaving behind him a line of miniature graves right down to the water. After burying the last slight imprint of Nina's slipper* he stood up, and, turning his face towards the headland where he had last seen the prau, he made an effort to shout out loud again his firm resolve to never forgive. Ali watching him uneasily saw only his lips move, but heard no sound. He brought his foot down with a stamp. He was a firm man—firm as a rock. Let her go. He never had a daughter. He would forget. He was forgetting already.

Ali approached him again, insisting on immediate departure, and this time he consented, and they went together towards their canoe, Almayer leading. For all his firmness he looked very dejected and feeble as he dragged his feet slowly through the sand on the beach; and by his side—invisible to Ali—stalked that particular fiend whose mission it is to jog the memories of men, lest they should forget the meaning of life. He whispered into Almayer's ear a childish prattle of many years ago. Almayer, his head bent on one side, seemed to listen to his invisible companion, but his face was like the face of a man that has died struck from behind —a face from which all feelings and all expression are suddenly wiped off by the hand of unexpected death.

They slept on the river that night, mooring their canoe under the bushes and lying down in the bottom side by side, in the absolute exhaustion that kills hunger, thirst, all feeling and all thought in the overpowering desire for that deep sleep which is like the temporary annihilation of the tired body. Next day they started again and fought doggedly with the current all the morning, till about midday they reached the settlement and made fast their little craft to the jetty of Lingard and Co. Almayer walked straight to the house, and Ali followed, paddles on shoulder, thinking that he would like to eat something. As they crossed the front courtyard they noticed the abandoned look of the place. Ali looked in at the different servants' houses: all were empty. In the back courtyard there was the same absence of sound and life. In the cooking-shed the fire was out and the black embers were cold. A tall, lean man came stealthily out of the banana plantation, and went away rapidly across the open space looking at them with big, frightened eyes over his shoulder. Some vagabond without a master; there were many such in the settlement, and they looked upon Almayer as their patron. They prowled about his premises and picked their living there, sure that nothing worse could befall them than a shower of curses when they got in the way of the white man, whom they trusted and liked, and called a fool amongst themselves. In the house, which Almayer entered through the back verandah, the only living thing that met his eyes was his small monkey, which hungry and unnoticed for the last two days, began to cry and complain in monkey language as soon as it caught sight of the familiar face. Almayer soothed it with a few words and ordered Ali to bring in some bananas, then while Ali was gone to get them he stood in the doorway of the front verandah looking at the chaos of overturned furniture. Finally he picked up the table and sat on it while the monkey let itself down from the roof stick by its chain and perched on his shoulder. When the bananas came they had their breakfast together; both hungry, both eating greedily and showering the skins round them recklessly, in the trusting silence of perfect friendship. Ali went away, grumbling, to cook some rice himself, for all the women about the house had disappeared; he did not know where. Almayer did not seem to care, and, after he finished eating, he sat on the table swinging his legs and staring at the river as if lost in thought.

After some time he got up and went to the door of a room on the right of the verandah. That was the office. The office of Lingard and Co. He very seldom went in there. There was no business now, and he did not want an office. The door was locked, and he stood biting his lower lip, trying to think of the place where the key could be. Suddenly he remembered: in the women's room hung upon a nail. He went over to the doorway where the red curtain hung down in motionless folds, and hesitated for a moment before pushing it aside with his shoulder as if breaking down some solid obstacle. A great square of sunshine entering through the window lay on the floor. On the left he saw Mrs. Almayer's big wooden chest, the lid thrown back, empty; near it the brass nails of Nina's European trunk shone in the large initials N. A. on the cover. A few of Nina's dresses hung on wooden pegs, stiffened in a look of offended dignity at their abandonment. He remembered making the pegs himself and noticed that they were very good pegs. Where was the key? He looked round and saw it near the door where he stood. It was red with rust. He felt very much annoyed at that, and directly afterwards wondered at his own feeling. What did it matter? There soon would be no key—no door—nothing! He paused, key in hand, and asked himself whether he knew well what he was about. He went out again on the verandah and stood by the table thinking. The monkey jumped down, and, snatching a banana skin, absorbed itself in picking it to shreds industriously.

"Forget!" muttered Almayer, and that word started before him a sequence of events, a detailed programme of things to do. He knew perfectly well what was to be done now. First this, then that, and then forgetfulness would come easy. Very easy. He had a fixed idea that if he should not forget before he died he would have to remember to all eternity. Certain things had to be taken out of his life, stamped out of sight, destroyed, forgotten. For a long time he stood in deep thought, lost in the alarming possibilities of unconquerable memory, with the fear of death and eternity before him. "Eternity!" he said aloud, and the sound of that word recalled him out of his reverie. The monkey started, dropped the skin, and grinned up at him amicably.

He went towards the office door and with some difficulty managed to open it. He entered in a cloud of dust that rose under his feet. Books open with torn pages bestrewed the floor; other books lay about grimy and black, looking as if they had never been opened. Account books. In those books he had intended to keep day by day a record of his rising fortunes. Long time ago. A very long time. For many years there had been no record to keep on the blue and red ruled pages! In the middle of the room the big office desk, with one of its legs broken, careened over like the hull of a stranded ship; most of the drawers had fallen out, disclosing heaps of paper yellow with age and dirt. The revolving office chair stood in its place, but he found the pivot set fast when he tried to turn it. No matter. He desisted, and his eyes wandered slowly from object to object. All those things had cost a lot of money at the time. The desk, the paper, the torn books, and the broken shelves, all under a thick coat of dust. The very dust and bones of a dead and gone business. He looked at all these things, all that was left after so many years of work, of strife, of weariness, of discouragement, conquered so many times. And all for what? He stood thinking mournfully of his past life till he heard distinctly the clear voice of a child speaking amongst all this wreck, ruin, and waste. He started with a great fear in his heart, and feverishly began to rake in the papers scattered on the floor, broke the chair into bits, splintered the drawers by banging them against the desk, and made a big heap of all that rubbish in one corner of the room.

He came out quickly, slammed the door after him, turned the key, and, taking it out, ran to the front rail of the verandah, and, with a great swing of his arm, sent the key whizzing into the river. This done, he went back slowly to the table, called the monkey down, unhooked its chain, and induced it to remain quiet in the breast of his jacket. Then he sat again on the table and looked fixedly at the door of the room he had just left. He listened also intently. He heard a dry sound of rustling, sharp cracks as of dry wood snapping, a whirr like that of a bird's wings when it rises suddenly, and then he saw a thin stream of smoke come through the keyhole. The monkey struggled under his coat. Ali appeared with his eyes starting out of his head.

"Master! House burn!" he shouted.

Almayer stood up holding by the table. He could hear the yells of alarm and surprise in the settlement. Ali wrung his hands, lamenting aloud.

"Stop this noise, fool!" said Almayer, quietly. "Pick up my hammock and blankets and take them to the other house. Quick, now!"

The smoke burst through the crevices of the door, and Ali, with the hammock in his arms, cleared in one bound the steps of the verandah.

"It has caught well," muttered Almayer to himself. "Be quiet, Jack," he added, as the monkey made a frantic effort to escape from its confinement.

The door split from top to bottom, and a rush of flame and smoke drove Almayer away from the table to the front rail of the verandah. He held on there till a great roar overhead assured him that the roof was ablaze. Then he ran down the steps of the verandah, coughing, half choked with the smoke that pursued him in bluish wreaths curling about his head.

On the other side of the ditch, separating Almayer's courtyard from the settlement, a crowd of the inhabitants of Sambir looked at the burning house of the white man. In the calm air the flames rushed up on high, coloured pale brick-red, with violet gleams in the strong sunshine. The thin column of smoke ascended straight and unwavering till it lost itself in the clear blue of the sky, and in the great empty space between the two houses the interested spectators could see the tall figure of the Tuan Putih, with bowed head and dragging feet, walking slowly away from the fire towards the shelter of "Almayer's Folly."

In that manner did Almayer move into his new house. He took possession of the new ruin, and in the undying folly of his heart set himself to wait in anxiety and pain for that forgetfulness which was so slow to come. He had done all he could. Every vestige of Nina's existence had been destroyed; and now with every sunrise he asked himself whether the longed-for oblivion would come before sunset, whether it would come before he died? He wanted to live only long enough to be able to forget, and the tenacity of his memory filled him with dread and horror of death; for should it come before he could accomplish the purpose of his life he would have to remember for ever! He also longed for loneliness. He wanted to be alone. But he was not. In the dim light of the rooms with their closed shutters, in the bright sunshine of the verandah, wherever he went, whichever way he turned, he saw the small figure of a little maiden with pretty olive face, with long black hair, her little pink robe slipping off her shoulders, her big eyes looking up at him in the tender trustfulness of a petted child. Ali did not see anything, but he also was aware of the presence of a child in the house. In his long talks by the evening fires of the settlement he used to tell his intimate friends of Almayer's strange doings. His master had turned sorcerer in his old age. Ali said that often when Tuan Putih had retired for the night he could hear him talking to something in his room. Ali thought that it was a spirit in the shape of a child. He knew his master spoke to a child from certain expressions and words his master used. His master spoke in Malay a little, but mostly in English, which he, Ali, could understand. Master spoke to the child at times tenderly, then he would weep over it, laugh at it, scold it, beg of it to go away; curse it. It was a bad and stubborn spirit. Ali thought his master had imprudently called it up, and now could not get rid of it. His master was very brave; he was not afraid to curse this spirit in the very Presence; and once he fought with it. Ali had heard a great noise as of running about inside the room and groans. His master groaned. Spirits do not groan. His master was brave, but foolish. You cannot hurt a spirit. Ali expected to find his master dead next morning, but he came out very early, looking much older than the day before, and had no food all day.

So far Ali to the settlement. To Captain Ford he was much more communicative, for the good reason that Captain Ford had the purse and gave orders. On each of Ford's monthly visits to Sambir Ali had to go on board with a report about the inhabitant of "Almayer's Folly." On his first visit to Sambir, after Nina's departure, Ford had taken charge of Almayer's affairs. They were not cumbersome. The shed for the storage of goods was empty, the boats had disappeared, appropriated—generally in night-time—by various citizens of Sambir in need of means of transport. During a great flood the jetty of Lingard and Co. left the bank and floated down the river, probably in search of more cheerful surroundings; even the flock of geese—"the only geese on the east coast"—departed somewhere, preferring the unknown dangers of the bush to the desolation of their old home. As time went on the grass grew over the black patch of ground where the old house used to stand, and nothing remained to mark the place of the dwelling that had sheltered Almayer's young hopes, his foolish dream of splendid future, his awakening, and his despair.

Ford did not often visit Almayer, for visiting Almayer was not a pleasant task. At first he used to respond listlessly to the old seaman's boisterous inquiries about his health; he even made efforts to talk, asking for news in a voice that made it perfectly clear that no news from this world had any interest for him. Then gradually he became more silent—not sulkily—but as if he was forgetting how to speak. He used also to hide in the darkest rooms of the house where Ford had to seek him out guided by the patter of the monkey galloping before him. The monkey was always there to receive and introduce Ford. The little animal seemed to have taken complete charge of its master, and whenever it wished for his presence on the verandah it would tug perseveringly at his jacket, till Almayer obediently came out into the sunshine, which he seemed to dislike so much.

One morning Ford found him sitting on the floor of the verandah, his back against the wall, his legs stretched stiffly out, his arms hanging by his side. His expressionless face, his eyes open wide with immobile pupils, and the rigidity of his pose, made him look like an immense man-doll broken and flung there out of the way. As Ford came up the steps he turned his head slowly.

"Ford," he murmured from the floor, "I cannot forget."

"Can't you?" said Ford, innocently, with an attempt at joviality: "I wish I was like you. I am losing my memory—age, I suppose; only the other day my mate——"

He stopped, for Almayer had got up, stumbled, and steadied himself on his friend's arm.

"Hallo! You are better to-day. Soon be all right," said Ford, cheerfully, but feeling rather scared.

Almayer let go his arm and stood very straight with his head up and shoulders thrown back, looking stonily at the multitude of suns shining in ripples of the river. His jacket and his loose trousers flapped in the breeze on his thin limbs.

"Let her go!" he whispered in a grating voice. "Let her go. To-morrow I shall forget. I am a firm man, ... firm as a . . . . rock, . . . firm. . . ."

Ford looked at his face—and fled. The skipper was a tolerably firm man himself—as those who had sailed with him could testify—but Almayer's firmness was altogether too much for his fortitude.

Next time the steamer called in Sambir Ali came on board early with a grievance. He complained to Ford that Jim-Eng the Chinaman had invaded Almayer's house, and actually had lived there for the last month.

"And they both smoke," added Ali.

"Phew! Opium, you mean?"

Ali nodded, and Ford remained thoughtful; then he muttered to himself, "Poor devil! The sooner the better now." In the afternoon he walked up to the house.

"What are you doing here?" he asked of Jim-Eng, whom he found strolling about on the verandah.

Jim-Eng explained in bad Malay, and speaking in that monotonous, uninterested voice of an opium smoker pretty far gone, that his house was old, the roof leaked, and the floor was rotten. So, being an old friend for many, many years, he took his money, his opium, and two pipes, and came to live in this big house. "There is plenty of room. He smokes, and I live here. He will not smoke long," he concluded.

"Where is he now?" asked Ford.

"Inside. He sleeps," answered Jim-Eng, wearily.

Ford glanced in through the doorway. In the dim light of the room he could see Almayer lying on his back on the floor, his head on a wooden pillow, the long white beard scattered over his breast, the yellow skin of the face, the half-closed eyelids showing the whites of the eye* only. . . .

He shuddered and turned away. As he was leaving he noticed a long strip of faded red silk, with some Chinese letters on it, which Jim-Eng had just fastened to one of the pillars.

"What's that?" he asked.

"That," said Jim-Eng, in his colourless voice, "that is the name of the house. All the same like my house. Very good name."

Ford looked at him for awhile and went away. He did not know what the crazy-looking maze of the Chinese inscription on the red silk meant. Had he asked Jim-Eng, that patient Chinaman would have informed him with proper pride that its meaning was: "House of heavenly delight."

In the evening of the same day Babalatchi called on

Captain Ford. The captain's cabin opened on deck, and Babalatchi sat astride on the high step, while Ford smoked his pipe on the settee inside. The steamer was leaving next morning, and the old statesman came as usual for a last chat.

"We had news from Bali last moon," remarked Babalatchi. "A grandson is born to the old Rajah, and there is great rejoicing."

Ford sat up interested.

"Yes," went on Babalatchi, in answer to Ford's look. "I told him. That was before he began to smoke."

"Well, and what?" asked Ford.

"I escaped with my life," said Babalatchi, with perfect gravity, "because the white man is very weak and fell as he rushed upon me." Then, after a pause, he added, "She is mad with joy."

"Mrs. Almayer, you mean?"

"Yes, she lives in our Rajah's house. She will not die soon. Such women live a long time," said Babalatchi, with a slight tinge of regret in his voice. "She has dollars, and she has buried them, but we know where. We had much trouble with those people. We had to pay a fine and listen to threats from the white men, and now we have to be careful." He sighed and remained silent for a long while. Then with energy:

"There will be fighting. There is a breath of war on the islands. Shall I live long enough to see? . . . Ah, Tuan!" he went on, more quietly, "the old times were best. Even I have sailed with Lanun* men, and boarded in the night silent ships with white sails. That was before an English Rajah ruled in Kuching.* Then we fought amongst ourselves and were happy. Now when we fight with you we can only die!"

He rose to go. "Tuan," he said, "you remember the

girl that man Bulangi had? Her that caused all the trouble?"

"Yes," said Ford. "What of her?"

"She grew thin and could not work. Then Bulangi, who is a thief and a pig-eater, gave her to me for fifty dollars. I sent her amongst my women to grow fat. I wanted to hear the sound of her laughter, but she must have been bewitched, and . . . she died two days ago. Nay, Tuan. Why do you speak bad words? I am old—that is true—but why should I not like the sight of a young face and the sound of a young voice in my house?" He paused, and then added with a little mournful laugh, "I am like a white man talking too much of what is not men's talk when they speak to one another."

And he went off looking very sad.

* * * * *

The crowd massed in a semicircle before the steps of "Almayer's Folly," swayed silently backwards and forwards, and opened out before the group of white-robed and turbaned men advancing through the grass towards the house. Abdulla walked first, supported by Reshid and followed by all the Arabs in Sambir. As they entered the lane made by the respectful throng there was a subdued murmur of voices, where the word "Mati"* was the only one distinctly audible. Abdulla stopped and looked round slowly.

"Is he dead?" he asked.

"May you live!" answered the crowd in one shout, and then there succeeded a breathless silence.

Abdulla made a few paces* forward and found himself for the last time face to face with his old enemy. Whatever he might have been once he was not dangerous now, lying stiff and lifeless in the tender light of the early day. The only white man on the east coast was dead, and his soul, delivered from the trammels of his earthly folly, stood now in the presence of Infinite Wisdom. On the upturned face there was that serene look which follows the sudden relief from anguish and pain, and it testified silently before the cloudless heaven that the man lying there under the gaze of indifferent eyes had been permitted to forget before he died.

Abdulla looked down sadly at this Infidel he had fought so long and had bested so many times. Such was the reward of the Faithful! Yet in the Arab's old heart there was a feeling of regret for that thing gone out of his life. He was leaving fast behind him friendships, and enmities, successes, and disappointments—all that makes up a life; and before him was only the end. Prayer would fill up the remainder of the days allotted to the True Believer! He took in his hand the beads that hung at his waist.

"I found him here, like this, in the morning," said Ali, in a low and awed voice.

Abdulla glanced coldly once more at the serene face. "Let us go," he said, addressing Reshid.

And as they passed through the crowd that fell back before them, the beads in Abdulla's hand clicked, while in a solemn whisper he breathed out piously the name of Allah! The Merciful! The Compassionate!

THE END

EXPLANATORY NOTES

'Author's Note'

lxi *a lady*: Alice Meynell (1847–1922), poet and essayist, who knew most of the literary figures of the late Victorian period, including Tennyson, Francis Thompson, Meredith, and Coventry Patmore.

disapproval of: aversion from (MS and H)

'decivilized': Alice Meynell published a short essay under that title in the *National Observer*, 24 January 1891, reprinted in *The Rhythm of Life*, 1893, a collection of her essays. In it she attacks literature on colonial subjects for its concern with degraded human beings and for preferring newness of effect over continuity. See David Leon Higdon, 'The Text and Context of Conrad's First Critical Essay', *Polish Review*, 20: 2–3 (1975), 106–22.

judgement:: judgement that: (MS and H)

seem: MS and H; seems (SD and D)

Only: But (MS and H)

lxii *Their hearts . . . our folly*: MS sets off this sentence as a separate paragraph. Thereafter, following it and slightly indented, H adds: 'I wrote the above in 1895 by way of preface for my first novel. An essay by Mrs Meynell furnished the impulse for this artless outpouring. I let it now be printed for the first time, unaltered and uncorrected, as my first attempt at writing a preface and an early record of exaggerated but genuine feeling.'

Text of Almayer's Folly

1 *T.B.*: Tadeusz Bobrowski, Conrad's maternal uncle and guardian, born 1829, died 10 February 1894 (or 29 January 1894 Gregorian style). On 18 February Conrad wrote to Marguerite Poradowska: 'Mon oncle est mort le 11 [sic] de ce mois et il me semble que tout est mort en moi. Il semble emporter mon âme avec lui.' ('My uncle died on the 11th of this month, and it seems as if everything has died in me. He seems to have carried my soul away with him.') (*Letters*, i. 148).

2 The epigraph is taken from the *Journal Intime*, or introspective diary, of Henri-Frédéric Amiel (1821–81), a Protestant pro-

fessor of philosophy at the University of Geneva. He kept the diary for over thirty years, selections from which appeared in 1883–7. Conrad quotes from the 24 April 1852 (p.m.) entry: 'Who among us has not had his promised land, his day of ecstasy and his end in exile?' He quoted, it seems, from memory, for the exact phrasing of the original is: 'Qui de nous n'a sa terre promise, son jour d'extase, et sa fin dans l'exil'.

3 *Makan*: Malay for 'Let's eat' (Winstedt).

Almayer: phonetic transcription of (Charles) Olmeijer, the prototype of Conrad's 'Almayer' in *Almayer's Folly*, *The Outcast of the Islands* (1896), and *A Personal Record* (1912), the fourth chapter of which describes Conrad's first meeting with him. For further details, see Appendix.

Pantai: the name given at the time of Conrad's visits to East Borneo to the river now known as the Berau. 'Pantai' is Malay for 'shore' or 'beach' (Winstedt).

gold: a report by J. A. Hooze on the mining prospects in the Berau region published in Holland in 1886 mentions Olmeijer ('the Dutch agent of the firm of Linggard & Co.') as an inveterate prospector (Allen, 216, 222).

Nina: when Conrad met Olmeijer in 1887 only his two youngest children were living with him—a small son and a daughter of five. In the *Straits Times* of 17 July 1951, one A. K. Suki wrote that 'nina', the Spanish for 'girl', had been absorbed into Malay from the early Spanish colonists, and was sometimes used in lieu of a proper name (Allen, 221).

4 *Dain*: according to Sherry, 'Dain' (properly spelt 'Daeng') was a title of distinction with the Malay Bugis tribe (Sherry, 140); according to Haverschmidt (see Appendix), Conrad's 'Dain Maroola', though a Balinese rajah, may have owed his name to one Dain Marola, a Buginese clerk working in Berau (Allen, 233). However, in Conrad's narrative, 'Dain Maroola' is a pseudonym (pp. 123 lines 17–18; 184 line 25).

house: according to Haverschmidt, Olmeijer built himself a large house in 1881, but neglected it. Haverschmidt located it well up the settlement, and not near the point of land marking the confluence of the two rivers, as in the novel (pp. 4 lines 26–7; 14 lines 26–8). See Allen, 194–6, 218.

Celebes . . . Macassar: at the end of the nineteenth century,

Macassar (now Ujung Pandang) consisted of the Dutch port (Vlaardingen), with a large quay, big warehouses, broad streets, and imposing public buildings; and the Malay city, which lay back from the shore. The town had been opened to foreign trade in 1848, and had become not only the principal outlet for the produce of Celebes, but the chief transshipment port of the eastern archipelago. Its main exports were agricultural and forest products, its main imports cotton, woollen, and silk goods.

5 *godowns*: warehouses, from Malay *godong* (Winstedt).

Hudig: Sherry failed to trace a merchant of that name in Macassar, and this editor has not taken up the challenge, especially as he has not found any evidence to suggest that Conrad ever went there. However, while waiting to embark on the *Highland Forest* in Amsterdam (see Appendix), Conrad would visit a merchant called 'Mr Hudig'. In his recollections, 'He was a big, swarthy Netherlander, with black moustaches and a bold glance. He always began by shoving me into a chair before I had time to open my mouth, gave me cordially a large cigar, and in excellent English would start to talk everlastingly . . .' (*The Mirror of the Sea*, 51). This Hudig shares traits with the Macassar Hudig.

Botanical Gardens of Buitenzorg: Buitenzorg was the name of a great estate south of Batavia (now Djakarta) established as the Governor's country residence; in 1811 it was converted into what quickly became one of the leading botanical institutions in the world (Vlekke, 218, 176).

long easy-chair: an unnecessary retranslation of what is already known in English as a 'chaise-longue', i.e. a sofa with a rest for the back at one end only (see also p. 65 line 15).

It was . . . dealer there: TS reads: 'It was an important epoch in his life for on that day began a new existence for the son of a subordinate government official employed on the staff of the Botanical Gardens in Buitenzorg—as glad, no doubt, to place his son in such a firm—as was the young man himself to leave the poisonous shores of Java, and the meagre comforts of the parental bungalow, where the father grumbled all day at the stupidity of native gardeners; and the mother—from the depths of her long easy-chair—bewailed the lost glories of Amsterdam where she had been brought up, being indeed the daughter of a cigar dealer there.' Conrad revised this laboured sentence in the proofs, and the result is a model of syntactical and rhetorical clarification (Higdon, *Proof*, 410).

Manchester goods: perhaps more commonly known as Manchester wares, these were essentially cotton goods manufactured in that city.

6 *Mr. Vinck*: this figure seems quite unrelated to the Mrs Vinck with whom Nina boards in Singapore (p. 27 line 31).

punkah: a large swinging fan made of cloth stretched over a rectangular frame, suspended from the ceiling and worked by a cord.

rattan: climbing liana palms, with long, thin, jointed pliable stems. They were regularly used for tying, for plaiting, and for basket work (see e.g. p. 106 line 4).

bonies: ponies. In *A Personal Record* (p. 46) the original 'Almayer' imports a pony as a status symbol. All the Lesser Soenda Islands, including Bali mentioned here, were known for pony-breeding. Before the advent of the motor car, most planters and officials possessed teams of 'sandalwood' horses (*Handbook*, ii. 207).

schooners: a schooner is a small sea-going, two-masted, fore-and-aft rigged vessel carrying square-rigged topsails.

7 *Tom Lingard*: this figure, a major character in *An Outcast of the Islands* (1896) and the protagonist of *The Rescue* (1920, begun 1896), is modelled on the trader-adventurer William Lingard, active in the Archipelago from before 1850 to about 1884 (see Appendix).

Rajah-Laut: *raja* is Malay for 'ruler', *laut* for 'sea' (Winstedt). William Lingard was known by that title throughout the Archipelago, and he gave it to his last ship.

Sulu pirates: the Sulu Archipelago, consisting of about eighty small islands between North Borneo and the southern Phillipine island of Mindanao, was a notorious pirate stronghold. (For an authoritative summary of nineteenth-century piracy in the region, see Hall, 497–505.) In 1954 G. Knijpenga found in Macassar newspapers for 1875 reports that William Lingard and his wife had successfully repelled a pirate attack off the mouth of the Pentai/Berau river after a two-hour engagement (Allen, 211). Moreover, Conrad owned Fred McNair's *Perak and the Malays* (London, 1878) in which, on p.

277, he would have found the following: 'The late Captain Edye, of H.M.S. *Satellite*, also brought down a little captive girl, who had evidently been taken by these people [the pirates] from one of the vessels they had destroyed. She was a Eurasian, and only about ten years of age, having in all probability been taken when quite an infant, for the language she spoke was very mixed, and she had no recollection of her capture . . . On her arrival at Singapore, she was first placed in the girls' school attached to the late Mr Keasberry's mission . . .' (quoted Sherry, 150). At least this may have persuaded Conrad of the plausibility of *his* incident.

prau: the characteristic boat of the Archipelago about 30 feet long, and propelled either by sails or by oars. The classic *prau* or *prao* has both stem and stern sharp, one side conventionally curved, the other flat (to act as a lee board) and steadied by a small canoe rigged parallel to it. It is exceptionally manœuvrable and fast-moving.

discovered a river: William Lingard did not discover the Pentai/Berau, but he was the first to survey it and to establish a trading post in Berau. The *Eastern Archipelago Pilot* of 1893 states: 'Below Guning Tabur [Berau], the Berau river has a breadth of from 660 to 1300 yards, its mean depth at ordinary low water being 18 feet, with a minimum depth of 12½ feet at a spot on the west side of Sandang-besar island, known as "Lingard's Cross"' (quoted in Sherry, 124).

Sunda Hotel: the Sunda Straits, which divide Sumatra from Java, provide a plausible name.

8 *cargo*: having researched Dutch records, G. Knijpenga in December 1954 and January 1955 published in the Amsterdam periodical *de Uitlaat* some articles entitled 'Archipelago Trade in the Past' in which he described the activities of the 'Rajah Laut' William Lingard: 'He called at various stations, making trade arrangements with the chiefs. The products he secured from them he sold elsewhere, calling regularly at Singapore. What he loaded at Singapore he delivered at islets and small coastal settlements. He was too much of an adventurer to adhere strictly to import regulations, drawing the lines himself between what was lawful and unlawful' (quoted Allen, 213).

brig: (short for 'brigantine') a two-masted square-rigged

vessel, with a lower fore-and-aft sail on the main mast. William Lingard never possessed a brig of that name.

roadstead: the anchorage or 'roadstead' at Macassar is bounded by a coral reef about half a mile from the shore.

gutta-percha . . . gum-dammar: gutta-percha is raw rubber, much in demand as insulation for underground and undersea cables; rattans are flexible stalks (see note to p. 6); pearl is 'mother of pearl'; birds' nests are the nests of swifts cemented in limestone caves with bird saliva and prized as a condiment for Chinese soup; wax is beeswax used for candles etc.; gum-dammar is the so-called 'cat's eye resin' used as fuel for Malay torches, for making varnish, etc. The *Eastern Archipelago Pilot* for 1893 reports on Berau trade as follows: 'The principal articles of export are rattan, gutta-percha, and dammar. . . . The principal trade is with Singapore, chiefly in the vessels of Messers Lingard & Co.' (quoted Sherry, 128). More particularly, the *Naval Handbook*, i. 219 notes: 'A few miles above Tandjoengredeb [Berau] is a tributary, the Birang, famous for its edible birds' nest caves.'

hidden sandbanks and coral reefs: the Berau estuary presented a genuine obstacle to navigation. The *Naval Handbook*, i. 224 describes the coast running north-west to the Berau delta as 'mainly low, flat and marshy, and overgrown with mangroves, with an occasional rocky headland. A coral reef fringes most of the eastern part'. The delta itself is, in the words of the *Eastern Archipelago Pilot* (ii. 468–9), 'formed by many uninhabited islands, with various passages between them . . . the channels through the estuary are only suitable for small vessels with local knowledge' (quoted Sherry, 123–4).

9 *Sourabaya*: main trading seaport of the eastern end of Java and, at the time, the naval and military headquarters of the Dutch East Indies.

intended: U has 'was going'. Why Conrad made this alteration remains entirely unclear.

10 *marry . . . daughter*: for the family link between William Lingard and Charles Olmeijer see Appendix.

11 *stockade . . . compound*: a Dutch administrative report produced *c.*1920 out of the archives of the sultan of Gunung Tabur (Conrad's 'Sambir') shows that the province, which had been

divided since the eighteenth century into two sultanates, Gunung Tabur and Sambaliung (see Appendix), had long been split by tension and rivalry between them. The compounds of the rajahs were therefore fortified as a matter of course, usually by means of stout wooden stockades and brass cannon. (See Allen, 214–15.)

12 *freshet*: river-flood.

Abdulla's: the Arab owner of the *Vidar*, Al Joffree, had placed his eldest son, Syed Abdulla, in Berau to supervise his trading house. Conrad's 'Abdulla' is an old man who has brought up his nephew as his successor.

Man: this seems an unnatural exclamation. It is the case that the typist had difficulty with Conrad's handwriting over Malay names, and regularly rendered 'Tuan' as 'Man' (Higdon, *Typescript*, 103). Conrad made all the necessary corrections except, perhaps, here. However, although at p. 52 line 16 Almayer addresses Dain as 'Tuan' and treats Abdulla and his agents with ostensible, if forced, respect, 'Tuan' is scarcely more plausible than 'Man'.

13 *Tuan*: a Malay term indicating deference. It was used regularly in addressing Europeans and Malay superiors.

Drop down: U has: 'But you are too far here. Drop down.' This focuses the scene and underlines the cross-purposes.

Orang Blanda: Malay for 'Dutchman'; *orang* = person, *blanda* (or *Belanda*) = Dutch (Winstedt).

Lakamba: the 1920 Dutch administrative report (see note to p. 11) shows that at the time of Conrad's visits to Berau the Rajah of Gunung Tabur was a youth of 21 named Mohamad Siranoedin, and dominated by an unscrupulous older cousin who acted as regent and governed the river (Allen, 231). Conrad's 'Lakamba' bears very little resemblance to this figure, except perhaps for his dependence on a more astute confidant. Jean-Aubry was told by Captain Craig (see Appendix) that 'Babalatchi and Lakamba . . . were two natives of the Celebes established as merchants at Broeuw' (*Life and Letters*, i. 97–8). Craig added that they were much respected by the inhabitants and that their remarkable appearance attracted Conrad's attention. The reliability of Craig, at least in this respect, was confirmed by the discovery among Conrad's papers of a bill of lading dated 1887 recording a shipment of gum by a Babalatchi via the *Vidar* to Celebes. Babalatchi is, of course, the name given by Conrad to Lakamba's 'prime minister, harbour master, financial adviser, and general factotum' (p. 38 lines 15–16).

bowman: the rower nearest to the bow, or fore-end of a boat.

14 *Sambir*: Conrad's name for the settlement as a whole (Berau) and for that part of it between the two rivers (Tanjong Redeb). He may have derived the name from 'Sambur-akat', a settlement 10 miles down river; but it is clear he wished to preserve the anonymity of the location.

The main stream . . . over the river: for an outline of the modifications brought by Conrad to the topography of Berau—both place and river—see Appendix. Conrad's topography is difficult to follow here: he seems to suggest that the Pantai divides into two streams to form an 'island', Almayer's house being at the point where the streams re-unite. Elsewhere (e.g. at p. 28 lines 20–3, where up-country canoes are obliged to round the point) Conrad implies that the branches are two separate rivers meeting to form, as it were, a promontory between them. Conrad's revision of U's 'main branch' to 'main stream' does not clarify the topography, for it merely removes a verbal echo ('branches . . . branch').

15 *Abdulla bin Selim*: Abdulla son of Selim. This man (in the form 'Abdullah bin Selim') remains Almayer's 'enemy' in *A Personal Record* (p. 82). The historical Abdulla's father, Al Joffree, was not called Selim.

Lingard & Co: this, the name of William Lingard's Berau trading company, was still cited in official documents in 1893 (Sherry, 127–8).

16 *the place*: after this sentence, U adds: 'Great red stains on the floor and walls testified to frequent and indiscriminate betel-nut chewing.' The deletion weakens the description: the details may be disgusting, but they are consistent with Mrs Almayer's domestic habits (pp. 27 line 14; 29 line 32; 41 lines 7–8, etc.).

genever: gin or 'hollands'. 'Genever' is the Dutch word for juniper, the berries of which are used to flavour the spirits.

17 *looked out*: U omits 'out'; the addition directs the gaze.

I heard nothing: U has 'No. I heard nothing.' This perhaps makes the slowness of the utterance more plausible.

Promised to: U has 'Will', which makes Almayer more gullible.

18 *She was as tall*: U has 'She was nearly as tall'. The deletion sharpens the contrast with the previous line.

fist: U has 'clenched hand'—a bizarre, and certainly less angry, locution.

he whispered tenderly, kissing: U has 'he whispered, tenderly kissing'—a pointing perhaps more sensitive to what follows.

unmoved: U has 'with her face unmoved'. The deletion entails no loss, and is therefore a gain.

19 *And motionless . . . merciless force*: this descriptive passage caused Conrad considerable trouble: all five versions (TS, U, M, SD, and H) underwent modifications, but the most significant were the alterations made by Conrad in 1916 to U for the proposed SD, the basis of the text of this edition. The U text read as follows: 'And motionless . . . before the furious blast of the coming tempest, the upper reach of the river whipped into white foam by the wind . . . she could hear afar off the roar of the wind, the hiss of heavy rain . . . the storm reached the low point dividing the river, the house shook in the wind, and the rain pattered loudly on the palm-tree roof, the thunder spoke in one prolonged roll . . .'. The replacement of U's 'blast of the coming tempest' with SD's 'blast of wind' (a much more economical and vivid phrase in context) entails the consequential deletion of the word 'wind' in three places, with expressive advantage in the last two ('the driving roar and hiss' and 'the whole house shook while the rain').

20 *rainy monsoon*: Conrad clearly believes that Borneo is subject to monsoon variations. However, according to the *Naval Handbook*, i. 225, in East Borneo the temperature varies very little from 80°F throughout the year, rainfall is consistently high, there is no true dry season, and thunderstorms accompanied by torrential downpours can be an almost daily event. Conrad's brief visits to Berau allowed him to experience the weather but not the climate.

21 *fore-deck*: deck forming the roof of the crew's quarters at the forepart of the ship.

poop: aftermost part of a ship over the captain's quarters, or 'cabins'.

22 *surroundings*: at this point, U adds: 'Being fourteen years old, she realised her position and came to that conclusion, the only one possible to a Malay girl, soon ripened under a tropical sun, and not unaware of her personal charms, of which she heard many a young warrior of her father's crew express an appreciative admiration.' The removal of this passage in the later editions greatly weakens the presentation of Mrs Almayer. Her youthful seductiveness and eroticism explain her sense of betrayal by Lingard, her resentment of Almayer, her extra-marital liaison with Lakamba, and (in part) her transformation into a harridan. One can only assume that the older Conrad was overcome by a fit of decorum.

23 *fiat*: Latin for 'Let it be done', repeating God's originating command, 'Fiat lux' ('Let there be light').

Europe, the young convert: U has 'Europe, the centre of an interested circle of Batavian society, the young convert'. The deletion is pure loss, for it removes the social pressure (the 'circle' admires the convert while remaining conscious of her race) so necessary for an understanding of her predicament.

law: U has 'laws'; the singular suggests the whole ethos, the plural specific regulations.

Batavia: today called Djakarta, it is situated in north-west Java; it was the capital of the Dutch East Indies.

24 *gold and diamonds*: the MS shows that Conrad originally envisaged for his Almayer the recovery of 'the big diamond and the gold nugget' buried by Lingard (Gordan, 128). He toned down this melodramatic prospect into that of a 'rich gold mine' (p. 62 lines 11–12), and removed from the TS all references to diamonds in the perspective of Almayer's plans. The retention here is deliberate, for what is in question is general credulity—a point reinforced several times in the course of the narrative, e.g. 'They . . . wished him many big diamonds and a mountain of gold' (p. 35 lines 24–5) and, more explicitly, 'The coast population of Borneo believes implicitly in diamonds of fabulous value, in gold mines of enormous richness in the interior' (p. 39 lines 4–6). In the nineteenth century, Borneo 'promised well as a source of gold and diamonds' (*Handbook*, i. 202). More generally, the Neth-

erlands Indies had been known since the sixteenth century as the land of gold and silver, and the first European travellers had brought back tales of diamonds in Borneo. Although gold and diamonds were always more important in legend than in fact, towards the end of the nineteenth century there occurred a speculative boom that seems to have infected the fictional Tom Lingard, if not the historical William Lingard. In fact, what gold there is in East Borneo occurs both in veins and alluvial deposits; and some Dyaks found small quantities of gold and occasional diamonds in sand and gravel deposits in river beds. (See *Handbook*, ii. 247–67.)

the godowns: U has 'the big godowns', which balances 'the . . . little house', and motivates Almayer's sudden excitement.

Chinese carpenters: by the eighteenth century, the Chinese had established trade with Borneo. After 1870 Dutch rule attracted a large number of Chinese artisans and semi-skilled workers, a fair proportion of whom eventually returned to China. There are no Chinese women in *Almayer's Folly*. (See Furnivall, 213.)

The Arabs . . . river: Conrad's next novel, *An Outcast of the Islands*, attributes this to the treachery of Willems, a character in part based on one Carel De Veer, a young Dutch alcoholic drifter whom Olmeijer had taken under his wing in Berau. There is no basis for this in fact: William Lingard was first into Berau; he was eventually followed and overtaken by Al Joffree.

green turban: see note to p. 44.

25 *Syed*: a Moslem title (strictly *Saiyet*, cognate with 'El Cid') indicating descent from Mohammed's grandson Hasan, as *Sherif* marks descent from the Prophet's younger grandson, Husein (Allen, 234).

fishermen: Conrad's continuous references to fishing, fishing boats, and fishermen in the novel reflects the fact that the Berau, like other rivers in East Borneo, teem with a great variety of fish, which are a central source of food. The native inhabitants catch fish by netting, baskets (Babalatchi at p. 116 line 11), and even by poisoning the water with the root of a creeper (*Handbook*, i. 227).

fishermen of Sambir . . . common to Malays: U has 'fishermen of Sambira [*sic*] . . . common to aristocratic Malays and with a malicious pleasure in the domestic misfortunes of the Orang Blando [*sic*]—the hated Dutchman.' If the deletion is a gain, stylistically, it is also a loss in that it dilutes the racial tension. The talk is, of course, about Almayer's cuckoldry, to which the novel refers only indirectly (e.g. pp. 21 line 27; 38 lines 12–14; 135 line 34–136 line 3; 136 lines 21–4).

banker . . . failed: Norman Sherry thinks that the historical William Lingard was a victim of the collapse of the Singapore Oriental Bank in 1884, after which he ceased to trade (Sherry, 111). In *The Rescue* (the third of the 'Lingard' novels, but the first in terms of narrative chronology), Tom Lingard loses money through the collapse of the 'Occidental Bank' which Conrad now locates in Singapore, not in Macassar where Hudig's is.

outbursts: U has 'floods'. As Higdon says, '"Outbursts" explode without warning from "sulky silence"' (Higdon, *Collected*, 92).

26 *burning the furniture*: an apparently gratuitous act on the part of Mrs Almayer, until one realizes that it is a gesture of cultural vandalism. By European standards, Eastern houses are underfurnished, and their owners sit on mats or rugs. Abdulla boasts of his European furniture to Almayer when seeking Nina's hand for his nephew. See also pp. 90 line 26–91 line 4.

quarter-deck: upper deck extending from the stern to the after-mast, and used as a promenade by the officers.

27 *whale-boat*: a long, light boat, sharp at both ends, and usually steered with an oar.

betel-nut: *betel* is the leaf of a plant used as a masticatory when wrapped around the parings of the *nut* of the areca palm, and flavoured with lime. See p. 81 lines 8–13.

compound: enclosure around a building complex or a residence (from Malay *campong* = fenced-in space). See note to p. 11.

Providence, the old ruler: U has 'Providence and the help of a little scientific manipulation, the old ruler'. Again, the deletion is an impoverishment, diluting both the sense of Lakamba's murderousness and the tone of religious cynicism. For the first, see p. 88 lines 4–10; for the second p. 109 lines 23–8.

Mrs Vinck: see note to p. 6.

28 *no relation . . . besides*: the '*but* little else besides' sounds odd

after 'no relation living'. MS reads: 'saying he was ill, had only found one relation living—a young man—but little else besides' (Gordan, 128–9). There are traces in MS to suggest that Conrad envisaged at one point a role for a young 'white man'; be that as it may, he suppressed it from the TS, at the cost of the local clumsiness here.

swallowed up: on the apparent disappearance of William Lingard, see Appendix.

Sumatrese: Sumatra is a major island of the Archipelago, separated from Malaya/Singapore by the Strait of Malacca.

verdigris: green deposit naturally formed on copper or brass.

Jim Eng: according to Haverschmidt, Jim Eng was the name of a Chinese trader in Singapore who shipped goods to Berau on the *Vidar*. Moreover, one Po Eng Seng had a shop in Berau at the time of Conrad's visits where Olmeijer and his friends spent their time drinking (Allen, 233). Allen's documentation is not sufficiently clear, however, to know how seriously to take these claims.

opium: the export of mass-produced opium to China by the West in the nineteenth century created addiction on a national scale.

29 *Straits Settlements*: a British colony, adjacent to the Strait of Malacca, comprising parts of the Malacca peninsula, Penang (established 1786), and Singapore (founded 1819).

steamer: according to Norman Sherry, it was steam that put William Lingard out of business. In *Sixty Years' Life and Adventure in the Far East*, i. 82, John Dill Ross reports that William Lingard reproved his father for going in 'for a damn steamer instead of the good old sailing ships that made the money' (quoted Sherry, 110). The steamer owned by an Arab trader and plying regularly between Singapore and Berau is clearly modelled on the *Vidar*. Moreover, the use of that steamer for gunpowder contraband is far from implausible. The KPM archives in Amsterdam hold a report by a Dutch officer who visited Berau on 24–6 July 1892, which says: 'The import of guns and powder by the *Vidar* . . . was a matter of investigation but my efforts drew a blank; it is a fact that many natives have firearms but one cannot call it smuggling since no one inspects unloaded cargo or what incoming ships carry. Nevertheless, it is forbidden to export arms from Singapore, or to import them into the Netherlands Indies' (quoted Allen, 223). The activities of Ford's steamer reflect this situation with surprising fidelity.

30 *Captain Ford*: Ford seems clearly modelled on Captain Craig, master of the *Vidar*, also an Englishman showing the same traits of kindliness, reliability, and adventurousness. According to Jean-Aubry, who interviewed him, Craig 'had navigated the dangerous rivers of the islands for ten years and had come into contact with European, half-caste, Arab, and Malayan traders. Few men could have been better qualified than he to enlighten the curiosity of his mate . . .' (*Life and Letters*, i. 95–6). In *A Personal Record*, Conrad speaks of 'my good friend and commander Captain C——' (p. 75).

31 *discussed eagerly*: U has 'eagerly discussed': the distinction is extremely difficult to perceive.

levées: assemblages of visitors (from French for 'rising', as in a reception of attendants on a Prince's rising from bed).

Ubat: Malay for 'medicine', often with magical properties (Winstedt).

Mem Putih: 'Mem' (from Madam?) is a polite term of address; 'putih' means 'white'. Mrs Almayer, who is also referred to as 'old Mem', earns the sobriquet as the wife of a white man.

32 *Dyaks*: name of the native inhabitants of Borneo, popularly known as head-hunters (see p. 39 line 10) and blow-pipe users. They were driven inland by Malay settlements on the coast (the word 'dyak' signifies 'inlander'). Their religion requires belief in tutelary powers and non-human ancestors, which suggests totemism; social relations are based on the family; cultivation is general, but of a low grade and mostly shifting. (See *Handbook*, ii. 23.)

33 *British Borneo Company*: in Borneo, British interests established themselves in the north-east. Sarawak was taken over by a humanitarian adventurer, Sir James Brooke (1803–68), who became its rajah in 1841, and cleared the coasts of pirates (see p. 206 lines 30–4). In 1878 Sarawak became a British Protectorate. In the previous year, another imperialist, W. H. Treacher, had secured North Borneo for British trade, though against the wishes of the Colonial Office. Yet despite this, in 1881 the British North Borneo Company was estab-

lished by Royal Charter. Protests from Holland, which felt threatened, proved unavailing. See Hall, 538–9.

confiding: this sounds like a gallicism. The French *confiant* does not distinguish between confident (= self-assured) and confiding (= trusting); both seem required by the context, but the English word can only deliver 'trusting'.

sarongs: the sarong is the Malay national garment, consisting of a long strip of cloth worn tucked round the waist like a skirt or kilt.

34 *The claim . . . abandoned*: Holland was forced to accept the British North Borneo Company as a *fait accompli*, but she remained concerned about her frontier in eastern Borneo. In 1884 both countries agreed to establish a Joint Frontier Commission. Whether or not such regions as Berau ever felt really threatened by British territorial ambitions, the fact is that this Commission put a term to British expansion into Dutch Borneo.

slaves: slavery officially ceased to exist in Indonesia on 1 January 1860, but unofficially persisted unabated. In 1878 the Dutch Resident of East Borneo persuaded the sultans of Gunong Tabur and Sambaliung (see note to p. 11) to forgo the import and export of slaves (State Contracts quoted Allen, 224). However, the *Straits Times Overland Journal* of 26 March 1883 (five years before Conrad's visits) reported of Berau: 'Slaves are met with in almost every house . . . The authorities allow this, in spite of Art. 115 of the Government reg. whereby slavery in Netherlands India has been abolished . . . The number of these unfortunates yearly sold at Gunong Thabor is estimated at 300. These people are bought in or kidnapped from the islands of Sooloo and the other Philippines, and then bartered for gunpowder, muskets, revolvers, lillas, cloths, calico, opium, Dutch candles, etc.' (quoted Sherry, 130); and Haverschmidt reported that the practice continued at Berau well into the new century (Allen, 224).

frigate: a warship, next in line and equipment to ships of the line, formerly carrying a minimum of 28 guns. No ship of that size could enter the Berau.

the great Rajah's: the Governor-General of the Dutch East Indies.

35 *Commission*: this Dutch visit involves more than a show of

strength; the officers are presumably representatives of the Commission referred to in note to p. 34.

lame armchairs: literal rendering of the French phrase 'fauteuils boiteux' (= 'rickety armchairs').

36 *anent*: in respect of, or in relation to. The legal flavour is appropriate here.

37 *Siamese girl*: it is a mark of her social insignificance that she is only given her name, Taminah, at p. 61 line 28. Haverschmidt reports that Carel De Veer (see p. 24 lines 17–18 note) had a Malay wife who earned a living by selling cakes (Allen, 226). Siam is, of course, the modern Thailand.

Bulangi: this rice farmer does not appear in person in the narrative, but his property plays a decisive part in it. It is some distance downstream: how far we are never told directly, but at p. 65 lines 31–2 Nina, who has an assignation with Dain in its vicinity, calculates that she must start at 4 a.m. if she is to meet Dain at sunrise.

38 *That gentleman*: see note to p. 13 for possible sources. Babalatchi has, like Mrs Almayer, a piratical background.

39 *quarrelling*: for the cause of tension between Dyaks and Malays see note to p. 32; for their possession of gold, see note to p. 24.

in his quality of: literal translation of 'en sa qualité de' (= 'in his capacity as').

better relations . . . tribes: according to Haverschmidt, the forest Dyaks had great respect for Olmeijer (Allen, 221).

40 *grandfather*: U has 'grand-father, Datu Besar!'. The Malay phrase means 'revered elder' (Winstedt), but perhaps Conrad excised this bit of linguistic local colour on the grounds that it sounded like a proper name.

surat: Malay for 'letter', 'writing', or 'memorandum' (Winstedt). Originally from Arabic, where it is a name for a chapter of the Koran.

41 *Djinns*: from Arabic and Malay 'jin' (cf. 'genie'): a middle ranking spirit able to assume human or animal form in Muslim demonology.

outfit: TS had 'baggage', U has 'luggage'. Perhaps 'outfit' is marginally less appropriate for the 'road'.

Protestant: for the education of Olmeijer's daughters see Appendix.

42 *Brow*: variant of 'Berau' current at the time. This is an authentic Freudian slip in that it lets the cat out of the bag: Conrad wrote 'Sambir' but thought 'Berau' in this novel.

her mixed blood: at this point U has: 'She had tasted the whole bitterness of it and remembered distinctly that the virtuous Mrs. Vinck's indignation was not so much directed against the young man from the bank as against the innocent cause of that young man's infatuation. And there was also no doubt in her mind that the principal cause of Mrs. Vinck's indignation was the thought that such a thing should happen in a white nest, where her snow-white doves, the two Misses Vinck, had just returned from Europe, to find shelter under the maternal wing, and there await the coming of irreproachable men of their destiny. Not even the thought of the money so painfully scraped together by Almayer, and so punctually sent for Nina's expenses, could dissuade Mrs. Vinck from her virtuous resolve. Nina was sent away, and in truth the girl herself wanted to go, although a little frightened by the impending change.' Here, the SD narrative resumes: 'And now she had lived . . .'—It is, to this editor, inexplicable that Conrad saw fit to remove this magnificent passage in his 1916 revisions. Gordan thinks that he wished to avoid repeating the information already provided by Ford at p. 30 lines 20–8; but the passage, in its sardonic indignation, is not only much more powerful, but presents the incident from Nina's point of view, and so both justifies her distrust of European civilization and explains her acceptance of her Malay inheritance and opportunity. In any case, it plays a significant part in the analysis of racialism sustained throughout the novel.

breathed: U has 'breathed in'; the omission of the preposition tightens the image.

43 *cathedral*: Conrad would have known St Andrew's Cathedral with its white spire, facing the esplanade and the sea, for he stayed at the Sailor's Home just behind it after leaving the *Vidar*.

dollar: familiar term for 'multifarious' foreign coins of equivalent value; but see note to p. 66.

44 *Syed Reshid*: see note to p. 25; 'Reshid' is a common Arab name.

green jacket: in *Personal Narrative of a Pilgrimage to El-Medinah and Meccah* (1879, ii. 259n.), which John Lester has demonstrated Conrad read closely (*Conradian*, 13 (1981), 163–79), Richard Burton writes: 'The green turban is an innovation in El Islam. In some countries it is confined to the Sayyids. In others it is worn as a mark of distinction by pilgrims.' Whether Lakamba's 'green turban' (p. 24 line 33) constitutes such a mark is unclear, given the context; but there is little doubt that Conrad took the wearing, or the display, of green as a sign that the greater pilgrimage to Mecca had been undertaken. See *The Shadow Line* (1917), p. 4: 'an Arab owned her, and a Syed at that. Hence the green border on the flag.'

Hadji: from Arabic *hājj*, pilgrimage. This title is given to those who have made, always on the 8th to 10th days of the 12th month, the greater pilgrimage to Mecca.

lame chairs: see note to p. 35.

Commissie: Dutch for 'Commission'.

46 *salaam*: the Arabic salutation *as-salām 'alaykum*, 'peace be upon you'. In the East it is accompanied by a low bow with the palm of the right hand placed on the forehead.

impassible: the French for 'impassive'. H amends accordingly.

48 *southwest monsoon*: see note to p. 20, and p. 57 line 14: generally, the west monsoon is wetter than the east monsoon, which often brings dry spells.

Straits Times: published in Singapore, it was and is the leading newspaper of the region.

Acheen war: Acheh (or Achin, Atjeh, etc.), the ancient kingdom of North Sumatra, had been since its revolt against Portugal in 1526 a centre of Islamic Malay nationalism. In 1873 the Dutch, partly in response to imperialist competition and partly to rid the region of Achinese piracy, started hostilities against Acheh that continued to fester at dreadful cost to themselves until 1903. Initially the war dragged on to 1880 (roughly the period to which Conrad refers here), when the Achinese began to show signs of capitulation and Batavia decided to put a civilian in charge of the administration of Acheh. Instantly, however, violence flared up again, and in 1881 two Dutch invasions were repulsed. Acheh victories were regarded by the whole Islamic world as the sign of a revival of Muslim power. (See Vlekke, 318–28, and, more ambitiously, C. Snouck Hurgronje, *The Achinese*, 2 vols., trans., London, 1906.)

Nakhodas: Malay, from Persian, for the leaders of trading crews (Winstedt).

stoppage of gunpowder: see note to p. 48. Until about 1870 Batavia followed a policy of limited interference in large areas of the Archipelago, especially Borneo and Celebes; but thereafter it began 'to press its claims to sovereignty and "to punish" the local rulers who ignored Batavia's advices [*sic*] or continued to interfere with shipping on Indonesian seas' (Vlekke, 317).

Princess Amelia: the Princess Amelia (or Amélie, princesse d'Orléans) was the daughter of the Count of Paris; her marriage in 1886 was the European social event of the year, and her name became fashionable.

against Almayer: according to Haverschmidt, Olmeijer (unlike Conrad's Almayer) was reputed to sell muzzle-loaders to the Dyaks of the interior (Allen, 222).

49 *splashing of*: U has 'splashing as if of', implying that the sound is unfamiliar.

Nipa palms: a coastal palm with a very short stem and feathery leaves of 18 feet or more forming a dark green belt along the shore line, contrasting with the lighter green of the mangroves. Nipa is especially well established along the tidal rivers of Borneo (*Handbook*, i. 380). They are also called 'water palms', as below.

alligators: these are the American saurians; one would have expected 'crocodiles', which abound in the rivers of Borneo.

yards squared: to square the yards (or spars on masts to support sails) is to line them up with the keel.

50 *Stopping . . . house*: this sentence was missing from the TS (which served as printer's copy) and from M (the first American edition). It was added by Conrad to the proofs from the MS, which read: 'She stopped her course by a rapid motion of the paddle and by another swift stroke sent it whirling away from the wharf and into a narrow rivulet leading at the back of the house' (Higdon, *Proof*, 89). It is almost certainly to this omission that Conrad referred in his letter to W. H. Chesson, one of the Unwin readers, in early January 1895: 'In reference to paragraph (of 2 sentences) left

out in the setting of Almayer I must own that the fault is mine entirely. The typescript is in error not the printer. If it can be rectified without too much trouble I would be very glad' (*Letters*, i. 198).

51 *Soldat*: Malay, from Portuguese *soldado* and Dutch *soldaat*, for 'soldier'.

Son of Heaven: the title of the ruling princes of Bali (see note to p. 80).

52 *but the occasional*: U has 'but the breathing of several men, the occasional'. The reason for the deletion remains obscure.

siri-vessels: spittoons, as on p. 61 line 1.

53 *Chelakka*: Malay: here the meaning is 'scoundrels' (Winstedt).

Inchi: Malay: an honorific for persons of superior rank (Winstedt).

Veil your face: traditional Moslems believe this practice to have been instituted by the Prophet: '. . . say to thy wives and daughters / and the believing women, that they draw / their veils close to them; so it is likelier / they will be known and not hurt' (*Koran*, xxxiii. 59). The belief was, and is, that women should not be seen by potential husbands, who might otherwise be roused to *fitnah* (disorderly behaviour). Not to be veiled would be a sign of shamelessness in that it would indicate a desire to provoke sexual response. (Soraya Altorki, *Women in Saudi Arabia* (New York, 1986), 35–6.)

54 *hair in disorder*: literal translation of 'cheveux en désordre' (= dishevelled).

kriss: a Malay dagger, straight- or wavy-bladed, to which magic properties were attributed.

55 *heavy short sword . . . horsehair*: Indonesian swords are short, weighty instruments, designed to be wielded rather like machetes. They have elaborate handles and scabbards, especially in Bali, and are worn on formal occasions with decorated belts and rich attire. See Sir T. Stamford Raffles, *The History of Java* (1817, repr. Oxford, 1965), i. 295–6 and illustrations.

as he thought: a clumsy emphasis on the subjectivity of Dain's response, as at p. 62 line 32 ('when his eyes beheld this—to him—perfection of loveliness'). Perhaps the syntax betrays an unaccommodated tension in Conrad between romantic self-surrender and realistic scepticism.

56 *Sumatrese*: the coastal Malays of Sumatra were regarded as unusually powerful physically (*Handbook*, ii. 15).

stern sheets: the space in a rowing boat between the thwarts (rowers' benches) and the stern.

rubbish: U has 'rubbish and broken bottles'. Why Conrad chose to sacrifice a detail which vividly implies Almayer's demoralized drinking remains mysterious.

57 *trepang*: a type of mollusc, also called 'sea-cucumber', 'sea-slug', 'sea-swallow' and 'bêche-de-mer', eaten as a luxury by the Chinese.

Bugis: the principal traders among the Malay tribes. They were very conscious of their ancestry and regarded themselves as an élite. They emigrated to Berau from Celebes. (Rodney Mundy, *Narrative of Events in Borneo and Celebes* (London, 1848), i. chs. 3–12.)

coral reefs . . . mainland: see notes to p. 8.

Bali, and a Brahmin: Bali, an island south of Borneo and east of Java, remained remarkably independent of the rest of Indonesia. With parts of neighbouring Lombok, it alone withstood the spread of Islam in the fifteenth and sixteenth centuries, retaining a unique admixture of Hinduism and Buddhism (Brahma is the supreme Hindu deity). Largely because of its commercial isolation, it avoided Dutch rule into 1849. In the nineteenth century, the Balinese state consisted of a fragile pyramid of kingdoms defined by ceremony and prestige; power was sacramental and the palace functioned as a temple. The Balinese were regarded as among the proudest and most graceful people of the Archipelago. (See Clifford Geertz, *Negara* (Princeton, NJ, 1980).)

58 *refusing all food*: Brahminism forbade the eating of food that had not been duly consecrated by the offering of a portion of it to the god, the 'beings' (prophets) and the 'manes' (ancestors).

60 *the vertical sun*: the Berau is 100 miles north of the Equator.

62 *loyalty*: presumably to the Dutch (cf. p. 82 line 1).

63 *mango trees*: common in Borneo.

65 *made his way*: U has 'made his way stealthily', suggesting a certain duplicity, or at least a lack of dignity.

long chair: see note to p. 5.

66 *guilders*: originally a gold, now a silver, coin.

Mexican dollars: from the Flemish *daler* and the German *thaler*, the familiar terms for the Spanish 'pieces of eight'. These were withdrawn in 1821, surviving only in the Mexican dollar. Originally, Chinese junks carried porcelain, silk, and other goods to Manila (capital of the Philippines) for transshipment to Mexico, earning in exchange large quantities of silver Mexican dollars which became standard currency in the South China ports. This dollar, in fact, circulated throughout the Archipelago until well into the present century. Being received by weight, it was bought and sold as bullion. In Hong Kong and the Straits Settlements, it was also known as the British Dollar. (See Brian Harrison, *South East Asia* (London, 1966), 134.)

he will give more: Conrad is sociologically exact. As a Balinese prince, Dain adheres to the Hindu custom of paying the dowry to the parents (in this case the mother). See Richard Winstead, *The Malays, a Cultural History* (London, 1950), 47, which distinguishes between the Hindu bride price paid to the parents, and the Muslim given to the bride.

Ranee: from Hindi *rānī*, fem. of *rajah*.

67 *time of start*: a clumsy gallicism (French 'l'heure du départ') for 'time of departure'.

69 *gunwales*: in boats a piece of timber extending along the top of both sides of the hull.

70 *white birds*: almost certainly egrets, prevalent in Borneo; they have white plumage and flock at dawn to feed in marshes, rivers and shallow wetlands (*Encyclopaedia Britannica*, 15th edn.).

71 *dense foliage*: the rain forest in equatorial regions like Borneo is a dense growth of tall heterogeneous trees, unlike the deciduous or monsoon forest as in Java where the east monsoon brings a dry season. Conrad evokes a species of the rain forest known as the swamp forest, typical of the East Borneo coast-line. It is obstructed by thick undergrowth, fed by decaying matter, festooned with a variety of lianas, and loaded on its upper branches with parasitic plants, such as

orchids and ferns. Conrad's further references to this forest on pp. 165 lines 1–18 and 167 lines 1–12 are accurate (*Handbook*, i. ch. 12).

immense red blossoms: this romantic petal shower may owe more to literature and symbolism than to observation and life; yet the fact remains that Borneo has over 10,000 species of flowering plants, including parasites with flowers up to a yard across. Tropical flowers, however, are generally without scent (*Handbook*, i. ch. 12).

sleeping water: another gallicism ('eau dormante' = 'still water'), but here producing a fresh metaphor. See also p. 175 line 24.

72 *kiss*: what surprises and delights Dain is more than Nina's sexual boldness, so transgressive of Indonesian traditions of feminine decorum; it is also the 'strange and hitherto . . . unknown' form it takes. The anthropological position is succinctly summarized by a recent authority: 'the labial kiss, which is so much taken for granted in Western societies, is not at all a universally practiced custom, for it was unknown to the majority of primitive peoples as well as to large segments of Asiatic cultures until introduced to them by Westerners' (Nicholas James Perella, *The Kiss Sacred and Profane* (Berkeley, University of California, 1969), 1).

73 *Kajang-mats*: The Kajan are a leading tribe in Central Borneo (*Handbook*, ii. 23). The production of straw mats was widespread among the Dyaks: presumably, the Kajans used them for barter. The Kajan river (also known as the Boeloengan) is some 40 miles north of the Berau.

74 *abandoned*: this odd epithet may have been prompted by the French 's'abandonner' (= to lose courage), as the use of 'abandon' below suggests. Certainly the 'discouragement' has not been 'abandoned', as the syntax suggests—quite the reverse. Conrad means 'hopeless' or 'unresisted' discouragement.

76 *bitcharra*: the Malay *bichara* signifies 'deliberation', 'discussion', or 'argument' (Winstedt).

78 *each on their own purposes*: strictly, this should be 'each on his own purpose'.

fire-ship: a native term for 'gun-ship', not a burning ship set adrift among enemy vessels.

79 *fireballs*: cannon-balls, not projectiles filled with combustibles.

80 *Anak Agong*: Malay *anak*, 'child' with *agong* 'exalted' (Winstedt). This, the title of the ruling powers of Bali, is rendered 'Son of Heaven' by Conrad.

81 *siri-box*: not the 'siri vessel' of p. 52 line 6, but the portable container of the ingredients; referred to as 'betel-nut box' at p. 86 lines 30–1.

independent Rajah of Bali: strictly, Bali was not ruled by a single potentate, but by a consortium of princes; its independence was *de facto* real enough, however. The formal agreement by the rajahs of Bali in 1841 to respect Dutch suzerainty was essentially a fiction. The Dutch expeditions of 1846 and 1849 met with fierce resistance; in 1849 the Dutch annexed some territory and exacted another gesture of recognition from the chiefs of the remainder; but the proud, independent attitude of the rulers of Bali remained undaunted. In 1884, the Dutch complied with a Balinese ultimatum requiring them to withdraw their ships within eight days, and did not reassert their power for 10 years (*Handbook*, ii. 82, 94; Hall, 546).

Sumatra: see note to p. 48.

Dutch resident: 'Resident' was the title of the governor of a residency in the nineteenth-century Dutch East Indies. The residency for the NE coast of Borneo was at Samarinda (see Map 1).

82 *Gunong Mas*: Malay *gunong*, 'mountain' with *emas*, 'gold' (Winstedt).

85 *Ada*: Malay word, equivalent to 'at your service', usually in a tone of urgency.

86 *Poulo Laut to Tanjong Batu*: the first is an island off the SE corner of Borneo; a coaling station, it was a regular port of call for the *Vidar*, to which Conrad refers in *A Personal Record* (p. 76). The second is a settlement at the north end of the Berau estuary.

at the pit: why not 'in the pit'? Perhaps because of the French locution 'au creux de l'estomac'.

87 *Sheitan*: Arabic *shaitan*, 'satan'; in popular credence, the whispering tempter.

89 *Trovatore . . . Leonore*: the most famous moment in Verdi's *Il Trovatore* ('The Troubadour'), first performed in 1853, is the

'Miserere', a duet with chorus between the condemned Manrico, imprisoned in a tower, and his lover Leonora [*sic*] who hears his voice floating above her singing: 'Ah! che la morte ognora / E tarda nel venir, / A chi desia morir. Addio, addio, Leonora, addio!' ('Ah, how unknown death is slow to come to him who longs to die. Farewell, Leonora, farewell.') Only H alters 'Leonore' to 'Leonora': but she is 'Leonore' in the French version.

91 *raft*: houses in river settlements in East Borneo are built on rafts as well as piles (*Handbook*, i. 216).

92 *bourrouh*: not a Malay expletive, but a slightly Frenchified rendering of 'brrr'—the audible shudder of discomfort.

93 *official get up*: Babalatchi is dressed as befits a man charged with a state execution.

96 *defiled myself before eating*: fear of a corpse, particularly one unprotected by ritual mourning, is reflected in the ceremonial uncleanliness acquired by contact. See e.g. Numbers 19: 11 ('He that toucheth the dead body of any man shall be unclean seven days').

97 *his foot*: H alters to 'its foot'; 'your feet', below, makes it clear that the alteration is mistaken.

98 *Hai*: an exclamation expressing mingled surprise and regret; see also p. 148 lines 29–30.

eater of pig's flesh: 'These things only has he forbidden you: / carrion, blood, the flesh of swine, / what has been hallowed to other than God' (*Koran*, ii. 169–70, v. 1–5, vi. 145–50).

99 *formless*: TS and M have 'inform' (Higdon, *Proof*, 415), but U's correction of TS's 'inform' is surely correct. A gallicism seems to be lurking here: the French 'informe', an ordinary word, should be rendered as 'formless' or 'shapeless', and not as the near-archaic 'inform'.

104 *Kaffir*: Arabic *kāfir*, 'infidel'.

strong water: the Koran's interdiction of alcoholic drink is of course unambiguous: 'They will question thee concerning / wine. . . . Say: "In [it] / is heinous sin' (ii. 215); and 'O believers, wine. . . . [is] an abomination, / some of Satan's work; so avoid it; haply / so you will prosper' (v. 90).

105 *lips and forehead*: see note to p. 46.

106 *painter*: a line attached to the bow of a boat to make it fast etc.

108 *deer*: wild deer are abundant in Borneo, along with monkeys of many kinds and wild pig.

109 *the Merciful, the Compassionate*: every surat of the Koran opens with the words: 'In the Name of God, the Merciful, the Compassionate'; these are the divine attributes.

110 *jamb*: all editions have 'lintel', which is the horizontal support placed above the door, and not the jamb, which is the vertical side-post. Conrad never learnt the meaning of that word: he was still misusing it in 1917 in *The Shadow Line*.

112 *whom*: H alters to 'which'. This is grammatically more acceptable, but it could be argued that the palms are personified, given their identification with Taminah.

113 *blocks*: a block is a pulley, or set of pulleys, mounted in a case.

120 *leeward*: directed away from the wind.

122 *scientific explorer*: according to Haverschmidt, there was a fourth European (in addition to Olmeijer, Jim Lingard, and De Veer) living in Berau at the time of Conrad's visits: a heavy-drinking old Russian who seems to have combined the activities of a naturalist with those of an orchid-hunter. But there is also evidence that occasional semi-scientific prospectors came and went (Allen, 218).

geese: Conrad remembered the historical Almayer's geese in *A Personal Record*: '"See these geese?" With the hand holding the letters he pointed out to me what resembled a patch of snow creeping and swaying across the distant part of his compound. It disappeared behind some bushes. "The only geese on the East Coast," Almayer informed me in a perfunctory mutter without a spark of faith, hope or pride.' (p. 85). See also p. 203 lines 6–9 below.

126 *coxwain*: a petty officer having permanent charge of a ship's boat and its crew.

130 *southern mouth . . . main entrance*: the Berau delta offers three, not two, main channels: 'The principal channel of approach leads through . . . the upper reaches of Muara [Malay for 'estuary'] Garoera (Garura). . . . There are also navigable approaches through Muara Pantai, on the southern side of the estuary, and Muara Tidoeng on the north side. . . . Muara Pantai is now seldom used' (*Eastern Archipelago Pilot*, ii. 468–9, quoted Sherry, 123–4).

Ampanam: in MS Dain comes from Lombok; in TS he comes

from Bali (Gordan, 49). As Ampanam is a port on the west coast of Lombok, an island to the east of Bali, it represents an uncorrected anachronism. There is no evidence that Conrad visited either of these islands, but he had enough information about them to know which of the two would better serve the interests of his novel.

133 *amok*: from Malay *āmoq*, 'homicidal frenzy'; in English more usually 'amuck'. For Conrad's representation of the phenomenon, see pp. 167 line 31–168 line 14.

Madura: an island just off the north-east coast of Java. Babalatchi may have feared deportation to a place characterized at the time by the forced labour or *corvée* system. See F. Fokkens (ed.), *Eind resumé van het . . . onderzoek naar de verplichte diensten der inlandsche bevolking op Java en Madoera*, 3 vols. (Smits, Batavia, 1901–3).

nothing pressed: literal rendering of the French phrase 'rien ne pressait' ('there was no hurry').

134 *Canton*: one of the first cities of China, north-east of Hong Kong. Cantonese is of course a language, not a dialect.

135 *Inside the passage*: U has 'Inside in the passage', which is more explicit if not clearer.

136 *guessed at many things*: for the things guessed at, see p. 25 lines 9–18.

138 *Arab slander*: see p. 36 lines 11–18.

140 *freak*: whim, prank, caper.

147 *vast silence*: 'One of the most striking things inside the [virgin] forest is the extraordinary stillness of the air; except during squalls which generally precede thunder storms . . . smoke ascends quite vertically and small scraps of paper never blow away' (*Handbook*, i. 381).

149 *woman god*: presumably the Virgin Mary; Mrs Almayer was brought up in a convent.

152 *and touched lightly*: U has 'and hesitatingly touched lightly'. If Conrad's deletion was prompted by the thought that the two adverbs jarred, he was surely mistaken.

156 *burnt the paper*: Conrad has not imagined this superstition. Chauvin, in *Bibliographie des Ouvrages Arabes*, v. 244, no. 143 refers to the practice of calling up a genie by writing his name on papers and burning them. The practice of burning paper,

wood, fish, hair, etc., in order to lay a ghost, is a standard theme of folk belief. Clifford Geertz, in *The Religions of Java* (London, 1964) 68, writes: 'The dead must be burned quickly because the spirit of the dead man is flying around loose until he is buried.' Richard Winstedt, in *The Malays, a Cultural History* (London, 1950), says that it is common in the Archipelago 'to ascribe malignity to the spirits of murdered men and suicides' (p. 20).

165 *expanse . . . rice-shoots*: in Borneo rice is grown in clearings without irrigation (*Handbook*, i. 226).

wild pigs: see note to p. 108.

166 *wide-open eyes*: U has 'wide-open eyes, and at every deep breath the fine white ash of bygone fires rose in a light cloud before his parted lips, and danced away from the warm glow into the moonbeams pouring down upon Bulangi's clearing.' What is wrong, if anything, with the deleted passage is not that it requires symbolic recoding to make sense (Higdon, *Collected*, 84), for the ash of old fires is easily disturbed; but that the writing is too highly coloured, that ash blown upwards in this way would first, like cigarette smoke, be breathed in, and that the winds of heaven would have cleared the site of such light ash anyway.

167 *pink and blue flowers*: 'Tropical rain forests are not a mass of brilliant and varied coloured flowers. Plants with showy flowers do exist, but they are not common. . . . The forest as a whole is sombre green' (*Handbook*, i. 381).

sounder . . . pig: M mistakenly amended 'sounder' to 'sound': Conrad has used the correct collective noun for wild swine. TS had 'pigs', which is more natural, just as 'pride of lions' is less stilted than 'pride of lion'.

fury: see note to p. 133.

173 *and his faults*: U has 'and all his faults'. The excision of this 'all' damages the antithesis, though the antithesis is perhaps a bit facile.

his own island: Dain's ensuing description of Bali is effective as a contrast to the atmosphere of Sambir. It may lack the precision of first-hand observation (see note to p. 130) but it is generally accurate. The sickle-shaped range round the northern part of Bali rises to the 10,000 feet of the cone-shaped Goenoeng Agoeng. The southern part is tilted in a southerly direction from 2,000 feet to sea level. It is crossed by torrential streams which fill or empty according to the monsoon. The exceptionally fertile soil was terraced and irrigated long before the advent of the Dutch. The Balinese are descendants of the Hindu–Javanese who emigrated from Java between the ninth and sixteenth centuries. (*Handbook*, i. 285–63.)

177 *I was not afraid*: H has 'I was much afraid'. This is a compositor's error almost certainly prompted by the 'much' five words before. In any case a confession of fear here is not plausible: Dain fears emotional collapse (p. 168 lines 15–32) but is supremely confident when dealing with a physical emergency.

178 *the dowry*: see note to p. 66.

in English: Almayer does not want to be understood by Dain; Nina, of course, has been brought up in Singapore.

180 *made a step*: gallicism for 'took a step' (French 'faire un pas').

181 *of their destruction*: U has 'for their destruction', a more direct and vivid phrase.

he will betray: H has 'he will betray us'. 'Betray', without the pronoun, is more menacing, suggesting as it does that Almayer is in danger of turning into the personification of treachery.

182 *Ada*: see note to p. 85.

184 *all over the island*: U has 'all over the islands'. In *A Personal Record*, Conrad remembers the historical Almayer as having been the object of 'the disrespectful chatter of every vagrant trader in the Islands' (p. 88). Perhaps Conrad decided to limit the range of Almayer's notoriety to the East Coast to justify his notion that he would avoid disgrace by letting Nina escape to Bali.

whatever your name may be: the Dutch lieutenant has told Almayer: 'He passed here under the name of Dain Maroola' (p. 123 lines 17–18).

185 *row-locks*: a device (either a notch, or two pins, or a rounded fork) on the gunwale of a boat to form a fulcrum for the oar in rowing.

Way enough: nautical for 'stop'. 'Way' is the progress of a boat or ship through water.

186 *the Straits*: the Macassar Strait, separating Borneo and Celebes.

mangrove . . . cliffs: see note to p. 8.

Tanjong Mirrah: Malay *tanjong*, 'cape' and *merrah*, 'red'. Probably a pseudonym for Tanjong Mangka, the major promontory stretching southwards of the Berau towards Celebes. This well-known landmark would have given away the location of 'Sambir'.

188 *access of*: literal translation of the French 'accès de' ('fit of' or 'attack of').

"What do you want?" asked Almayer: U has '"What?" said Almayer.' The expanded version may have seemed a more natural response to a gesture interrupting a train of thought.

194 *Dapat*: Malay for 'to get', as Conrad indicates (Winstedt).

195 *Tanah Mirrah*: 'Tanah' is a familiar variant of 'tanjong'.

slipper: H alters to 'slippers', but this is to miss the force of the generic singular.

200 *like that of*: U has 'like of'; here Conrad's revision tidies the syntax.

202 *monthly visits*: while with the *Vidar* Conrad visited Berau four times in just over four months.

205 *eye*: H alters to 'eyes', but this, again, is to miss the force of the generic singular.

206 *Lanun*: the Lanuns, or 'Pirates of the Lagoon', came from a great bay in the south of Mindanao, the southernmost Philippine island; they also had headquarters in NW Borneo. They and their neighbouring rivals of the Sulu Archipelago (see note to p. 7) set out annually with fleets of up to 200 praus, each manned with crews of 40–60, and raided most parts of the Malay Archipelago. They were the most feared of the sea-robbers. (Hall, 498–9.)

English Rajah . . . Kuching: the rajah in question was Sir James Brooke (see note to p. 33). Brooke mounted a scientific expedition to Sarawak in 1839, befriended the Sultan of Brunei, pacified rebellious Dyaks, and was rewarded with the Governorship of Sarawak in 1841, ruling the territory as a benevolent despot from its capital Kuching. Piracy, which had threatened the whole of the East Indies trade, had been quelled by a deployment of naval power in 1837; but it quickly saw a recrudescence of activity, particularly on the part of the Lanuns from North Borneo, and the Sea Dyaks from Sarawak. Brooke secured a warship and destroyed the strongholds of the Sea Dyaks in 1843–4; and a naval squadron crushed the Lanuns in 1845. As Babalatchi's nostalgic 'silent ships with white sails' implies, it was steam power that broke the back of Indonesian piracy. (Hall, 500–2.)

207 *Mati*: Malay for 'dead' (Winstedt).

made a few paces: see note to p. 180.

APPENDIX: 'ALMAYER'S FOLLY' AND THE EAST

THE actual place that, however loosely, can be regarded as a source of *Almayer's Folly* was finally identified no less than half a century after the appearance of the novel. This was partly because of the obscurity of the location itself, but also partly because of Conrad's reluctance to make disclosures that might encourage reductively biographical readings of his work. Indeed, the closest he ever came to identifying the 'Eastern River' of the novel's sub-title was a pencil sketch of a tropical shoreline, with palm trees, estuaries, headlands, and horizon, drawn on the title page of a first edition presented to Edward Garnett, now at the Free Library of Philadelphia. But the scene is, alas, completely anonymous.

In 1924, Conrad's first biographer, G. Jean-Aubry, met the 70-year-old Captain James Craig, who had been master of the SS *Vidar* when Conrad served on her in the Sea of Celebes at the end of 1887, and who told him that the action of *Almayer's Folly* was located in Bulungan on the north-eastern coast of Borneo (*Life and Letters*, ii. 94–6). The second investigator into that part of Conrad's life, John Dozier Gordan, visited Bulungan in 1939, but to discover that the alleged models of Conrad's characters had lived in Berau, 150 miles to the south; he was however able to interview a Mrs Andrew Gray, one of the surviving children of Charles Olmeijer, the prototype of Conrad's 'Almayer' (*The Making of a Novelist* (1940), 36–46). Field-work in Berau itself, however, was finally undertaken only in 1952 by M. Haverschmidt, a mining official living a few miles down-stream, at the instance of Dr J. G. Reed, a surgeon in Malaya who had met the granddaughter of William Lingard, the prototype of Conrad's 'Tom Lingard'. The results of this research appeared, fully but uncritically, in Jerry Allen's *The Sea Years of Joseph Conrad* (1965), 187–240. Independently, Norman Sherry, who was able to interview descendants of William Lingard and Charles Olmeijer, confirmed or qualified these findings in *Conrad's Eastern World* (1966), 89–170.

The circumstances of Conrad's contact with Berau can be briefly summarized. On 16 February 1887 he was appointed First Mate on the *Highland Forest*, a sailing ship bound for Samarang, Java. During this, the sixth of his deep-sea voyages to the East or Australia, he was injured; and on reaching his destination, he was ordered to a Singapore hospital, leaving with the SS *Celestial* on 2

July, and arriving on the 6th. During these four days he struck up an acquaintance with the *Celestial*'s First Mate, one F. H. Brooksbank, the son-in-law of the locally celebrated sailor-adventurer William Lingard. After his discharge from hospital, Conrad secured, on or near 20 August, and probably through the offices of Brooksbank, the position of First Mate on the SS *Vidar*, owned by an Arab trader in Singapore, Al Joffree, but sailing under the British flag and commanded by an Englishman, the Captain James Craig mentioned above. Craig, together with his two engineers, Allen and Niven, were very familiar with the places marking the ship's run—Banjarmasin, Pulau Laut, Donggala, Samarinda, Berau, and Bulungan, returning to Singapore via Pulau Laut (see Map 1, p. lix). Between 22 August 1887 and 2 January 1888, when he signed off, Conrad made four trips with the *Vidar*; given that Al Joffree's eldest son, Syed Abdulla, ran a branch house for his father at Berau, and a younger son another at Bulungan (Sherry, 107; Allen, 233), it is likely that these were treated as major stops. Apart from Syed Abdulla, at Berau Conrad would have found two of William Lingard's agents, Charles Olmeijer, and Lingard's nephew Jim.

What Conrad was able to discover during that period, and what use he put it to when he came to write his first novel, is discussed in the notes to this edition. As a guide to these notes an outline of the main findings is in order.

Conrad calls his river the 'Pantai'; its entrance is a complex of islands with at least two main channels (p. 186 lines 10–11); his settlement he calls 'Sambir', which he locates 'thirty miles' upstream (p. 36 line 24) at the juncture of two rivers, or two branches of the same river, the main branch being called 'the Pantai', the lesser one 'the Sambir reach' (p. 14 lines 24–31). The actual river was also called the Sambir in Conrad's time, but is now known as the Berau; it has three main outlets through the delta at its mouth; thirty-four miles upstream, at the juncture of two rivers respectively called the Segah and the Kelai, clusters a settlement generally known as Berau from the name of the sultanate in which it is located; the main station, situated on the promontory formed by the juncture of the rivers, is called Tanjong Redeb (Conrad's 'Sambir'); across the northern branch (the Segah) is Gunung Tabur (where Conrad locates his rajah); across the southern branch (the Kelai) is Sambaliung (which does not feature in the novel). Like Conrad's 'Sambir' Tanjong Redeb lines a single road or path, with houses over the water standing on stilts; the disposition of the principal houses, however, including Syed Abdulla's, and Jim Lingard's and Charles Olmeijer's mansions, is quite different.

Conrad's 'Tom Lingard' who discovered and navigated the 'Pantai', installed 'Almayer' as his agent in 'Sambir', prospected for gold, and finally disappeared, is in part modelled on Captain William Lingard, whom Conrad never met (on 31 March 1917 Conrad wrote to Mr W. G. St Clair: 'Old Lingard was before my time but I knew slightly both his nephews, Jim and Jos [Joshua], of whom the latter was then officer on board the King of Siam's yacht' [quoted Sherry, 317]). William Lingard may have been active in the Archipelago as early as the 1840s; in 1864 he married Johanna Olmeijer; in the early 1880s he surveyed the southern channel of the Berau; in 1886 he established an agency, Lingard & Co, in Berau (Tanjong Redeb), appointing Charles Olmeijer to it in about 1869, and his nephew Jim Lingard in about 1880; he undertook exploratory voyages in the waters of the Archipelago, had several bloody encounters with pirates, and became known as the Rajah Laut (and owned a ship of that name); he was, to his disadvantage, prejudiced against steam ships, may have lost money in the collapse of the Oriental Bank of Singapore in 1884, and after 1887 disappeared from all printed records and the memory of his descendants.

Conrad's 'Kaspar Almayer' is a Hollander from Java and Macassar, married to the adopted Malay daughter of 'Tom Lingard', and manager of 'Lingard & Co' in 'Sambir'. Charles Olmeijer was a Eurasian, related by marriage to William Lingard, who appointed him resident trader in Berau at the age of 22 in 1869/70; he was born in Java in 1848, spent some time in Macassar (probably at another Lingard trading house) before coming to Berau, married another Eurasian, Johanna van Lieshout, in 1874, and between 1874 and 1892, when his wife died, produced eleven children. The eldest daughter was brought up a Protestant in Macassar; her five sisters received a convent education in Surabaya. Olmeijer prospected for gold, smuggled arms and powder, and is alleged to have constructed an extravagant house in about 1881. He died of cancer in Surabaya hospital in 1900, aged 52.

Every character in the novel and much of its setting reverberate in the actuality of the time; and many of these echoes will appear in the notes. It is clear that Conrad's first-hand and hearsay experience of Berau during the last four months of 1887 decisively influenced his book; it is equally clear that the novel is in no way constrained, let alone determined, by the facts of that experience.

As Conrad's greatest biographer, Zdzisław Najder pungently observes: 'to the readers of *Almayer's Folly* it is immaterial whether Nina Almayer owes her name to her aunt Ninette Olmeijer' (Najder, 99). The meaning of a novel is positioned by its structure, and cannot be reduced to its sources, which are finally coextensive with the whole of a particular life at a particular time. Yet to disregard the world out of which linguistic art emerges, especially when that art is, as this edition tries to show, 'thus near, and familiarly allied to the time', is to run the risk of receiving it in impoverished terms, where not only the fiction, but also the history, and the relationship between the two, dissolve into schema and abstraction.

THE WORLD'S CLASSICS

A Select List

HANS ANDERSEN: Fairy Tales
Translated by L. W. Kingsland
Introduction by Naomi Lewis
Illustrated by Vilhelm Pedersen and Lorenz Frølich

ARTHUR J. ARBERRY (Transl.): The Koran

LUDOVICO ARIOSTO: Orlando Furioso
Translated by Guido Waldman

ARISTOTLE: The Nicomachean Ethics
Translated by David Ross

JANE AUSTEN: Emma
Edited by James Kinsley and David Lodge

Mansfield Park
Edited by James Kinsley and John Lucas

Northanger Abbey, Lady Susan, The Watsons, *and* Sanditon
Edited by John Davie

HONORÉ DE BALZAC: Père Goriot
Translated and Edited by A. J. Krailsheimer

CHARLES BAUDELAIRE: The Flowers of Evil
Translated by James McGowan
Introduction by Jonathan Culler

WILLIAM BECKFORD: Vathek
Edited by Roger Lonsdale

R. D. BLACKMORE: Lorna Doone
Edited by Sally Shuttleworth

KEITH BOSLEY (Transl.): The Kalevala

JAMES BOSWELL: Life of Johnson
The Hill/Powell edition, revised by David Fleeman
Introduction by Pat Rogers

MARY ELIZABETH BRADDON: Lady Audley's Secret
Edited by David Skilton

ANNE BRONTË: The Tenant of Wildfell Hall
Edited by Herbert Rosengarten and Margaret Smith

CHARLOTTE BRONTË: Jane Eyre
Edited by Margaret Smith

Shirley
Edited by Margaret Smith and Herbert Rosengarten

EMILY BRONTË: Wuthering Heights
Edited by Ian Jack

GEORG BÜCHNER:
Danton's Death, Leonce and Lena, Woyzeck
Translated by Victor Price

JOHN BUNYAN: The Pilgrim's Progress
Edited by N. H. Keeble

EDMUND BURKE: A Philosophical Enquiry into the Origin of our Ideas of the Sublime and Beautiful
Edited by Adam Phillips

FANNY BURNEY: Camilla
Edited by Edward A. Bloom and Lilian D. Bloom

THOMAS CARLYLE: The French Revolution
Edited by K. J. Fielding and David Sorensen

LEWIS CARROLL: Alice's Adventures in Wonderland *and* Through the Looking Glass
Edited by Roger Lancelyn Green
Illustrated by John Tenniel

CATULLUS: The Poems of Catullus
Edited by Guy Lee

MIGUEL DE CERVANTES: Don Quixote
Translated by Charles Jarvis
Edited by E. C. Riley

GEOFFREY CHAUCER: The Canterbury Tales
Translated by David Wright

ANTON CHEKHOV: The Russian Master and Other Stories
Translated by Ronald Hingley

Ward Number Six and Other Stories
Translated by Ronald Hingley

JOHN CLELAND:
Memoirs of a Woman of Pleasure (Fanny Hill)
Edited by Peter Sabor

WILKIE COLLINS: Armadale
Edited by Catherine Peters

The Moonstone
Edited by Anthea Trodd

JOSEPH CONRAD: Chance
Edited by Martin Ray

Typhoon and Other Tales
Edited by Cedric Watts

Youth, Heart of Darkness, The End of the Tether
Edited by Robert Kimbrough

JAMES FENIMORE COOPER: The Last of the Mohicans
Edited by John McWilliams

DANTE ALIGHIERI: The Divine Comedy
Translated by C. H. Sisson
Edited by David Higgins

DANIEL DEFOE: Robinson Crusoe
Edited by J. Donald Crowley

THOMAS DE QUINCEY:
The Confessions of an English Opium-Eater
Edited by Grevel Lindop

CHARLES DICKENS: Christmas Books
Edited by Ruth Glancy

David Copperfield
Edited by Nina Burgis

The Pickwick Papers
Edited by James Kinsley

FEDOR DOSTOEVSKY: Crime and Punishment
Translated by Jessie Coulson
Introduction by John Jones

The Idiot
Translated by Alan Myers
Introduction by W. J. Leatherbarrow

Memoirs from the House of the Dead
Translated by Jessie Coulson
Introduction by Ronald Hingley

ARTHUR CONAN DOYLE:
Sherlock Holmes: Selected Stories
Introduction by S. C. Roberts

ALEXANDRE DUMAS *père*:
The Three Musketeers
Edited by David Coward

ALEXANDRE DUMAS *fils*:
La Dame aux Camélias
Translated by David Coward

MARIA EDGEWORTH: Castle Rackrent
Edited by George Watson

GEORGE ELIOT: Daniel Deronda
Edited by Graham Handley

Felix Holt, The Radical
Edited by Fred C. Thompson

Middlemarch
Edited by David Carroll

HENRY FIELDING: Joseph Andrews *and* Shamela
Edited by Douglas Brooks-Davies

GUSTAVE FLAUBERT: Madame Bovary
Translated by Gerard Hopkins
Introduction by Terence Cave

A Sentimental Education
Translated by Douglas Parmée

FORD MADOX FORD: The Good Soldier
Edited by Thomas C. Moser

BENJAMIN FRANKLIN:
Autobiography and Other Writings
Edited by Ormond Seavey

ELIZABETH GASKELL: Cousin Phillis and Other Tales
Edited by Angus Easson

North and South
Edited by Angus Easson

GEORGE GISSING: The Private Papers of Henry Ryecroft
Edited by Mark Storey

WILLIAM GODWIN: Caleb Williams
Edited by David McCracken

J. W. VON GOETHE: Faust, Part One
Translated by David Luke

KENNETH GRAHAME: The Wind in the Willows
Edited by Peter Green

H. RIDER HAGGARD: King Solomon's Mines
Edited by Dennis Butts

THOMAS HARDY: A Pair of Blue Eyes
Edited by Alan Manford

Jude the Obscure
Edited by Patricia Ingham

Tess of the D'Urbervilles
Edited by Juliet Grindle and Simon Gatrell

NATHANIEL HAWTHORNE:
Young Goodman Brown and Other Tales
Edited by Brian Harding

HESIOD: Theogony *and* Works and Days
Translated by M. L. West

E. T. A. HOFFMANN:
The Golden Pot and Other Tales
Translated and Edited by Ritchie Robertson

HOMER: The Iliad
Translated by Robert Fitzgerald
Introduction by G. S. Kirk

The Odyssey
Translated by Walter Shewring
Introduction by G. S. Kirk

THOMAS HUGHES: Tom Brown's Schooldays
Edited by Andrew Sanders

HENRIK IBSEN: An Enemy of the People, The Wild Duck, Rosmersholm
Edited and Translated by James McFarlane

Peer Gynt
Translated by Christopher Fry and Johan Fillinger
Introduction by James McFarlane

HENRY JAMES: The Ambassadors
Edited by Christopher Butler

A London Life *and* The Reverberator
Edited by Philip Horne

The Spoils of Poynton
Edited by Bernard Richards

RUDYARD KIPLING: The Jungle Books
Edited by W. W. Robson

Stalky & Co.
Edited by Isobel Quigly

MADAME DE LAFAYETTE: The Princesse de Clèves
Translated and Edited by Terence Cave

WILLIAM LANGLAND: Piers Plowman
Translated and Edited by A. V. C. Schmidt

J. SHERIDAN LE FANU: Uncle Silas
Edited by W. J. McCormack

CHARLOTTE LENNOX: The Female Quixote
Edited by Margaret Dalziel
Introduction by Margaret Anne Doody

LEONARDO DA VINCI: Notebooks
Edited by Irma A. Richter

MIKHAIL LERMONTOV: A Hero of our Time
Translated by Vladimir Nabokov with Dmitri Nabokov

MATTHEW LEWIS: The Monk
Edited by Howard Anderson

JACK LONDON:
The Call of the Wild, White Fang, and Other Stories
Edited by Earle Labor and Robert C. Leitz III

NICCOLÒ MACHIAVELLI: The Prince
Edited by Peter Bondanella and Mark Musa
Introduction by Peter Bondanella

KATHERINE MANSFIELD: Selected Stories
Edited by D. M. Davin

MARCUS AURELIUS:
The Meditations of Marcus Aurelius
Translated by A. S. L. Farquharson
Edited by R. B. Rutherford

KARL MARX AND FRIEDRICH ENGELS:
The Communist Manifesto
Edited by David McLellan

CHARLES MATURIN: Melmoth the Wanderer
Edited by Douglas Grant
Introduction by Chris Baldick

HERMAN MELVILLE: The Confidence-Man
Edited by Tony Tanner

Moby Dick
Edited by Tony Tanner

PROSPER MÉRIMÉE: Carmen and Other Stories
Translated by Nicholas Jotcham

MICHELANGELO: Life, Letters, and Poetry
Translated by George Bull with Peter Porter

JOHN STUART MILL: On Liberty and Other Essays
Edited by John Gray

MOLIÈRE: Don Juan and Other Plays
Translated by George Graveley and Ian Maclean

GEORGE MOORE: Esther Waters
Edited by David Skilton

MYTHS FROM MESOPOTAMIA
Translated and Edited by Stephanie Dalley

E. NESBIT: The Railway Children
Edited by Dennis Butts

ORIENTAL TALES
Edited by Robert L. Mack

OVID: Metamorphoses
Translated by A. D. Melville
Introduction and Notes by E. J. Kenney

FRANCESCO PETRARCH:
Selections from the Canzoniere and Other Works
Translated by Mark Musa

EDGAR ALLAN POE: Selected Tales
Edited by Julian Symons

JEAN RACINE: Britannicus, Phaedra, Athaliah
Translated by C. H. Sisson

ANN RADCLIFFE: The Italian
Edited by Frederick Garber

The Mysteries of Udolpho
Edited by Bonamy Dobrée

The Romance of the Forest
Edited by Chloe Chard

THE MARQUIS DE SADE:
The Misfortune of Virtue and Other Early Tales
Translated and Edited by David Coward

PAUL SALZMAN (Ed.):
An Anthology of Elizabethan Prose Fiction

OLIVE SCHREINER: The Story of an African Farm
Edited by Joseph Bristow

SIR WALTER SCOTT: The Heart of Midlothian
Edited by Claire Lamont

Waverley
Edited by Claire Lamont

ANNA SEWELL: Black Beauty
Edited by Peter Hollindale

MARY SHELLEY: Frankenstein
Edited by M. K. Joseph

TOBIAS SMOLLETT: The Expedition of Humphry Clinker
Edited by Lewis M. Knapp
Revised by Paul-Gabriel Boucé

STENDHAL: The Red and the Black
Translated by Catherine Slater

LAURENCE STERNE: A Sentimental Journey
Edited by Ian Jack

Tristram Shandy
Edited by Ian Campbell Ross

ROBERT LOUIS STEVENSON: Kidnapped and Catriona
Edited by Emma Letley

The Strange Case of Dr. Jekyll and Mr. Hyde
and Weir of Hermiston
Edited by Emma Letley

BRAM STOKER: Dracula
Edited by A. N. Wilson

JONATHAN SWIFT: Gulliver's Travels
Edited by Paul Turner

A Tale of a Tub and Other Works
Edited by Angus Ross and David Woolley

WILLIAM MAKEPEACE THACKERAY: Barry Lyndon
Edited by Andrew Sanders

Vanity Fair
Edited by John Sutherland

LEO TOLSTOY: Anna Karenina
Translated by Louise and Aylmer Maude
Introduction by John Bayley

War and Peace
Translated by Louise and Aylmer Maude
Edited by Henry Gifford

ANTHONY TROLLOPE: The American Senator
Edited by John Halperin

The Belton Estate
Edited by John Halperin

Cousin Henry
Edited by Julian Thompson

The Eustace Diamonds
Edited by W. J. McCormack

The Kellys and the O'Kellys
Edited by W. J. McCormack
Introduction by William Trevor

Orley Farm
Edited by David Skilton

Rachel Ray
Edited by P. D. Edwards

The Warden
Edited by David Skilton

IVAN TURGENEV: First Love and Other Stories
Translated by Richard Freeborn

MARK TWAIN: Pudd'nhead Wilson and Other Tales
Edited by R. D. Gooder

GIORGIO VASARI: The Lives of the Artists
Translated and Edited by Julia Conaway Bondanella and Peter Bondanella

JULES VERNE: Journey to the Centre of the Earth
Translated and Edited by William Butcher

VIRGIL: The Aeneid
Translated by C. Day Lewis
Edited by Jasper Griffin

The Eclogues and The Georgics
Translated by C. Day Lewis
Edited by R. O. A. M. Lyne

HORACE WALPOLE : The Castle of Otranto
Edited by W. S. Lewis

IZAAK WALTON and CHARLES COTTON:
The Compleat Angler
Edited by John Buxton
Introduction by John Buchan

OSCAR WILDE: Complete Shorter Fiction
Edited by Isobel Murray

The Picture of Dorian Gray
Edited by Isobel Murray

MARY WOLLSTONECRAFT:
Mary *and* The Wrongs of Woman
Edited by Gary Kelly

VIRGINIA WOOLF: Mrs Dalloway
Edited by Claire Tomalin

Orlando
Edited by Rachel Bowlby

ÉMILE ZOLA:
The Attack on the Mill and Other Stories
Translated by Douglas Parmée

Nana
Translated and Edited by Douglas Parmée